Praise for **Neruda on the Park**

"With the grit of Gloria Naylor's **The Women of Brewster Place,** the fierce insights of Kate Chopin's **The Awakening,** and the exploration of immigrant mothers and daughters of Amy Tan's **The Joy Luck Club . . .** Cleyvis Natera is the real thing: a warrior storyteller who had me in her thrall from beginning to end. . . . A novel that speaks to so many of the current challenges confronting our global community and does so with generosity, moral imagination, grace, and—never to be downplayed—wickedly good, page-turning storytelling."
—Julia Alvarez, nationally bestselling author of **Afterlife** and **How the García Girls Lost Their Accents**

"Natera's prose is intricate, tender, and perfectly calibrated—the Guerrero family will stay with me forever. This is a tremendous debut novel from a profoundly gifted writer."
—Kimberly King Parsons, National Book Award–longlisted author of **Black Light**

"What Natera has given us with **Neruda on the Park** is a book so honest, so implicating, so liberating that it is at once beautiful and terrifying. **Neruda on the Park** is a loud triumph that caresses like a whisper."
—Robert Jones, Jr., **New York Times** bestselling author of **The Prophets**

"Natera is a writer to watch. Her excellent debut novel is lyrical, absorbing, and slyly funny."
—JENNY OFFILL, **New York Times** bestselling author of **Weather**

"**Neruda on the Park** is unlike anything I've ever read before. It is as poignant and perceptive as it is sexy and thrilling, the rare book that manages to be chilling and fun and profound all at once. . . . A remarkable feat of imagination from a wholly original writer."
—NAIMA COSTER, **New York Times** bestselling author of **What's Mine and Yours**

"A dazzling triumph . . . Every beat of Natera's gorgeous prose pulses with urgency, humanity, and a whole lot of heart."
—ZAKIYA DALILA HARRIS, **New York Times** bestselling author of **The Other Black Girl**

"**Neruda on the Park** strikes all the right notes—captivating characters, lyrical language, and a story line that captures your imagination and refuses to let go. Combining all this with insights that linger and questions that challenge, Cleyvis Natera makes an unforgettable debut!"
—TAYARI JONES, **New York Times** bestselling author of **An American Marriage**

"Natera has written a powerful and arresting novel with unforgettable characters. **Neruda on the Park** is the book we need and the reason I read."
—ANGIE CRUZ, author of **Dominicana**

"Armed with wit and a warm sense of humor, Natera deftly scales questions as huge as the luxury building that looms over her characters' lives. But pulsing at the heart of **Neruda on the Park** is a story more intimate, tender, and timeless. . . . A beautifully observed and propulsive debut."

—DAWNIE WALTON, author of
The Final Revival of Opal & Nev

"Tenderly written, **Neruda on the Park** is an insightful narrative that sifts through the layers of the family, lovers, and places we choose to find home in."

—ELIZABETH ACEVEDO, National Book
Award–winning author of **The Poet X**

"A wondrous debut . . . Natera's novel, which artfully, imaginatively, convincingly explores home and the lengths one goes to protect it; love and womanhood; class and the promise of the American dream, is a compelling, crucial work of fiction."

—MITCHELL S. JACKSON, Pulitzer Prize–winning
author of **Survival Math**

"Probing questions of race, class, and displacement, **Neruda on the Park** is clear-sighted and full of heart as it traces all the ways a community—and a family—can fall apart and seek their way back to one another."

—GABRIELA GARCIA, **New York Times** bestselling
author of **Of Women and Salt**

NERUDA ON THE PARK

NERUDA ON THE PARK

A Novel

Cleyvis Natera

RANDOM HOUSE LARGE PRINT

Copyright © 2022 by Cleyvis Natera Tucker

All rights reserved.
Published in the United States of America by
Random House Large Print in association with
Ballantine Books, an imprint of Random House,
a division of Penguin Random House LLC, New York.

Cover design and illustration: Cassie Gonzales
Cover images: Ohlamour studio/Stocksy (girl), Simon
Desrochers/Stocksy (bench), Bonninstudio/Stocksy (woman),
Cafe Racer/Shutterstock (background), Westend61/
Shutterstock (building)

The Library of Congress has established a
Cataloging-in-Publication record for this title.

ISBN: 978-0-593-55911-6

www.penguinrandomhouse.com/large-print-format-books

FIRST LARGE PRINT EDITION

Printed in the United States of America

1st Printing

This Large Print edition published in accord with
the standards of the N.A.V.H.

Para mis difuntos
  Mi abuelita, Regina "Masona" Lucas
  Mi padre, Bienvenido Natera
  Mi abuelito, Silvilio Lucas

And for Penelope and Julian

Who would have said that the earth
with its ancient skin would change so much?
—Pablo Neruda, "How Much Happens in a Day"

Remember—you are the trunk, not a branch.
—Regina "Masona" Lucas

PART I
DEMOLITION

CHAPTER ONE

Luz Guerrero

WHITE OUT, WASHED OUT

The sound of split wooden frames, shattered glass windows, and fractured brownstone woke her. Luz imagined a huge crash, her body hurling toward a windshield, or some other kind of hurt. Then, as silence followed, she burrowed deeper into her covers, relieved. It was only moments before her wind-chime alarm, before Mami handed her a cup of coffee and Papi looked on at her, so very proud. She left their apartment, ready. Today—the biggest day, the day that would set everything in motion.

Luz walked out into Nothar Park, where she watched a wrecking ball swing back and forth from a crane. She picked up part of a brick that had skittered out to the sidewalk, noting how close to her own skin tone it was, a color Eusebia, her mother, called casi puro cafecito. Hardly any milk there, she always said, with an edge of concern, finding it impossible to simply use the word **Black.** The crane's neck moved, and the metal rope swung the ball forward, striking again. The noise grew noticeably louder. The wall resisted. But the force of the pressure caused a crater where it hit, and from it, tiny lines extended like wrinkles.

This the sound that woke her.

The cold air was thick with mist. Luz turned away from the noise and rubble, making her way through Nothar Park toward the subway, intent on her destination and determined not to be distracted. Her boss, Raenna, had texted her late last night.

I got news to share, she wrote. Meet me at TSP before work.

What's the big news? Luz responded.

Raenna hadn't texted back.

As Luz reached the stairs down to the subway, the escalating noise made her pause. The wrecking ball had finally broken through the stubborn wall—the fracturing now complete. Dust rose into the damp air rapidly, then hung softly above the trees.

Was Luz upset to witness the beginning of the destruction of her neighborhood? Nope. Qué va. She was focused on a rare moment of elation. Would today be the day she'd be offered junior partner? Of course it would. Over the last five years, she and her boss had had an agreement. The minute the promotion was a go, she'd be the first to know. She pushed forward.

Although Luz wasn't upset about the crashing

wall, she did worry about her mother. Eusebia often looked onto that old, burnt-out tenement building and spoke about maybe putting together a community campaign to purchase the grounds—for a garden, no less. Luz and her father, Vladimir, remained mute to Mami's inquiries, hiding conspiring smiles behind cupped palms. They both knew how hard it would be, to pull that off. The obscene asking price for the shell—over ten million dollars. They thought it would remain as it had—abandoned, neglected, unwanted—since they arrived from the Dominican Republic twenty years ago. Who would bother?

Plus. Vladimir had cashed out his retirement investments, and Luz had contributed all her savings from the bonuses she'd gotten over the years, all to build Mami's dream home back in the Dominican Republic. Mami remained oblivious to their secret scheming. Just last week, Luz and her father pored over the pictures of the terrace overlooking the sea with the hole in the ground that would soon become an infinity pool. In just a few months, the house would be completed, her parents would retire and move back, and Luz would finally be able to live her own life. Move to Central Park West, that corner building on Seventy-ninth Street she'd had her eye on since she graduated law school.

It was ironic, really, that now that she was so close to finally leaving the neighborhood, change had reached it instead. A miracle it had taken this long for the gentrification of New York to reach

Nothar Park. The Lower East Side, Chelsea, Hell's Kitchen, Harlem, Washington Heights, and especially Brooklyn, washed out, white out, everything forever changed. At the firm where she practiced law as a junior associate, she had friends who'd moved into those same neighborhoods, awed at how amazing the space (actual space!) was—friends who just a few years back would have been too scared to walk down the street they now lived on. She knew what would happen when the neighborhood changed. Some of it good, some of it not good. Now here they were, at the cusp. Belowground, the turbulence of the train entering the station prompted her to hurry on. She put the neighborhood out of her mind. Her future life was waiting.

A BODY CAN SURVIVE GREAT PAIN

The Secret Place, a members-only restaurant in midtown Manhattan, wasn't listed in any online apps, didn't accept reservations. As she waited for Raenna to arrive, Luz noticed the dining room space as if for the first time. Every wall painted black, including the tall ceiling. The vases, in contrast, had an ombré gold tint and were filled with oversized tree branches sprouting yellow flowers. They enhanced Luz's feeling of pure light. She held fast to the edge of the table lest she float away. Luz tried to place the soothing, hip music flowing discreetly out of hidden speakers. Underground Portugal? Brazil?

She had often felt out of place. Just a few nights ago, at dinner with colleagues, they'd been served eel in a reduction of lime that made the flesh writhe. Nodding along with everyone else, she'd said it was delicious, while worrying that others could sense her growing discomfort and nausea. But not today.

Today, Luz ordered the expensive champagne, knowing it was ridiculous to do so at 8 A.M. Raenna would sigh at the impropriety, but find it charming nonetheless.

"Should I bring it now?" asked Henry, their usual server, with honey in his eyes, honey in his smile. Around them, bussers moved with the efficiency of those under constant threat of being fired, removing sweaty water glasses from unoccupied tables and replacing them with fresh ones.

Luz shook her head. "Let's wait until she gets here."

She stood and went to the bathroom.

Looking in the mirror, she applied another coat of lipstick. She fixed a strand that had escaped her tight bun, pushed the pinchos further in place—wincing at how tight the hairpins were, how much they hurt. It was worth the pain. She practiced how she would stand in front of her peers when they made the announcement later—each associate would clap, while drilling her with their eyes, especially those who'd been waiting to hear it was their turn.

In the dimness of the bathroom, a familiar sadness

neared at the thought of all the hours, all the work, all the sacrifice, her hand first up to volunteer on extra cases—spending every weekend in the office, getting home later and later every day. Not now, she thought, pushing that sadness away. Today, it insisted. In the mirror, on her face, the outline of that emptiness. Where did it come from?

Luz didn't answer that question, was cautious to not ask it of herself a second time. Emptiness, she knew, was a human-sized shape inside each of us—you could fill it with slimming suits or sky-high heels; one way or another, it gets filled. Older women—Raenna and Mami—never spoke of such. They wanted her focused, relentless. From their lives to hers, the wrong corrected. But the emptiness remained, persisted.

"Diablo," a loud voice said behind her, outside the frame of the mirror. She had to turn to see.

"Where's the runway?" Angélica said. "You look like a model."

Angélica, who lived in the basement apartment of her building, who'd been her best friend until Luz went away to college. At twenty-nine, Angélica's round face was still exactly the same as when they were teenagers. Her blond hair in stark contrast with her dark eyes. Luz had given her the first dye when they were both fifteen, then immediately tried to talk her into going back to her natural brown hair. But Angélica loved it and said she'd never go back, twirling bangs over her forehead. Today, her hair tucked behind an ear showed the scar on Angélica's forehead she'd always been so self-conscious of, the shape forever reminding Luz of a centipede.

"Are those red-bottom shoes?" Angélica said, grabbing hold of one of Luz's legs and lifting her foot off the ground.

Luz stumbled, caught herself against the vanity. She gently pushed Angélica's hand away, lifted her own foot, showed her the bottom. She had bought these shoes just last week, after she noticed Raenna had them. Hadn't even blinked twice at the price as she extended payment.

"Must be nice to be rich," Angélica said.

"They hurt, a lot," Luz said. She caught herself slouching and straightened up. "And please, I'm not rich. What are you doing here?"

"Nice to see you, too," Angélica said.

"Sorry," Luz said. "I'm just surprised. How are you?"

Eusebia had said something about Angélica getting a new job. How Angélica's mom hoped she'd stick with this one for a while. Luz never thought her dizque friend would end up working in the place she had dinner several nights a week.

"All the people who eat here are jerks. You fit right in," Angélica said.

Luz shook her head. She took a step around Angélica, headed out the door, and held it as it closed so it would make no sound. Didn't bother

with a fake goodbye. No one was going to take
away this feeling of elation. Not today.

In the dining room, across the way, Raenna sat
at her table. Their eyes locked, and instead of offering her usual warm smile, Raenna busied herself with her phone. Weird. Henry rushed across
the room, holding a champagne bottle in one hand
and two flutes expertly crossed at the stems in the
other. Behind him, another server followed, carrying a bottle chiller and stand.

Her shoes were not designed for rushing across
a room.

When she finally made it to the table, she knew
the meeting wasn't about a promotion.

"You ordered champagne?"

Raenna's bone-straight hair was twice its natural
volume because of the weave she'd had put in over
the weekend. With those huge green eyes, pale skin,
and tiny frame, no one would ever suspect where
she was from. South Side of Chicago, she would
volunteer, right after correcting their pronunciation
(Ray-nuh). Luz knew it was code for people to understand she wasn't white, never mind what her fair
skin, green eyes, and straight hair implied.

"What's the news?"

"Luz, let's sit together for a minute before we get
to that."

"Why are we here, Rae?"

Raenna took a sip of the champagne. "Will
you please bring orange juice," she said to Henry,

who rushed away to the kitchen. To Luz she said, "Please sit."

Luz couldn't sit down. She reached for the glass. Took a sip of the champagne. She thought the more expensive champagne should be sweeter than this dry, tart thing.

Raenna raised the flute to her lips. When she put the glass down, it was empty. She stood up, and though Luz towered over her, her confidence made her appear bigger than her five-foot-two-inch height. There was a peplum on Raenna's blouse like petals of a white flower, unfurling. Her tailored pants elongated her legs. Same shoes Luz wore, only Raenna's were in taupe. Grooming, flawless. Clothes, always exquisite. Luz modeled her life after Raenna's.

Underneath the makeup, there were large dark circles around Raenna's eyes. There was pigment discoloration around her jawline spreading toward her ears; an accident involving a fire had left the scarred tissue much darker than the remainder of her skin. Green veins were visible all the way up to her forehead. Makeup covered it well but not fully. In spite of the scar, or maybe because of it, Raenna was stunning. The scar was a sign of fragility, yes, but also a testament to the fact a body can survive great pain. Luz had never worked up the courage to ask what happened.

"At some point today," Raenna said, "you will lose your job."

Luz sat down. She couldn't force any more of the

bitter drink. She placed the glass on the table but missed. The glass fell on the floor.

"It didn't break," Henry said. As he reached their table, he placed a carafe filled with orange juice between the two women. "That means it's your lucky day."

Raenna raised a hand, shook her head at Henry. Not now.

"What did you say?" Luz asked her.

Raenna's lips were moving but Luz had a hard time understanding the words. Was she whispering? Mumbling? She had a bad habit of mumbling when her brain was moving fast. No, this was a slur. From one glass of champagne?

Then Raenna grew silent. Henry went away, and neither woman knew what to say. Henry returned moments later with a fresh basket of the most delicate croissants and a new flute. He made Luz a mimosa, then called Angélica over. She bent down to wipe the wet floor with a startlingly white cloth. Henry didn't speak, and when Angélica made to say something, he held an index finger against his mouth.

"I'm so sorry," Raenna said.

"I don't understand," Luz said. "What are you talking about?"

Luz grabbed a croissant, then put it back. Its warmth lingered on her hand. Angélica continued scrubbing the floor with exaggerated diligence.

"I think I need to hear you say it one more time."

"It's better if we focus on the future," Raenna said. "I know this is shocking. I wish we had more time to let you absorb it, but we have to go soon."

"I know," Luz said. "Okay. I'm listening."

Luz wasn't listening. The blackness of the room contracted, and the room's objects fell into sharp relief. The branches in the vases thickened, choking the space around them. She felt heat spreading upward under her clothes. Don't cry, she commanded, don't cry.

"It's better if you resign," Raenna said. "That's why I'm telling you."

"Is this a joke?" Luz asked.

Raenna touched her scar. Some of her makeup came off on her fingertips, exposing the rigid tissue underneath.

"I wish it was a joke," she said, then, to Angélica, "I'm sure you got it." She made a dismissive gesture.

Angélica reacted by slowing down, wrapping the cloth around two fingers and wiping the floor with renewed force. Henry cleared his throat at her.

"I just found out last night," Raenna said. "They know I'm your mentor. That's probably why they kept me out of it."

"How could you find out last? I work for you."

"You don't work for me," Raenna said sharply. "You work for the firm. You know the trouble I can get into for talking to you about this?" She caught herself, softened her tone. "I just wanted to warn you," she said. "You should resign, that will make it easier to get another job. Don't let them fire you."

Henry cleared his throat at Angélica again, and she finally stood, satisfied. She looked right at Luz before she walked away, with a little smile that lifted the centipede's belly. Did that mean she would tell Mami? Mami. Luz remembered the hole in the ground that would become a pool, overlooking a breathtaking view—all ocean and sky. During those long days at work, she'd imagined Mami and Papi sitting on the edge of that pool, lightly touching the surface of the water. She reminded herself, daily, how hard they'd worked, how much they deserved a break.

"This makes no sense," Luz said.

"We're just not making margin. Top-heavy."

"So, get rid of associates?" Luz said.

"Not plural," Raenna said. She poured herself more champagne, and her Adam's apple slid up and down as she took a sip. "This is just you."

"Oh," Luz said. It was the smallest sound she'd ever uttered. The heat, now at her neck, threatened to set her face on fire. How could she be the only one?

"Why me? Everyone knows Duvall is on probation. There are, um, people who have made mistakes."

Behind her eyes, pressure burned. How many times over the last year had she heard this or that associate talk about a missed statute of limitations?

Raenna opened her mouth as if to speak but

shut it immediately. She examined the bubbles in her glass. One after the other, in rapid succession, each rose to the surface, joined others in a necklace around the glass, then disappeared. Luz felt rage surfacing beneath the humiliation. She got up.

"Let's just go," she said. She thought about heading into the office, sitting at her neat desk. Doing the million things she was supposed to do until HR called her into a conference room. She decided she wouldn't pay for the champagne. Raenna had a business account. No checks ever had to be signed.

Then she stopped. Raenna buttoned up her camel coat, held a small purse in the crook of her elbow.

"Did you try to stop it?"

"There was no stopping it."

"Who picked me?"

"You think I'd do this to you?"

In private moments, away from the office, Raenna always told Luz the only way to change the world was to take it over, rip it out of the hands of those holding on for dear life. Nobody is going to give anything willingly, she would say. We have to take what belongs to us. It was hard to reconcile the person who said those words, most recently just last week, with the person who stood in front of her. She was hiding something from her. What was it?

"In my heart," Raenna said, "I know you're meant for better things."

At the words, the tears fell. Raenna reached in her purse and took out a small cloth handkerchief and handed it over. Luz wiped her tears. Who even went around with cloth anything these days? she thought. Of course: Raenna, who was unlike anyone she'd ever known.

Raenna reached over, gave her a hug. Once Luz calmed down, Raenna told her again. It would be better if she quit.

"I haven't done anything wrong," Luz said. "Why would I quit?"

If Luz had been a wall in that old building being demolished in Nothar Park, Raenna would have seen the crater forming, followed by a line that cracked her skin. But she wasn't a wall. The sound of her own voice reminded Luz she was solid, so she went ahead, not waiting for Raenna to lead the way as she usually did. Nothing would break her down.

THE TONGUES

When she made her way up the subway stairs back in her neighborhood, it was late afternoon. Neighbors stood side by side around Nothar Park. Their commute home had been halted by these new machines. Tight faces peeked out from the windows of apartments all around the park as blinds were raised. Luz's face tightened as her eyes watered, stinging from the dust that spread as the wrecking ball continued its attack. She wove past neighbors.

She pretended nothing out of the ordinary had happened to her at work. She'd been doing the same pretending all day, from the moment she and Raenna arrived in the office, to the interminable day that extended to 4 P.M., when just as she'd grown sure Raenna had played a terrible prank on her, she was called into a conference room. And just as Raenna had forecasted, she'd been let go.

Now Luz turned in front of the eight-floor stone façade of 600 West. The Tongues, her mother's bingo-playing friends, stood outside. The triplets, identical with their white hair and matching eyeglass chains, kept most in line with the threat of exposure. Eusebia had nicknamed them the Tongues because of how much they liked to gossip.

"Buenas tardes," Luz said.

All three women turned to her, then back to the noise across the way.

"This look like a good afternoon to you?" one of them said, in Spanish.

Their jaws were hard-set, angry. Luz didn't bother responding. She'd never figured out why they disliked her so much. But she certainly had no time for their shade today. Instead, she turned her attention to the park. Trucks and cars and trees and people blocked the view. Even the land itself sloped in such a way that Luz and the Tongues were unable to see clearly. In front of them a group of volunteers in matching bright green shirts were picking up garbage in the park. She tilted her head to get a better view and couldn't. She left the sisters.

On the way into the building, Luz slipped, and

braced her fall with a hand against the brick wall.
When she pulled her hand away, it was wet with a
sticky white film. Disgusted, she brought it to her
nose. It smelled clean, like powder. She wiped her
hand against her suit, without thought, and then
winced. She'd have to get the suit dry-cleaned.

The Tongues sucked their teeth at her. As always, they shook their heads, disapproving, as if
they couldn't wait to put the word out, Radio Mil
Informando, that they saw Luz wiping the neighborhood off her fancy lawyer clothes.

EACH BRICK, TRASH

Upstairs, Luz opened the door to her home. The
long, dark hallway stretched in front of her. Her
bedroom with the smells she loved—figs, vanilla,
bitter orange, and the bed freshly made—was to her
left. Her mother changed the sheets every Monday,
for Tuesday was laundry day. Up ahead, to the
right, the kitchen. Luz wanted so badly to go inside
her room and lie on the bed, discarding all she'd
brought from outside. To recapture the moment
before Raenna showed up. She'd been about to float
from that lightness. But if she went into her room
first, it would be suspicious. She never changed out
of her work clothes without saying hello.

Her mother was talking to someone on the phone,
someone who'd obviously just described gringos
painting a mural in the park. She was oblivious as

Luz went farther into the apartment. There was the clank and clink of a pot being stirred—no doubt something delicious on the stove top. From the living room, children's laughter, high-pitched and continuous, accompanied cartoons on the television. Luz called out her mother's name. She didn't respond.

When Eusebia turned toward her, she let out the smallest of shrieks. Her hand went to her heart and her eyes widened so much Luz had to rush to her side and reassure her.

"It's just me, Mami. Just me."

Eusebia gave her a stern, serious look.

"What are you trying to do?" she yelled at Luz in Spanish. "Give me a heart attack?"

"Never," Luz said, in English.

This is how they spoke to each other. Her mother had learned enough English to understand Luz, but her body had refused to speak it. The words themselves a trespass, an allergic reaction that thickened the tongue and made her accent impossible to understand. For her part, Luz had lost all but a bit of her Spanish—was unable to write it or read it.

Luz examined Mami's face for a sign of knowing.

Her mother's forehead took up a generous portion of her face, and that, coupled with those wide, large brown eyes, gave her a childlike quality. It was Eusebia's mouth that made her appear womanly, one of the first things her father said he'd noticed about her. Her lips are perfect bows, thick and sensual, he always said, which made Luz wince. But when her mother smiled, as she did now taking Luz in, she'd be back to looking like a kid because of her tiny teeth, a few of which, both at the bottom and the top, here crowded together, there shifted stubbornly apart.

There it was, just love. Mami didn't know what happened today.

Everyone said Luz was the spitting image of her mother, though her mother had a petite, hourglass figure, while Luz was small-breasted, statuesque. Her mother had that milky fair skin; Luz was dark. Over six feet tall, she'd inherited her height and skin color from her father. Braces had straightened her teeth, retainers kept them in line. For work, her hair was always pulled back in a tight bun; at home, she let her kinky curls free. With relief, she picked the pinchos out one by one, loosened the bun.

Kenya and Paris, Angélica's twin daughters, rushed into the kitchen. Eusebia watched them occasionally, whenever their grandmother Isabel had super duties or running around to do. They held on to each of Luz's legs, pulling her down for kisses. Luz put the purse on the back of a chair in the kitchen and kneeled down to give them both hugs. Even though she didn't see the girls often, they were always so affectionate, so sweet. So different from their mother.

Eusebia turned her attention back to the stove,

adjusting the flame on the three pots from high to low. Then she fixed her entire body on Luz.

"What are you doing home so early?" she asked, looking her all over.

Luz busied herself with the girls so that she didn't have to make direct eye contact with her mother. She touched their hair, told them how pretty they both looked. Called them by the wrong name on purpose to make them laugh. Asked them how old they were, knowing full well they'd just celebrated their fifth birthday. Both hands up, all fingers outstretched. Ten? she asked. They punched her chest with small fists.

"You're so silly," they said.

"A few lawyers got out of court early today," Luz said, which she figured wasn't untrue. "Won another big case. Everyone's been killing themselves, so they said take the rest of the day off."

Luz didn't usually lie to her mother. She had a very small window to make eye contact, otherwise Eusebia would know something weird was going on. So she did it, shrugging her shoulders in a nonchalant way, the entire time wondering why she didn't just say the truth. She'd lost her job for no good reason, through no fault of her own. And what did she have to show for all that hard work and dedication of the past five years? A laughable severance package, one paycheck for each year worked. At least they'd prorated the mid-year incentive bonus to account for a full six months of anticipated billable hours, even though it was late April. She fumed again, remembering how it had taken the entire business day for her to be called into the conference room—as if they couldn't help but milk a few more hours out of her. We strongly encourage you to review the documents with a lawyer before you sign, Laura, the HR director, had said. Stupidly, Luz had said she was fine, grabbed the pen to sign the severance documents on the spot, wanting to get the hell out of there as quickly as possible. But Laura stopped her, hand over hand, and insisted that she take the documents and read them over at home. Send them through the mail, Laura had said. Take your time reviewing them.

"You hungry?" her mother asked, left eyebrow slightly raised, as if she wasn't quite convinced what Luz said was true. See, whenever Luz was worried about something, she couldn't touch any food. But for some reason, at the thought of food, the space underneath her tongue filled with saliva and her stomach growled loud enough that it made her mother nod in appreciation. The girls hollered in delight, poking Luz in the belly.

"Guess that's all the answer I need," Eusebia said, satisfied. "Food will be ready in a few minutes. I've been calling you all day. Thought we were having an earthquake."

It was Luz's turn to raise a suspicious eyebrow. The girls went back to the living room, then started running in a circle from there to the front door, down the hall to the kitchen, and back to the living room.

"You better stop running or I'm going to beat you," Eusebia yelled the next time their circle brought them to the kitchen. The girls ran on, unconvinced, unthreatened. Eusebia was incapable of the least amount of violence, even two five-year-olds knew that. "Fine then, no habichuelas con dulce for neither of you."

The girls marched back to the living room. The threat of denying them that creamy, sweet treat was enough to still their bodies in front of the television. From outside, the noise of men yelling at each other carried across the park, penetrated the closed windows.

"Go on!" Eusebia said, pushing Luz to the fire escape. "Tell me what's happening."

"The fire escape is wet," Luz whined. "It's pretty nasty outside. I haven't even changed."

"Please," Eusebia said.

Luz went into her bedroom. She avoided the pile of unopened packages by her closet as she changed out of her work clothes and into yoga pants, a thick hooded sweatshirt. What was in the pile? Shoes, purses, tailored suits? She had no memory of what the boxes held. Couldn't remember what she'd spent. But as always, knew it was a lot. Should she return those packages? But wouldn't that be admitting she was scared? Worried?

She hurried away, sat on the fire escape. They'd closed down the entire northern side of the park. There were trucks and dumpsters and many men working on the demolition of the old building. The twins started screaming that they wanted to go outside on the fire escape with Luz. Eusebia bribed them with food to quiet down.

"What's happening now?" Eusebia shouted from inside the apartment.

"The same thing that was happening five minutes ago," Luz said, feigning lightheartedness. "Only now there's, wait, let me count, ten more bricks inside the dumpster."

"Remind me to tell your dad if I go first you can't write my obituary."

"They have pills that can cure you, Mami," Luz said. Half a joke.

Her mother snorted. She stood on her usual spot, on the other side of the living room, as close as she was willing to get unless the window that led to the fire escape was shut, the blinds drawn, the metal accordion gate that led outside locked. Eusebia had come down with a mean case of vertigo the first time she looked out of that same window when they'd arrived from DR. Back home, Eusebia used to say, everything is on the ground floor, where it should be.

Up on the fire escape, looking around, Luz noted how little had changed in all the years they'd lived there. Nothar Park occupied an entire city block in width, two city blocks in length, and it had seemed enormous to Luz when she was a child. The brownstones around the park, converted into apartments, vibrated with loud merengue and bachata. There were groups of men on the street, speaking loudly enough for her to hear as they leaned against lampposts, gesticulating with their arms toward the biggest change to strike Nothar Park in decades—that old tenement building being destroyed without a thought. Every few minutes, there was a booming collapse. Luz's building, which dominated at eight stories, seemed a sponge, absorbing the tumult around it.

"You know," her mother yelled, returning to her corner in the living room, "this is all connected to those americanos in the park."

"Ma," Luz said. "You think the construction is connected to the volunteers?"

"I don't think," she said. "I know."

The phone rang. By the tender way her mother's hand touched the wall next to the phone, Luz could tell it was her father. Eusebia told him the world was coming to an end.

"They're tearing down the old building," she screamed over the construction into the phone.

Across the way, the volunteers had finished the mural. From the fire escape, Luz had a perfect view of the various oversized people holding hands painted in various shades of brown. Words swayed above their arms—**Amor, Familia, y Comunidad.**

The vibrant colors stood out even more because it was such a dreary day. The few remaining volunteers were packing up the art supplies. A woman with a streak of bright blue in her blond hair made wide circles with one arm while an athletic-looking white man with startlingly black hair picked up paint buckets. For a brief moment, the man looked up, staring in Luz's direction. He waved at her. She ignored him.

The old tenement building tugged at Luz. As teenagers, she, Angélica, and their friends from the block would get tipsy in there. They laughed and dreamed about the future—how one day they would all travel the world, move far, far away.

She touched the wet bars on either side of her legs. The metal bars of the fire escape flaked; layers of black paint peeled like brittle nails and gave way easily as she pulled at them, down to the corroded, rusty orange center. Those spots, finally free of years of coats of paint, looked like sores.

When she glanced up again, dusk had fallen, and the park was softly illuminated in streetlight.

"It's never a good sign"—her mother kept going like there'd been no pause—"when the americanos are the ones doing the cleaning. You think this is a coincidence? Demolition and a park cleanup on the same day? I'm telling you they have their eye on pushing us out."

Off the phone, she had inched just a step closer to the window.

"Ma," Luz said, "we don't know what they're going to build. It might be good for the neighborhood. It doesn't have to suck."

Mami didn't get it, how inconvenient it was where they lived. Any time she wanted to do anything—go to the bank, go to the gym, go to a healthy food market, get a nice glass of wine, buy fresh flowers—she had to hail a cab or pay train fare. She told her that.

"You think that's what we'd get in exchange?" Mami said, suddenly serious. "The world is a harsh place. Why do you think only Dominican people live here? We stay close to each other not just to belong, but to be safe."

When they first arrived in this country, Eusebia had insisted Luz not forget their true home had been left behind, that this new place, with its hard ground and impossible language, was hostile. But over time, Eusebia had created an entire new world in it. Listening to her now, Luz marveled at the change, wondering exactly what it was about this place that had won her mother over.

Because Luz knew the truth about the way a city responds to a community of folks who may not even be eligible to vote, who didn't have the know-how to demand change, even of the smallest kind. It was mirrored in schools, in garbage pickup times, in police response times. She didn't want to get into a fight. Because that's what would happen if she told her mother what she actually thought.

She didn't feel like she belonged here. There was hostility toward her, in the neighborhood, and she'd often felt like an outsider, especially when she went off to college. It only got worse after she graduated from law school.

Luz already knew how this story ended—the neon-colored storefronts that lined their side of the park with their loud-ass blinking lights would transform as if by magic—cue in yoga, juice bars, endless mimosa brunch places with lines out the door.

On the street level below, Christian, Angélica's brother, walked with his head down toward the entrance of the building, backpack slung low over one shoulder, a plastic bag of groceries in hand. He was finishing his senior year of high school. He walked slow, like an old man, then turned in the direction everyone faced, toward the menacing, silent machines. He glanced up directly at her fire escape and, after a moment, waved at her. Startled, she managed a small wave. Did he often look up, searching for her? There had been a time years ago, when he was a tween crushing on her, that he was like her shadow. He made his way out of her vision, into the building through the side door that led to the basement.

HOME

Eusebia placed a man-sized serving on a plate in front of Luz and waited for her reaction. The rice was a white mountain topped with pollo guisado, steamy with the sweet aroma of tomato sauce. On the side, in a small bowl, she placed black beans garnished with chopped raw cilantro. A single plate with all the fixings together would have been fine, but the way the food was presented was a reminder Eusebia considered her daughter king of this house. Luz smiled at her, winked with exaggeration at the pomposity of the display.

Satisfied, Eusebia went back to the kitchen and returned with a tall glass of water, a smaller plate topped with green salad, and a slice of ripe avocado. She turned around and went back to the kitchen, returned with a napkin.

"Mami, sit down, you're making me dizzy."

Eusebia sat down, eyes intent on Luz as she ate, nodding approvingly as her daughter shoved spoonful after spoonful in her mouth. The food so soothing. Luz closed her eyes against the pleasure of her mother's talents. This was love, in her mouth, filling her body.

"Wow, Mami," Luz said. "This is the best thing in the world."

"There are better things," Eusebia said. Wicked look, eyebrows up and down like a comedian. Luz understood immediately, even without the facial shenanigans.

"Ay, Mami!" Luz said. "You're gross."

Her mother never ate with Luz or Vladimir. She liked to watch them as they ate, and only served herself once they were finished and needed no second servings. She often put whatever was left in a small bowl and ate it standing in front of the sink. Luz had never given the practice much thought, either. Now she put her spoon down, drank the water in long gulps, and rested her eyes on the hollow space inside the cup. When she lifted her gaze, her mother's face was tight with tension, searching.

"What's wrong?" her mother asked.

Luz shook her head. She turned the TV's volume higher. Watched her mother's profile as she stared at the screen. When was the last time she'd really looked at Eusebia?

On the television, the whale whose baby calf had died swam on. She'd been carrying him on her glossy head for weeks. Eusebia's eyelids hung heavy. Luz wanted to ask her mother if her own life had turned out the way she wanted, if she would change any of it given the chance. But the question got stuck on the ridges at the roof of her mouth. As if the spell, that promise that kept both of them in place, would splinter were she to ask such a simple question.

Over at the china cabinet, her mother's most treasured possessions. None of it china. Instead, the shelves held school pictures of Luz from every year since third grade, when she'd first arrived from DR, and all the plaques she'd been awarded and the medals in national colors that had hung from her neck. She was the star of photos that her mother insisted on to track her success. The only anomaly was her father's old book of poems by Pablo Neruda.

Now was the time for truth.

Should she tell her now?

She'd remained here, with her parents, in this same apartment, when everyone her age had their own place. It wasn't that unusual, around the neighborhood, to stay home until a woman got married, even in this day and age. But that wasn't the reason Luz stayed behind. She'd been too embarrassed to tell those who dared ask the truth. She couldn't pay for the shoes, the purses, and the suits, help her father out with the house on the mountain, and also afford to live on her own. She'd told herself it would just be a few years, to pay them back for all they'd done. They deserved a happy ending.

But there was more. She felt bad for her father—so often gone on police business—who looked more miserable as time went on. She felt bad for her mother, too, who had nothing else to do except take care of everyone.

"Something is wrong," Eusebia insisted. "Why won't you tell me?"

How to explain they'd both sacrificed so much for a purpose now gone?

Luz looked up at a painting on the wall. Vladimir had painted the picture as a present for both of them when they got to the USA. It depicted a peaceful, if somewhat cliché, campo scene. A man wearing a sombrero, with his back to the viewer, held a rope tied around the neck of a little donkey. Behind him, a road that forked, and because Vladimir hadn't fully mastered the art of perspective, the gorgeous little house, river, and trees that would have been impossible to see ahead of the campesino were right at the top of the canvas. It gave the entire painting an amateur, flat feeling. The home he'd painted was on a mountain in the countryside where Eusebia and Vladimir were born and fell in love as they grew up—the land where their new house was going up. She often wondered how he'd done it. What about the line, the softness of it, made her feel such melancholy? That campesino was happy to be home.

Eusebia extended her hand to Luz's cheek, caressing it, and gave her a quick peck on the forehead as she rose from the table, gathering the dirty plates.

"I'm here when you're ready," she said over a shoulder as she left the room.

From the kitchen, Luz heard the radio play a beautiful bolero from the Buena Vista Social Club. Mami sang along, off-key. Tomorrow, she thought. She'd tell her tomorrow for sure. She imagined the remains of her meal sliding off with the suds of the dishwashing liquid as her mother squeezed the sponge, imagined it all swirling down the drain to the accompaniment of such sad music. Did it matter to Luz, what was about to be lost? What already had been? Mami had asked her if she understood what was at stake. As if, already, Mami found Luz lacking because she'd been able to thrive in the face of their early loss. Home, she told herself, could be a place, a person, a feeling; at times, a profession, the end result of a long pursuit. A fluid thing, for sure, but precious. She did care about Nothar Park, just as she'd cared so deeply for her job. But wasn't the whole point of life to turn each loss into a win? If that was true, then what was the use of wasting time mourning?

CHAPTER TWO

Eusebia de Guerrero

HALIDOM

Eusebia sat up—tried not to disturb Vladimir on his side of the bed—and swung her bare feet into a puddle of water so cold her nipples hardened instantly. Radiator broken, again.

She went to the kitchen. Put water and coffee grinds in the greca, set it on the stove. Took the sliced bread out of the plastic bag and slid three pieces into the four-slice toaster. Removed eggs from the refrigerator and put three in a small pot filled with water for Luz, who would only eat the egg whites, and left three on the side for Vladimir, who would only eat his fried over hard. Vladimir's eggs needed to reach room temperature before she dropped them in the pan. Later, she'd place each fried egg on top of not-too-toasted bread.

The sound of magical wind chimes came from down the hallway. Luz's phone alarm. Eusebia heard kitchen noises below and knew Verónica García must be standing right where she stood, doing exactly this.

During the night, she'd heard Luz make her way to their bedroom. The doorknob turned. She sat up in bed, ready to receive and soothe. But Luz never opened the door. Eusebia did not stand. She did not follow. Whatever happened yesterday, better to wait until Luz was ready to say it.

Eusebia took the moment before Luz came for her coffee to wash her face, hastily brush her teeth. Were they sending Luz to Europe again? Permanently? Last year, they made her go to London every two minutes to support the lawyers that worked there, because apparently some lawyers didn't know everything they needed to know to do their job. Luz's boss was the expert and Luz's job was to help her boss. Eusebia worried. Who would make sure Luz ate in the morning before going to work? Not her boss. Every story Luz ever told about Raenna went the same way—Luz the one catering while the boss consumed.

It isn't the way here, to care, to be selfless.

Back in the kitchen, she focused on the boiling eggs and the rising coffee. Tried, for just a moment, to slow it all down before the day pulled on her. This moment—with how the vapor exited the spout and filled this entire kitchen with the smell of coffee, with how it made her forget herself—only lasted the shortest bit.

She served herself a cup of coffee and took the first sip, so sweet the rush dilated her pupils. She put it to the side. She needed to get to the more important work first.

Luz arrived silently, eyes barely open. She extended a hand toward Eusebia, who already had the coffee cup ready to go. Eusebia couldn't understand why anyone would drink the coffee that bitter. Luz headed back to her bedroom, cup in hand. There she would sit, drinking her coffee on the edge of her bed, eyes glued to her phone, thumb drawing an eyelash over and over as she scrolled on the screen.

In the bathroom they all shared, Eusebia turned the hot water on all the way, then left the room. It would take a while to warm up. Moments later, she heard Luz gently close the door to the bathroom, then the shower started to run.

She peeled the eggs and cut them in half. Removed the yolks. The egg whites were firm and perfect except for one piece, which had a small veiny string that bunched like thread. She pulled at it and removed the tiny attached lump. Luz got grossed out easily; it was Eusebia's job to remove all imperfections. She took the mango out of the refrigerator—the most delicious mango she'd tasted in years. Yesterday, on first bite, Eusebia had set it aside for her daughter, knowing this reminder of home could momentarily erase whatever was wrong.

Eusebia carried the plate to Luz's room. Left it on the dresser. Back in the kitchen, she grabbed a mop and Vladimir's cup of coffee, which was just like hers, puro rico cafecito. In their bedroom, Vladimir lay in the fetal position; the blanket around him made him a caterpillar, only his handsome face poking out. Usually, his warm hand would reach for her hip as soon as she neared the bed, pulling her toward him. But today, his body remained immobile, still deeply asleep. She shook him gently and he blinked hard.

"Muñeca, five more minutes," he said. He turned his back to her, caterpillar cocoon split open as his body expanded, took over more than half the bed.

She mopped the mess by the radiator, retraced her steps, and found them disappeared. Yesterday was a bad day for Vladimir. She could always tell by how long it took for his gun and badge to leave his body. If he went straight to the bedroom, changed his clothes, and put the gun away in the safe—secret safe code 1125 for the day she and Luz arrived in New York City, the happiest day of his life, he always said—she knew it was a not-so-terrible day. Yesterday, he had sat down on the couch—didn't even bother switching the channel from the orca still swimming with that baby on its back—and stared listlessly into space. He'd shoveled the dinner she served him into his mouth without once looking up. Finally, he'd taken a shower and gone into the bedroom, putting gun and badge into the safe as an afterthought right before he slipped into bed, falling asleep immediately. Not two words to keep each other company had left his mouth. On bad days, he forgot she'd been waiting all day to speak to him.

She had turned the channel to the local news. A tractor-trailer parked in an abandoned warehouse in the Bronx. Over one hundred people found but more than half were dead. They'd been traveling for days and had made the long journey all the way from Mexico to Texas, then Texas to the Bronx, without appropriate supplies, the air running out. A search was on for the driver. She stared intently at the screen, always vigilant for Vladimir's cameo, but he was never on the news. Police detectives were hardly ever seen on camera.

On bad days, Eusebia knew to leave Vladimir alone. No gossip about the neighborhood or news of her sister, who had left over a year ago to attend a fat camp and get plastic surgery in DR. No update on the tenement going down across Nothar Park or how all those volunteers spent all day cleaning up their mess, painting a beautiful mural that was so bright she'd had to touch it. Most of all, she wouldn't speak about their daughter, who showed up looking sad enough to make her wonder if her promotion would put her in another continent. She couldn't put another worry on his mind, after the day he had. She would just give him time to rest, and then slide beside him, the warmth of her body sanctuary, the wetness a vessel.

She would ease him into the next day quietly,

holding his hand firmly, to remind him that what stood out from the bad day wasn't the worst part but the best part, that there was a lot of love left over in this horrible world. That the brutality he saw on a bad day could always be bested by what waited for him when he returned home. He'd been having a lot of bad days back-to-back.

DESCENT

Eusebia's daughter was simply stunning. Luz stood in the kitchen's doorway, wearing a navy-blue suit. The unbuttoned jacket revealed a pink form-fitting shell tight on her lean body. A silk scarf with birds and branches drawn on the fabric was tied around her neck with the prettiest of bows. She didn't need to wear makeup. Her face was rosy from the shower and her hair bun, so high on her head, made her cheekbones stand out. A small rivulet of water from her still-wet hair curved from hairline to clavicle, darkening the silk scarf. Luz leaned her weight from one leg to the other and looked distractedly at her watch, then at the television, then back at her watch. Anywhere but Eusebia's eyes. Luz placed the plate on the table. Eusebia reached for the greca, topping off her daughter's mug.

"What's up with the whale?" Luz asked.

"The baby is still on her head," Eusebia said, peeling her eyes away from Luz to the television.

She shrugged. Took Luz's plate, noticing half

the egg whites were still there. The grapefruit untouched. But she did eat all the mango. Standing this close, she could tell Luz had been crying. "Querida, what's wrong?" Eusebia asked.

"I have to go," Luz said.

"Dímelo. A mother knows."

Luz undid the knot at her neck. The scarf hung loose for a moment, then slid off. Impossible, how slow it descended. Luz didn't bend down to pick it up. A tear sloped down her cheek and onto her pink shirt. The fabric absorbed the moisture, magnified it into a wider circle. Eusebia cupped her face, then wiped her daughter's cheek with her thumb. A great surge entered Eusebia's body through the place where their skin touched.

Luz shook her off, removed her shoes in one quick motion.

"I'm not going to work today," she said. Her bedroom door closed quietly moments later. It took Eusebia time to move. She knew Luz better than anyone else. That feeling she'd just had, of sadness and rapid descent, came right from her daughter's body. All she had to do was touch Luz to be right there with her, feel what she felt. Eusebia picked up the scarf.

"Let me in," she demanded at Luz's door. She raised her voice, knowing it might wake Vladimir and steal sleep he badly needed.

"Not now," Luz said.

Eusebia realized Luz stood against the door. She

gently touched the spot where she thought her head might be.

"What can I do?"

"Nothing," Luz said.

Imagine that, she thought. Help by doing nothing? Ridiculous.

"Whatever it is, mi'ja," Eusebia said, "we'll get through it."

"Please," Luz said, low enough that Eusebia could hardly hear her, now clearly choking on her tears. "Please, Mami. Just let me be for a little bit."

So, she didn't get promoted. So what. She'd have other chances, other triumphs.

At the other end of the hall, Vladimir called.

"Is everything okay?"

"Of course," Eusebia said, walking away from Luz's door, toward Vladimir. "I just made more coffee."

THE WORST PART

Eusebia held Vladimir's hand in both of her hands, then his face. She kissed him with a smile, just a hint of teeth grazing his lips, so he would know it was pure joy, getting to be near him. Still, when she was done, he was quiet.

She went to the kitchen. Prepared the toast, with the eggs on top, fried so hard the edges were charred. Just the way he liked them. And she saw his effort, as he, just like Luz, avoided her eyes. His shoulders were so tight she could hardly see neck.

"Start with the worst part," she said.

"No way," he said, finally a spark. He made a show of how much he had to chew, so she wouldn't ask him to talk.

"You chew like a goat from Sancho Panza's farm," she told him. Sancho Panza was the old man who still lived, Dios lo bendiga, next to her mother's house on the mountain back in DR. Vladimir had nicknamed him Sancho after reading **Don Quijote,** because of his easygoing manner, because he seemed like the kind of person who went along with whoever had a plan.

Now Eusebia reminded Vladimir how they'd spent hours back then, hypnotized by the slow chewing of those goats, jaws moving side to side, drawing half-moons. Vladimir, stick in hand, drawing houses, their future, on the red dirt as the old man calmly petted his goats, checking them for ticks, walking so slow from one to the other Eusebia wanted to scream. Vladimir would put a dusty hand on her mouth to prevent her. Then. Remember? We climbed trees, Vladimir said. We walked down by the beach, swam for hours, Eusebia said.

His skin had grown dull of late, so many more fine lines by his eyes. His robe fell open, exposing the soft hair of his chest. Such beautiful circles, perfectly duplicated, perfectly made. She drew their outlines in his skin. Vladimir smiled finally, out of his funk.

"I'm probably going to be gone a few days," he said. "The truck driver is on the run."

For once, she welcomed his absence. She'd be able to deal with whatever was going on with Luz. It'd be resolved by the time he got back. She wouldn't let it touch him.

"Noooo," she said, the way she always reacted when he said he had to run after some criminal. She took the finger that was tracing circles, moved it down his stomach, then down more. He shook his head, mumbled something about being exhausted. She told him, "If I run away with the milkman, it's your fault."

It was his turn to fold her hand in both of his, bring it to his lips, kiss it.

"There are no milkmen here," he said. "So if you run away with one, I'd be very suspicious."

Finished with breakfast, he took a last sip of that too-sweet coffee. Got up from the table, headed for a shower.

"The worst thing," he said, over his shoulder, "was the smell." The lines of his shoulders, softer now, showed neck. She pictured the trailer, with the dead people in it. She invoked the stench that slapped him on the face. Sensed the stress flowing out of Vladimir's body, into hers, like a fume through a chimney flue.

She made a soft, pained sound.

"So many bodies," he said. "All kids, women.

The men survived. They didn't stop much, and so the back of the trailer was kitchen, bedroom, bathroom . . ."

". . . grave," she finished.

He pivoted back to grab his plate and coffee mug but she pushed him away, a little harder than she meant to. He paused, surprised at her roughness.

"You weren't put on earth to clean up after people," she said. "That's my job."

"You should tell my boss," he said, full smile on. Fortified to take on this new day.

LOCUSTS

Eusebia pushed the laundry cart out of the building. It was so heavy she had to use the strength of her entire body as she got it through to the sidewalk. The noise from the construction started at exactly 7 A.M., as she crossed the street into Nothar Park. It was deafening. There was hammering and yelling, and huge machines that amplified all the noise. The dust that covered the cars, sidewalk, swings, trees, made its way to her eyes, her nose. She inhaled it. It scraped her nostrils, then her throat when she swallowed. The dust was a force that tried to slow her down, attacked her body particle by particle. She sped up, cutting through the dirt and avoiding the paved concrete path. The grass was yellow and dry, but the volunteers had planted various beautiful tulips, already in bloom, with pastel colors like ice cream. Peach on the outside, pineapple up top, inside. She wanted to peel off a petal, eat it.

She had to admit it. The park looked great.

There was something sharp about this day. Like an optometrist's lens machine had rotated right in front of Eusebia's eyes. Click: it was clean and bright. Click: they'd even painted the garbage cans the deepest of blacks. Click: it couldn't be good news, having white people over here, cleaning.

Two decades ago, when they'd arrived on a November day, she'd been shocked at the lack of color in the neighborhood. Every tree a dull brown. Every building a variation of that same color, though some tended toward a bit of red. All around, gray and brown—the colors of things on their way to death. Now Eusebia often found the muted colors soothing. This was the color palette that left her room to think. The tulips were a reminder that spring would grab full hold within weeks, maybe even days—fogging the clarity she so enjoyed.

She forced her cart over the roots that stuck out of the ground, bruising them as she went. A cold wind tunnel came from the direction of the construction and lifted her hair all around her face. She quickened her step.

The wrecking ball struck the building, and a gigantic piece of concrete collapsed. Eusebia's distress grew. Months before, she sat next to an older Dominican woman who talked to the roof of the bus they traveled on, lamenting she had to move to Reading, Pennsylvania, with her cousin because she couldn't afford her rent anymore. At one point, she looked directly at Eusebia. Have you heard of Reading, Pennsylvania? Eusebia shook her head. What should I do? I don't want to leave my home, the old woman said. Eusebia held the strange woman's hand in silence. That day, she'd been sure it would never happen to her. Why had she thought they were immune?

Maybe it wouldn't be so bad. Maybe this construction wouldn't yield displacement. Luz could get her fancy coffee, more options for dinner right by the park. But what else could they be building but luxury apartments? Fancy, expensive, and meant for people who didn't look like any of them. Where would they all go, if they were pushed out of their homes?

How would she fix this mess?

She wasn't paying attention as she pushed the cart. It stopped short at the root of a honey locust tree and toppled over, pulling her down. She let it go but not without a jerk toward her first. She thought for a moment that she might be able to reverse time, keep the cart and herself upright. Both hands went out instinctively to break her fall; one touched the trunk of the tree, the other slipped on the dirt. A loud thud as her head hit the ground. Then a stinging pain, and the weight of the cart on top of her, all that weight on her head. A gash opened. Eyes closed, she felt blood down her neck, soaking her shirt, the scarf, and the coat. Eyes opened, the blood spread not down like it was supposed to but out, right around her, dispersing into the air. As if the air were made of water. Back when she still had a period, this was the full expression on the third day of her flow: out of her body the brightest of reds spreading in the bowl of the toilet—unstoppable eggs, uselessly escaping her body—a reminder that the beginning of life and death were often inked the same. This red in the air just as vibrant, just as gorgeous, infused the brown of the dry earth, penetrated the root of that offensive tree, became the deepest red she'd seen. The hand that touched the trunk now touched the root. Mesmerized, she watched as that arm attached to the hand, then her entire body, went completely red. Then the park. Then the buildings. Then the sky. How had she never noticed the sky itself was an inverted bowl?

Her friends the Tongues appeared above her. All of them tainted red, too.

"Should we call an ambulance?" one of them asked, but their voices sounded far away.

She shook her head, then felt for the cut, searched for the wound, and tentatively, on finding it, put a fingertip inside the dampness. She had to pull away fast, because from the one hand that still touched the root of that tree and the fingertip inside the wound there was no difference in texture. Inside the gash, inside her skull, unmistakably, it felt like tree bark, growing.

"She don't look too good," the women said to each other. "We should call an ambulance."

Calm down, she commanded herself silently. Then. She blinked hard to right the world. No change: all still red. Blinked harder still. Stop it, she told herself, as panic rose, as the world deepened to the heart of a beet root. No need to make a big fuss. At the third hard blink, the world went back to normal. Finally, all that red gone. Fingertips went on the side of her head and felt for a wound that wasn't there. Not even a cut. Just a tender spot, swelling.

"Let's go to your house," Eusebia said to the women. Her voice thicker, deeper to her own ears. Could they hear the difference?

Her friends offered a hand, but she shooed them away. She stood up and wiped away the dirt from her bruised hand, wiped more dirt from the side of her hip. She offered the women a small smile so they would know she was fine. She touched the side of her head again, the part that pulsed, with cautious fingertips, pressing it to make sure. She was relieved—and confused—when she still found no blood.

She took a step. Stumbled. Two of the women reached for her, then held her by each arm, while the third righted the laundry cart, bending to pick up and put back all the clothing that fell out. Humiliated. Now they all knew her daughter didn't wash her underwear by hand.

Halfway through the park, the women noticed a

large moving truck parked in front of their building; on the side of the truck an English sign said BETTER MOVE in red bold letters. There were lines that made those letters seem as though the truck was already in motion, hightailing it out of Nothar Park faster than a Dominican lotto winner heading back home.

"Luz got fired yesterday?" one of the women said. Her tone a non-question.

Eusebia didn't respond. Her daughter fired? It made no sense and it made complete sense. Fired over what?

They didn't push. But all three stared at her, waiting.

How did they find out?

She shook her head at them. It could have meant no, she didn't get fired. It could have meant, in the motherly resignation all of them knew so well, that kids ultimately were put on earth to shame, to disappoint. But then Eusebia firmed her mouth into a line so interpretation would be clear. The shake meant leave it alone.

It had gotten colder. Without gloves, Eusebia felt the cold accumulate around her nail beds, making her fingertips stiff. The bruise from the fall on her palm became a slight, throbbing pink.

As they crossed the street, a set of men made their way out of the building with a brilliant white couch, still covered in plastic, a true tell of who was moving out. Verónica García always trying to be upscale—but she'd put a plastic cover on her sofa just like they all did.

Eusebia had been wrong that morning, while making breakfast, when she imagined Verónica doing the same thing she'd been doing. While Eusebia prepared breakfast for her family, Verónica had been preparing hers to depart. Eusebia's hip pinched, pulled, made the opposite knee give. Her shirt felt wet with invisible blood.

"Angélica heard the boss tell her it was going to happen yesterday," one of them said to the white couch.

The Tongues were always right. The only source of news she'd never questioned. But where had Angélica been to overhear? At the new restaurant where she worked? Maybe when everyone left work early to get wine?

Why had Luz meant to deceive her?

"Verónica's moving," one of the women said, letting her silence win.

"Remember when," another responded.

This was them being kind.

Eusebia remembered when. She wished the women would stop talking for a bit.

The Tongues sucked their teeth.

"Verónica is the queen of the crickets." The women went on to distract, to make light.

It worked because it was true. Verónica, a member of a long tradition of women referred to as crickets in DR. Why would others call them sirens? These women who would drop their panties for men—single, engaged, married, these women didn't care. These women were named crickets because their bodies created so much noise, so much distraction. And just like their insect namesake, with its strong hind legs, once they caught what they wanted, they consumed, devoured. Years ago, the Tongues saw Verónica put a hand on Vladimir's shoulder, and that hand stayed there longer than was necessary. Such a simple gesture, such a clear invitation. But Vladimir took a step away, out of her reach.

"Good riddance, cricket," one of the women said to the couch.

At the entrance of the building, the women were greeted by more cold as the drilling from across the way grew ever more insistent. The entire building being without heat made the dust that now lived inside weigh more, a sting to the eye that forced repeated blinks. A pile of envelopes had been delivered while they were gone. From the landlord. One of the women reached for Eusebia's, handed it over. The Tongues' envelope was at the very bottom of the pile.

The letter was in Spanish. Had the landlord ever bothered translating a single document for them before? Of course not. They knew it meant trouble.

The three women lifted their eyeglass chains and put their readers on.

The building was turning all apartments into condos. Each resident would be offered a generous buyout of the lease. Or, sure, they could buy the apartments. Either way, their days as renters were numbered. The noise across the park quieted. They didn't know why the machines had been turned off. Each of the three women turned to Eusebia. The question hung between them delicate as a single string from a spider to the wall.

How to fix this mess?

Inside the Tongues' apartment, it was warmer than the lobby but still cold. They didn't take off their coats. They wheeled the cart and left it off to the side, outside their door. Their apartment was exactly like Eusebia's, facing out toward the park. Except the Tongues' home had too much furniture. A couch and a love seat and a single chair set of imitation French Louis XV tufted velvet in an olive green. There were too many cushions for a person to sit comfortably but Eusebia tried.

One sister rushed to the bathroom and got a wet cloth, wiped away the dirt from Eusebia's forehead. Then tended her bruised hand. The water so hot it steamed.

"Can you check the back of my head?" Eusebia said, sounding childish to her own ears. "It feels like there's a cut there."

One of the women parted her long hair, searched and found nothing suspicious except a big tender bump. The throbbing on her palm crawled halfway up her forearm now, like the spider, climbing.

"We should take you to the hospital just to make sure," the women said, then waited.

All four of them equally suspicious of doctors, trusted no medical establishment.

"I'm fine," Eusebia said.

Relieved, one of the women was already on the way to the kitchen to make coffee, while another turned the television on. Moments later, coffee in hand, all the women stared at the whale with the baby on its back. The camera closed in on her. In the background, a scientist's words, dubbed in Spanish, explained this was unprecedented footage. Do all whales experience grief as humans do?

"What are we going to do?" one of them finally said to the ceiling.

The throbbing in Eusebia's hand had by then taken over her entire arm. She felt a slight numbness spreading to meet that side of her head, where she still felt the trickling of blood. She reached up, touched it, astonished to find it still dry.

On the television, when the whale's baby slipped off her head, instead of dipping low into the water as before, the mother swam on. Instinctively, Eusebia stood up. It was her turn to put a hand to heart.

"She'll go get him," one of the women said. All of them stared at the television as the whale swam away.

They sat in silence for a very long time. The women's question pulsed the air. Eusebia could taste salt in the air, could smell it as if she'd been standing at the foot of that mountain where she'd grown up, where it gave way to a beach. What were they going to do?

Then, as Eusebia stood waiting for the whale to dive into the water, the television's image changed. Breaking news. The image of a young naked boy, no older than Luz when they'd first arrived in this country, flashed onto the screen with his name: José García. He'd been shot numerous times, the reporter said, left with a message carved into his back: **Go Home.** He was in the hospital, in critical condition.

Eusebia sat down. She felt light-headed. There wasn't much more of this day she could take. On the screen, the whale was back, swimming on. Where had the calf gone? Where would the current take him? And this young boy, shot so many times? Who would do such a terrible thing?

The three women spoke to each other and to her, but she could no longer listen. From very far away she heard them say "1992." They were speaking of a young Dominican man by the same name as this boy. That José García had been shot dead by a plainclothes policeman. They spoke of violence as rapture, how Dominicans spilled out in the streets in protest, arms outstretched in fervor. One closed fist ready to fight, the other closed over branches of palm trees.

One of the women left the room, returned with

a folder, put frail newspaper clippings ready to disintegrate into Eusebia's hands. Metro section of **The New York Times.** She stared at the words. Some so unfamiliar, others clearly the same as in Spanish with minor syllable differences.

Surprise

Police

Erupts

Calm

"I have to go upstairs," she said.

She picked up her manila envelope, gave the women one last look before she left.

"I'll come back later. We're going to figure this out. We're going to stop it."

"Stop what?" one of them said, eyes on the screen. Viewer discretion was advised before a flash of horrible images of the boy's back appeared. Is it a hate crime? the reporter said to the audience, then gave them a phone number to text their answer to. One of the women reached for her phone, responded to the flash survey. Yes.

Eusebia considered the word **home,** carved on the boy's back. Who had the nerve to proclaim a young boy, born in this country, an outsider? When Eusebia first arrived in Nothar Park, she'd been an outsider. In every sense of the word. Now, facing this attack, she felt fiercely connected to the neighborhood, to her people.

"We're going to stop all of it," Eusebia said. "The

building across the street, them trying to sell our apartments. Them trying to push us out of our homes. We're going to find a way to stop it all."

The women looked at her, incredulous.

"What do you mean 'we'?" one asked.

"The four of us," Eusebia said, "we're going to stop it."

The women were distracted by the past. They weren't focused on what was most important. But Eusebia would help them. She felt certain she would find a way.

In the elevator, her phone rang. Vladimir was on his way upstate. She told him she could hardly hear him, that she would try him back. But he insisted she stay on the phone, walk to the kitchen, where he'd left her a surprise.

"I'll be back tomorrow" is what she thought he said, before the line went dead.

She tried him. It went straight to voicemail.

Upstairs, in her apartment, Eusebia parked the laundry cart in the hallway. She went back to check on Luz, whose door remained locked. She considered grabbing a butter knife, jimmying the lock, and confronting her daughter about losing her job. But the throbbing in her head intensified. She decided to leave her daughter alone. Luz was being melodramatic. It would all work out. If there was one thing Eusebia was certain of, it was her daughter's prospects in life. She'd been to college, was a lawyer. Why did they fire her? Well, it didn't really matter. Her daughter would find another job. Slowly, she made her way to the kitchen, where she found Vladimir's surprise: a replacement mango. She'd told him about the mango, how it reminded her of home, how she'd given it to their daughter. She bit into it without washing it, skin and all. Her sweet Vladimir.

She went to her bedroom and lay down in un-accustomed light. Had she ever taken a nap during the day in this country? No, of course not. But today, her head found the sun-warmed pillow, and she drifted off to the sound of a wrecking ball striking that building yet again, replaying the memory of the entire world stained such a deep red, tasting in her mouth the flavor of home, and asking herself over and over again, "How?" How would she stop this mess?

WAS SHE DYING?

When Eusebia woke up, her bedroom was pitch-black. It stayed that way—even past the time when her eyes should have adjusted. Frightened, she reached for Vladimir, hand searching the bed for his body. How much time had passed? She reached for her phone and found it was minutes past midnight. She'd made no dinner, had abandoned the laundry, for the first time in her life had slept an entire day away.

Her head felt fragile, as if made of glass. She was

scared to touch it again; who knew what she might find? Would it break? Or worse? That rough texture of bark unlike anything she'd ever felt before.

Instead, she extended her reach farther for Vladimir and still couldn't touch him. Why couldn't she reach him? Her heart beat wildly. Her head pulsed, the pulse lifted her eyelids. A tremble from her fingertips into the faint heartbeat at her throat.

"Is the world trying to destroy us?" she said in the direction of the place where his body should be. No answer. She got out of the bed, and crashed into the floor. Then raised herself off the floor with great effort.

"Vladimir," she cried out.

"Luz," she said. But her throat so dry it was hardly a moan. No one came to help.

AMPHISCIANS

Eusebia thought herself the whale. She thought about the dead boy, with those words carved on his skin. She thought of her own dead boy, from so many years ago. On that king-sized bed, she squeezed her legs shut—knees bolted, ankles glued—so her feet became a tail. She said to the whale: I am just like you. I know the pain of death, of loss. She moved this new tail from side to side slowly, sheet now water, the lines in the fabric forming shapes in a shifting current. Vladimir was gone; Luz couldn't hear her. She was alone.

Her body, in that moment weightless, reminded her of the place she once considered home. As a kid in DR, she'd sneak down that mountain by herself, ignoring her mother's shouts in the distance. Who's got eyes on Eusebia? her mother would ask. Nobody, she'd yell back, running as fast as she could. Past the wooden houses, sheds really, and past the toothless grin of old Sancho Panza, before she called him that. Muchachita. Don't run so fast, he'd say, te vas a matar.

What did an old man know? She was immortal. Through a dark, cavernous dirt tunnel whose mouth led to a hidden beach, she'd emerge into the light. No palm trees on her beach. No white sand. Just crowds of short bushes with thorn branches lining the small path a human once made, cutting those bushes with a blade. The shore had gathered sharp-edged pebbles as a defense, adapted them into weapons as a response, serrated enough to shred feet. But they were no deterrent for a wild six-year-old with soles hard as stone. Her body had adapted, too. She would sprint, then leap—above waves ready to break—into the warmest seawater. Body a spear, she dominated whatever got in her way. Eyes closed, arms tight by her ribs, all forward movement came from her legs. The farther she went, the deeper she swam. Until. Salt water so dense shoved her small body off the ocean's floor, then up. Nature had a way of winning, too. But floating, like swimming, was its own kind of release. Its own kind of triumph. Eyes squinting from the salt sting, she'd always come to the same thought looking at that sky: This world is mine.

Earlier, in the Tongues' apartment, she hadn't allowed herself to think deeply.

Eusebia lost her boy before she met him. He died on his way out of her body. For decades she'd pushed any thought of him away, buried him in her flesh. Truth? She'd avoided looking at the whale's dead baby. She'd focused instead on the immense power of the whale. That body behemoth, so black, with only a bean-shaped white spot on her belly, would elicit fear just by being. Let him go, Eusebia silently commanded the whale each morning that first week, to no avail. Eusebia knew. She knew once that weight was gone, the whale would be able to glide through the water, gain enough strength to jump out in great arcs. Once she let go, she'd be able to indulge her greatest instincts—to hunt.

Eusebia's bed the ocean, she imagined swimming next to that great body, six times her length, thousands of pounds heavier. She moved her tail in an ess. Repeated it. Again.

The ripples behind them, trailing in the water, were sure to disappear from the surface almost as quickly as they appeared. From above, the indistinct shadows of their moving shapes resembling sisters. Traceless, they would swim on. Both of them, as one. The hunger, awake.

CHAPTER THREE

Luz Guerrero

JOSÉ GARCÍA — AGAIN?

Luz couldn't remember a time Mami had slept an entire day away. She'd been expecting a butter knife through the slit of the closed door moments after Eusebia had entered the apartment, followed by a firm hand on her forearm to force a confession about what she'd been hiding. So when she heard Mami's retreating footsteps, and hours later still no sign of her, she'd gone searching in the apartment. She'd been surprised to find her deeply asleep and left the room quietly so she wouldn't wake her. About time she got some rest. But when night fell, and Mami remained in bed, Luz leaned over her, shook her until she got a response. Mami half woke and made an odd guttural sound like a wild animal caught in a trap.

"Mami," she said, "are you okay?"

Luz felt Eusebia's forehead, sensed no fever. While

Luz debated whether to call someone for help, Eusebia suddenly sat up, spoke clearly: "I need to go back to the sea for a while longer, okay?"

Luz smiled, sensing the warm ocean water Eusebia must be floating in, in a dream. She kissed Mami on the forehead, told her it was okay, left her alone.

While Mami slept and slept, Luz had turned a corner. She stopped crying. Vowed to get her life back on track. She'd spent the entire day looking up her law school friends, making a list of everyone she needed to reach out to, make coffee dates with, send an updated resume to. Hours into her search, she'd had to stop, take a deep breath. It was startling. Most people she went to law school with weren't even practicing law. And then, more shocking, for each woman who had a good, solid job—law related or not—two had left the workforce altogether. Why had these women stopped working? Spying on their social media pages showed lives carefully curated—bachelorette outings, wedding pictures, honeymoons, pregnancies, babymoons, and now babies; so many of them had followed the same path. Dismissing them altogether, she made a separate list of the people she knew who would help her. It felt so embarrassing, lame even, to work the network when she had made absolutely no effort to stay in touch after school. Why was she stressing this much about it? She signed up for a few agencies, went through job postings, and started applying directly herself. She cared little if it was anything she was actually interested in or would enjoy. She didn't allow herself to wonder too long about the interruption. She just wanted to get things back to normal as quickly as possible.

Her dizque friends from work reached out as Eusebia slept into the night. Texts from one, then another. All of them fake-worried about her. All asking veiled questions trying to figure out what happened. She couldn't be bothered to respond to anyone. She had to get moving, find a better job fast, so they'd know she was fine. Better than fine. She'd venture out in the next few days—buy a new bag or a new pair of shoes she could selfie with to still their tongues. Raenna had texted her late at night, to check in.

Let's drink all the wine, eat all the seaweed! Raenna wrote, inviting her over to her place after work.

Luz responded with a bunch of martini emojis and even threw in a couple of dancing women to show how unbothered she actually was, how unworried.

Today, on day three of demolition, the wrecking ball had largely been replaced by drilling. The loud voices of men yelling at each other outside got Luz out of bed. Cellphone in hand, she went into the hallway to find the apartment silent, cold. The heat still hadn't come back on. No pungent smell of coffee or stinky lingering boiled eggs in the air.

The kitchen was as it had been last night. Clean, cold, even the plates she'd used when she heated the leftovers for dinner last night still on the kitchen table where she'd left them. Mami hadn't gotten up all night.

Luz went back in Mami's room and found her face-up in bed. She'd kicked the blankets off her body, even though the apartment was so cold. Luz ventured closer. She quietly put the blanket back on Eusebia. Gently so as to not wake her. She obviously needed the rest.

In the living room, Luz turned the volume loud, surfed the channels. Maybe news of the whale would prompt Mami out of this deep sleep. But the whale was no longer on TV. A quick search on her phone answered why. The orca had let the baby go, and the world had immediately pivoted to something else. No one seemed interested in the remainder of her journey. Now it was the young boy on the news. His mother was on the screen, awkwardly answering questions about him, sounding robotic.

Luz's phone was as quiet as the apartment. She knew it was absurd to think that the jobs she'd applied to would get back to her so quickly, but she had to admit she'd been expecting her phone to buzz as quickly as she'd hit submit on the first application.

Through the doorway, Mami remained in the same position.

She called Papi on her phone. He picked up right away.

"Mi Dulce Luz," he said, the nickname that was only for her.

"Bendición," she said, out of habit, listening for sounds on his side. He was in the car, outside. She went on before he had a chance to respond. "Where are you?"

"Syracuse," he said.

"Did you catch the bad guys?" Luz asked, the way she'd been asking since she was nine years old.

"Not yet," he said. "Been texting your mom since last night. No answer."

"Mami's been sleeping since yesterday. Woke up for a quick minute, said something about needing to go for a swim in the sea."

Papi was quiet on the other end.

"The sea would be good for her right now," he said. "I'm sure she's going through . . . you know."

He coughed uncomfortably, then cleared his throat.

"God, Papi," she said, "it's just menopause!"

"We're on high alert," he said, abruptly changing the conversation. They were on the phone for a long time. He talked about how they might have to head all the way to the Canadian border, following some leads on the driver of the truck. But everyone was worried about this boy, who had died overnight. José García, dead again. There was a vigil tonight and everyone was talking about how it would be nothing but trouble. Already there was noise on-line, people asking if it was the police this time, too. Some had started using a hashtag, #justiceforjosé.

When he started talking about the incident from 1992, how a Dominican man had been killed by the police, Luz interrupted him. The last thing she wanted to spend time on was talking about the past.

"I got fired Monday," she said, to her own surprise.

On the other end, a deep sigh. Then complete silence.

"Papi," she said, "you there?"

"Yeah," he said. "Should I come back?"

"No, it's okay," she said. "Not why I'm telling you."

"How are you doing?" he asked. "You feel okay?"

"I don't know," Luz said. "I'm really sad. But then I feel like I'm going to be okay, maybe better than okay. But then I'm embarrassed, mad. And sorry I let you and Mami down."

Her voice did a strange thing then, breaking down, but she recovered quick, pretended to be stronger. What she couldn't tell him? About the worry, that feeling of dread back again, pressing hard on her. About the school loans, her savings depleted for the house in DR. She'd assured him there was a lot more where that came from.

"Your job is just a job," he said. "We're proud of who you are, fancy job or not. What did Mami say?"

Luz was silent, let him catch on.

"Do you want me to tell her?" he asked.

"No, I'm not that much chickenshit," she said. Mami would be furious if she learned that Papi found out first.

"I won't tell her you told me," he said, reading her mind. "When I get back, we can talk about it more. I told you before, I have contacts at the DA's. They'd love to have you."

"I don't need you getting me a job," she said. "I already applied to a bunch. Bet you I'll have an offer by next week."

That part was a lie, too. She didn't know how long it would take to find another job. On the other end, his partner's voice. Papi said something she couldn't hear. She realized she was keeping him from something important. He would never hang up first, it was one of her favorite things about him. No matter what, he always made her feel like she was the most important thing. "I gotta go," she said.

"Okay. Sure. But listen to me. You're not alone. We're a family. We take care of each other."

Luz reminded herself she was an adult, that she shouldn't cry at the first sign of kindness.

"Whatever you do," he said, "don't go to the vigil. It's probably going to be a hot mess."

Luz smiled in spite of herself, through her tears, at Papi's attempts to be cool, because no one said "hot mess" anymore. Luz promised him she'd stay put. She promised him she'd keep an eye on Mami and let him know right away if anything else happened. On the television, she stared at the image of that young boy, a strangeness stirring in her.

HIS PALM ON HER PALM, WARM

Luz broke her promise, left the apartment to go to the vigil. She paused at the devastation on the north side. Three days and the old building was gone. Machines with huge arms lifted large chunks of concrete, depositing them directly into trucks that then drove away. The voices of the men echoed across the park as they yelled directions, cursed, laughed at each other. Luz was shocked at how quickly they'd done this work—would the replacement building go up as quickly?

When she arrived at the vigil, she stood on the lower level of Riverbank State Park on 145th Street, awed at how many people had gathered on a Wednesday afternoon. A stage had been set up over by the BBQ zone, across from a parking lot that was teeming with people. The plan was to start by the river and then make their way to Nothar Park, one of the organizers told the dense crowd. The Hudson River was their backdrop. It was a brilliant sunny day. The water perfectly still above a clear, cloudless sky.

Within moments, the crowd swelled as hundreds and hundreds of people converged by the river. She heard various languages spoken around her. The loss wasn't singular, Dominican. Immigrants had come from every borough to say we're all neighbors, this is our loss, too. Someone handed her a candle that blew out in the wind. Others carried posters of José's blown-up second-grade picture, missing front

tooth a promise of a future that would never come.
The posters said "Our Lives Matter" and "This Was
His Home" in both Spanish and English. "Home"
was underlined many times. Off to the side, people
were translating the signs into other languages, lips
set in tight lines as their hands made the ink dance.
"We're done being treated like shit," a woman said
somewhere to her left. When Luz turned to find the
voice, she couldn't.

Standing a few feet from the boy's mother, she
paused to consider yesterday's job search. She'd
been manic. Illogical. She wasn't going to take just
any job. She hadn't worked as hard as she had to
jump at any old thing. She would take today as
a day off from worrying about what to do next.
She wasn't going to check her email obsessively. She
wasn't going to keep applying for jobs she knew
were beneath her experience level. She had to trust.
Pretty soon, everything would fall into place. She
was glad she hadn't been able to talk herself into
wearing anything cute, or punishing her feet by
squeezing them into expensive shoes, just to im-
press Raenna, when she saw her later.

The microphone screeched, hurting everyone's
ears. José's mother was ushered to the steps near
the stage, and stood waiting as a political activist
spoke into the microphone. Luz got as close as she
could get to her. The woman looked stunned. Her
ponytail at a weird angle, like someone else had
tried to fix her hair in a rush. She was so much

smaller than she appeared on TV. Her other kids, all younger than José García, pulled at her limp hands, begged to be picked up. She didn't respond. She was surrounded by people who told her she had to be strong. Take comfort knowing he's home, someone said.

Luz wondered where the woman's real friends were, those charged with helping her cope. No one should be telling a grieving mother to be strong. There was no comfort to be had here. A young kid like that, murdered. Luz thought of José growing up; he could have been anything, gone anywhere. Now nothing. On the phone, Papi had said there were no suspects. Is it possible whoever did this would get away with it? Luz focused on the grieving mother, trying to comprehend her pain. No way, she thought. Impossible.

A woman with burgundy-colored hair offered her some gum. Luz shook her head.

"They're trying to kill us," she said directly to Luz. "They want to push us out of this country."

Luz recognized that voice. She was the one who'd said we're tired of being treated like shit moments before. People turned to look at her. With attention, she got louder.

"I say hell no," she said. "This is our house."

At first, only her voice could be heard, but within moments other voices joined—their cries an over-powering chant—arms outstretched, fists pumping, feet stomping. "Our house," they said. "Our house!" The guy onstage grew quiet at the commotion, then joined the shouting.

"This is our house," he said. "No one is kicking us out."

The chant echoed above them, over the river and into its reflection. Didn't those words, carved into a boy's flesh, command they all go home? That command amplified the chant.

A young guy wearing a Yankees baseball cap held a bat, walked toward some parked cars. He swung, struck the glass on the driver's side, hardly a crack. But he would not be deterred. He swung again, again. On the third try, the glass shattered. Everyone around him stopped, watching him, approving. This was the pain everyone felt. Luz could see it in the tight fists of the crowd—pain to anger to hunger. For destruction? Luz yelled at the kid with the bat, at the adults who soundlessly urged him on.

"Stop that," she said. The kid gave her a sideways middle finger. In a quick movement, he was atop the hood of the car, swinging harder on the front shield, looking right at her each time the bat struck. Was he threatening her?

The vigil was to show solidarity for the family, show community, not a rally to destroy some innocent person's car. What about following the rules? There were other people wielding bats, who went toward other cars, started replicating the anger. She took a step toward the kid with the Yankees cap, to make him stop. Someone grabbed her arm, pulled her back. She turned, found a white man she hadn't noticed. He was the tallest guy there. Maybe six foot five. His hair jet black, deep blue eyes. He wore a Harvard sweatshirt.

"You shouldn't go over there," he said. "They're agitators."

"Do I know you?" Luz stared at his hand, which moved from her forearm to her hand as he held it. His fingernails perfectly square, pristine. His palm on her palm, warm. Soft. Ready to slap his hand away, she was stilled by his eyes, unprepared for their transparency, their depth. How could those eyes appear heavy like liquid and at the same time light as air? It was a familiar color. The first time she'd seen it was back when she didn't know how to swim. Mami held her, assured her it was okay to float on the calm waves of the Caribbean Sea, as long as she rested on her arms. Luz's arms stretched out; she was awed at all the blue—above her, blue, around her, blue. She laughed as a swarm of birds made their way across the sky, dancing. She'd pushed Mami away, twisted to her belly, swallowed salt. She'd had an urge she couldn't name then. An appetite for freedom, a hunger to fly.

"Sorry," he said. He let go.

"It's fine," she said, recovering. "If we don't stop them, this is going to get ugly fast."

"It already is," he said.

The other young guys who had bats were systematically moving from one set of cars to another, smashing glass. Luz searched for José's mother, his siblings, but they were already gone. Stage cleared.

The police, who'd been standing watch on the other side of the park, moved toward the young kids holding bats.

"Harvard shirt," one of the cops said in their direction, "get the hell out of here. Vigil's over."

Luz followed the crowd out of the park. Within moments, she lost him. A little disappointed, she stood on tiptoes, hoping for a last glimpse. Now that the excitement was dying down, she could appreciate how handsome he was. And what was it about his hand? Her hand already missed its warmth.

GOTTACUTTHEUMBILICALCORD

Raenna opened the door, then ushered Luz inside her Harlem brownstone. She tapped the right side of her wireless headset to let Luz know she was on a call. She was dressed up. Hair done, makeup perfect, the only relaxed part of her a long-sleeve sweater dress instead of the suit she usually wore.

Inside, the house was warm. Raenna's home smelled amazing. Black currant floated with white jasmine and mixed with another scent, the pungent bitterness of coffee left out all day, that accentuated the sweeter notes.

"Take your jacket off," Raenna said, pointing to the closet. "I already opened the wine."

"I need food first," Luz said.

The main floor had a baby grand piano with a wall-sized original Kara Walker behind it. The black silhouette on a white background was of a Black woman sitting at the head of a conference table while a group of demon-headed men swirled menacingly around her. Past the piano, there was an all-white open-concept sitting room and kitchen that led to floor-to-ceiling windows in the back—four panels framed in black opened individually or folded into each other so the entire wall would be open to the patio. On the island in the kitchen, Raenna's work laptop was open, and next to it dozens of folders with pleadings, and yellow notepad upon yellow notepad filled with Luz's neat handwriting. A glass of red wine sat next to a bottle that was almost empty.

"You started the party without me?" Luz asked.

Raenna unmuted her phone and spoke into it. "We're dealing with a celebrity plaintiff here, Andre. The judge is unsympathetic to our client. We need to settle and shut this down."

Raenna grabbed a clean glass out of a cabinet, poured Luz the little bit that was left in the bottle. She grabbed an unopened bottle of wine. Luz motioned for her to stop halfway. Raenna gave her a dismissive look. She poured an obscene amount of wine.

"Yeah, Andre," she continued into the phone, "but it's my ass on the line. Not yours."

She took the headphones off, put her cell on speakerphone.

Luz heard several voices on the call, all talking over each other. The conversation, on its surface about strategy, was about posturing, about power. Whose ideas would prevail?

Luz recognized Andre, one of the named partners in the firm, and Mark, who was an equity partner like Raenna, but out of the London office. Mark was always trying to show Raenna up. Luz knew there were several other people on the phone call not important enough to speak. Just last week, she'd been one of those people.

Back then, Luz's heart would have quickened. She would have been in the office, handling the work while the partners called from home or on their way to a business dinner. She would have gotten everything ready for tonight's meeting, because it was the norm, that everyone went back to the office after work dinners, after popping home to tuck children into bed. But today, she nodded sympathetically, already bored. She turned to the Walker piece. The first time Luz had seen it, she'd been embarrassed to admit she'd never heard of the artist. Raenna had jokingly told her she was about to get her Black card and her Harvard card revoked. Then, more seriously, confided that aside from the home they stood in, that piece of art symbolized what success meant to her. You gotta pick your prize and don't stop until you get it, Raenna had said.

"I'll see you losers in the office in a couple of hours," Raenna said. Then, without missing a beat, turned to Luz. "I've been worried about you. But look at you. You're radiant. Practically glowing."

"It's called sleep," Luz said. "You should try it sometime."

Raenna smirked through the glass of wine. Her face was distorted by it, shrunken and diminutive. "Nobody took over the world in their sleep," she said. "Enough about work. Tell me what's going on with you. Did you start looking yet?"

It was Luz's turn to drink her wine slowly. It'd only been a couple of days.

Raenna waited. Grabbed a spicy tuna roll from the plate, popped it into her mouth.

"A little bit," Luz said, filling a plate with her favorite rolls. "Sent some emails to law school friends. Applied online to some in-house roles. Just wait and see, I guess."

"You're not going in-house," Raenna said, furrowing her brow. "I'll reach out to my contacts. We'll get you a job in no time."

Her phone rang. It was Andre. She sighed deeply. Pressed ignore.

Her phone vibrated with a text, then rang again. It was Andre.

"I finally finished my shoe closet," she said. "Go up. Let me get rid of this."

The brownstone was four stories high. Years ago, the first time Luz walked into this house, she felt in possession of a singular gift. Her future laid out so clearly, her goals in life crystallized without the slightest hint of a smudge. This, then, would be her life, if she worked hard and stayed on track.

Luz ate sushi and wandered into the library on the second floor. There were the usual law textbooks. A series of books on bird-watching. Random. Then off to a corner, in a small case by itself, a copy of Virginia Woolf's **A Room of One's Own.** Luz pulled on the case to find it locked. The red cover of the book reminded her of the mountain where Mami grew up in DR. The only times Luz played in the dirt were when she was at her abuelita's house. Luz wished she could touch the cover, turn the pages. She must have read the book back in college, but couldn't remember what it was about. Feminism, sure; independence, sure. It was crazy the cover of a book could evoke a memory so clearly, bring her back into a childhood she hadn't thought of in years. The sweetness of that dirt was in her mouth right now.

Days before they left for the United States, Luz had gotten so anxious about the trip she'd stopped eating. Eusebia had decided staying in the half-empty house in Santo Domingo wouldn't do. They left to spend a few days in the countryside, that mountainside where Eusebia and Vladimir grew up. It was there, as they stared at the vastness of the ocean and sky, that Eusebia had held Luz's hand—you have to be brave for both of us, she'd said. The breeze carried within it the soothing scent of salt. Luz felt fortified by the air and by her mother's words when she spoke of what awaited them in that strange new land. Even if we don't love it there, we'll make a good life, she'd told her. Was her mother scared? Eusebia's conviction that they'd be accomplices of sorts, choosing happiness no matter what, made Luz believe so. It also made her see her mother more clearly and love her more fiercely than ever. She understood, even as a nine-year-old, how the power dynamic was changing between them. Her mother needed her to be the one to take sure steps into the unknown. Her mother's need made her feel powerful, but her assurance made her feel safe, too. Especially knowing Eusebia would be a few steps behind her, a hand nudging softly any time Luz hesitated, redirecting if she took a misstep.

On the day they were set to go back to Santo Domingo, Luz's abuelita had taken her on a short walk away from the ocean, toward the parcela, to pick some things she needed to cook. Her abuelita, with that long, strong rope of braided hair, had been a tiny woman, so that at nine Luz already was taller by inches. They'd lazily plucked what she needed—sour oranges, bunches of limoncillos, spicy peppers, and fresh cilantro—all while her grandmother told her about her mother as a child, how wild and free she'd been. How she spent endless hours in the ocean, how Vladimir was the only one who could get her out without complaint. They'd parted at some point, Abuelita heading back to prepare food so they'd eat before they left, and Luz had been left to wander on her own, awed again at how the dirt on the mountain always remained so brightly red. Bending down, she dug her fingers into the ground, not questioning the sudden longing to bring handfuls to her mouth. That dry dirt was the color of oxidized metal roofs. She loved how as she crumbled chunks of it, the sunlight made it liquid. Her eyes widened with pleasure as she tasted the sweetness there. And she thought it was fortifying her, too—not just the dirt itself but the wind that carried her grandmother's memories of Mami as a child. Eusebia called her name, breaking the spell. Luz called back, not bothering to stand, not bothering to stop eating the dirt. When she looked up, Eusebia blocked the sun, the sky. In her shade, Luz extended the sweet offering.

"I used to do the same thing when I was a kid," Eusebia said, laughing a little bit in wonder, taking the offering into her own mouth.

Now, staring at the cover of the priceless first edition, she called Mami's cellphone, then tried the house. No answer. She sent her a text. Are you ok? You won't believe what I just remembered. No answer.

She wanted to head back home, to check on Eusebia, but feeling obligated to Raenna, she went upstairs instead, to the third floor where the master bedroom had been gutted and redesigned to make room for a bigger closet. Luz whistled. There was an island in the center, Raenna's jewelry displayed in elegant glass cases. The walls were lined with rich brown shelves that held hundreds of shoes and purses, most of which looked unused. Her clothes were arranged by color family—from light to dark. Luz thought of her mother on that mountain, saying those things about courage as they prepared to tear down their lives in search of something better. Raenna was one of the bravest people she knew. This space was testament—a person only achieved this level of success by having complete confidence in the future and her place in it, regardless of the hard times sure to come. From downstairs, music reached her. Raenna was playing the piano. Had she forgotten Luz was in the house?

When she reached the landing, Raenna's mannerisms at the piano were manic. It reminded Luz of the way she'd been typing just the night before, applying to all those jobs as music blasted on her headphones. Raenna was crying, the way Luz had been crying. But where Luz felt childish for her reaction to being fired, she thought Raenna's problems were real, big, messy. Raenna's glass of wine had tipped over and was spreading slowly on the carpet. Mami always said when it came to drinking, you have to stop one before the last one. She could tell Raenna had gone a few past that point. She stopped playing when she noticed Luz.

"I never heard you play before," Luz said. "Don't stop. It's beautiful."

"I'll text my old protégée Frances," she said,

grabbing her phone. It took effort for her to send that text, maybe because as she typed, she kept talking. "Her firm is just a few buildings down from us. She'll get you in stat. I'm hot. Are you hot?"

Raenna stood up from the piano. Luz wasn't hot. She wished Raenna would go back to playing. She was masterful. Raenna stepped on the wet spot, and her footprints made tiny spots on the carpet, then the hardwood floor. When she reached the back, she opened the glass doors. The room got cold fast.

"What did Andre say?"

"Fuck what Andre said."

Raenna extended her arms, opened them wide. Started to say something, then stopped abruptly. Sweeping the whole room into her embrace, she was reaching for words. Sat on the couch. Patted the seat next to hers. Luz joined her. There was something about her eyes, the way she couldn't quite maintain eye contact with Luz. It was a moment that had happened before, happened often. And in that moment of stillness, of awkwardness, while Raenna struggled to find her train of thought, Luz understood, for the first time in the five years since they'd worked together, that Raenna was an alcoholic.

"Nobody wants to say this aloud, but I will," she said. "If you want to do anything worthwhile, you have to get used to being lonely. You can't trust nobody, always assume people will fail you. Gottacuttheumbilicalcord. If you wanna be free."

"Free to buy all those shoes," Luz said, trying to lighten the mood, not knowing what to think or what to feel or what to say. Should she tell Raenna she was worried? How frightening it was, to see her like this?

"Shoes?" Raenna said. "You think this is about shoes? You need to wake the fuck up and look around. We don't get time off. We don't get rest."

Raenna leaned back and closed her eyes. Her peaceful face reminded Luz of Mami's quiet body on her bed that morning. Such stillness. Within moments, Raenna was in a deep sleep.

In all the years she'd known Raenna, she'd never seen her so affected. So hurt. She wondered again what Andre had said. Luz tried to anticipate, to soothe Raenna when she woke up. Offer a slight bit of shade. But she came up empty. Raenna was always the one with all the answers.

Luz went to the kitchen, put her now-empty plate away. She unrolled paper towels and kneeled on the carpet, patted the wine spot. When she was done, she stood, considering Raenna's sleeping body. What now? Raenna was just having a bad day, not a bad life. Luz repeated this to herself a few times. Then Raenna opened her eyes wide, sat up. Her words carefully enunciated. Her face back to being itself. In sadness, Raenna looked both younger and older than she could possibly be.

"By the time it's your turn," she said, suddenly sober, "things will be so much better. Look"—she showed Luz her phone—"already a response from Frances. She said get ready for an interview next week. You'll be on the right track. The fast track. I gotta go take a bath. Wake myself up. Let yourself out."

She began to hum as she went up the stairs. Luz stood to follow—what just happened?

But her phone vibrated. Papi wanted an update on what was going on. Luz thought of Mami's stillness on that bed. Phoned her. No answer. What if something was really wrong? Her place was back home. She wouldn't admit it to anyone else at that moment, but she felt true relief she wasn't back at the firm.

CHAPTER FOUR

Eusebia de Guerrero

A LIST WOULD STOP IT ALL

On Wednesday afternoon, Eusebia woke up and left her apartment. Just like that. She didn't empty her bladder, she didn't bother changing out of the clothes she still wore from the day before, she didn't brush her teeth, she didn't knock on Luz's door. The slimy feeling that coated her teeth was familiar. From giving birth twice, from leaving her country to come to this new place. Those times, she'd ended up with a dirty mouth that lasted for days, too, even after she brushed her teeth.

Her head ached, pulsed, but she decided to ignore it. She should be thirsty. But she wasn't that, either. The world seemed a bit distant, and she really liked it. She'd pretend nothing was wrong until she got a handle on things, on herself. In her sleep, she'd solved the problem of how they'd stop the construction, how they'd stop the apartments from being sold. It came folded inside a terrifying memory of the last time she'd visited DR.

On the first floor, she rang the bell to the Tongues' apartment. One of the women opened the door.

"Let's go for a walk," she said. Her friend nodded, went to get the others.

Moments later, they were outside, where the day was bright. The weather warmer than it should be. Eusebia's body felt sore, as if she'd actually gone for a long swim. She moved gingerly. The noise from the construction site got louder as they approached. Huge chunks of concrete were being dropped into a metal dumpster, sending sharp chills from their teeth to the bones of their jaws. The dust still lingered in the air, and all four of them fanned at the sting in their eyes. The Tongues blinked repeatedly, tears rolling down their cheeks. They didn't wipe them away. Eusebia's eyes got red from the dust but none of her tears fell.

"What happened to you yesterday?" one of the women asked.

It was a strange way to ask the question. Eusebia turned the words in her mind. Had she heard what was said?

"I don't know," she said.

The women nodded like they knew what she meant. But she was sure they didn't.

"José died," one of the women said.

Eusebia didn't know who José was. "I'm really sorry," she said, searching her mind for that name.

"The boy," the three of them said at once, annoyed, hurt.

Go Home, someone had carved into the skin of the young boy's back. She remembered. The banging ahead culminated in a huge crashing sound. Because the empty space of the missing building was so wide, the echo was magnified. It shook them. The Tongues smiled self-consciously; how silly to be startled by noise.

"You feeling okay?" one of the women asked, all three of them eyeing her up and down. She'd stopped walking.

Better snap out of it, she said to herself. She shrugged, moved. How to describe it to her friends? She felt like herself but also as if something important had happened to that self and she could appreciate it from a distance. Like her body belonged to someone else. Had the fall loosened something, someone, within her?

She put the thought out of her mind. What she was about to say would be crazy enough. Her idea required them to trust she hadn't lost her mind.

The group decided to head up to the rooftop of 291 East Nothar Park, the building directly adjacent to the construction site, opposite 600 West. From the fourth-floor rooftop, the sisters leaned over the safety railings, elbows on metal, in an attempt to catch their breath. Eusebia hung back, her heartbeat pounding in her left eyelid, in her fingertips, in the slight trembling of her left cheek. This had nothing to do with her falling down. This was vertigo. It had been years since she'd forced herself to look down from any height.

Eusebia willed herself to stop that sensation of movement, of falling and twirling through the air in opposite directions at once, a nauseous feeling. Usually this was the moment that forced her to close her eyes and seek lower ground. Not today. On weak knees, she walked to where the women stood, and inhaled deeply as she leaned over. Beneath them, it was as if a bomb had exploded. Bricks, pipes, concrete, refrigerators, stoves—even, farther away, discarded toys: a doll with matted blond hair, a blue truck missing a wheel. She was puzzled at the sharpness of her vision.

How could they have done all of that in three days?

"How could they possibly have gotten that done so fast?" one of the women asked.

"They discarded that old building to make room for what?" the Tongues asked her.

Eusebia never imagined there would be this much space.

"I have an idea on how to stop all of this from happening," she said.

The Tongues looked at her curiously.

"What if we just scare everyone into thinking this neighborhood is really bad?" she said.

The women smiled, thinking it a joke. Brilliant in its simplicity.

"How would we do that?" they asked. Eusebia

could clearly see the unvoiced thought that it would be too easy to work.

Eusebia spoke in a confident way, as if this conversation had already happened. She explained she meant recruiting their neighbors, who would act out crimes throughout the neighborhood, with other volunteers who'd be victims of these crimes.

"You mean fake crimes?" they asked.

No. Not fake. Real. Who'd be crazy enough to move to a neighborhood amid a crime spree?

"What kind of crimes?" they asked.

Eusebia was quiet. She had come up with a list. But she knew if they participated, helped formulate it, they'd be in.

"What would scare you?" she asked. "What would be bad enough?"

"This is the kind of idea that can destroy a community," they said.

"That can save it," she corrected.

The women stared at her, worried. They understood she was serious. She'd moved too fast. Eusebia extended her arm around the neighborhood, lovingly sweeping all they could see—over by their side of the park, Raúl's shipping place, the cleaners owned by the chinitos who were born in DR, the liquor store, the dentist. She wrapped her arm around herself, signaling what they couldn't see— the smell of water boiling for root vegetables, of meat sizzling in pans, laundry being folded, children being kissed, phone calls back home, to people who needed help, who would be lost without the support of those who'd traveled here.

"We can just come up with a list of things people are scared of," she said.

The women exchanged looks. They spoke to each other with the simple speed of a blink. But now Eusebia was in on it. An eavesdropper. Questions floated among all four of them. Could it work? Was it worth trying? What else as an alternative? It was true. Fear would work. Fear always worked.

She turned her body away from them, to the park. Her phone vibrated in her pocket. Luz or Vladimir must be worried. But she'd care for them later. Now she turned her attention to the destruction beneath them. It tugged at something in the women, but Eusebia was the only one who called out the dead boy's name. She had a strange feeling of being anchored to the tarmac on the roof for a long while. It made sense when the blinding sky turned into a black sky and the sun was replaced by a yellow, pockmarked moon. There was complete stillness and silence in the work site. The men had gone for the day.

"If we don't stop it," Eusebia said, "it will not be stopped."

"This is the kind of idea that might destroy," they said again. Eusebia followed their gaze around Nothar Park as they took in the yellow light that pulsed softly from the windows of the brownstones that flanked the park, with halos of rainbows bordering the light. There was the sound of the television, of music, of laughter—the natural noises of a neighborhood, that shut the hostility outside what they'd made here. Somewhere far away, a baby cried—a newborn, by the sound of the urgency in its voice, as if underlining what was truly at stake. It wasn't just about them.

And so, impossibly, the Tongues agreed to go along. They came up with a list that would stop it all. It was exactly the list she'd come up with on her own, absent two. She tried to persuade them to write it all down. "You can't write something like that down," they said. "You speak something that terrible into the air, you tempt the devil."

She assured them it would never come to the point where they'd have to evoke every fear. No way they'd even get to number five! Why not add the last two? But the Tongues remained unshakable.

The List
1. Violation of privacy
2. Theft
3. Destruction of private property
4. Destruction of public property
5. Physical violence

The two items the women wouldn't let her add? Rape and murder.

THE TONGUES' INTERLUDE:

SPIRITUAL ILLUMINATIONS

Down the stairs harder than up for once in our lives. Slowed by bones that could hardly stand the weight of what came before, of what would come next. We took the long way, walking around the park instead of through. Passed blue walls that hid away the shameful construction, noticed all the signs. And there were so damn many. NO TRESPASSING. VIOLATORS WILL BE PROSECUTED TO THE FULLEST EXTENT OF THE LAW. POST NO BILLS. Every ten feet or so there was a silver sign with black bold letters: SACKETT GLOBAL DEVELOPMENT ENTERPRISES.

We wondered where else they'd intruded before. Who else they made feel like outsiders in their own homes. On the sidewalk, behind us, some murmured about the vigil. How a peaceful gathering had been stopped before it started. Thugs, a voice claimed on someone's car radio, a perfectly unaccented American voice belonging to someone who hadn't even been there. But us? We said fuck that. Damn likely undercover cops were the instigators, inventing an excuse to arrest, to scare people off a good fight.

Nothar Park had seen worse days, but it had also seen better, and we'd seen it all. Even after the blanquitos came to give it a face-lift the day they broke our ground, we knew underneath it was still rot; detected the faint smell of human piss, of shit—of neglect. Eusebia couldn't have known all we'd seen, living in Nothar Park that long.

We had the history sutured inside us, were selfish holding it in. We only shared our stories with each other. How when we started showing up six decades ago most Black people didn't even notice. Not until we opened our mouths and a different language came out. Most of us were the same exact skin tone as most of them. But a different language cleaved us. They closed their ears to us, grew suspicious, watchful.

Back then, a different set of three used to patrol the park. It'd always been women who protected this place. The Watkins sisters with their white-gloved hands and Bibles would stare down anyone needed staring down. They didn't talk much to us either, there was just an understanding when it came time for them to leave. That it was our turn to preserve, protect. One day, they walked away, left the beach chairs sitting there empty except for one, with a

Toni Morrison novel waiting. Not the Bible as we expected. We knew it was our turn because sitting, watching, protecting, felt like rest. The rest of our souls finally done searching for a calling, purpose.

Not sure why we failed, when it came our turn. We'd felt so ready.

The moon was full the night we agreed to go along with Eusebia's plan. It lit our way as we went around the park and not through it, thinking it over, finally arriving at our building. When we parted the curtains and lifted up the window shades, we were sure the moon was the brightest anyone had seen. We thought it must be a sign, how clear and beautiful the night turned out to be. If we were destined to go down this path, it must be illuminated by a spiritual sign of some kind. No? We're not idiots. We knew the risks. But it was clear to us Eusebia would be the next one destined to preserve, protect. We didn't know what to do to fix the mess. She was so full of confidence, radiated such fucking strength.

CHAPTER FIVE

Luz Guerrero

CARIBBEAN BIRDS

Luz let herself into the apartment. The weight of the evening with Raenna rested somewhere in the bottom half of her neck. Tiny needles made their way in and out of her upper vertebrae.

"Mami?" she called out.

She heard the house phone ringing, ringing. Mami still asleep? But when she entered the living room, Mami sat at the dining room table, erasing something on a piece of paper. She stared intently at the campesino heading home, sipped from a cup of coffee. The smell of nutmeg filled the room.

"We've been so worried. Why aren't you picking up?"

Eusebia quickly folded the piece of paper, fisted it. She tilted her head back to finish what was left in the cup. Luz worried she had burned her mouth. But there was no reaction of being hurt.

Luz leaned in, gave her mother a kiss on the cheek. Eusebia's face felt cold, as if she'd just come in from outside, too.

"I'm out of it," Mami said. "Go pick up the phone."

Luz stared. So abrupt, so bossy. She went to the phone. The caller ID said it was NYC Police Department. She picked up too late. She texted Papi. Mami's up, fine.

"What's going on with you?" Luz asked, back in the living room.

"I fell down in the park," Eusebia said. She showed her the bruised hand; it was a deep purple with some red in the center. It crawled from palm to elbow.

"Today?" Luz asked.

"No, not today," Eusebia said. "Yesterday."

"Was it bad?" Luz asked.

Eusebia nodded.

"And then you slept for an entire day?"

Eusebia shrugged.

"Did you hit your head?" Luz asked.

Eusebia nodded.

"What if you have a concussion? You're not supposed to go to sleep. We have to go to the hospital right away."

"I'm not going anywhere," she said. Then, to soften it: "I didn't go right to sleep. I was with the Tongues most of that day. I feel good. Strong. Don't worry."

Luz observed Eusebia, knowing she was lying.

Yesterday afternoon, she'd gone looking for her after she didn't jimmy the lock, and found her asleep. But she did look good. Something in her skin glowed, like she was lit by a great fire from within.

"You just said you're out of it," Luz said, unconvinced. She took her mother's arm in her hands, touched the bruised skin lightly. Her arm was swollen, tender to the touch. She could tell part of the bruise would become a scar.

"I haven't had anything to eat," Eusebia said. "I'll be fine once I eat something. But enough about me. Enough. Why didn't you tell me you lost your job?"

Luz sat down. How did Mami find out? Then she remembered Angélica wiping champagne off the floor, how she smiled at her shame as she walked away.

"Why did you get fired?"

Luz shook her head. She didn't know. She felt tightness in her chest. The campesino's back in the painting bent to sadness, not relief.

"It doesn't matter why," Luz said. "I already started applying to jobs. It's just a matter of time before I get a better one."

Eusebia nodded. Luz crossed her legs, to appear even more convincing.

"You just have to get right back on track," Eusebia said. "You shouldn't waste any time."

Luz was surprised at Eusebia's reaction. She was usually the first to offer comfort after disappointing news.

"That's exactly what I think," Luz said, feeling unsteady. "Raenna reached out to some of her contacts; one of them already said she'd get me in next week."

"All those long nights and weekends—you've worked too hard to give up at the first little bump."

They all had worked really hard to get Luz to where she was. Papi. Mami. She'd been the luckiest out of so many people she knew. And what of the relief she'd felt at Raenna's? At not going back into that life? She pushed that thought away. Everyone made sacrifices to get to where they needed to go. Just look at Raenna, and that endless shoe closet, and the beautiful house. Never mind those empty bottles of wine. And José García, who was only seven years old when he'd been attacked, murdered. He could have been anything. He could have gone anywhere. What did she owe him? What did she owe herself? She knew what she wanted. To find a way, to fulfill a promise without losing herself, to not have to move on to the next thing so quickly, without thinking, without feeling.

"You can't let the world defeat you," Eusebia said.

"I'm not defeated."

Luz remembered the sharp outlines of those tree branches in the restaurant as Raenna told her she was about to lose her job. How when she finally understood it wasn't a joke, the small trunks grew in girth, in strength. It was like the news had removed a dark film from her sight, sharpened it. And what of this day? With the guy at the rally, how his eyes had transported her to the ocean, her body craving the freedom of those Caribbean birds. And Raenna's house—with that red book cover, and the taste of dirt in her mouth?

"Terrible things can happen to wake you up," Eusebia said.

"I'm awake," Luz said to Eusebia. I've never been more awake, she said to herself.

Mami's hand gripped the piece of paper until it crumpled into a ball.

"What's that?" Luz asked. Eusebia smoothed it out, opened it. There were numbers, a list of words in Spanish. Luz didn't read it, couldn't understand it, waited for Mami to explain.

"It's my part," Eusebia said. "To make sure all our hard work isn't for nothing."

Luz thought about all those years, those long hours. Could she let that go to waste?

She couldn't sleep that night. Worried that time was passing while she neglected to do what she was supposed to do, she tossed and turned, and scrolled through the bright screen of her phone. She reminded herself that flawless selfies never meant a flawless life. That she didn't have to account for her time to anyone but herself. She felt like crap, but at least she didn't have to manually keep track of her billables. Didn't have to put up with the sense she was slowly disappearing into the human-sized emptiness in her body. Instead, she savored this new awareness—the outline of her body grew sharper, thickened in girth.

PENDEJOS

Luz slept in late the next morning, woke up only when her parched throat demanded it—the radiator whined and spewed way too much heat. When she made her way to the kitchen, there waited for her the usual—egg whites, half of a grapefruit, and a cup of now-cold black coffee. She gulped cold water, grateful for the alertness that flooded her body, ignored the meal Mami had made. On the stove, pots poised for the next meal; in the sink, inside a bowl, meat defrosted. In the living room, piles of clothes, neatly folded. Luz recognized her things. Eusebia had waited until she woke up to put her things away. The television was on, with the image of green and red balloons released into the air as the political activist Luz had seen the day before spoke into the mike.

"We will not stop seeking justice for the violence in our streets," he said. "We have been silent too long, willing to accept the unacceptable."

The segment ended with the newscaster saying there still were no arrests, that the investigation was ongoing.

"Ma," Luz called out, making her way to her

parents' bedroom. There, she found Eusebia, in dress pants and a pretty white shirt with lace around the collar, applying makeup.

"Where's the party?" Luz said lightly, remembering Eusebia's tone the day before.

"I have a video chat with your dad later," Eusebia said, giving Luz a wink. "Did you see your breakfast?"

Luz nodded, feeling relieved Mami sounded more like herself. "When's he coming back? You feeling better? How's your arm?"

Eusebia touched it through the shirt. "Still hurts," she said. "My head, too. But I'll be okay. Vladimir said it might be a few more days. Did you get any sleep?"

"A little," Luz said. They were both quiet. The collapsing and banging of concrete outside penetrated the living room. **Pendejos,** a neighbor yelled from somewhere nearby, **stop this fucking noise!**

"Pendejo," Eusebia yelled back, "stop being so loud." They waited for a response but none came. "This is going to be great."

They both laughed. "Let me warm up your coffee."

Luz ate her food in the kitchen. Eusebia put away the clothes. When they finished, they each wandered into the living room. Eusebia sat on the plastic-covered maroon couch; Luz lay next to her, placed her head on her lap. Luz scrolled through her phone as Eusebia ran her fingers through her hair. "We can't let this much time pass without oiling your scalp," Eusebia said. "It's like a desert in here."

She stood, went into her bedroom, and returned with a jar of coconut oil and a hair comb, then absentmindedly began parting Luz's hair, applying the coconut to her scalp, undoing knots she found with the gentlest touch.

"You shouldn't worry about the job," Eusebia told her.

Luz didn't respond.

"It happened to make way for something better, I'm sure of it."

How to tell her she didn't want better? That she wanted different? But Eusebia's voice, like shade, always soothed. Luz wanted to talk to her about what happened the day before. About how angry and tense she'd been. Why did she hesitate? Because she didn't want to disrupt this nice moment. Mami might be suffering a brain hemorrhage and she'd just rather let her keep scratching her dry scalp, and offering reassurances that her life wasn't falling apart, the way she had always done.

"You want to go to a doctor today?" Luz asked carefully. "I have some free time on my schedule," she added, trying to be funny. There, at least **she** wasn't a total pendeja.

"I'm fine," Eusebia said, an edge of sharpness in her voice, ignoring her daughter's attempt at a joke.

On her cellphone, Luz searched **dangers of**

an untreated concussion. She sat up, faced her mother. She listed them for her, raising each digit of a fisted hand: chronic headaches, dizziness, mood swings, memory problems, vertigo. At the last she raised her voice—"Mami," she said, "can you imagine worse vertigo?"

"I'm not going to see a doctor," she said. She showed Luz her palm, which had paled from the day before, the deep pink faded, the edges already turning brown. "I'm fine."

"Fine," Luz said. "I'll just tell Papi when he gets here."

Her mother pulled Luz gently by the shoulders, forcing her head back on her lap. The tooth of the comb felt a bit rough as it parted her hair, but the oil on Eusebia's fingers felt cool, nourishing on her scalp. "I'll make you a deal. If the headache isn't gone by tomorrow, we'll go to the doctor. But if it's gone, you'll leave it alone."

Luz accepted the deal. Her mother continued oiling her scalp and began to sing one of her favorite Buena Vista Social Club songs in her off-key voice. Luz, wrapped up in her phone, didn't notice how often Eusebia misspoke the lyrics to a song she'd known most of her life.

AWKWARD

The next day, Eusebia said her headache was gone. Did Luz do anything to verify it? Nope. She was happy Eusebia had fallen back into herself each day, until, by Saturday evening, Luz had all but forgotten the fall, the bruised hand, her mother's odd behavior. That night, while she ate, Luz described how every last piece of evidence of the tenement building's existence had been hauled far away from Nothar Park.

On Sunday morning, Luz set out to try hot yoga. She'd been wanting to try it for months but never could find the time. Now? Ninety minutes in the heat seemed like the perfect way to burn extra calories—she reminded herself that whenever she got back to work, she had to fit into her suits. Out early for her class, she was momentarily blinded by the sunlight. Another gorgeous, crisp day. The first day of May. An entire week since she'd lost her job. She crossed the street and walked up the central pathway of Nothar Park, which was lined with citrus-colored tulips. The world had gone from a monotone gray-brown to full-on color. The trees around her had sprouted new leaves, and everywhere there was a different shade of green. Budding flowers abounded—tiny blue ones close to the ground, cupped white ones extending from gently arched stems, pink ones the size of her fist.

The mural to her right had been defaced. It stopped her in her tracks, took the buoyancy out of her steps. Someone had painted breasts on the men, penises on the women, and pirate patches on the eyes of the children. They'd written **fuck** over each of the words that swayed above the hand-holding extended arms.

Fuck Love. **Fuck** Family. **Fuck** Community.

Around her, people hurried to catch a train to their weekend jobs. She remembered how often she'd headed downtown on weekends, too, putting in a few hours to get ahead for the week—expected minimum billable hours of two thousand a year were hard enough to meet. The office on the weekend was not that different than during the work-week, aside from the fact that people wore their expensive jeans instead of expensive suits—except for Raenna, who wouldn't be caught dead in jeans. What am I, thirteen? she asked any time anyone spoke of loosening up.

Raenna hadn't responded to any texts since they'd seen each other midweek. Without much plan, Luz called her. What would she say if Raenna picked up? Most of their interactions had been in person or via text. She wasn't sure they'd ever spoken on the phone, other than the interoffice line, when Raenna beckoned. The phone rang, and a beep to voicemail let her know Raenna had opted not to pick up.

"Raenna," she started, then felt foolish, calling her by her full name. "Rae," she started again, "I'm gonna just come out and say it. I'm really worried about you. I never saw you look so upset, so sad. Maybe I can come by later, and we can talk about how I can help? I don't know that you can keep going this way. Or that you should. Maybe you can find help or—"

The voicemail cut her off. Then, abruptly, the phone line dropped. She felt immediately embarrassed at how earnest she sounded on the voicemail, how clueless and young. How to check to see if it'd gone through? Should she text her, ask her? She decided to wait. If there was a reaction, she'd know soon enough.

Up ahead, Angélica was talking to her brother Christian. He was visibly upset, looking away from his sister, in Luz's direction, as he nodded. Angélica's back was turned so Luz couldn't see her face. As she got closer, Christian finally registered her approach and said something. Angélica turned around.

Both Christian and Angélica wore jackets that were too heavy for this weather. But Christian wore a skirt over his pants, and she noticed black nail polish on his fingernails. He had also pierced his septum. Where Angélica had their mother Isabel's round face with freckles on the nose and cheeks, Christian had a strong, square face and almond-shaped eyes. And skin exactly the hue of Luz's. As Luz got closer, their expressions changed. When she was a few paces away from them, Angélica said something Luz couldn't hear that made Christian laugh.

"What's up, Lulu?" she said.

Luz hadn't heard that nickname in a long time. She leaned up and kissed Christian, surprised that he'd grown so much since the last time she'd stood in front of him.

"Nothing's up," Luz said.

She looked away from Angélica, back toward home. She noticed a sprinkling of windows decorated with the Dominican flag's big white cross surrounded by red and blue squares. At least a quarter of the windows on their side of the block had hung the flag. That had to have happened in the last week or so. The Dominican Day Parade wasn't for months.

Then, not knowing which way to look next, she turned to the construction site, silenced by the weekend. Angélica's twins came out of nowhere and grabbed Luz's legs, pulling her down for kisses, while Isabel, their grandmother, followed closely behind.

Isabel gave Luz a tight hug.

"Did your mom tell you they're selling the apartments?" Isabel said. "Did she ask you if you can help?"

Luz shook her head.

"Maybe today you can read it? What they sent us?" Isabel asked. "Everybody is real worried."

"Of course," she said. "I'll read it as soon as I come back. I'm not a real estate lawyer, so I don't know if I can help."

"You can try," Angélica snapped.

"Easy," Isabel said to Angélica. Then she turned back to Luz. "We'd really appreciate it. People don't know what to do. It feels like there's nowhere left to go."

Angélica ushered the girls toward the playground. Isabel followed. Kenya was the first to jump up on the snake, swinging through its wavelike curves. Above them, birds sang, and the pretty sound momentarily eclipsed all other noise around the park. It made Luz realize how intrusive the construction had been over the last week.

Angélica remained quiet. Then she made eye contact.

"Listen," Angélica said, "I'm sorry about your job. I should have said it that day. That was real fucked up the way it went down. Did you get a lawyer yet?"

"Thanks," Luz said. "A lawyer for what?"

"You're the one who said Duvall was on probation. Let me guess? Duvall is a white man?"

"A white woman, actually. No, it's not like that. This wasn't about race." It couldn't be.

"If you say so." Angélica raised an eyebrow, unconvinced. Luz recalled that odd feeling she'd had about Raenna that day, that she'd been hiding something from her.

"How did you know about Duvall, anyway?"

"I was behind you at another table," Angélica said.

Luz took a step past Angélica and Christian. What right did Angélica have to be in her business, intruding in this way? The dumbest move for her right now would be to accuse her old employer of racism. She put it out of her mind. She said she didn't want to be late to yoga, moved away.

"Smarty-pants over here got into Cornell," Angélica said.

Luz brightened up immediately, stopped moving.

"That's such great news!" she said.

"Yeah," Christian said. "I can't wait to get the hell out of here."

Luz remembered being his age, having the same thought. Who was she kidding? She still regularly had that same thought.

"Slow your roll, player," Angélica said. "We got you for the entire summer. I don't know what we're going to do without him," she added, turning to Luz. "But we have a few months to work it out. I'm trying to talk him into going to City College."

"Not happening," Christian said.

"Cornell is a great school," Luz said.

"It's no Harvard," Angélica said, staring at Luz's emblazoned sweatshirt. "But we're real proud."

"I'm proud of you," Luz said. She went to give him a high-five, which sort of turned into a fist bump, and Christian was blushing and happy at the same time because she finally gave up and gave him a kiss on the cheek instead.

"You're still so fucking awkward," Angélica said, loud, with her back-in-the-day voice.

Around the same time that Luz found out she got into Harvard, Angélica found out she was pregnant.

She and Tony, both seniors in high school, had struggled with the right next step. Abortion? Marriage? It had been such a hard time for Luz and Angélica's friendship. As Luz prepared for what were supposed to be the best years of her life, her best friend got a quickie marriage and prepared for motherhood, only to suffer a miscarriage. Angélica had been so pissed Luz still left for college—left her. Had never gotten over Luz's choice. There had been a series of failures in their friendship through college. When they finally tried to make up with a night out on the town, after Luz graduated with her law degree, it had ended in disaster.

"I have to run," Luz said, glancing at her watch. "This probably doesn't make a difference now, but you should know that I'm sorry. I wish I could take that night back—it was sweet, what you tried to do. I don't want to wait another five years to tell you."

The wind rolled an empty can of grape soda to them and Angélica kicked it. Then, it seemed, Angélica didn't know what to do with her eyes. Five years ago, Angélica had taken her to one of those bars where migrant men pay three dollars a dance. She'd thought it'd be hilarious. Luz had been furious, accused her of taking advantage of sad and lonely men. Angélica had kept insisting it'd been a joke, that back-in-the-day Luz would have laughed, kept the dollars. That Luz is gone, Luz had said, wondering to herself if that Luz had ever really existed. Angélica had thrown her hands up: Makes two of us, she'd said. They'd never been able to find their way back after that.

Angélica kicked the empty air a second time. She was quiet as Christian went to join Isabel and the kids. Luz wondered where the hell that apology had come from. What was she apologizing for? First with Raenna and now with Angélica? Was there no off button on her mouth?

"Unemployed Luz Speaks the Truth," Angélica said, copying a game they played as kids, where they talked in newspaper headlines. "Melts Angélica's Heart."

"Woman's Heart Too Cold to Thaw," Luz played along. "Felt like a block of ice at the restaurant."

"That was mad childish," Angélica said. "I just have a lot on my mind lately."

"Like what?" Luz asked.

Angélica shook her head, pointing with her chin at her brother and her mom and her kids.

"What isn't going on?" she said. Then, "You should come by the house if you need a break. I can get some of that fancy red wine you like."

Luz said she would, knowing she wouldn't. Angélica reminded her of Eusebia in some ways. Pushy and comforting at once. Over her shoulder, she caught Angélica making her way to the bench, removing the lodged can, then tossing it like a basketball into a nearby garbage bin. There was grace in her movements as she made her way to her kids.

HUDSON

Luz went up the narrow stairs. At the top, there was a desk, and behind it, a mostly naked, thin white man with angular features and surprisingly large, sharp teeth. As she waited in line to pay for the class, a small dog with an elongated torso shaped like a hot dog licked her shoe. She noticed a distinctively unpleasant scent permeating the space. She wondered if it had anything to do with the little dog.

"Anna Karenina," the guy said, "leave the pretty lady alone."

Anna Karenina did not leave Luz alone. But the man grabbed the small dog so she wouldn't follow Luz into the changing room. Luz took off her sweatshirt, left her sports bra and her long tights on. When she stepped out, the toothy man shook his head.

"No, honey," he said. "You need to buy some shorts."

He held up a pair of shorts shaped like underwear.

"No, honey," she said, smiling. "That's not gonna happen."

"Don't say I didn't warn you," he said. He puckered his mouth. "It's hot as fuck in there."

All around her, women wore sports bras and tiny, tight shorts. The men were shirtless and wore their own version of tiny, tight shorts as well. They walked around very slowly, as if they were all quite pleased with themselves. There was so much confidence in such a slow gait, the kind of comfort Luz had never felt moving through the world in her own body. Not even when she was fully protected by her perfect clothes. As she rushed into the class, she couldn't make up her mind whether or not she was surprised that pretty much everyone in the studio was white. Everyone was very petite, even the men, and Luz was struck by the image in the mirror—she, the giant among them, some kind of slim-hipped Black Amazon invader. In Washington Heights. Luz the one who didn't belong. This is what it would feel like, once the blocks around Nothar Park changed. Over the last week, as those trucks hauled away the bricks, cement, pipes, she'd wondered how long it would take.

Stop it, she told herself. Seventy-ninth Street waited. That's where she belonged.

A passing car filled the studio with loud bachata, and the smell of fried, spicy meat traveled softly into her nostrils. Luz's stomach grumbled. She was hungry. It wasn't as hot as she thought it would be. But she'd begun to perspire slightly and made a conscious effort not to fidget.

"Please stand up," the thin man said, and introduced himself as Adam. As he began to speak about the class, Luz could tell he was stalling, and then she realized why. The man who walked in late was taller than everyone else in the room, including her. He was shirtless, like the rest of the men, but he wore loose shorts that lay low on his hips and stopped an inch or so below his knees. Luz was momentarily distracted by such a well-proportioned, attractive body. His shape that of an actor or model. She saw the way people in the room reacted to him, men and women alike. A communal intake of breath.

"Hudson," Adam said, motioning toward her, "why don't you stand next to Luz?"

There was something conniving in his tone, like he was playing matchmaker. It made other people in the room smile.

Hudson put his mat next to hers. It wasn't until he was right next to her that she realized this was the same white guy from the vigil. The one who held her arm when she'd tried to go stop those kids from taking bats to cars. He also stared at her, startled. She could tell he was trying to place where they'd met. She mouthed the word "Vigil," and then he nodded in recognition.

When Adam asked if anyone was new in the class, Luz was the only one to raise her hand, which made everyone in the room turn on their respective mats toward her.

"If you get confused or lost," he said, "just look at Hudson."

Luz had a feeling a lot of people would look at Hudson, confused or not.

As the class got going and the room became increasingly suffocating, Luz had a hard time staying upright, let alone focusing on anyone else. The sweat trickled down in rivulets. Through some of the positions, she became so dizzy she feared collapse. It took every effort to remind herself to breathe, to stay in that room, to just give the next pose a try.

She sat down a few times and Adam reassured her everyone had a tough time their first class.

"Have some water," Hudson said, handing her his unopened bottle. Hers was long finished.

Luz shook her head. Hudson gave her an encouraging smile.

Luz felt embarrassed. She wanted to leave the absurdly hot room, to be done with the stupid class and go back to the life she had before it all fell apart. She wanted to go back to working downtown, wearing suits every day, and complaining about the long lines at Starbucks. She wanted to go back to skipping lunch ostensibly because she was so busy, but secretly because she wanted to win ten thousand dollars in the firm's Biggest Loser competition, in which the real prize was not the money but the respect you got for proving you had the strongest will to win. She'd use the money to travel to amazing places all over the world. She wanted to be among people who did important things, who made a lot of money, who got to buy clothes and shoes and purses that sat unopened in their packaging for months by the foot of the bed or inside their closets, because they forgot what they bought moments after they confirmed the purchase. She wanted to be back with her friends, who had slowly

all become people from work, to indulge in dinners at the trendiest places where all everyone could
talk about was how busy they were, which meant
how important they felt. And she did feel important, among them. She wanted to go back to the
day she got fired, when she had a nagging feeling in
a bathroom that her life was empty but didn't know
how true it was.

By the time it was over, she understood why some
people became addicted to hot yoga. Her skin tin-
gled in a delicious way, and there was a sweet, spicy
scent she tried to place but could not. She inhaled
deeply, so glad she'd made it through the class. That
smell, in all this heat, reminded her of her childhood. It reminded her of home.

Within that moment, inside that scent, a certainty emerged from somewhere deep: she missed
what she missed, but she didn't really want to go
back to her old life.

When Luz walked down the stairs and out onto the
street, so exhausted and hungry she could hardly
muster the energy to throw that burgundy sweatshirt on, she found Hudson just outside the door.
Later, he would say he wasn't stalking her, that it
was a complete coincidence that he'd been tying
his shoelaces when she happened outside. Only
it'd taken a long time for her to leave, since she'd

decided to take a shower and there had been an excruciatingly slow-moving line.

She gave him a faint smile and walked on.

He trotted a few steps to catch up with her.

"Pretty intense, huh?" he said.

"That's an understatement," Luz said, drinking water out of a new bottle she'd bought. "I'm just happy snot didn't make its way out of my nose when I started crying like a five-year-old."

"You think you'll come back?" he asked.

"I'm not sure," Luz said. "Guess it'll depend on how I feel tomorrow."

They went down the hill.

"So, when were you at Harvard?" he asked, pointing at the sweatshirt.

She told him.

"A baby," he said. "What does that make you, twenty-seven?"

"Twenty-nine," she said. A chill ran down her body.

"I graduated exactly ten years before you," he said. "From Harvard, too."

Luz glanced at him.

"I saw your shirt at the vigil," she said.

"I'm an old man," he said, wrinkling his nose.

"Thirty-nine is not so old," she said, chuckling.

"So old?" he laughed.

"I mean, it's old but not **so** old." She smiled. "Do you live around here?"

"Yeah," he said. "Just down the street, on Sugar Hill. I also work around here."

They walked along quietly for a while. The street was busy. There was an elderly couple walking a fat chocolate Labrador, a guy who sold incense and body oils, a woman with a large wooden board filled with tiny holes through which she'd hung various earrings. Luz tried to guess what Hudson could possibly do for work.

In the middle of the next block, Luz stopped to buy a mango on a stick from a fruit stand.

"What do you do?" he asked, as if he'd already answered the question.

"I'm an attorney," Luz said automatically.

"Oh, I have a few buddies who work in law firms," Hudson said, watching as she bit into the mango. "Which one are you at?"

She had set herself up.

She squinted at the tartness of the mango—she never knew how to pick them like Mami did. "I'm in between firms right now. Actually, trying to find a different kind of job."

"Oh," he said. "Didn't mean to intrude. I just noticed your sweatshirt when you walked out and I thought it was a pretty unusual thing in this neighborhood, to see a Harvard graduate."

It didn't sit well with Luz, the way that came out. "You would be surprised," she said tightly. She remembered how often, at Harvard, guys went on and on about how they'd never met a Dominican woman before meeting her, always commenting how much they liked her accent. It was suggestive, the focus on her voice—what a rare thing it was, to meet a "first" of any kind. Columbia hadn't been much different, either, even though if anyone bothered to go just one mile north, they'd be in the heart of the biggest concentration of Dominicans outside DR.

"Sorry," he said. "I didn't mean it the way it sounded."

"Right," Luz said. This was the second time he'd apologized. The first time was when they were at the vigil. Had she ever heard another white man apologize? Nope. Couldn't remember it happening once. She listened closely to him.

He rambled about sports injuries, about how he'd come to love hot yoga. Luz was surprised at how nervous he seemed to be, how truly embarrassed he was at the earlier exchange. She decided to let it go. She would never have thought that someone who was that attractive was capable of being mortified. This, then, a first for her, too.

When they arrived at the corner where she would turn in to Nothar Park, she stopped and looked at him. Was he going to make a move? Awkwardly, he said it'd been a nice walk.

"I'll be there on Monday," he said. "Maybe I'll see you there?"

"Maybe," Luz said, so calm.

"Sorry, about before," he said again. "What was your name?"

"Luz," she said, though she had a feeling he knew it.

He did a little goodbye wave, even though he was just a foot away from her. She laughed and waved back. But instead of walking away, he just stood there, watching her. Luz understood, in an abstract way, that she was attractive. She'd had this kind of impact on men most of her life. Actually, if she was honest, she'd had it way earlier than she should have, when men two or three times her age told her the things they wanted to do to her as she walked across Nothar Park, barely out of fifth grade. Some of those same dudes, or younger duplicates of them, loitered in the park now, blasting music from parked cars, mixtapes that combined bachata with Motown.

Some threw her knowing glances, then pressed an elbow to whoever was nearby, as if it was to be expected, Luz talking to some white boy. There was resentment there, and she knew it was complicated because it was based on the fact they considered her beautiful, a prize. She knew that the impact she had on men didn't translate into her feeling beautiful. It was always a difficult thing to explain even to herself, as she was trying to do at that moment. It wouldn't be right to say she thought she was ugly, because on most days, she liked her body and what it could do, how strong it was, and how some of the lines she saw—like her collarbone or the shape of her neck when someone snapped a picture of her when she happened to turn her head just so, or when she was hot and was wearing shorts and she looked at the triangle shape her parted legs made on a chair—those were the images that made her think, This is what a body is supposed to look like. Still. There were some days when she couldn't diet enough or whiten her teeth enough or get enough gel manicures. There were days when she felt like she needed to conform to a version of herself that would never exist.

Her eyes grazed his body—remembering the warmth of his hand. At yoga, they'd done a pose that required lying flat on the stomach and raising both the arms and legs off the floor toward the ceiling. Adam had said to push forward and up, pull back and up. She'd stared at Hudson, trying to see what Adam meant. She didn't think she'd ever seen a man, in real life, with such symmetry in the strength and length of his muscles. He could easily pose as the ideal male figure in any textbook. Absentmindedly, she made a mental note to go shopping for those super-short shorts after all. And maybe also get a full-body wax. Would it be too much to get her hair done? Then she thought, Challenge the structures that make you waste so much time on grooming. Luz smiled at herself, in spite of herself. She was a mess.

He said her name, softly, bringing her back to the moment.

"Here," he said, handing her his card. "Just in

case you don't come to class. Maybe we can get a cup of coffee or something?"

"Maybe," Luz repeated, putting the card away without looking at it. She felt so smooth.

He finally turned and headed back in the opposite direction. She might have let him walk away, but right then, her phone vibrated with a text from Raenna.

WTF with this VM? You seem to be confused about the nature of our relationship. You focus on getting yourself on track. I got me.

The moment grew in significance. Her life, her time. And what use was it, if she wasn't willing to claim it?

"Hudson," she called after him. He turned to look at her. "How about dinner tonight?"

"Yeah," he said. "That would be great."

"I'll text you to coordinate?"

He nodded.

When Luz was safely inside the building, she looked at the card.

Hudson Sackett
Chief Innovation Officer
Sackett & Associates
Global Development Enterprises

On the back, he'd written his cellphone number. Make no mistake, she reminded herself, even if I lack confidence sometimes, I am irresistible! Up the stairs Luz flew, forgetting about her hunger. She couldn't stop thinking about those amazing eyes, about his shirtless body and how his awkwardness was somehow endearing.

Her cellphone rang and it was a number she didn't recognize. She let it go to voicemail.

Inside, the apartment was quiet. Her mother had left her a note next to her lunch, saying her aunt was coming back the next day and they were having people over to celebrate Cuca's return over in her aunt's apartment—Mami had left to start setting up for the party. Did Luz want to join her? Luz chuckled, thinking there was no way in hell she'd go clean up an apartment when she could have a date instead. She texted Eusebia.

Sorry, Ma. Already have plans. Sad face emoji, followed by martini emoji, followed by fork and knife emoji.

Mami was the one who said sometimes a terrible thing happened to wake you up. She couldn't say this to anyone else, but she could say it to herself: What if the terrible thing didn't happen so she'd work harder on the life she'd been building? What if triumph meant tearing the whole damn thing down, excavating deeply, to build something new?

PART II
EXCAVATION

THE TONGUES' INTERLUDE:

#1. VIOLATION OF PRIVACY

Eusebia overreacted. She said if we didn't take things seriously? It would blow up in our faces. But the thing is, after the first "crime" happened, how could we not laugh? We agreed a Peeping Tom terrorizing the women of the neighborhood, spying on our bodies, would be a good place to start. Who isn't afraid of invisible, scavenging eyes? Every act of aggression against a woman starts with a ravenous look.

Maritza, from the beauty salon, volunteered to call the cops. She was perfect for the job. Petite, with those huge brown eyes. Made us want to give her a hug just by standing there. But who knew the cop that showed up to monitor the situation would be so handsome? Michael B. Jordan incarnate, is what Maritza said. We thought he looked more like Sidney Poitier. Who could blame her for losing focus? During the exchange, she said she was a bit lonely, drinking a cold beer by herself in her empty apartment when the incident occurred.

The pervert, the cop asked seriously, what exactly did he do? She was supposed to say he exposed himself, that he pretended to ejaculate toward her, on the window's glass. But what would the cop have thought if she said that? Would he have asked her for her phone number anyway if she hadn't said it was scary, but there'd been no real threat? That the pervert only stared at her through the curtain, sitting on her fire escape, seemingly just as sad and lonely as she felt? There's an epidemic of loneliness in this city, the cop said, putting his pad away, leaning gently against a wall. Would you like un cafecito? she asked. He said yes. A perfect beginning for those two.

We understood. In his mind there would have been a stain if she would have stuck with the plan. Eusebia said we had better get our heads out of our asses before we started to smell like mondongo, and we agreed, chuckling. All these years, Maritza so lonely wanting a man. Look what it took! We went back and forth for a while, talking about how if we made a 911 dating app we wouldn't need those Social Security checks.

I just have to do the organizing myself, Eusebia said, fuming. And we agreed. Do it yourself, we said, laughing, we'll support you at the back end. It was unusual for her to be so outraged so fast. But there was much on her shoulders those days. Who could blame her? Unemployed daughter, Vladimir chasing after criminals all over the state, Cuca on her way back in God only knew what shape. Of course, we forgave her short temper, her unusually forceful manner. Do it yourself, we repeated, laughing—laughing the entire time.

CHAPTER SIX

Eusebia de Guerrero

As she walked through the quiet park to her sister's apartment, Eusebia marveled at the difference a week made in spring. All the trees were flowering; the grass—yellow with bald patches just a week ago, when she fell down—was an undeniable green. Her eyes hurt at all the shades of green at her feet and all around her—dark green of seaweed, light green of lime, warm green of avocado, cold green of pine.

At the door to Cuca's apartment, she found her spare key was no good. Juan Juan, her sister's husband, had changed the locks. What was he hiding, that he'd decided to change those locks? She headed over to his bodega. Sandwiched between Raúl's shipping business and the dentist's place, the crates overflowed with bright green plantains, the yucas brown with specs of dirt. She pushed the door open, absentmindedly noting that she couldn't even see a scar on her hand where she had fallen and scraped it. There was a tiny bit of pink discoloration on the palm that was hardly noticeable unless you looked for it. It was like the fall hadn't even happened.

Juan Juan greeted her with a warm smile, the bachata out of the radio behind him screeching about some lost love. He moved his head comically from side to side, those wide-set eyes darting just like a rat's—this was his happy dance. Their favorite girl would be back within a day. Eusebia tried to temper the rage as it rose; the sudden, uncontrollable urge she had to scratch, bite. Why was she angry at Juan Juan? She had no proof he'd done anything wrong—except maybe his actions of the past; he'd always been a sucio. She took a deep breath. She focused on the items that framed him. There were candy bars and packs of gum and various medicines sold in single-use packets. She reminded herself how every time she and Luz had come here, as her daughter grew up, Juan Juan had let her have the run of the place—eat candy and soda nonstop. It was wrong, because he knew Luz wasn't allowed, but it was well intentioned, his way of making sure that Luz enjoyed her childhood. That the strictness with which Eusebia brought her up didn't prevent her from enjoying being a kid, too.

"Cuña," he said, loudly, so happy to see her, showing her all his tiny, pointy teeth. This was the way it went. There was no way he didn't know how she felt about him. She knew how he felt about her. The throbbing in her head became pronounced as she remembered Cuca. "Nobody can stand a saint," her sister had once blurted out, and Eusebia knew those words, even in tone, had come straight from Juan Juan's lips, even if it was Cuca who mouthed them. But Eusebia and Juan Juan had long ago decided, in an unspoken way, to remain civil for Cuca's sake. He reached both hands toward her, through the partition, and she extended hers toward him.

"I need the key," she said, without greeting, pulling her hands from his quick.

Juan Juan reached behind him and grabbed a key ring with at least a dozen keys on it. He went about unwinding the right one from it.

"Are you feeling all right?" he asked. The concern in his eyes was real.

His hands were coated in a white, waxy substance. She tried to remember it; that consistency was so familiar. But before she could, his hands grew bigger. Rounded fingers swelled. She blinked. Commanded the pressure on her head to ease up. She knew the moment would pass. Had been aware, since she'd lied to Luz about her headaches being gone, that she was ignoring something she likely should not. Yet. She'd suffered debilitating headaches from time to time since she began menstruating and knew they eventually went away. So what, if this time the headaches had been constant with ever briefer reprieves? So what, when the visions—terrifyingly new—came and went, as long as she focused on breathing, and gave herself time to let them pass.

She would not bother herself with worry, there was already enough to fret about.

"I'm fine," she said curtly at his giant hands as webbing grew between his fingers and became wet with transparent shine. Saliva? Honey?

"Figured you could use some help getting the apartment ready," she said, finding calm in the sound of her own voice.

"I'm sure you're excited for Cuca's return, too," he said, struggling to get the key out, each impotent finger the size of a sausage. "I was going to ask you if you were thinking of going to get her from the airport? Because I don't have anyone to stay in the store? It being so last-minute and everything?"

"Oh, for heaven's sake," she said, grabbing the keys from him. With an expert twist of the wrist, she pulled the key right out. When she returned the key ring to him, his hands were their normal size, webbing gone—no shine whatsoever. See? As long as she made space for her body to do what it wanted to do, things eventually got back to normal.

"So, let me understand this right," she said, "you haven't seen your wife in over a year, didn't even bother to go when she almost died, and you're asking me if I can go pick her up from the airport? Do I have that right?"

"Cuña," he said, face flushed, searching the store for help. The Tongues were edging over from the refrigerated part of the store. She could practically see their ears quivering. One of them held a single-serving carton of milk in her hand, the kind they give children in school. Eusebia, annoyed, wondered if they would pay for it in pennies dredged from their collective pockets so they could linger and listen more. Maybe she'd have to start calling them Bats instead of Tongues.

He cleared his throat. "It's not a problem," he said. "I'll figure it out."

"Yes," she said, turning from him toward the door. "You will."

"Please forgive the mess," he was saying as she let the door close behind her.

As she'd turned from him, she'd seen the expression on the faces of the Tongues. There was something like concern and pride mixed in there. They knew that Juan Juan deserved the rebuke. They were adjusting to this new side of her. When she'd snapped at them about Maritza, it was the first time she'd ever spoken to them like that. Well, they better get used to it. The impatience was required if things were going to change. She felt terrible afterward for just a moment, but she shook it off. How else would things get done? She took a deep breath now, as she made her way to the east side of the park. She walked by the offensive tree, which had erupted with many bright green leaves on its skinny branches. She paused underneath it, right on the spot where she'd fallen. Found herself nervous to get closer to it, afraid to touch it. What was this imbecility? What was she afraid of? A tree? Small birds, too many to count, were chirping happily and hopping from skinny branch to branch. Above them, the sky was the lightest hue of gold. Her neighbors waved at her from across the street, their limbs more relaxed in this warmer weather that allowed their skin to absorb and reflect back the softer light. This was a time for renewal. Rebirth. She decided to savor that feeling, of having spoken up and said what she meant to say when she meant to say it. Old Eusebia would have accepted the charge to pick up her sister, knowing that it would have been heartbreak when Cuca arrived and found Juan Juan couldn't be bothered to pick her up. When her sister returned the next day, she would need her more than ever. Her need dug into Eusebia. That's all she would focus on.

007

Juan Juan's slithering, webbed skin: the way she'd often thought of him. Repulsive. Reptilian. But what if she was wrong? What if these visions were leading her to a place where all she focused on was the pain of the past?

Eusebia entered her sister's apartment, allowed her body comfort in getting to work.

Under the four-poster bed frame, no condoms. Neither were any twisted in the smelly sheets.

Though there were dried-up, cakey parts she was disgusted to touch, she had to admit that they might have signaled loneliness as much as anything else. In the closet, among his dirty underwear and his unwashed socks, no women's thongs or a discarded brassiere. In the bathroom, in the claw-foot tub, only his Irish Spring soap and a sad-looking razor with the thinnest, shortest hairs she'd ever seen. Did the man not wash his hair with shampoo? No signs of his infidelity. But she knew it was there, invisible though it remained.

There was a smell that still clung to this apartment. A smell of something, of wretchedness. In a frenzy, she sprayed, wiped, scrubbed—to be rid of it. Bathroom, living room, bedroom, kitchen. Eusebia took great pleasure in anticipating telling Cuca how she found, in the very back of the refrigerator, the meal she'd made to see her sister off over a year ago; how it had grown mold, and how the mold had grown tentacles with fuzzy white seeds like dandelions. She did not blow on it, as they'd done on the mountain as kids, letting it float toward the ocean, to rest on the surface of a wave. She buried it deep in the garbage. What a relief to feel the throbbing in her head ease up the harder she cleaned, now that she'd found the source of that terrible smell!

She mopped the floor not three but four times, and each time a new calm settled over her. The feeling of the stiff sheets and the sharp hair and the soft, mushy mold all dissolved from her hands as she wrung the mop dry. By the time she placed the sheets and dirty clothes in a laundry bag (laundry was where she chose to draw the line), she was so exhausted she sat on the faux-leather couch to catch her breath. As she rested, she allowed her hand to gently slip inside the fold between two cushions.

Ahhhh. There it was.

A triangle of lace.

It'd been worn for the first and only time the day it was taken off. Not worn long enough to leave a smell. Still a size smaller than the size her sister had gone through hell to become.

Her cellphone rang.

Vladimir, whose voice competed with hers in weariness, had a lilt that told her it was good news. One bad guy down. This happened often between them—somehow, regardless of how far away he was from her, he could intuit when she was distraught.

"Double-oh-seven," he said. "You got evidence?"

She stared at the underwear; the sadness torched her. It incinerated a body, always being right.

"No," she said. "It looks like the man is reformed for real."

Eusebia rested her eyes, thinking about her sister as she fingered a stranger's thong. The pulse in her head went from back to front, from faint to loud. A roar. What if the visions weren't her mind telling itself a lie, but showing her how to see the truth?

INTERNAL CLAUSTROPHOBIA

Cuca left for DR with the purpose of getting the "Ofrézcome Altagracia" Complete Makeover just a bit over a year ago, to Eusebia's dismay. Altagracia, patron saint of the Dominican Republic, had probably cursed the plastic surgeon who came up with the body overhaul. Patients spent six to eight months at an intense fat camp losing the recommended amount of weight, then plastic surgeons took over and offered an extensive menu of procedures: face-lift, nose job, tummy tuck, breast augmentation, excisional arm lipectomy, butt implants, a series of skin-bleaching treatments, and, as a bonus for those who got three or more "enhancements" but had been hardheaded enough to have refused the "husband stitch," they threw in a vaginal rejuvenation at no extra charge.

Before Cuca left for the Dominican Republic to get the makeover, she hadn't made it out of her apartment in months. Eusebia watched helplessly as her sister became a prisoner in her own body. Fat hung off her arms, folded the skin of her neck, and sometimes trapped dirt. Cuca's thighs rubbed painfully against each other, leaving bruised skin that peeled. She had the same gorgeous hair as Eusebia, but it had begun to thin and fall in chunks that left the sensitive skin of her scalp exposed. Her ankles had grown so swollen it was difficult for her to walk, and because Cuca was so embarrassed about this condition, Eusebia was the one who helped her sister use the bathroom, take a bath, scratch the itch in the middle of her back. Cuca received a motorized wheelchair from her Medicaid doctor, who advised her that she had officially reached the point considered morbidly obese in medical terms and that the government would pay for her to get her stomach stapled.

How did it come to that? On the rare occasions Cuca made it out of her apartment or allowed a visitor other than her sister to go into it (but always only when her sister was with her), she would point to her husband, Juan Juan, and say it was because of him, that cheating asshole.

Juan Juan—named after his mother's favorite Dominican political figure, Juan Bosch, and her favorite singer, Juan Gabriel, in that order—would throw his hands up, like someone was pointing a gun at him, and go to the kitchen to get Cuca a snack.

Cuca may have kept going the way she had been for years and years if a doctor hadn't used the words "morbid" and "stomach staples" when speaking of her body the same day Eusebia had said, offhand as she wiped her sister's ass before bathing her for the doctor's appointment, "I don't know how you live with yourself." Eusebia regretted those words immediately, said so carelessly.

Especially when Cuca showed her a brightly colored ad for a new clinical center in DR that claimed an impossible transformation within twelve months. "THEY WILL SCREAM 'OFRÉZCOME ALTAGRACIA' WHEN THEY SEE YOU!!!" went the catchphrase, followed by rows of before-and-after pictures. The more carefully Eusebia examined the pictures, the more convinced she became those pictured weren't the same people.

You can't go through with this, Eusebia said. It's crazy. I'll help you lose the weight.

This isn't about fat, Cuca said.

She had shown Eusebia a series of pictures on her phone.

Swiping left, Eusebia saw picture after picture of Juan Juan posing with beautiful young women, some maybe twenty, twenty-five at most. All had slender, youthful bodies. The background changed with each girl. There were bars, restaurants, and beach resorts with astounding views of ocean and sky that went on forever.

You have to listen to me, Eusebia had said, as she handed the phone back. Even if you spend the next year going through all that painful stuff, there is no guarantee Juan Juan is going to stop cheating on you. He was cheating on you when you looked just as beautiful as these girls.

Eusebia knew sometimes it was up to the people who love you the most to tell you the most painful truths.

Cuca didn't believe she'd ever been that beautiful, though Eusebia was witness she had. Cuca was willing to do whatever was necessary to keep her man. I can't live with myself anymore, she said.

The weirdest part? Though she insisted she did it for Juan Juan, it wasn't true. She did it because of what Eusebia told her. And that part made Eusebia angry in equal parts at herself and her sister. Cuca stopped speaking to her sister when she booked her flight, when she made that down payment on the "Ofrézcome Altagracia" Complete Makeover.

During the first few months Cuca was gone, Eusebia had beaten herself up for letting the conversation get so out of hand. How could she have said such a terrible thing? Her sister had been able to live with herself and she had no right to change that. She wished she'd told Cuca it'd do her no good to get cut up because there was something at work here bigger than the two of them. She wanted to tell her that from where Cuca stood, Eusebia might appear to be beautiful but she often had those same feelings of not being good enough just like Cuca did. Eusebia herself couldn't put her finger on why she felt that way. Her husband desired her, loved her. Men often, even as she advanced in age, asked her to dance at parties, offered to buy her a beer if she happened into a bar by herself. The women in the neighborhood often came to her for advice not only about taking care of their families, but also beyond that—clothes, recipes for growing thick, lustrous hair, how to keep their lovers' eyes fixated on them and only them. Even when she looked in the mirror, when she first woke up in the morning, there was a sense she had that she liked what she saw, that she liked herself. But it was at the end of the day, when she took her nighttime bath, when she washed the grit off her face, that the thought surfaced: Maybe there was something off about her. Eusebia didn't say those things to her sister. Deep down, she knew it'd be a waste of time saying those things, because her sister was determined to become someone else.

HAPPINESS HURTS

Nine months into the one-year journey, Eusebia received a phone call from the hospital where her sister was staying in DR. They were sorry to inform her that the surgery hadn't gone as expected and her sister was in critical condition. They urged her to get there as quickly as possible.

There was no one else in the two-bed hospital room when Eusebia arrived. The place was disgusting, dirty, with hospital furniture that appeared to have been picked out of a dumpster. She spent the entire day there, and every single staff member was consistently tired and pissed off.

Her sister had been unconscious, and as Eusebia stood there, staring at the mummy on the bed, afraid to touch the dirty sheets, lifting first one foot, then the other off the sticky floor, she was overcome with a sense of her own responsibility. She could have done so much more to prevent this from happening in the first place. Over the next few days, as much as Eusebia spoke to her and held her hand, Cuca remained completely unresponsive.

Through the lump of fear in her throat, Eusebia could, objectively, review the progress of her sister's botched transformation. Even beneath all the bandages, it was obvious she was hundreds of pounds lighter. From that point forward, regardless of the consequences, her sister would take significantly less space in the world. The bandages covered her face, her arms, and her legs. Spots of blood made their way through the tiny holes in the gauze, congealed the fabric as it dried, changing the brightness of the red to a dull brown. That blood carried her sister's insecurity, yes, but also something more. Her stubbornness, her drive. Eusebia was certain her sister would be okay. She couldn't have made it this far to be knocked down by an infection. No way.

Eusebia couldn't figure out if the hospital was helping or making things worse. The treatment is working, the doctor said, when they met at Eusebia's request. It's just going to be a little worse before it gets better. This is very unusual, I assure you of that.

Eusebia didn't appreciate the way the doctor's eyes took such an interest in her figure, as though he was analyzing how she might benefit from his skill.

Cuca woke up on Eusebia's fourth day. Eusebia felt an immense sense of relief, and that swallowed lump of fear dissolved into a rush of anger that in-flated in her belly. Why would Cuca do this to her-self? To Eusebia?

Do you feel okay? she asked, pushing down on that feeling.

Cuca just shook her head.

Later, when she could speak, Cuca said she wasn't sure if it was the drugs, or lying flat for as long as she had, but she felt like a visitor in her own body.

I thought that was what you came here to fix, Eusebia said, before she could stop herself.

I'm sure you'll feel like yourself soon, Eusebia continued, trying to recover. She'd bought Cuca a dress with a wild pattern of tropical birds and flowers, the kind of ridiculous pattern they used to laugh at when they were younger, would have called Caribbean cliché. Wear it when you come back home, Eusebia said. You're gonna knock him dead.

Don't make me smile, Cuca said, happiness hurts so much.

Eusebia winced.

I regret nothing, Cuca said at the hard thing that floated between them. This is my happiness hurt. For my love. You wouldn't know it.

Eusebia stayed by her sister's side for another week, until Cuca finally stabilized. Each time the bandages had to be changed, Eusebia was asked to leave the room. So, in all that time, she never had gotten to see her sister without them. And all those days, in that hospital room that reminded her of a different hospital room, she kept thinking about love. Cuca's love, Juan Juan's love, Vladimir's love, her own.

Did Eusebia know anything about love? She remembered the sweetness of new love, the electricity that traveled up and down her body when Vladimir touched her those very first few times. She remembered the anxiety of love, when he'd first told her he wanted to spend the rest of his life with her and she realized she loved him more than anyone else, even her own mother or sister or father. Maybe even herself. She remembered the weight of love, when they'd first had Luz and had both stared at their newborn. It was in the shared love they felt for the child that their purpose had become so real, so serious. Their focus now less on each other, more on her. She remembered the loneliness of love, after great losses fell on them, and she was the one who had to carry their dead son. Then it was the dullness of love, how it had faded as the months passed and became years when Vladimir had left for New York. She remembered the awkwardness of love, when they reunited after being apart so long, and how she exercised her love for Luz then, how for her sake she tried to feel something more than the familiarity she felt for him; that love so changed she thought she needed to call it something else. She remembered the generosity of love, how Vladimir had known the distance between them for what it was, and how he decided to reignite their love and had found so

many ways to do so. An old salsa song, an invitation to the old women of the building, whom she'd
eventually call the Tongues, who as a housewarming
gift brought Eusebia a copy of Neruda's love poems
and a pot of caramelized chicken. Vladimir devel-
oped a new habit, overnight, of reading aloud from
that collection of poetry by Pablo Neruda. That last
one her favorite, because it reminded her of when
they were kids, how he loved to read, and would do
it aloud because she couldn't stand sitting still and
staring at a page. And the way he did it, just like it
wasn't a big deal, but in his tenor a note of despera-
tion. To have sacrificed as much as they both had to
have it fall apart? No. Those poems were about love,
all different kinds of love, and through listening to
what Vladimir was saying in recitation, which was
really what he couldn't possibly have ever said with
his own words, she'd been transported to an earlier
version of herself, an earlier version of them both.
A time when neither needed words. Eusebia had
been overwhelmed by the gratitude she felt that he
had chosen her at the beginning, that throughout
their relationship it had always been a little skewed,
how much more he seemed to love her than she
him, and how he never hid it from her, or others,
or himself. There was great comfort in knowing that
he would never hurt her. That she would never have
to hurt herself to make him happy. That in the ways
she'd chosen him, and Luz—really the family—it

had never been an expectation from them more than a given, had never felt like a sacrifice to her for what she might have had instead. People don't ever get it, Cuca said, in that cold hospital room. When it's done for love, it hardly ever feels like anything other than happiness, even if it hurts. Eusebia had been quiet. She couldn't possibly tell her sister she knew exactly what she meant.

SHADOW

In the pristine apartment, Eusebia crumpled the lace thong in one hand, took it and buried it inside the garbage bag. Tomorrow her sister would be back, and it would be of no use to anyone to do anything other than pretend all she'd gone through had been worth it.

On the way home, Eusebia dragged the garbage bag out. Even though it was late afternoon, she tried not to overreact at how darkness had fallen around the park—when she knew deep down it should still be lighter out. Instead, she focused on the stench. It was garbage day in the neighborhood. The black bags on the corner made her hurry her step, cut across the park even though that would make it a longer walk. She hadn't been walking longer than a few feet when she stopped dead. Right next to that offensive tree, a shadow moved, a shadow walked toward her.

"You got spare change?" a familiar voice crooned.

When he took a step forward, Eusebia took a step back.

"Jesús, René," she said, feeling the sting in her eyes, in her nostrils, in her throat, when he got close enough for her to see him.

"Thought I'd be less insulting on garbage day," he said, lifting an arm, taking a sniff.

"Garbage would be insulted to smell you," she said. She searched in her purse, gave him the first bill that she came across, relieved the shadow was human. His eyes lit up.

René was the first person Eusebia ever saw high. Just months after his father was killed in the September 11 attacks, René went out to run an errand and came back changed. The first hit was free, he would tell her later. She'd found him in the park, leaning against that same tree, moving back and forth as if a string pulled, then released him.

"You got any spare work?" he said. It was a trick. He would ask people if they had work for him, knowing it might prompt a second reach. But on this day, Eusebia told him she actually did have work. After the explanation, he gave her a nonchalant nod.

"And you're going to pay me?" he asked.

She told him a few dollars, sure.

"And what am I supposed to do with the stuff I steal?" he asked.

"Whatever you want," she said.

"When do I start?" he asked.

"No time like the present," she said, and gave him the addresses of the women who'd said sure, they had renter's insurance, no big deal. Anything to stop the noise across the street, to keep the neighborhood safe.

CHAPTER SEVEN

Luz Guerrero

HOW MUCH HAPPENS IN A DAY

It was the first truly warm day after a brutal winter. Beneath the glow of a golden sky, they went to Hudson's favorite Indian restaurant down in the East Village. They got there early, but the place was already full. In the tiny dining room, there were only a dozen tables. Outside, in the garden, there were half as many. The periphery of the garden was walled off by cherry laurels, leaves glossy and fresh.

The tablecloths were made of a light cotton in jewel tones. Theirs an emerald green. The waiter brought them water and wafer-like crisps with red spicy and sweet sauces. Hudson ordered a bottle of wine. He asked what she was going to eat. Luz said she wanted meat samosas, naan, chana masala, and chicken tikka masala.

"Is that for both of us?" he asked.

Luz shook her head. "Ever since I stopped working,

I can't stop eating," she said. "It's like I'm making up for all the years I starved myself."

"Why were you starving yourself?" he said.

"To be skinny," she said. "The culture at my firm was crazy."

She told him how they used to do these Biggest Loser competitions. Never mind that no one really needed to lose any weight. How the longer you went, the less you ate, the more everyone respected you.

"I'm sure you can't wait to get to your next job. That place sounds awful."

Raenna's friend Frances was the one who'd called from an unknown number earlier, who'd left a voicemail. Luz had returned the call and they'd spoken for close to an hour. Luz thought it was going really well, then Frances stopped abruptly, as if distracted by someone in the room. She'd said there were no current openings, but anyone Raenna recommended this highly had to be considered. We'd create an opportunity if the interview worked out, she'd said. Can you come in Tuesday? she'd asked, then transferred her to her assistant before Luz responded affirmatively. The exchange left Luz feeling uneasy. She wondered if they played the Biggest Loser there, too.

"I never understand why women do that," Hudson said. "Most men like women who look healthy."

"Since when?" Luz said.

"I'm serious," he said. "Women do these things to themselves because you're competing against each

other. Not for us. I'm surprised. I thought culturally, it would be different."

Luz didn't respond.

"Because," he said, "you know. Latinx women are
supposed to be curvier?"

"Curvier?" Luz said.

"I mean," he said, "it's more culturally acceptable
to be, ummm—"

"Fat?" Luz said.

The waiter came back, opened the wine. Hudson
asked Luz to taste it.

"It's really good wine," she said.

"Sorry," he said. "I didn't mean—"

"No," Luz said. "Don't apologize. People think
that. But it's not true. Everyone feels the same pressure. No matter how different things are when
you get home. Sure, maybe there's more spectrum
where I'm from about what's considered desirable,
but pressure is pressure. You don't escape it based
on zip code."

She thought about Tía Cuca. When Cuca asked
Luz, before she left, if she was crazy to get all that
surgery, Luz had been adamant in her response—
women's choice meant you do what you want, forget the society that makes you feel like shit for not
fitting the standard and then criticizes you when
you try. The pressure was everywhere. But she wasn't
going to get into that with Hudson. She wasn't on
this date to be political. He was wearing a button-
down short-sleeve shirt. From his open collar, she

could see his hairless chest. It didn't look like he was wearing an undershirt. They were both too tall for the table, and their knees kept touching. Each awkwardly shifting the knee away but not too fast.

He was asking her something. She hadn't heard him.

"What are you going to eat?" she asked.

He was a vegetarian. She drank an entire glass of wine while they waited for the food to come. She began to feel giddy. When he finished sipping his wine, he wiped the rim where the wetness remained. He stared at her glass, at the liquid on the rim. She wondered if he expected her to do the same thing. How weird was that?

When the food arrived, she bent over her plate and ate as if she hadn't eaten in days.

He sat back, staring.

"What?" she asked. "Didn't anyone teach you it's rude to stare?"

He blushed and turned his attention to the food.

"Does it gross you out when you see people eat meat?" she asked, in between bites of delicious chicken.

"No," he said. Then, a few moments later, carefully: "I don't think there's anything you could do that would gross me out."

Wepa!

By the time they finished the first bottle of wine, she found out they were both only children. He'd grown up in Manhattan but had spent most of his time away from here. He'd been shipped off to boarding school at Andover when he was fourteen years old. She furrowed her brow, thinking the poor thing had been abandoned by cold, uncaring parents, but he dismissed the gesture. That wasn't his life. His mother, a poet who'd grown up in Boston and had attended the same school, hadn't missed any opportunity to visit, staying at least a weekend out of each month, regardless of where business took his father. They were great parents, he insisted, loving to a fault.

He'd decided to stay in Boston afterward, when he got into Harvard. Because of a girl he loved, who had also gotten in. They'd been engaged since freshman year. Both sets of parents begged them to wait until after graduation to get married, then the wedding kept getting put off. They moved to the city and started working, building a life he thought they both wanted, but then the whole thing fell apart.

Luz didn't ask why.

He took a break from his life. Left the country and lived abroad for a few years. Traveled through Asia, then the Middle East, later settled in London, where his parents were living at the time.

"Nobody gave you a hard time about taking time off?"

His parents encouraged it. They were relieved the relationship had fallen apart. Thought they were too young for that much commitment. Since his father had a global development firm, it was expected he'd eventually return, whenever he was done bouncing around, to carry on the family legacy.

"That's how I found my passion was climate work," he said. There were years and years of grass-roots work, mobilizing people to demand change from the government, organizing boycotts of the biggest corporations causing harm.

"But now you work in real estate development? At your father's company?"

"Yeah," he said, "it's bizarre. But it was a tough lesson. We couldn't compete, to make real change, because the corporations had the resources, so much more money, lobbying could undo what it would take us months, even years to organize. And I knew then the biggest way to fight back was to fund the effort the way corporations do. I get to re-cruit, funnel more funds from people who care but feel helpless. Everyone is overwhelmed. And when people are overwhelmed, they become paralyzed."

"Do you miss it? Being on the ground?"

"Sometimes," he said. "It was so exhilarating, all of us in our twenties—rallies, protests, just like those kids with the bats! We were going to burn it all down. We were certain we'd be the generation that finally made a difference. But passion doesn't change much. I realized our best bet is to slow cor-porations down. To become obstacles. Only capital can do that."

She thought about it. He sounded defeated. But

still—look at his life. Years off work, following his heart—so what if he ended up doing exactly what his parents wanted? Some people had the freedom to carve their own path.

"Are you taking a break from work right now?" he asked.

"We don't do that," she said, thinking that is how Mami and Raenna would both say it.

"Tell me more about your climate work," she said, changing the topic.

"But do you want to take a break?" he asked, not letting up.

"It's hard to say," Luz said. Christmas lights were turned on overhead. The illumination around the garden made everything soft, made her want to touch him, made her tell him the truth. "There's a part of me that knows the life I've been living isn't the real life I'm supposed to live. I get this pain sometimes, in the lower part of my neck." She tapped the spot with her index finger. "I was thinking the other day that it's probably from not looking up. I've just been following rules, following the playbook. But I'm looking up now."

She grew quiet. Scared to speak honestly, to put her hopes into words.

"Keep going," he said.

"I've been wondering who I would be if I wasn't who I've been up to now. The last few days have been so strange. And my mom and my boss, I'm really close with both of them, they're so invested in who I will be. I don't know if they're scared for me or themselves."

"The people who love you most are the ones who will do their best to control you."

Luz was quiet. Hudson was quiet.

Then he said, "It's not my place, you take it or leave it, but you know, when something bad happens sometimes it's to make way for something really great."

She didn't respond. Didn't tell him Mami had said pretty much the same thing.

"Don't rush back to the life you had," he said. Such authority.

"I wasn't asking for your permission," she said sharply.

"I wasn't giving it," he said. His brow furrowed. "Just 'cause you wanna be chickenshit, don't take it out on me."

She laughed at his slang. He laughed at himself. Their knees touched under the table. Neither moved.

"So, you sell out, start working for the man," she said. "But I guess you're working at your own company, so it's like **you're** the man! What are you doing right now?"

A new luxury condominium at Nothar Park.

"You mean the demolished tenement?" Her voice was so loud a few people around them turned. "You're building luxury condos? There?"

He nodded.

Nothar Park. Washed out, white out, everything forever changed.

He spoke in such a contained, calm way that it put Luz in a trance. As if he were talking about owning a pair of new sneakers. Her heart beat wildly in her chest. Why? Why couldn't he be an investment banker or a douchey hedge fund guy? Why did he have to be the guy who threatened her entire neighborhood? Everyone is scared, Isabel had said, it's like there's nowhere left to go. Luz sighed deeply.

"Is that a problem?" he asked.

She leaned an elbow on the arm of the chair, covered her eyes with her hand.

"Is it that bad?" he asked.

She shrugged, finished the wine in her glass. He went to serve her more, but the bottle was empty. "People in my neighborhood are scared," she said. "It's hard to know what to expect except displacement."

"We're working hard to do it differently," he said, signaling for the waiter to come back, placing his hand on her hand. Again, there was so much warmth in his body. "That building burned down over twenty years ago. We purposefully picked a space in the city that was unoccupied. And there are other things we can do to ensure representation, like the percentage of flats we're going to allot below market price, to accommodate the community. In a way, we'd be creating more housing than exists now, you know."

She narrowed her eyes at him, measuring his effort to warm the chill in the air that had settled between them. She acknowledged to herself, if not to him, it wasn't usually the first building that was the problem—it was what happened in the aftermath.

The waiter came over. "More wine?" he asked.

Hudson waited for her to respond. Was she going to single-handedly stop this new building and the inexorable ravages of commercialism in New York City? Probably not. But she could enjoy a night out with this handsome man, just one night. Who would even find out?

"More wine," she told the waiter.

"Are you sure?" Hudson asked.

"Yes, I'm sure," she said. For once, she would listen to her body, not her mind. She was going to give her body what it wanted.

By the time they finished the second bottle of wine, darkness had descended around them. The waiter lit the candles on the tables. The May evening air had become markedly cooler.

Her phone rang. Her father, asking where she was.

"Just having dinner with a friend," she said.

He wanted to know if her mother had spoken to her about what was going on with the building, that their apartment was up for sale. There were some documents she needed to read, to help them figure out what their options were.

Hudson's hand rested on her hand, lightly touching her index finger with his index finger. She felt the flutter of a strong current between them, right where his finger touched her skin. Was the rest of his body as warm as that hand? Would his stomach burn her tongue?

"I'll read it as soon as I get home," she said. "Just tell Mami to leave it on top of my bed."

Her father wanted to make sure she was all right. His tone, that seriousness, sobered her momentarily. Luz sat up, aware all the other tables had changed over. Once? Twice? People kept stealing glances at them.

"Papi," she said, "I'll talk to you later. I'm not in a good place to talk."

He was about to ask her something else when she hung up the phone.

"Everything okay?" Hudson asked.

She nodded. "People are staring at us," she said. "Are you famous?"

"No," he said, noticing the same thing. "Are you?"

She laughed. He paid. They left.

KEY CHAIN

The thing about the first warm night after an endless winter? Brings everyone out to play! Even as the chill descended, people acted like it wasn't true. Winter was behind them. They didn't care. From outside the car, no one would know Luz sat in the passenger seat, that the entire city reflected on her. She felt charged by it, by them. They hustled on the streets, selling "I ♥ NY" T-shirts to the tourists or other things, harder things for those wanting. The kids—too young to be outside—with old-school radios on shoulders, danced for coins. This is the city in constant retrospective. Old is new, new is old. All the time. College-aged girls linked arms in groups of four or five as they made their way to dinners or bars or clubs. They wore platform shoes and short pants, much too short for the weather, that accentuated their too-thin legs. They threw their heads back when they laughed, as someone snapped pictures with a phone. Real or pretend, Luz had never allowed herself such abandon. Hudson drove without asking questions, but every few minutes he looked away from the road, letting his eyes rest on her.

"I love New York City," she said. A surge of joy thickened her voice.

"Why?" he said, then, smiling, went on. "You sound like a cheesy tourist key chain."

"You win this city and it's like you conquered the entire world. I always feel this pull, you know, this rush, a yearning for more, to have all of it."

He smiled the way Vladimir sometimes smiled at her, like she was very young. He responded quietly, in a contained way. His feeling was the opposite, he told her. More and more, he felt like he didn't even belong in this city. It seemed to him that unlike what she felt, that pull and yearning, the energy of the city was pushing at him, a palpable pressure nudging him away. He grew quiet and for a moment the feeling she'd had at the restaurant, knees touching, electric, came back. Some kind of pull from his body to hers.

"You should stay with me tonight," he said.

She noticed how different he was from the way he'd been during their walk after yoga. He was so confident, so assured, she wondered briefly if the way he'd been acting on their walk had been a pretense. But when she looked at him, to see if it was a farce, if she needed to worry, there was that same face: open, honest, kind. His eyes were on her, waiting for a response.

She nodded. She didn't want the night to end.

WHO THE CONQUEROR?
WHO THE CONQUERED?

Hudson went up Central Park West and it was as if they'd suddenly traveled to a desolate, enchanted place. The branches of the trees extended down majestically, almost touching the road. There were hardly any people on the street. When they neared the corner of Seventy-ninth Street, she asked him to pull over, and pointed to the building she wanted to move to. He nodded, saying it was nice.

"Do you know anyone who lives there?" he asked.

"I did," she said. "I had a law school friend who lived there when I was at Columbia. It had been in her family for generations. And I remember thinking that it was wild, you know. That apartment sitting empty—just waiting for anyone to use it. And I thought that would be my contribution to my future family. An apartment like that, in the best city in the world."

He didn't respond, but his eyes lingered on her before he accelerated the car, drove them away. And she felt young again, but this time, she liked it. Maybe he could use a reminder about ambition, about desire.

When they got to his block, which was just a few blocks over from Nothar Park, he pressed a button that opened a set of gates on the right, and swerved into an entryway between what appeared to be a row of unassuming brownstones. She expected they'd entered a building, and on leaving the car they'd be in a garage, but they were in a cobblestone courtyard with a fountain in the middle. It featured a little nymph holding a carafe that overflowed with water; two iron benches with ornate backs and claw-feet sat on opposite sides of it. He parked the car next to it. They went inside his house. Luz's jaw dropped.

"Jesus Christ, Hudson," she said. "Is this where you live?"

They went up a grand staircase that curved and curved. The lower floors were dark; their rooms appeared hardly furnished.

At the top floor, a kitchen, a living room. He went for another bottle of wine and Luz shook her head. No more.

"One more glass," he said, and she could tell it was much more to put himself at ease. He looked almost fearful of her reaction to the surroundings.

"Whose house is it?" she asked.

"It's mine," he said. "A labor of love for a really long time."

"I live with my parents," she said, laughing to herself, sipping slowly from the glass of wine he'd given her. She wet her lips and put the glass down. She knew her limits.

She walked over to a bookshelf, drawn by the elephant tusk displayed on top of it. The tusk was held up by two small metal arms in a dark wood base. There was an inscription on the base:

Who the Conqueror?
Who the Conquered?

Next to it, a picture of a young boy, maybe ten years old, next to two big men. One of the men held the tail of the elephant; the boy held the tusk. She turned to him.

"Is this boy you?" she asked.

"Yeah," he said.

"You killed an elephant?" she asked.

"I'll tell you about that another time," he said. He placed the picture in exactly the same spot it'd been before. His face clouded over and she wanted to go back to before she'd seen the tusk, to the energy they had before this sudden heaviness. As he handed her the wineglass again, taking her free hand, he led her to a wraparound terrace. It faced the courtyard with the fountain and the nymph, and if she didn't know they were a couple of blocks away from Nothar Park, she would have thought they were anywhere but there, maybe in Italy.

"I can't believe you don't have a table out here," she said. "I'd eat dinner out here every night."

When she turned around, she bumped into him and spilled most of her wine on his shirt.

"So sorry," she said, covering her mouth with her hand.

He left to get her water. She heard the sound of the faucet. But when he returned, he had an unopened blue bottle of Saratoga sparkling water. His face was a little bit red, like he'd splashed water on it and had dried it quickly, the towel irritating the skin. She got this sense about Hudson then, as he let her watch him open the bottle of water and pour some into a glass. He was incredibly lonely, just like she was.

She felt light, and close to him, so it wasn't hard to start talking. But she made sure to focus on the early years, careful not to go back to that talk of what she was going to do with her life right now, or Nothar Park, and what was ahead there, either. It'd been a long time since she'd thought about her childhood, and then, in the last few days, it was a constant presence. Those memories were like old photographs, bent and faded around the edges, so fragile she moved guardedly from one to the other, lest they fall apart in her hands.

That yearning she'd had, the sadness she often carried, she wondered, aloud to him, if it had to do with the land itself, the earth she used to eat by the handful as a child. She had the feeling in the hot yoga class, something to do with how the heat and the sweat opened a memory that contained the feeling she hadn't even known was there. Or how just a few days ago, she'd seen the cover of that book, and the memory had slammed into the roof of her mouth. She could taste so much sweetness surging from her past, making way like a great dam fallen apart.

"I could love you," he said. Then, as if surprised he'd said so aloud, stared straight at the curve of water from the little nymph as it fell.

"Because I'm talking about eating dirt?" she said. "Wait till I put it on you."

"Put what on me?" he asked.

"It," she said. He glanced at her and she puckered her mouth, pointed to her crotch with her pretend beak.

"Are you drunk?" he asked.

A little bit, she thought.

"I don't want you to worry," he said. "If you stay, nothing will happen."

You are very wrong about that, Luz thought.

"Why?" she said.

Look at him. The expanse of his chest, the strength of his arms, the flatness of his stomach. She'd been inside her head for days and days and days. Now? Time to get out of her own way. She went to him and let him fold her in. She inhaled deeply, willing the room to stop spinning so fast, so she could enjoy the evocative smell. Then, in delight, she knew. It'd been his scent she couldn't name in the yoga studio: he smelled like ginger. When they kissed, his hands were light on the small of her back. She was the one who led him back inside, to the room she thought was the bedroom, that ended up being a bathroom.

He shook his head.

"We're both a little drunk," he said.

Luz shrugged and undressed without looking away from him. All that drinking had made her bold. She stepped into the shower, turned the shower on, let the water rain on her.

He took a deep breath and left the room.

She wrapped herself in a towel and went to find him. She sat on his lap and kissed him hard. Him fully clothed, her body wet and naked when she opened the towel and let it fall. She tried to undo the buttons on his shirt but her fingers were clumsy, she couldn't get it done.

"Take that off," she said.

He held her hands, stood her up.

"Another time," he said.

He put a robe on her, something girly and soft; a bright mint color overlaid with the word **love** in many languages. She smelled it and couldn't detect a scent, found **amor** right by her belly button and traced it with a fingertip. He led her to his bed. The sheets were vibrant white. The comforter as soft as his mouth. He put his arm around her and within moments, by the evenness of his breath, she knew he was asleep. In bed, she was never self-conscious or shy. There are things our bodies know to do, if we only let go, she thought. She let herself drift asleep, wondering with disappointment why he'd stopped her.

CHAPTER EIGHT

Eusebia de Guerrero

WHAT THE HELL HAVE YOU DONE TO YOURSELF?

Eusebia told the Tongues there was absolutely nothing to worry about.

"Why is your eye twitching?" one of the women asked.

Juan Juan and Cuca should have arrived over an hour ago, but there was nothing to worry about, nothing at all. There wasn't a speck of dirt anywhere, so instead, she fidgeted with the pans filled with food and changed their locations on the table. She'd made pernil, moro cooked in coconut milk (the way Cuca preferred it), and potato salad. Isabel was supposed to come later with a garden salad.

Eusebia moved the curtains out of the way, to allow light into the room. Yesterday's golden hue had intensified—it was a deep orange today and cast the entire apartment in a potent, thick atmosphere.

Eusebia had a hard time catching her breath. She went to the bedroom and called Luz. Voicemail. She hung up. She wasn't going to talk to the Tongues about how Luz never came home last night, hadn't been home this morning when she left to do the grocery shopping.

"Everyone will be here today," one of the women yelled at her from the living room.

Eusebia nodded even though they wouldn't be able to see her response. Today would be a good day to talk to a few people about their plan. Get more volunteers, pick up the pace. Even though it was Monday, no workers had shown up to the construction. Instead, they saw some city inspectors surveying the grounds, taking samples of dirt in vials. The construction was moving forward, step by step. What about their plan?

Eusebia wanted to remain calm. That was the person she'd been in this neighborhood. For years, she'd been the one who organized prayer circles when there was a terrible blow that struck one of their own. Hell, even Dominicans beyond their own neighborhood. She understood the power of prayer, of community, to transform pain and despair from the seemingly devastating hopelessness of fate. Into what? She often didn't know. But it had been enough for her, to help others accept what couldn't be changed, settle into patience as virtue. Eventually, another path opened. Even when they ended up speaking mostly about their fears and not praying at all, each person left the circle reinforced for the days ahead.

On Saturday, as Luz had searched the internet for jobs, Eusebia had made an arepa. She'd put extra corn, added Carnation evaporated milk and condensed milk to the cornmeal to make it superrich. It'd been one of the best arepas she'd ever made. When she cut it into two-inch squares and distributed them to her friends around the park, she'd ended up flabbergasted. No surprise that her landlord, who owned many of the buildings around the park, had delivered the same manila envelopes to so many of her neighbors. The shocking part was how resigned everyone appeared. Grateful, even. At least they're willing to pay us out, she heard, over and over again. When she ended up at home, after delivering the treats to her friends around the park, she'd had to admit she was part of the problem. Hadn't she spent years convincing people the best response to hostility was inertia?

She tried Juan Juan's cellphone again. No answer.

She went back to the living room and sat next to the Tongues. She wished she could speak to her friends about these thoughts, about how consumed she'd been by this realization: They'd been wrong. All of them, but mostly her, for assuming acceptance would eventually yield a better life, fairer treatment. She trusted her hesitation. Whatever she felt, she knew she had to keep it inside. As much as she loved her friends, she knew they were all talk and no action. If she let them know how each day her outrage grew, they would get scared, maybe even try to stop her. And then what? What would come at them? They'd end up in a shitty place where none of them wanted to be, that's what.

When she reached for the remote control to turn on the television, her hand trembled.

"You gotta calm down," one of the women said. "You know she's perfectly fine. It's bad news that travels fast."

The doorknob turned. Eusebia almost jumped out of her skin with anticipation. She was fully un-prepared when Juan Juan walked in with a stranger who happened to be wearing a wild-patterned Caribbean cliché dress.

When the newly improved Cuca went up to her and gave her a big hug, Eusebia hugged her back and smiled wide, holding the hand this Cuca ex-tended to do a full turn and show everyone the goods. It was Eusebia's turn to admit that she also felt like a copy of herself. She knew the smile she sported on her own face was all teeth, no eyes.

Everyone's mouths fell open, and if it weren't for having Juan Juan there, saying "Can you believe it, can you believe it?" Eusebia would have thought it was some kind of prank. But then Cuca opened her mouth and there was no mistaking her voice.

"You better believe it," she said.

Eusebia had an eerie feeling. This is what wet blood on a dry shirt would have felt like if it'd been sound.

Her sister had lost 258 pounds, making her smaller than she'd ever been, even when she was a teenager. The thong Eusebia found tucked between the cushions would be too big on her.

She was hovering somewhere between a size six and a four. She had a short haircut that accentuated her new features. Was it possible that all that thick shining hair was hers? Cuca had taken pictures of her favorite actress and had modeled her face after her. But interestingly enough, she had a cute button nose and eyes that were wider, making her resemble, of all people, Eusebia herself, even more than before. Cuca used to have thin lips but now she'd worked it so the lower lip was just slightly thicker than the upper, and with those high cheekbones, after further inspection, she did look like a version of Sophia Loren or a duck. Her eyebrows were thick and full and seemed just a tad high on her forehead. Overall, even if the parts themselves were meticulously constructed, she had that man-made look people have when they've had plastic surgery.

Juan Juan rushed out to the bodega for some beer. For the flight home, Cuca had tried to sneak bottles of rum in the folds of her packed clothes, but the airline had misplaced her luggage. She didn't even seem bothered by it.

"I'm going to need an entire new wardrobe," she said coquettishly.

The minute the door closed behind him, she took off her dress to display what the money had bought her. She took off her bra and Eusebia noted how the Tongues didn't blink, looked at the new body with an intensity equal parts curiosity, equal parts disgust.

Eusebia tried to look away. But how could she? The breasts were a perfect 32D; they were perky and full. Cuca's belly was flat, and they had somehow managed to put in there the appearance of muscle. These doctors must have made a pact with the devil, because even her legs had the appearance of a young girl's, if you overlooked the scars.

And there were many scars. Underneath her breasts and up, then around the nipples. On the inside of the arms all the way to the armpit. On the inside of her thighs and the back of her calves. Right underneath both armpits there was a round dark spot, like she'd been branded. Across the bottom of her stomach, from hip to hip, like a C-section scar, only longer, thicker, still appearing raw. Even to their inexperienced eyes, it was obvious the work had been done by someone without much experience.

"I've given birth to myself," Cuca said.

She assured them the scars would fade with time.

The bleaching cream they'd used on her worked. She certainly was much lighter than she'd been before but not any human shade Eusebia could easily recognize. It was yellowish, with discolored spots, and Cuca said proudly she had to spend five hundred dollars every couple of months to keep up the treatment.

"Otherwise," she said, "I'll go back to being una negra." She turned to Eusebia. "Can you zip me up?"

Eusebia had the smile plastered on her face and hadn't spoken a word. As she zipped up her sister's dress, she tried not to touch Cuca's skin.

"And I have an extra surprise for Juan Juan," she said. Eusebia braced herself. What else could she have done for the man?

Instead of the vaginal rejuvenation, she had insisted they do a new procedure the doctors marketed as revirginization.

The Tongues leaned forward. Eusebia's smile dropped as she fell back.

"The medical term is hymenoplasty," Cuca said, and stood up. Eusebia stood, too, panicked her sister was about to take her panties off. But she had merely stood to get a glass of water from the kitchen. Cuca spoke from down the hall.

"I told the doctor he hit the golden goose with me. If this surgery works the way he said it would, I'll be a regular."

No one spoke. No one looked at each other. What procedure could be left? Eusebia sat back down. She knew her sister. She talked this much when she was nervous. She was waiting for Eusebia to tell her it'd all been worth it. That she was beautiful. Could she do it? Could she lie to her sister?

"It's a little painful when I pee," Cuca said, coming back, drawing a circle in the air around her crotch. She went over to the windows, closed the curtains, to keep the mystery alive, she said. She turned on the radio, and immediately, when an old merengue song came on, she began dancing by herself. Her point of focus, at the turn of each revolution, was Eusebia. "Juan Juan won't have eyes for nobody else."

Witnessing Cuca's antics forced Eusebia into further introspection. She recalled her annoyance that day in the bathroom. How upset she'd been at her sister, allowing herself to become practically immobile because of a man who hadn't shown her the care or respect she deserved. Then, when she'd decided to go to these extremes, Eusebia had been mortified but also, deep down, she'd been relieved. She had to admit it. She thought if her sister found a way toward self-acceptance and self-respect, she'd know better than to remain at the emotional whims of a man who did nothing but hurt her. Now here they were. She'd gone through hell, to land in the same position.

Juan Juan returned. He brought plenty of liquor and had found Vladimir and Luz along the way. Vladimir, as promised, had arrived from his manhunt in time for Cuca's party. He'd gone back to the apartment, had showered, shaved, and wore the shirt and pants she'd left ironed for him on the bed. When he came over and gave her a tight hug and a long kiss, she tried to hold his gaze, to connect with him momentarily about this bizarre situation, but he turned to Cuca straightaway, hardly noticing Eusebia's need.

"Wepa, Cuca," he said, the only one who got close enough to actually touch her face, shaking his head in dismay. "What the hell have you done to yourself?"

"You look so young," Luz said, trying to cover for her father. "You look like somebody completely different."

Cuca turned to Eusebia again. Her silence palpitated between the two of them.

"Is there any pain left?" Eusebia asked.

"I'm perfect," Cuca said in a high-pitched voice.

"I can stay with you for a few days," Eusebia insisted. "So you don't strain yourself. Your body has been through so much."

"That's sweet," Cuca said. "But I'm fine. Juan Juan will be taking care of me."

Who the hell could figure people out? A minute ago, Cuca'd been practically begging for acceptance. Perplexed, Eusebia stood up, opened the various trays of food. She went to the kitchen and removed the chicken she'd been roasting and the pork shoulder she'd heated up. It had been left out for too long and she could see how dry it was now, almost ruined. The skin, crispy and tough, curled away from the flesh at the edges. Of course, it was great that Cuca was feeling so well. She had achieved what was important to her. It was great that Cuca didn't even need her. Sure, become someone else, slice your face off and pay someone to do it. Fake or real, her sister felt good about her body. She should be happy about that. The window in the kitchen, which faced an interior wall only a few feet away, showed the growing darkness outside. Instead of bricks, it reflected Eusebia's image back to her. Was she really about to cry? She felt enraged, not sad.

She relaxed her jaw. Eusebia admitted to herself she was waiting for her sister to give her credit for initiating this transformation. Why? She found herself at once proud and revolted by her influence on her sister. What the hell was going on with her? Eusebia slammed some lids into the sink. But because it was a shallow sink, one lid boomeranged out, landing on her foot.

"Coñazo," she yelled.

She loosened her fist, pressed her palm on the soft leather of her shoe where the lid had landed. She had to get herself under control. Why was she this upset? Over the years, she'd lost count of how many times she'd been disappointed by her sister's ridiculous choices. Now, her face burned with anger.

Luz came into the kitchen. Vladimir followed closely behind.

"Ma," Luz said, rushing to her. "What happened? Are you okay?"

She dismissed the worry with a fluttering of a hand.

"If she's happy," Vladimir said, without waiting for her to say anything, "then you have to be happy for her. What other option do you have?"

Sometimes she hated how well he knew her. "Está horrible," Eusebia said, thinking of the odd shape of her sister's mouth. Her smile, always so pretty, now gone, forever.

"It isn't horrible," Luz said, getting two bottles of beer out of the refrigerator. She flipped the caps off with the magnetized opener that bore a flag of DR, and offered one beer to her father. Both tilted their heads in identical gestures, swallowed hard. "The whole world wants women to conform to impossible standards, and then when we try, they blame us for not being confident enough to love ourselves the way we are. What's horrible is we can't ever win."

Luz, so young. Cuca had told Eusebia that Luz had said the same thing to her.

"If you'd seen her in that bed, almost dead, you wouldn't be talking about standards."

"I'm talking about what put her in the bed, Mami, the pressure that came before that."

"Juan Juan," Eusebia whispered, glancing toward the hallway. "That's who put her there."

"You can't blame him, Ma. No matter how much you hate his guts."

"What? How can you—"

Vladimir did cheers with Luz, said, "To freedom." But Eusebia asked herself whose freedom they were toasting.

Luz drank with the ease of a person devoid of worries even though she'd just lost her job. Vladimir's success at catching the driver vacated the memory of that truck filled with dead people. Must be nice, this ability they both shared, moving on so quickly from devastation.

Vladimir put a hand on Eusebia's shoulder, heavy and calming. Reassuring? Or was it just to shut her up?

"She seems happy," he said. From the living room, Juan Juan called to him, saying they were ready to start the game. Vladimir squeezed her shoulder, threw Luz a knowing look, then left the kitchen.

Luz stayed behind, her hand now on Eusebia's shoulder, replacing Vladimir's. Were they patronizing her? Pretending she was the one acting like a delusional child?

"Why don't we go back to the party?"

Eusebia shrugged. "I don't feel like it."

"You want to talk about it?"

Eusebia shook her head, turned away.

She picked the lid up off the floor and faced the sink. There were dirty pots that needed washing.

Luz stood next to her, found a drying rag, and

began to help as her mother washed, placing the pots in any random cabinet where there was space. Eusebia didn't correct her. From the window, they heard the soft sounds of raindrops hitting the glass.

"It's raining," Luz said. Eusebia didn't respond. Luz took a few strands of Eusebia's hair and tucked it behind an ear. "I'm not saying it's not fucked up."

"Then what are you saying?" Eusebia asked, with an edge.

"She's a grown-up," Luz said, and laughed a little awkwardly. The laugh grated on Eusebia's nerves. "We're all grown-ups here. She gets to decide how to live her life. Not you, you can't decide that for her, even if you know better."

"Where did you spend the night last night? Why didn't you pick up my phone calls?"

Luz's cheeks reddened immediately. "I stayed with a friend."

"What friend?"

Luz focused on the pot she was drying. She cleared her throat. "A new friend?"

"You couldn't let me know, so I wouldn't worry?"

"Ma, have you had something to eat? Since when do you worry if I sleep out?"

"Since you're unemployed and have nowhere to go."

Luz took a step back. "Well, lucky for us, I have an interview tomorrow, so that won't be an issue much longer."

She left the kitchen without a second glance at Eusebia.

Eusebia refused to consider why she'd been rude to Luz. There were boxes and boxes of beer that needed to be placed in the now-clean bathtub. Bags and bags of ice that needed to be emptied into the tub. In the bathroom, her hand lingered at the very bottom of the tub, where the water was freezing. She liked how the ice numbed her hand. How on the way to feeling less, the pain multiplied, became endless.

Before she left on her trip to DR, Cuca told anyone who had ears she was doing it all for her man, and after Eusebia got back from the hospital in DR and told her sister's husband how badly she was doing, Juan Juan said he couldn't go until weeks after because of work. It was okay to sacrifice for love, Eusebia thought, you just have to be sure you do it for the right person. Now, as she returned to the living room, Juan Juan was the picture of affection and love. A hand on Cuca's new face, another on her neck.

Was Luz right?

Eusebia sat next to her sister, held the free hand, and was glad it still felt like the hand she'd held since they were children. It was a little skinnier but those were her fingers and her fingernails—the ring finger with that odd curve from an injury she'd gotten as a child that never healed quite right.

"What do you really think?" Cuca asked, so quietly only the two of them could hear.

"I think it was worth it," Eusebia said, exactly

the opposite of what she thought. "I think you look beautiful."

Her sister smiled wide and leaned her head on Eusebia's shoulder.

People from around the park arrived. Angélica brought more beer. Isabel brought the garden salad. Others came, each carrying more food.

Luz made herself a plate worthy of three grown men. Eusebia looked at her, questioning, but Luz's head was down, her focus completely on the food. Cuca served herself a chicken breast (without the skin) and some green stuff. She said she would not be touching rice anytime soon, patting her flat belly as she sat next to Luz. Plates on laps, the two had similar postures, even the bend of their necks a duplicate; so was the way they raised their forks to their mouths, greedily taking in the food with such pleasure that it must have been hard-coded into their DNA.

Luz's phone vibrated and she took it out of her pocket. Cuca leaned toward her, reading the text as Luz turned the phone slightly in her direction. Cuca whispered something in Luz's ear, and by Luz's secretive smile and whispers back, Eusebia could tell they must be talking about men. Cuca had always been better at that than she had. As close as Eusebia and Luz were, there was a line. Sex, relationships, Luz's single life and her lackadaisical approach to men, had been the line. Eusebia had struggled between pride and shame at her daughter's disregard for men. Luz was always focused on what was important, and Eusebia agreed it shouldn't be a husband just yet, or children just yet. Long ago, Eusebia decided to leave it to Cuca to sort whatever guidance Luz needed to navigate men, while Eusebia focused on helping Luz chart ahead with the rest of her life. Why? Cuca would act as a warning about what not to do, that was for sure.

Luz started tapping the screen of her phone. Eusebia heard her tell Cuca that the number one thing US parents were gifting their newly graduated college daughters was breasts. Cuca said something Eusebia couldn't hear while pinching right underneath one of Luz's small breasts.

"I like my body the way it is," Luz said. "But no judgments. Everybody should do whatever makes them happy. More breasts? More ass? Get it."

Cuca pinched Luz again, this time much closer to her nipple. Luz shrieked and pushed Cuca away, letting her giant plate of food fall to the ground as she laughed. Eusebia imagined saying she liked Luz's body the way it was, too, but those two were having such a silly, fun time she felt completely left out. Cuca gave Juan Juan a look and he immediately went to the kitchen, got the broom and a bunch of paper towels, and picked up the mess. That must have been the first time he ever cleaned up the floor in the house. Luz went to the kitchen and returned with another plateful. She said she had to leave soon, and Cuca winked at her in a knowing way.

The Tongues stared at her daughter, at the food on the plate, as they finally got up to serve themselves. Cuca and Luz continued their girlish nonsense, giggling as if they were twelve-year-olds. Cuca went on and on about how her doctor had urged her not to go for a natural look, to make sure the size of the breasts was just slightly too big for her new frame, the ass contoured so perfectly there'd be no doubt it was man-made. Even the lips, he'd insisted, should look just a bit off. It has to be obvious you've had surgery done if it's to be any kind of status symbol. Dozens of women perched on their seats, enraptured by the revelations.

Luz came over to her then, kneeled in front of her. "I have to head back home. Get some rest for the interview."

"Okay. I'll get up with you, get your power breakfast ready."

Luz smiled at her hand quotation marks around the word "power." She stood up and gave her a kiss on the cheek. "You gotta get some dinner in you, Ma. Stop acting hangry."

Eusebia had plenty of reasons to be angry and no appetite at all. She didn't realize how many people had arrived until Luz left. On and on, Eusebia listened and surveyed the women, wishing she could shake away her weariness and shake some sense into them instead. We shouldn't give in, she wanted to tell them. We shouldn't all become the same.

The Tongues cleared their throats, then sucked their teeth. "You all sound like a bunch of idiots," one of them said. Eusebia sighed deeply. Did that phrase come from her, to them, or the other way? She remembered saying the same thing to Luz, when she was talking about the women starving themselves for a few dollars. Eusebia's own body felt heavy, inadequate.

Vladimir glanced at her from his dominoes. "What's wrong?"

What had she been doing that he noticed?

"My head is about to explode," she said.

"Have you eaten?" he asked her.

Why was everyone paying so much attention to her eating? She tried to remember the last time she ate, and could not. "Of course I ate," she said.

She stood to leave. The Tongues walked discreetly up to her, asked about the plan.

"Pick some more of the women," she told them sharply, not glancing back. "Do what we said. This is the easiest one."

When Vladimir rose to leave with her, she shook her head definitively.

"Are you sure?" he asked.

"Of course," she said, growing even more annoyed. Then, softening her tone, she reminded him Luz was already home, to help if she needed it. She wanted to be by herself. She'd spent the entire

NERUDA ON THE PARK   185

weekend with most of the women who lined these walls, listening to their fears though they all were resigned to accept whatever came, to scatter like baby roaches when a bright light was turned on. They'd all seemed so young, defenseless, that she'd become even more determined to go through with their plan. She'd need rest if she was going to be any help to them.

She'd go straight to bed, she told him. He nodded consent. The music was loud and the people were louder. They gulped loudly, chewed with open mouths. Every few moments, someone remarked how amazing Cuca looked. Everyone was having such a good time she felt completely out of place. As Eusebia walked out, one woman asked how much it had cost. And shrieked at how cheap it was, I'm def next, she said, and then another woman said, No, I am, and then a third. Her sister said something about her breasts, how numb they were, that she couldn't really feel them anymore, but who cared? She had better breasts than when she was a teenager. You want to feel them? she asked someone. From somewhere, Juan Juan said, Yes, yes. Eusebia let the door slam behind her. As she left the building, Cuca shouted her name. It had stopped raining, but the sidewalk was still dark with it, and there were deep puddles that lined the street. When Cuca came up to Eusebia, held her hand, and said, "I'm happy I did it," Eusebia was still thinking how much a person could miss by staying indoors.

"Are you? Happy?"

Cuca seemed to take a step back from her, though she didn't move.

Eusebia embraced her. This was her sister. Who was funny and outrageous and always danced to her own tune. Her sister, who was more than a body. She gave her a tight squeeze, reassuring? In solidarity? Reminding herself what had been done couldn't be undone. From the apartment, Juan Juan called after Cuca to come dance. Muffled against her shoulder, Cuca spoke to her. My life may not look like yours but it's still a good life? Or maybe, A life doesn't have to look like yours to be a damn good life? She hurried away before Eusebia could ask what she said, or catch the reflection of her face.

CHAPTER NINE

Luz Guerrero

SPINE

The conference room had a stunning view of Central Park. To Luz's right, with a clarity that made her dizzy, an entire wall of floor-to-ceiling windows. Through those windows, on each side of the lush greenness, buildings of varying shades of tan put the world into scale. Outside, another early May day, sky clear with hardly a cloud to be seen. Inside the offices of Luca, Santorini & Associates, the temperature was a cool 66 degrees. Maybe it was the comfort of the temperature, or how high up they were in this building. Whatever it was undeniably magnified Luz's sense of expansiveness, of immortality. This office was so much more impressive than her last. She thought how small Nothar Park was compared to this park. She reminded herself the building she wanted to live in would have a version of this view.

Frances, the woman who was interviewing her, had mastered the chin-in-cupped-hand stance. With her free hand, she manipulated two stainless-steel stress balls. They made a wind-chime sound any time they bumped against each other, which was often. Frances was Amazonian in stature, with a short afro and a chin that dimpled when she smiled. Her engagement ring was absurd, seemed only slightly smaller than a golf ball. She nodded appreciatively when Luz walked out of the elevator wearing the same outfit she had on. Same suit in tan, same shoes (hers were black, Luz's brown), same Michele watch. Standing in front of each other, they were the exact same height. You'll fit right in, Frances said.

Now she stared with mouth agape, showing just a hint of an overbite. Her teeth were perfectly straight and dentist-bleached, blinding white.

"Come again?" she said.

"Work-life balance," Luz repeated. "I'm just curious how the firm cultivates an environment that encourages a balanced life. So employees don't burn out?"

Frances took a look at her fingernails. Claws of the steeliest shade of gray.

"I just took my first vacation in ten years," she said. "On average, I bill fifty hours a week, so I must be putting in at least seventy. We expect our associates to keep up."

The words came out coarse but pleased the ear.

Her voice's hoarseness—like she'd been out drinking too long or screaming at a concert—hinted at something uncontained. Wild. Outside, a fire truck's engine sounded faint, like the hiccup of a sleeping child. They were so far up. Luz felt powerful breathing the same air as Frances. She could learn things from her. She knew she'd said the wrong thing, talking about balance, tried to strategize how to get out of this jam.

In the earlier part of the interview, Frances asked specific questions about the cases Luz had been involved in, the motions she'd written, her appearances in depositions, in court. Here, she said, everyone pulls their own weight. Last night, Luz had left Cuca's party early to call Raenna and ask for guidance on preparing for the interview, both of them acting like the voicemail-text exchange had never happened. Raenna told her to play into the culture, make sure she got offered the job, even if a better one came along later and it was a short stint. Make them all want you, she had said, play to win. Luz reminded herself of Mami's words. All the hard work couldn't be for nothing. Luz had a new strategy now: she'd take this job but ensure there was enough room to explore other options.

"This may not be the right fit," Frances said, filling the now too-long silence, "if you're looking for balance."

"I prefer no sleep," Luz said. "Makes it easier to justify all the drinking."

Frances nodded in agreement, sighed relief. Both women noticed as one of the assistants walked by carrying a tray of giant-sized white-lidded cups— the smells of pungent coffee and sweetness of flavored syrup filled the room. The assistant looked into the conference room, gave Luz a tight-lipped smile as she rushed away.

"You had me worried there for a minute," Frances said, stress balls bumping into each other. "I was about to call Raenna and be like, 'Hashtag WTF. Your protégée wants balance?'"

"I've been in a fast-paced environment my entire career," Luz said, falling into step. "I wouldn't know what to do with free time."

The sound of the metal balls remained in the air, an echo.

"Then why ask that question?" Frances said.

Luz stared across at Central Park, at the buildings that flanked it. Like alabaster, some of them. Standing in place for hundreds of years. Those buildings would never be touched, torn down, replaced.

"I'm interested in doing more pro bono work," Luz said. "Use more of my time to further the causes important to my values."

"There you go," she said. "Much better. It wouldn't be New York if half the firm wasn't running around trying to correct the criminal justice system or the immigration system or the atrocities of public education. It's what we'd all be doing full-time if we didn't have mortgages or kids or a desire to see the world." Here, Frances winked.

"We all get it done," she continued. "It's incredible. Save the world but don't starve to do it. How about I take you around to meet the rest of the team?"

Just then, the assistant who'd carried the tray of coffees stuck her head into the conference room, opened her mouth as if to speak. Frances immediately pointed with an index finger, flicked it as if she had a booger on it, and the assistant went away. Oh boy. Frances said something about hating interruptions, and a bit of spit flew out of her mouth and landed on Luz's cheek. They both knew it happened, but instead of apologizing to give Luz a chance to wipe it off, Frances ignored it. Luz left it there, feeling it unmoving, slowly growing in size.

If Luz was offered a position, her office would be bigger than it used to be, with a view of all those trees, all those pale bodies sunbathing out of view, on the Great Lawn. She'd have a private bathroom, with a closet that opened into a Murphy bed. She'd have her own paralegal assistant, to double her productivity and develop leadership skills. The firm would provide lunch, dinner, a private driver for anyone who worked past nine each night.

"Which is all of us," Frances said, matter-of-fact. She stopped and stared at Luz.

"You can start immediately, yes?" she asked.

Luz stopped. Nodded. Didn't wipe her face, even as Frances walked ahead of her, because Frances had a habit of twisting her long neck to glance at her every few steps.

When her phone vibrated, Luz took a quick look. Thinking of you, Hudson texted. Frances noticed the phone. Luz put it away but did not apologize. She could already tell Frances got annoyed easily by women who apologized too much. As they walked through the kitchen, past a refrigerator that Frances said was fully stocked with snacks, fruit, and energy drinks, Luz saw a bulletin board with at least twenty people's names, a distance ranging from 10K to 30K next to each. In the upper left corner, a printout of a funny-looking pot, with dollar amounts and a 5K in it.

"What's that?" Luz asked.

"Oh, it's a running challenge," Frances said. "No one's managed to beat me at a workweek hustle since we started competing months ago. Do you run?"

"Not yet," she said.

"I would plan to go sneaker shopping soon," she said, a deep dimple making an appearance on her chin. "Most people go their whole lives walking less than a thousand feet each day. Can you believe that? Hardly far enough to see anything worthwhile, wouldn't you say?"

On Luz's face, the spit began to dry in place. Frances walked her back to the elevator bank, and when Luz made a left instead of a right, Frances held her lightly by the elbow, directing her body. Even when they got to the elevator, and Luz pressed the down button, Frances didn't let go. She spoke to her from behind.

"I want to show you something," Frances said.

Elbow in her hand, she directed Luz to an enormous office. She only let go when they reached the windowsill. On it sat a framed photograph next to three books—**Their Eyes Were Watching God** by Zora Neale Hurston, **Killing the Black Body** by Dorothy Roberts, and **Sula** by Toni Morrison. Luz recognized the texts from a Black Feminist Thought elective at Harvard. She turned to Frances, admiring how bold it was, for someone like her to display books like that so prominently in this office, in this building, in this city—each spine at the eye level of whatever client or colleague happened by. Luz was so taken by those books she almost missed the picture next to them. She paused momentarily for a clue from Frances, to see if she'd meant for her to comment on the books or the picture. But Frances was watching her, expressionless, waiting.

Luz stared at the five stunning women in the photograph, Frances at their center. Like an advertisement for luxury brands that purported a gold standard—for watches or dresses or a certain kind of life. The women ranged in skin tone, nationality, age. The backdrop a beach and a deep purple sky with hints of pink, orange. Each woman extended her left hand toward the camera, showing engagement rings, the right hand holding a flute filled to the brim. But it was Frances she stared at, Frances in a low-cut silk dress, with a thick scar in the center of her chest. Luz wanted to ask her where the scar was from, wondered if that's how she and Raenna had first bonded, over a wardrobe malfunction, Frances's button undone to display some hidden horror.

"Everyone got engaged on the same trip?" Luz asked, instead.

Frances nodded. "Not one man to be found among the lot of us," she said. "We got engaged to ourselves, to our careers. Same jeweler designed each ring, and we put them on our own fingers during this glorious trip to Bali."

Luz brought the picture closer to her face. Were they true, those smiles?

"Raenna is a kingmaker," Frances said. "Never wrong when it comes to talent. Look at me, named managing partner, first Black woman to have the run of this place. There are so few of us. But we're going to grow. We're the ones saying fuck the old way. Our way. We won't be distracted by a world that tells us our ambitions aren't right, that we should be trying to have it all. We're focused on the one important thing. You know what it is?"

Luz nodded, not knowing what the one important thing was, but sure she'd figure it out, once she came to work with Frances.

"I always thought I was Raenna's last king," Frances said.

She gave Luz that opening, positioning her for her own bold move, but Luz didn't bite. She put the picture down next to the books. She picked up each of those books, held their weight, tried to remember the concepts of equality or parity or whatever else was in those pages. She knew she'd read them, had opinions at some point about them, enough to earn her straight A's from a professor notorious for never handing them out. She regretted how easily she'd moved past the philosophy that lay at their nucleus. She'd been engulfed by the brutality of her path. The parts she didn't allow herself to think about when Mami tried to remind her of all the hard work. How lonely those nights, getting no sleep, studying without really knowing how to do it—shocked that her valedictorian status left her befuddled and overwhelmed. But she'd listened to Mami, who'd reminded her she wasn't there to flounder. Find the help, Mami had said. And so she'd gone to Student Life, and found herself a tutor, and suffered through the embarrassment of having to be taught how to study, how to organize, how to manage time. And with each A, the feeling of warmth spreading in her body, consuming her; to be the best meant everything.

And that same warmth followed her to law school, but by then she was good, keeping her head down, not worrying about networks or law review, just focused on getting those A's. And then it was a full-blown, manic seduction by the bar. But by then, she was an expert. No memory of the originating brutality by the time she became an associate, as she'd been focused only on her cases, on being the one who stood out. Who needed sleep? Who needed to eat regularly? Who needed a life outside of those walls? Only the strongest could survive a career in the law, in corporate America, at the pinnacle of the global framework. To be part of this club meant you were not just the brightest, or hardest working, or the wealthiest. It meant you were safe, protected, sheltered—too important to be touched.

Next to her, Frances cleared her throat.

"Come on," she said. "You have a lot to see."

Maybe she mistook Luz's silence for aloofness, because she didn't seem displeased. The next hour went by in a blur. Luz met so many people. The men and the women ageless, so fit. Everyone dressed so well, smelled so good. Their voices all sounded the same. Like a new species.

At the elevator bank, Luz smiled brightly at Frances, so seduced by the place. She kept thinking of the picture, of that small group of women on their once-a-decade vacation. She imagined them around a table, drinking wine, solving problems collectively when they were meant to be competitors. These were the women Raenna meant when she said power had to be ripped out of the hands of those who held on for dear life. These women could do it—were doing it. She could hear their controlled, singular voices as they posed for that picture: We won't stop until the entire world is ours.

"Thanks for coming by," Frances said.

The elevator opened, and Luz walked in, pivoted, gave Frances her best smile. Then she made an exaggerated gesture of wiping that spit off her cheek, and pressed the button so the doors would close on her last words.

"You're not Raenna's last king. I am."

The doors closed, as Luz had intended, on Frances's look of pure delight.

UNEXCAVATED

On the train uptown, a set of kids yelled, "Showtime!" With wild movements and loud clapping, each of them danced for coins. One guy came up to Luz, striking a sexy pose in front of her, his crotch way too close to her face. She tried hard not to laugh, finally gave in and handed over a dollar.

Would she be happy, working in that office? No, she would not. But she had a strong sense she would do well. She'd work all the hours of the day. She'd fall into step right behind Frances. In ten years, no doubt she'd be invited on the trip.

She flipped through her phone

Thinking of you, Hudson had written when she'd been sitting next to Tía Cuca at the party last night. She hadn't written him back. He had re-sent the exact same text while she'd been speaking with Frances. Now Luz texted back. I miss your mouth on mine. He didn't react to that, but wrote her immediately, asked how the interview went instead. Guess no sexy texting with Hudson. She told him she did okay. Only ok? he asked. She picked the emoji with the hands in a wide V, I dunno. But she did know. She killed it. This was her chance to pick up where she'd left off, maybe a little further along. Wealth, power, linked to women who would do whatever it took to ensure everyone reached the top. Infiltration, domination. This! The stuff fast-paced TV series were made of. So. What with this feeling of dread?

What are you doing tonight?

I'm very busy.

For real?

No, of course not. I'm unemployed. I have nothing to do.

But that wasn't true. She needed to be home, read the documents about the apartment. Help her parents figure out what to do next.

There's a place I like in UWS, he said.

Can we order in instead? Watch a movie?

She waited for him to respond. Five minutes went by, then ten. Nothing.

HIS TEETH BIT INTO HER HIPBONE

Yesterday morning, as the sun peeked through his curtains, Luz must have bumped into Hudson in her sleep, because they'd both woken up, startled and disoriented to find themselves in bed. She had slowly remembered her disappointment that he'd been uninterested in taking things further the night before. But there was no hesitation that morning as he leaned over and kissed her, ran his index finger from the nape of her neck, down her spine, stopping here and there, giving her small kisses before he went on around her body, like a rope. Slow, so slow, so she could tell him to stop. But she didn't.

When he spoke, Luz could feel his lips lightly touching her hip.

"You're a wonder."

Then his teeth bit into her hipbone, and a current from his mouth went into her. She was lifted, buoyant, ready to be filled with him. She pulled him up, urgently, and felt him hard, opened her legs wide for him. But he pulled back, resisted.

"Why are you in such a rush?" he asked.

What exactly did he think she was there for? How to ask how come he wasn't rushing, too? And how to tell him how sad she'd been feeling, how long it'd been? How to explain she was hungry? How to say that these things never last anyway, that they should have fun while they could?

"I want to see you tonight, and tomorrow night, and the night after that," he said. "We can take our time."

She pushed him off, away. Why was he the one setting the pace? Why didn't he want to give her what she wanted?

"I gotta go," she said. "Should prepare for tomorrow's interview."

He looked confused, hurt. She held his face in both her hands, kissed him, said, "Maybe we can finish next time?"

Then she got up, put her clothes on, left.

DIG IN, NEITHER BUY NOR MOVE

In Nothar Park, the sounds of new machines greeted her. It was terrible. There were jackhammers now, breaking down the existing foundation beneath the ghost tenement building. Luz hadn't made it but halfway through the park when she heard her father's voice calling her name. She swung her head from left to right, up and down the park as he kept calling her.

"Pa'rriba," he said, directing her.

He sat on the fire escape, his own balcony, a cup of coffee in hand, oblivious to all the noise from the construction, all the dust floating about, leafing through papers on his lap. The Tongues were holding court on beach chairs in front of the building, even though the day was still on the chilly side for May, but they sat, like always, with their multi-colored beaded eyeglass chains sparkling on their necks, with their eyes loaded with judgment, fired at Luz as she walked by, the only thing out of their mouths the residue of smoke. The empty non–beach chair next to them told her Mami lurked nearby.

Today, Luz didn't bother saying hello to the women. She rushed past, took the stairs two at a time. Out on the fire escape, she pulled all the pinchos out of her hair so it spread up, out, whichever way it wanted to go. She'd swapped the suit for leggings and her favorite tank top, with the outline of Frida Kahlo's face, flowers as headpiece, red lips ready to say, Whatever, world, I'm doing things my way.

"How did it go?" Papi asked.

He handed her the stack of pages, and Luz had to reorder them so she could start at the beginning.

"The lady liked me a lot," Luz said. "I could tell. But it just felt like I'd be going back to the same kind of place. Same life."

"What's wrong with that?"

Vladimir asked questions to understand and not to respond like three-quarters of the world. She'd been taught to ask questions in order to lead people to say specific things, or as a way to gather intelligence ("What is it someone else knows, and what does that tell us about what they will likely do?" Raenna had instructed), so she could appreciate that purity in her father's mind. That kindness. It was the weight of his experience, how he didn't rush to make up his mind. She was sure this was the singular skill he'd learned as a police detective. To patiently let facts guide your understanding of the world, and not the other way around.

"Do you ever regret the way your life turned out?" Luz asked.

Papi nodded. "I regret things every day," he said. "If I could go back, I'd make a million different choices."

"Like what?"

"My main regrets are the times when I wasn't there for the people I love. But I know a different choice would have led to a different regret. Wondering if the choices I didn't make might've been the right ones? You just do your best each day with what you got."

In her back pocket, her phone buzzed.

Negotiate hard, Raenna said. Frances loved you. I'm proud of you. But next time, skip the worklifebalance bs.

Another text came through from Raenna with three bright red hearts, two champagne flutes crossed at the stems, a bottle of champagne, popped. As soon as you say yes, we'll get to toast and finish the entire bottle, she wrote.

It would be time to celebrate soon. Of course. Everything back on track, to the way it was. That's what she wanted. Of course.

Luz wrote her back. So excited. Frances is a beast. Got a number for a running coach? LOL.

Around the park, people were setting up illegal charcoal grills on the sidewalks. Tupperware filled with beef patties, hot dogs, chicken legs with adobo and oregano leaves darkening their dimpled skin. Rafael, from the hardware store, waved his hand to get the smoke out of his eyes. She remembered how he'd come back from somewhere down south, obsessed with smoking meat and forcing everyone who walked by to taste a sauce he'd created that combined mango and passion fruit with BBQ spices. Why didn't he make the food in his own apartment? she wondered. Such a hassle just for the chance to be outdoors.

"Maybe I'm being ridiculous," she said. "I have privilege, opportunities—"

"Nothing wrong with taking time to think it all through," he said. He handed her the cup and she drank the little bit of coffee that was left. It was mostly sugar, and after the liquid was gone she stuck her finger in the cup to scrape what remained. That sweetness in her mouth went right to her head, made her think of Hudson. She checked her phone again. No response. Was she coming on too strong?

"Put the phone down," Papi said. "Tell me what you think."

The memo was an offer to buy out their lease. There was no amount specified, but a phone number was provided that they could call to discuss the details. A separate document let them know they also had an option to buy the apartments, as is. The same phone number was given on that one.

"Should we call them now?" Papi asked.

Luz shook her head. She explained they had to do research before they spoke to anyone about anything. On her phone, she searched for a range of lease buyouts and learned in Washington Heights people had gotten as much as $80K for apartments much smaller than theirs. Vladimir's eyes widened in response.

"More than my whole life's savings," he said.

Luz told him she'd reach out to some of her friends in real estate law.

"They don't offer this option but there is another choice. An invisible choice: dig in, neither buy nor move."

"That's not an option for us," Papi said. His eyes rested on the Tongues' heads, then darted across to the park, obviously looking for Mami. He handed Luz his phone, showed her the progress of the house. Excavation complete, they'd built the filtration system in a matter of days. They had just finished pouring concrete for the pool, had moved on to placing the pretty blue tiles she'd chosen as a frame. Mami won't be able to tell the difference between pool, sea, and sky, Luz had thought when she chose it.

Across Nothar Park, small clouds of powdered concrete lifted out of the worksite. The jack-hammers vibrated through the air, a tremor.

"This noise is going to be the death of me," Papi said.

His hairline receded as he pulled at his forehead with both hands. He was tired, she could tell. All he wanted was to go back to DR, live in this crazy house, and enjoy the acres upon acres of land they'd bought, where he said he planned to get back to basics. Just a few chickens for fresh eggs and a couple of pigs as pets and so many fruit trees they'd have more than they could ever eat. He talked about how peaceful it would be, for both him and Mami, to go back to the life they had when they were kids.

"The pool is so much bigger than I thought," Luz said, handing the phone back to him.

"Imagine when you have kids? They'll love coming to visit us," he said.

"What kids? I'm going to enjoy the hell out of that pool," she said. "Watch."

"Grandkids would be nice," he said.

Luz groaned. Whenever he drank too much, Vladimir said, Time for a husband, for babies, you gotta let me off the hook. You're not on any hook, Papi, she'd been telling him since she graduated college. This isn't 1950.

Beneath them, a car parallel parked right in front of their building. Within moments, the trunk was opened, merengue blasting out of speakers. Vladimir shook his head. "How can anyone think, listening to music so loud?"

"Stop acting old, Papi."

Sometimes Luz worried about her parents. On their last trip to DR, Mami confessed how torn she'd been about going back, how little she'd liked it. Luz had been surprised. For years and years, all those two spoke about were their plans to move back home. Luz asked why she didn't tell Papi the truth. And break his heart? Mami said. So, lie instead? Because you love him? Luz asked. One day you'll understand, Mami said, in the way old people spoke sometimes, like they knew best. Sometimes we lie to spare, to protect. At Luz's eye roll, Mami shook her head. We can't afford to go back there for years anyway, she'd said. Thank God for that, she'd finished.

Meanwhile, Papi had confessed he didn't want to wait. Luz gave him all the money in her savings account. It had been her idea, to do it as a surprise for Mami. Because deep down, Luz feared Mami would call the whole thing off if they told her early on.

Down below, Mami came back from the direction of the bodega with a bag of oranges and sat next to the Tongues. Moments later, they saw Tía Cuca in the park. Mami and the Tongues each peeled an orange as Cuca made her way toward them.

"Is Cuca wearing a catsuit?" Papi asked. "Ofrézcome."

"That's why the doctor called it the 'Ofrézcome Altagracia' Make—"

"Okay," Papi said, interrupting her. "Once we have all the information, we'll make a decision as a family."

"I'm not getting caught up in that. I abstain from voting."

Her father patted her head, like she was crazy.

"We'll make the decision together. Your name is on the lease, just like ours. Each of us gets one vote."

Luz stared at Papi's eyebrows, how his forehead protruded out. Did he know, already, Mami didn't want to go? Should she tell him it might take time to talk her into it?

"Plus, we should split it. You'll have some more cash for your move to Seventy-ninth Street; we'll have some extra for furniture."

Her phone buzzed again and she glanced at it, thinking it'd be Raenna again.

Sorry, Hudson said. Been in meetings all day. Are you still up for hanging out tonight?

Luz contemplated telling him she was busy; she knew how to play hard to get. Her gaze fell on Frida's outline on her shirt. Would Kahlo deny her body what it wanted? Nope. Frida wouldn't let anything or anyone stop her from doing what she wanted. Luz thought about the current from Hudson's mouth, how it traveled into her body, from his teeth on her hip. Those aftershocks were with her now. If she hadn't been so impatient, things would have escalated naturally.

I'm dying to see you, she wrote.

She stared as the three dots bolded and lightened, showing his typing. I'm already dead, he wrote. She bit her lips. It was going to be on tonight!

"Luz," her father said, "did you hear what I said? We should have a family meeting, make a decision, tonight."

"Not tonight," Luz said, dragging her eyes away from her phone.

"Why not?" he said.

Below them, Mami called to them. "Come down," she shouted. "Let's drink." Mami sounded happy. It was a nice sound.

"Why not tonight?' Papi insisted.

Want me to pick up vegan? Hudson asked.

Ugh, vegan. Well. She had to do what she had to do. Vegan sounds great, she wrote.

"Luz," Papi said, putting his hand over the screen of her phone. "Why not tonight?"

"Papi," Luz said, "I have to do research on the buyout. We need all the information before we decide. We have to get as much money as possible. Right?"

He got up, took the empty coffee cup from her. "You're right, of course. What's another few days when I've waited decades to go home? I'll talk to Eusebia tonight, make sure she's ready."

Oh boy. Now **this** was a hot mess. She had to tell Mami what was coming.

"You coming?" he asked.

On her phone, Hudson's last text came through. Three kissy-face emojis, mouths puckered with hearts for lips. See? Already she was wearing him down. They'd be sexy texting in no time.

Vladimir cleared his throat.

"Yes," she said. "I'm right behind you."

She'd wait for the right moment to speak to Mami. Retirement on a beautiful island, with the husband she loved, that was what Mami should want. Why would Mami be so torn about it anyway? Was it because she thought Luz couldn't handle her own life? She thought of their exchange at Cuca's party last night. There'd been a tightness in Mami's face, a stiffness that pointed at something else. It was as if she'd grown tired of all the emotional support Luz needed from her. And it was true. When was the last time she'd functioned independently, when she didn't require as much from Eusebia?

Her phone froze her in place halfway into the apartment. It rang with a 212 number and she stared at it. Let it go to voicemail. The message was only a few seconds long. She clicked on the button that let her see the transcription. There it was, clear as day. **Hi Luz! This is Frances. Call me back. Let's lock this down.**

CHAPTER TEN

Eusebia de Guerrero

#2. THEFT

The pressure in her head eased up a bit and Eusebia felt enough like herself that she considered calling the whole thing off. The string of robberies had started out well enough, with some of the women happy they'd gotten rid of the old couches, televisions that didn't connect to the internet, lamps that had gone out of style. But once the insurance adjusters began calling people, and it became clear what they would pay for was the value of the lost merchandise, and not what it would take to replace it, a lot of people were pissed off. It was as if they didn't understand some sacrifice was required to save their neighborhood.

"Where am I supposed to watch my fucking telenovela?" Ximena told the Tongues, who told Eusebia.

How about at a neighbor's house? These weren't

real problems, Eusebia thought. Well. The robberies hadn't made the TV news. But! In the newspaper, they had run an article about the increase in petty crimes. Had called Nothar Park by name. That was worth something. The next crime would make the nighttime news. She was sure of it.

Today, the construction site went silent at exactly 5 P.M. Right as Luz emerged and greeted everyone. Earlier, she'd changed out of her interview clothes but hadn't taken the enormous diamond earrings off. She tugged at her ears now, the way she had as a child, when she was tired or nervous. With her kinky hair out, she somehow seemed younger, free.

"Ma," Luz said, "you want a beer?"

Angélica had brought a cooler, and Luz handed each of the women a beer. Eusebia refused. She didn't want to disrupt this newfound steadiness. But she was happy to see Luz sitting outside. Luz laughed in a light way she hadn't seen in years. She tilted her head just then and Eusebia noted a softness in the line from her cheekbones down to her jawbone. Since Luz had been out of work, she'd been eating like a normal person, and though it wasn't visible anywhere else, the few pounds she'd gained softened her. Maybe that was why she appeared younger. Maybe it was the laughing, too. Eusebia could always see what a person looked like as a child when they laughed. Vladimir, standing off to the side chatting with some of the men, noticed the same thing at the same time, and found his wife's eyes at the sound of Luz's laughter, a reassurance. It had been years since they'd spent a moment like this together.

When he came down ahead of Luz, Vladimir told her that their daughter had a good interview, that she was on her way to going back to her old life. He said it in a way that meant she would be okay, that Eusebia shouldn't worry anymore. And she was glad for that. But not for the question behind that reassurance. When would they go back to DR? He'd apprehended the truck driver. Had come back home earlier than expected from handling all the related paperwork that day—had placed the gun and the badge in the safe right away, had pulled her to him in a way that said yes, he'd pushed through another day. But her body, even on good days, wasn't enough relief.

One of the men stood, ceding his place at the table. Vladimir's hands moved fast over the dominoes, and just like that, the moment was gone.

"Luz," Eusebia said, "what happened with the interview?"

"I got the job!" she said.

Angélica and Cuca made a lot of congratulatory noise.

"You accepted the job?" Eusebia pressed on. Why did Luz furrow her brow?

"I'll call the lady later," she said.

"Why don't you call her now," Eusebia said, "before you start drinking?"

Luz stared at the beer in her hand.

"Something else going on?" Eusebia asked.

"No," Luz said. She stood and walked away from them into the lobby. Eusebia saw her through the glass. She paced back and forth. Seemed animated as she spoke into the phone, then turned sharply to face inside the building. When she came back moments later, she shrugged her shoulders against Eusebia's questioning look. "Busy line," she said. But Eusebia knew she lied, that she had in fact gotten through. It wouldn't have taken that long just to leave a message.

Cuca's high-pitched voice dominated the conversation among the women. While the men played on, dominoes noisy like so many high-heeled shoes, Cuca was complaining about her surgery, how something went terribly wrong.

"So, let me get this straight," Luz said, "you spent a whole year changing your entire body over, and now you can't use it?"

"That shit isn't funny," Cuca said, laughing along. "He couldn't even get it in halfway."

"And if you can't get it all the way," Angélica said, "what's even the point?"

"Amén," Cuca said.

"Jesús," one of the Tongues said to them, "have some respect."

But by the lift of their eyebrows, it was obvious even the old women were enjoying the outrageous conversation. The crickets were out in the park, and one of them pulled out a phone, to make a video, while another put hands on knees, ass toward the camera, ready to dance.

Isabel came over then with a foil pan full of pastelitos. The air hung heavy with the smell of fat, of well-seasoned meat. They were gooey with cheese, and some had chicken or beef. Everyone grabbed one and the women were quiet for a bit, chewing, swallowing.

"Tell me about your new man," Cuca said. She winked at Luz.

"Never mind about that. What are you going to do?" Luz asked.

"Are you going to see him tonight?" Cuca said.

"You can't live in pain," Luz said. "You get that, right? You have to go back to the doctor, see a specialist, and let them see what went wrong. It could be an easy fix. You never should have gone to that dollar-store surgeon."

"Relationships are so exciting at the beginning," Cuca said. "All that fire, all that passion. JJ and me, we used to be so wild. We coulda gotten arrested a few times, the stuff we pulled."

Eusebia knew it to be true. And since the surgery, they'd gone back to being horny teenagers.

"I read an article just yesterday," Luz went on. "Women are notorious for not getting themselves to the doctor. Half dead, we walk around like it's not a big deal. It has to stop. You have to pick yourself. Sometimes you have to say no to every demand that comes your way and take a stand for what you want."

This would have been a good time for Eusebia to say she, in fact, was one of those women. She should have said she needed a doctor the day she fell in the park, that the pressure in her head had in fact persisted. But because of that pressure, she was finding new space inside herself as well.

From that bright, gorgeous burst of red had emerged a new reality. She'd all but lost her appetite, but unlike in the past, when lack of nourishment had made her weak and lethargic, she was now focused and deliberate. So what if she swung from feeling powerful and effervescent to disoriented and unsure? Eusebia knew she was meant to yield all this new energy and the rage it often birthed into the plan—to keep everyone she loved safe in their homes. She had to admit there were moments, like now, when the rage dissipated and left in its stead the sad certainty it was all futile. How could she, of all people, stop them from being forced out? And worse still, what if she ended up hurting instead of helping?

If she didn't take steps to save her community, no one would. That truth had to be worth the risk. What she'd often found charming about her people—the joy that flowed through everyone's veins even when times were most difficult, how they drank and partied and bullshitted even when the more prudent thing to do was act in revolt—wasn't resilience in action but acquiescence. Knowing that, accepting that, meant she couldn't do anything but stay the course. So, what of the visions? Of her growing impatience? Of the ways in which she slowly recognized a voice from somewhere inside her that said do whatever it takes to make sure it ends where it should? This was the voice she had enough presence of mind, still, to recognize as an unstoppable reckoning.

To stop it would require her admitting what had happened over the last week. Spread-eagle under a doctor's eyes, as he tested and prodded and treated her like she didn't know her own body, her own mind.

"I'll do whatever the hell I want to do," Cuca said to Luz, snapping Eusebia back to the moment. "If that means not playing martyr, keeping my ass at home, then so be it. Do you understand what I just went through under the hands of some butchers who pretended to be doctors? And now I'm supposed to voluntarily put myself in the same position? Hell no. Please get off my case. I'll go when I'm ready."

Luz sipped at her beer, grunted, acknowledging her aunt was partly right. She gestured to Angélica to look down the block in the other direction, where Tony was headed toward them. Handsome Tony with his bulging arms, a black panther tattoo on his bicep, who'd grown into a man overnight,

Eusebia had noticed, serious and hardworking yet still always making jokes.

Angélica stood when she saw him, then surveyed the area for the girls. The twins always went nuts as soon as they saw their father. And there they were, about to run across the street to meet him. "Don't," she yelled at them, but it was too late. They had already entered the street. A car was driving fast toward them. The only sound was of the twins, yelling "Papi, Papi," and the car, which was almost upon them.

Every single person stood up. Eusebia felt the ground give way underneath her at the thought of the collision.

Christian came out of nowhere, scooping each kid under an arm.

"Jesus fucking Christ," Angélica said, as if speaking through cotton, rushing toward the girls. When she reached them, and held them both so tight in her arms, that's when the entire block went silent. Eusebia couldn't understand how it happened. The music that had been playing was paused, the voices of people screaming and talking and laughing all went mute. She looked around to see others' reactions, but everyone kept speaking, hands to hearts, and she knew it was only her ears that stopped working.

What a lovely thing, this silence.

Troubling, too, but glorious. She stared at the

things that usually made noise. The cars with their open trunks blasting music, the kids running around, laughing—all of it soundless. Luz in front of her, saying something. Vladimir must be hungry.

Eusebia went into the building; Luz followed her, beer in hand. In the elevator, Luz fidgeted with the tank top's hem. I have something to tell you, she said, and Eusebia could hear again.

"Why do you have to announce yourself?" Eusebia said, smiling. "Say what you have to say."

But Luz didn't say what she had to say. Eusebia turned to see if the silence was back. But heard the noise from outside. She didn't push. What new drama now?

In the apartment, Luz forked into the bathroom, while Eusebia went right to the kitchen, put a pot full of water on the stove. In the freezer, she searched for the stack of pasteles, found only two left. She'd have to make some more tomorrow. Her body re-coiled at the thought. It would be hours and hours of work—mashing raw vegetables, cooking meat, folding the entire thing into plantain leaves—but in the end this gift. A full meal inside each plantain leaf; no more effort after that initial exhaustion. Drop some inside a pot of boiling water, sit down for an hour, and voilà!

She dumped the two pasteles in the pot, didn't mop the water that fell on the floor, didn't even wipe the stove's surface, where it stared at her. In the fridge, she found the ketchup bottle had nothing left. In the cabinet where she kept extra, found none. Another thing for the shopping list tomorrow. She called Isabel, asked if she had some ketchup. When Isabel said of course, who doesn't have ketchup, Eusebia told her abruptly she'd send Luz in a bit. Then, without lingering on that disturbing silence from moments before, Eusebia went into the living room and turned on the TV. Sat down. **Primer Impacto** was on.

Then a stirring in the air. Luz, a phone outstretched toward her. She hadn't dried her hands after using the bathroom, and from her fingers, small drops of water accumulated, then fell.

It was a house. A beautiful mansion by the sea. Something so familiar about its surrounding greenery, where it was perched on a cliff.

"Wow," Eusebia said, trying to place it.

And then, unmistakably, the words. Even with perfect hearing, she didn't comprehend what Luz said.

"It's your house," Luz repeated, swiping through a series of pictures that showed the view she knew so well, of that sky, and that beach, and those mountains. Off on the side, out of the frame of these photos, a cliff, made of rocks that plummeted down to the sea. Her mother never let them walk toward them, never let them swim close by. Why? An old wives' tale of a woman who swam too close to the rocks, who died when the undercurrent dragged her until her body was battered to a pulp.

"How?" Eusebia asked. She didn't allow her mind

to race or her heart to quicken. This wasn't real. She understood, then, what Cuca had felt when she first came across those pictures years ago, with those pretty women.

"Papi's worked hard enough, don't you think? He's given up so much for us."

"I told you I couldn't live there," Eusebia said. "This is my home now. Where did the money come from? To buy a house like that?"

"Nothar Park isn't going anywhere," Luz said, explaining the concrete hole would soon be a pool. The land this new house occupied cut past the boundary her parents had owned. The pool had been built where Sancho Panza's house used to be, where the goats used to roam. Where did the old man go?

"Papi deserves rest," Luz insisted, "and so do you. I mean, who knows, maybe you just need to live there to remember how beautiful it is. Look at it. Remember how much you hated it when we first got here? Your hands never got warm that first winter. Fingertips . . ."

Luz rambled on. Eusebia turned her hands palm-up. Now what? A nearly finished house. A husband pulling. A daughter pushing.

On the television, the segment was an exposé of child prostitution in a small town. She missed what country it was in. It had taken years of suspicious comings and goings for the neighbors to uncover the fact that the father was prostituting his three young girls. The oldest seven, the next five, the youngest two years old. Eusebia stared at the bodies of those young girls, how only their faces had been blurred. Look at the five-year-old, with a stomach so inflated, like she'd just eaten a huge plate of white rice, followed by a glass of unpasteurized milk. The two-year-old, still wearing diapers, held a doll by the matted blond hair. That doll, with an embroidered green dress, a knitted hat, socks, shoes, gloves. Armored.

"Animals," Eusebia said. "The neighbors, too. How could they not know?"

Luz talked and talked. Maybe $100,000 they could get for the apartment lease buyout, she said. This was her daughter's gift: terrible things could happen right next to her and it didn't affect her. Eusebia turned off the television. Eusebia couldn't stand the thought of those girls.

"The money from this apartment will set you up. You can get some help with cooking and cleaning. I will send you money every month. It would be a good life."

I'm not going anywhere, Eusebia thought.

"What happened on the phone?" Eusebia asked.

"I told you—"

"Tell me the truth," Eusebia said.

"She offered me the job and I said no," Luz said, crossing arms over her chest. "I've been thinking of just taking some time. A break."

"What do you mean, a break? From what?"

"Maybe to figure out if I want to do something else?"

"Like what? Sounds like a waste of time."

"Ma," Luz said. "It's my life. I decide if I want to waste time."

"All those years? You're ready to throw it all away?"

"I'm not throwing anything away," Luz said.

"Do you remember how often you called me? Crying? Because you had no friends and you got no sleep and you were so stressed out?"

"I remember you telling me I wasn't there to make friends, that I could have all the sleep in the world when I came home for the holidays, or was finished with law school or when I made partner. Because all you've ever cared about is me being successful, right?"

"Independent," Eusebia corrected.

"As long as I was dependent on you," Luz said.

Eusebia felt her body grow in height. Eye-to-eye level, the two of them. That new house, with those enormous windows, it would take an army to keep it clean.

"All I've ever done is take care of you," Eusebia said.

"That's not all you've ever done," Luz said.

The pasteles boiled over. The water fell into the burner, making a hissing sound from the kitchen. Eusebia went into the kitchen, turned the fire down low. Luz followed her, stood off to the side looking small, scared.

"What else have I done?" Eusebia asked.

Luz didn't respond. Her face red from the beer, or the conversation.

"What else have I done?" Eusebia asked again, slowly.

"You've never wanted me to be independent," Luz said, speaking with hesitation, like she was discovering the right words only as she spoke them. "You've only wanted me to rely on you, to only run to you for help. The last thing you want is for me to think for myself. Be on my own."

"Claro," Eusebia spat out. "Because it's so much fun having a grown woman incapable of making decisions. You're the one who likes running to me. To solve all your problems. 'Mami,' she mocked, in a baby voice, 'what major should I choose, I'm so tired, the people at work don't like me, what should I do?' That's you, Luz. Confused, helpless, lost. The only reason you are where you are is because of me."

"Not true," Luz said, shocked.

To freedom, they had toasted at Cuca's party. But freedom to do what? Whatever the two of them wanted. Always at her expense? Not this time.

Eusebia left the kitchen; Luz followed her again, like a puppet unable to do anything but be pulled by strings. Eusebia pointed to the china cabinet. Dramatically, she pulled out each framed photograph, each medal, each trophy, and placed it on the dining room table.

"If it wasn't for me," Eusebia said, "you would be another Angélica. Raising kids, not able to keep a minimum wage job, cooking and cleaning and taking care of others. If it wasn't for me, you'd be a total loser."

Luz placed a hand on the back of her neck, took a deep breath.

"Right, Mami. You're such a genius mastermind, this terrible life you guided me away from is the same one you live every day. Your life."

Stunned, Eusebia sat on the couch. That first winter, her hands never did get warm. She felt it now, hands in so much pain, she feared if she bumped into a wall, fingers might detach, frostbitten, shatter to pieces. If she stood now, smacked Luz across the face, would the shards rip that precious skin?

"You need to go downstairs," Eusebia said, barely above a whisper. "Isabel has some ketchup for your dad."

Luz left without another word.

CHAPTER ELEVEN

Luz Guerrero

THE PEOPLE'S LAWYER

Luz's hands shook as she rushed down the stairs.
Then the trembling spread down her entire body
as she made it out of the building. What the hell
was that? How had things escalated so quickly? She
reminded herself it was necessary. That it might
hurt a bit but Mami needed to let her go. Mami
deserved her own freedom.

Truth? Luz felt overwhelmed. She inhaled and
the smells of Nothar Park filled her, calmed her,
and her mind turned to how mortified she'd been,
when she'd called Frances back from the lobby, at
her low-ball offer, nearly half what she used to
make. Frances on the phone, acting like she was
doing Luz a favor by offering her this opportunity.
Some would come work for me for free, she said
before she hung up.

Her phone vibrated in her pocket. Frances says you turned down the job, Raenna wrote.

She offered me less than I used to make, Luz wrote back, fingers still trembling as she headed to Isabel's place. I'll keep looking.

Do you have any other leads? Raenna wrote.

Not yet. She didn't respond.

Don't be foolish, Raenna pressed. Take the job and then you can keep looking.

I'm good, she wrote. She was tempted to write her back, to say maybe Raenna needed to butt out of her life. But then she thought better of it. Last thing she needed was to piss Raenna off. If I get a better offer, won't Frances be compelled to match? she asked.

Maybe. Or she might be annoyed. Let me think this through. This feels like the wrong move for you.

Luz wanted space. I'll give you an update when I have a solid plan, she wrote. The three dots darkened, lightened up, then went away. Raenna, annoyed. Mami, hurt. She didn't have time to worry about Raenna. How would she fix what she'd done upstairs? Should she? She sped up until she made it to the door with the sign that said B E NT, the space around each missing letter that originally spelled Basement Apt. outlined in the gray of old glue. The bell was one of those loud ones that sounded like a fire alarm. It got stuck when Luz pressed it.

"Whoever's ringing that bell better pay half this fucking rent," Angélica said from inside, swinging the door with such force it slammed hard against the wall behind it. Her angry expression changed to annoyed surprise as soon as she saw Luz.

"Isn't the super's apartment rent-free?" Luz said.

Angélica chuckled. "Lulu, always a smart-ass."

"Sorry, I couldn't get it to stop," Luz said.

Angélica bumped Luz out of the way with her hip. "That piece-of-shit bell is always getting stuck."

"Where's the party?" Luz asked.

Angélica had gotten done up in the time Luz had gone upstairs with Mami. Tight jeans and a pretty orange blouse that twisted like rope on the back, exposing her upper and lower back, showing that she wore no bra. The heels were the most impressive. Four-inch stilettos with a peep toe that showed a bedazzled pedicure. "I gots to be tight to keep him locked," she said.

"Nice shoes," Luz said.

"They hurt," Angélica said.

They were both quiet as they each thought of their encounter in that bathroom at the Secret Place restaurant, when Luz had said the same thing.

"You got the ketchup?" Luz said.

Angélica headed through the living room to the kitchen. Luz followed. Noticed how much had changed in all the years. They'd torn down walls, replaced wooden floors, upgraded their countertops and appliances, replaced cheap cabinets. This is what people did when they rented an apartment they never intended to move out of.

On the stove, three giant pots plus a frying pan.

"How many armies are you feeding?"

"You forgot how much Tony eats?" she said. "Plus mac and cheese for the kids. They won't eat Dominican food unless it's your mom's habichuelas con dulce."

"They get an option?" Luz asked.

Angélica put her hands up. "I'm a sucker when it comes to those two."

In the frying pan, four pork chops, meat bleeding from the joints. Crimson liquid bubbled and clotted in the hot oil. It was a repulsive sight. Yet, the smell that floated up was fragrant with citrus and salt.

"You know how squeamish you are," Angélica said. "Don't look at it or you won't be able to eat it later."

It was strange that even after all these years Angélica remembered that.

"Oh, I'm not staying that long," she said. "I just came for the ketchup."

Angélica turned toward the stove, flipping the pork chops one by one.

"Why can't you stay to eat? You don't have shit to do," she said. And then, before Luz had a chance to react, she went on. "I'm glad you came over. Everyone is freaking about the apartments going for sale. Chris found the website for the new construction across the street—Hudson's Yard. Even the name sounds expensive."

As if on cue, far off, the insistent pounding of machines digging through concrete started back up. It was after 5 P.M. Why would the work still be going on? The tumult brought with it a reminder of all the other things she had to do. There was paperwork she still hadn't signed for her old job to make the separation final. There was the lease buyout document, and all the phone calls she'd have to make to her old colleagues to figure out what to tell her parents. And now she was supposed to advise the entire neighborhood?

"People are freaking," Angélica repeated. "It's better you get involved now. Maybe calm people down."

"Calm people over what? Why panic? Either buy the apartment or get a bucketful of cash to leave. Have you heard what they're offering? That's a down payment on a real home."

Angélica didn't turn around to face her but her back stiffened, making her an inch taller.

"This **is** our real home," she said. "Do you understand what's at stake?"

Luz wasn't about to get into this conversation with Angélica; she'd done fine enough to avoid it with Mami the first time it came up. Instead, she lifted her phone closer toward the window to get a signal. In this basement apartment, she had zero bars.

Exasperated, Angélica showed her anger in the

curve of her hip, jutted out like someone ready to throw the first punch. But Luz wasn't going to entertain the attitude, engage further in this conversation. The line would go around the park three times if she started offering people free legal advice, which she wasn't even qualified to give.

"Okay," she said to appease, "I'll look into it."

"You could use a few more pounds," Angélica said, turning toward her. The moment when the smile faded, there was so much sadness in her face Luz thought she saw the unresolved remnants of the fight that had caused the rift between them five years ago, a tag visible, itching their skin, and neither willing to tuck it back in. But maybe she imagined it.

"Do you remember what happened to me years ago, when I first graduated law school?" Luz asked.

"Who could forget?" Angélica said.

Within days of Luz graduating Columbia Law, people from the neighborhood came to her with all kinds of legal questions, which turned into legal demands—for her to handle their divorces, real estate transactions, small business conflicts, adoptions, even wills and the drafting of estate plans. International estates in DR! People hadn't then understood that she didn't have intimate knowledge of all the areas of practice under law. They didn't even get that she wasn't, practically speaking, a "real" lawyer until she passed the state bar exam.

"La abogada del pueblo," Angélica said, snickering. "You were stressed but you liked it, too."

Luz recalled the stress, not the feeling-good part. It was Eusebia who finally told her she had to stop trying to help everyone, to instead route them to Legal Aid or another organization that had the resources to help. Mami convinced her that her main job was to focus on studying, passing the test, and to turn those pariguayos loose on some other victim.

"I just remember that one time you were up so late studying immigration law and at the end you were like, as long as the Rosarios became citizens while the kid was under eighteen, then we're good. And then come to find out those dumbasses sent the kid back to DR crazy scared of ICE."

Luz remembered that day. She remembered all the days. There had been some really good days.

"I'm not really here for that," Luz said, careful not to romanticize the past. "I'll help you guys as much as I can, but I'm not here for everyone else."

"Shocking," Angélica said.

"Where's this ketchup?" Luz said, standing up, tired of the dynamic.

Angélica jerked her forearm away from a flying drop of hot oil. "Why are you in such a rush?"

"I have a lot to do today."

From the living room, the girls screamed they were thirsty, hungry. Angélica went to them with water, small plastic pouches with green apple slices. Luz checked her phone. No bars. No texts.

"So never mind the lease stuff, then. I actually need you to talk to Christian," Angélica said.

"What's going on with Christian?" Luz put the phone away.

"Brace yourself," Angélica said. "Christian decided he's dizque a nonbinary, gender-nonconforming individual. Because it's not hard enough to be poor and Dominican and Black. Now not male or female? What the hell is left? I would rather go back to when we all thought he was a fag."

"Don't use that word," Luz said.

"He uses that word," Angélica said. "You should hear him. 'It's empowering, to take control of the oppressor's language.' That's how he fucking talks."

"Take it easy," Luz said. "Why are you so worked up?"

"I know how hard life is going to be for him," Angélica said. She put the fire on low, covered the pan with a lid, came over to the table. The meat erupted in tiny explosions under the lid. Angélica ignored it. "I only wish I could shake him, tell him to stop being so weird and act normal for a while. Maybe you can do that? Tell him it'll be easier for him in college if he tries to fit in."

Luz was speechless. Although she understood that Angélica, too, felt as despairing and overwhelmed as she herself felt only moments ago, Luz was struck by the implication of her friend's request: Luz as the authority on selling out.

Don't be so self-centered, Luz told herself. It was hard for Angélica to ask for help. It always had been. Angélica had taken over Christian's upbringing after their father died. Back when Nothar Park was a dangerous place, when drug dealers roamed the park, Angélica's dad had been making his way home from work when a bullet hit him. Isabel had been so taxed taking over as super and trying to keep their small family afloat that she'd let the kids raise themselves mostly; raise each other.

"College," Luz said, "is the best place on earth to be gender nonconforming. They'll have all the time to figure theirself out over there. I wouldn't worry if I was you. I advise you to stop calling Christian 'him,' though, if they told you their preference."

Angélica let out a loud sigh.

"That's your advice? Don't worry? Call Christian 'they'?"

"Yes," Luz said, "college isn't a job. It's a place to learn and grow. Trust me. Chris will be fine."

"Since he was a kid," Angélica said, "I've been worried about him. I wish I knew how to stop. He spends so much time writing in his notebooks, drawing instead of paying attention to figure out how he's supposed to act. You know what I was thinking about before you got here? How no one ever taught me how to make my way in the world. Isn't that the worst part? Our parents, they're waiting for us to teach them the rules. Or they try to get us to play by rules they learned back home, that are useless. And now here I am. I can't teach him shit, either."

She covered her face with both hands, only her

nose and mouth visible between them. Luz wondered if she was crying.

"I don't know what to tell him," she said, voice breaking with emotion. "I'm amazed he even has the opportunity to be out there with the rich people, like you. He can have a completely different life than anyone who's come before him. If he can just survive four years. What am I supposed to do to keep him safe?"

"It doesn't stop at four years," Luz said.

She still remembered Angélica having to skip school to take Christian to pediatrician appointments, going with her mom to get public assistance. Angélica came back from one appointment so pissed that when she grabbed her hand, she made Luz yelp in pain. The women are always the worst, she'd said. It's like they want to humiliate us for being poor. I'll die of hunger before I let Mami go on food stamps, she said. That's when she decided to forgo college, to start working full-time. She succeeded. They didn't have to go on food stamps. But her life had been so much harder for it. Had Luz tried to get her best friend to stay in school? She couldn't remember.

She'd had difficult times. But she knew it was a different thing, making her way through college, then through the corporate world, than what most people dealt with around the park. Wasn't it? She thought of her work at the firm over the years, how often her words and ideas had been usurped; she'd never complained to Raenna, worried that making an uproar would be unwise for her career. Thought of Frances's offer as a door back into her old life. How upset she'd been to be undervalued, herself a different kind of entitled.

Angélica removed her hands from her face. Her eyes were dry and clear, but her face was bright red. She turned off the stove, got a large serving plate, put paper towels on it, and then laid four perfectly golden pork chops atop. She set them on the table next to Luz.

"It's surviving and figuring it out every step of the way," Luz said to the plate of meat. She reached for a chop, stopped herself. "We're lucky," she went on. "We get to make our own way. We're free to discover a path that's never been plodded. It's scary and hard but at the end we get to say, 'My life, not theirs.' You can see it as a burden. Or not."

"There's something so beautiful about Christian, so gentle," Angélica said. "The world is going to break him down, devour him, you know?"

"Maybe," Luz said. "Maybe they'll break the world, then rebuild it."

"You still talk like that," Angélica said, amazement in her voice. There was something soft yet complicated in her tone. "You and him are the same. Life is beautiful, blah, blah, blah."

"What do you say instead?" Luz asked.

"Life is so fucking hard," she screamed. "So let's numb away the pain!"

She danced to the refrigerator, twerking to the music from the street, as she reached for two beers. She opened them and gave one to Luz.

"Oh, no," Luz said, "I'm good."

"Bitch," Angélica said, "drink the fucking beer. I haven't spent time with you in like five years. Truth is he may have to defer, so I should just chill. Maybe you're right. The worry is for nothing."

"Why would they defer?"

"If we have to move," Angélica said, "he'll have to work. Things at Tony's job are bad. Pendejo boss put him on a plan so it's only a matter of time before he gets fired. And he doesn't make enough money to pay all those bills. My contribution, well, you get it."

Luz hadn't realized what moving would mean for them. But her heart ached, thinking of Christian giving it all up.

"You know if Chris defers, they likely won't go at all."

"Family first," Angélica said. "We all make sacrifices. How do we get around it?"

There was no way around it, Luz thought hopelessly. "I don't know."

The beer was cold, so cold a frosted coating descended the bottle's throat all the way to the ridged base. When they were teenagers, they used to call the frosting vestida de novia, dressed as a bride, draw designs with fingertips, planning a double wedding right outside in the park. Luz tilted her head back and swallowed. Their eyes met and they kept drinking, both adhering to the superstition that it's bad luck to break eye contact during the first sip after a toast. Both drank on, waiting to see which one would stop first. Just like the old days, Luz was the first one to lean forward, choking on the beer.

"Wimp," Angélica said, putting her empty beer on the table.

Beer must enhance the sense of smell. Luz couldn't resist reaching over, pinching a piece off that meat. Her eyes widened. Ambrosia. The meat practically melted in her mouth, so tender.

"Eat more," Angélica said. "Get some ass."

"I never get complaints," she said, thinking of Hudson's hands. She felt a burst of small pleasure from the memory. Beer in her head, Hudson's phantom hands on her body, it was Luz's turn to stand up. To the beat of the music blasting out of the car's trunk outside, she did a silly dance that finished with a slithering-snake move.

"Ewww," Angélica said, "you dance like a white girl now."

Luz laughed loudly, from somewhere deep in her belly. She probably did dance like a white girl now. She got two more beers out of the fridge. When Angélica raised her eyebrow at her first unfinished beer, Luz told her she'd catch up.

Angélica examined her, eyes lingering on her earrings. Luz knew what she looked like. Messy hair,

and no-makeup face, and those perfectly manicured nails in a pretty shade of pink. But it wasn't
about that or the designer shorts she'd switched to
or the tank top or the flip-flops. Angélica must be
wondering how they'd ended up being so different
from each other. There was a time when they were
the same person. Angélica stood, reached into the
cabinet, brought out a giant, unopened bottle of
Heinz ketchup. She placed it on the table between
them. Finally releasing her.

"You've always been so beautiful," Angélica said.
"Perfect skin, not a scar in sight. Perfect life ahead,
nothing to prevent that."

Angélica had always known when Luz worried,
and known how to make her feel good—even if
they never spoke of the concern directly. Like now,
all this time and not once a question about the job
search, about what she meant to do. Just this reassurance, that all would be fine, that Luz would end
up fine no matter how shaky everything felt right
now. And with that much confidence, how could
Luz not believe, not be reassured? She felt better.
In her heart, she knew it wasn't the path for her,
working for Frances. She had to accept it—admit
it wasn't about the money but about how senseless
it all seemed now. What would she do with her life
instead? Well, she didn't really know. And for now,
that was okay. All she had to do was buy herself
some time. But how?

She came up blank. Stared at Angélica, asked

herself a serious question. What had she ever done to help Angélica? She'd hardly known what to do with Angélica's tough exterior, knowing inside there was such heartache. How to mend a friend's heart? How to reach across such vast space when you've let too much time pass? How to ask forgiveness when you aren't sorry for moving on, for leaving them behind? How to explain sometimes the only way to grow is to sever from those who tether you in place, knowing they stay behind ever more shackled in such a dark place? Luz didn't know. Instead, she held Angélica's hand in her hand, the way they did when they were nine years old. Angélica responded, relaxing for the first time that afternoon. Angélica's hands were warm from cooking, the skin on her palms tough from life. Luz had thought it often of Eusebia's hands.

Luz put a squiggly line a third of the way down the beer's body, making a waist, drew another line where the ankles would be, and added a line down the center, making it pants. Then she tilted her head, staring at Angélica's throat as she swallowed. The beer tasted good on the way down. She wasn't going to take that lame job from Frances. She wasn't going to feel bad for taking whatever time she needed to find a better, purpose-filled life. She would push hard on Mami, be harsher if required—just to show she wasn't lost, confused. She was capable of forging her own path forward. Angélica choked on the beer for the first time ever, stopped midway, left eyebrow raised appreciatively as Luz went on without her. Finished the entire thing, then slammed down the bottle, triumphant.

"Didn't think you had it in you," Angélica squeaked, laughing so hard the tears came down. And when she didn't stop crying, Luz leaned in, offered her a hug, and when Angélica shook her head, trying to dismiss the emotion as a silly outburst, Luz gathered her in. Luz didn't let go. Angélica cried quietly for a long time. It felt good to not say anything, to not have the answers, to just offer her old friend a hug.

CHAPTER TWELVE

Eusebia de Guerrero

#3. DESTRUCTION OF PRIVATE PROPERTY

Night fell. Eusebia carried two plates that each held a pastel. One for Luz, who'd materialized from the basement with a lightness that was a real shocker, and who hadn't bothered to apologize even as she took the plate. Vladimir took the other plate without saying thank you. She stared at her husband. He'd been lying to her for months, maybe an entire year. Vladimir glanced over, smiled a big foolish smile, gave her a thumbs-up. For months they'd been plotting against her, probably laughing at her.

Raúl came out of the building, toward his shipping business. He threw her a questioning look, to make sure the plan was on, and she nodded. Hard.

She searched for René, Raúl's brother, the other part of the plan, but didn't see him anywhere. Would Vladimir stop things, get in the way of her plan? Always the savior, always trying to clean up a mess. But fate was on her side this time. Because just like magic, Vladimir said he had to go upstairs, and so the only one who'd know enough to stop what was about to happen was gone.

"A guy like that!" Cuca was saying. "I'm sure a guy like that, with so many resources, has a, umm, rather large art collection?"

"He does," Luz said. "He has some really nice pieces."

"Right," Cuca said, with the mischievous look Eusebia knew so well. "Would you say his art collection is large or a normal size?"

"Cuca," one of the Tongues said. "For heaven's sake."

"Let her answer," Cuca said.

"The art collection is a very good size," Luz said, cheeks flushing. One would never know she'd just finished insulting Eusebia. Look at her, giddy, drunk.

Raúl stopped in front of the group to wish them all a good evening. He gave Eusebia a nod, and she nodded back. Should she stop him now? She could.

"But let's be more specific," Cuca said, dismissing their talk. "If we had to put it in terms of how a viewer would feel about it, would you say it's so large it might hurt the viewer?"

Luz, obviously buzzed, said the amount of pain would depend largely on the viewer, and how accustomed she was to handling such a fine piece of art.

Cuca rolled her eyes with pleasure as the Tongues stood and huffed away from them.

Unbothered Luz. Hardly affected by the conversation they'd had.

Eusebia sat down next to them, in the seat Angélica had occupied, to get a better view of the action. Raúl came out of his shipping store and went inside the building. As planned, René walked out with a crowbar in hand. Eusebia noticed his distinctive gait, those knees and lower legs that seemed to lean backwards on themselves. Ten months apart, Raúl and René had features so similar everyone confused them for twins. The way they walked was the main distinction people used to tell them apart growing up. These days, it wasn't as hard—René with that terrible smell, rotted teeth from too many drugs.

Eusebia was proud of René's purposeful stride. Not giving the impression of walking backwards but ahead. No one paid him much mind. Good. In front of the shipping store, he swung the crowbar against the glass. It was terrific, how he broke open the front door and kicked it in, how it startled everyone, including Luz, into standing, into silence. Eusebia rose as well. They stared as he went inside the store and they heard him destroying everything inside it. Even amidst all the noise around the block, the sound of the alarm in the store made everyone look in that direction. She felt vindicated by the noise. Vladimir, Luz, they all thought they could move her around like a rag doll. She was no rag doll.

"What the hell is going on?" Cuca asked.

Luz shook her head. "Who knows?" she said. "Just family issues, I guess."

"Someone should call the police," Eusebia said. And at the same time, a tall white man stood next to the group of women.

"Someone should call the police," he said, in English.

Luz's eyes widened. Cuca laughed loudly.

"Where did you come from?" Luz said.

"My car is on the other side of the park," he said. "I went to check on the excavation—we had a rogue worker who decided to work past shutdown. Figured I'd come check on you, offer you a ride."

"Oh," Luz said.

Cuca, who could care less about the incident in progress, stood and introduced herself.

"I'm sure you've heard all about me," she said. "I'm Lucía, Luz's aunt. Everybody calls me Cuca. This is Luz's mom."

"Hudson. It's nice to meet you," he said, extending a hand to Cuca, then Eusebia. "Sorry, I'll be right back. Let me see what's going on."

"Who is he?" Eusebia asked Luz.

The tall white man went in the direction of Raúl's store. René ran out of the store and across the way, through the park, and down the stairs to the train station before anyone could blink. Hudson made as if to follow him.

"Wait," Luz said, after him. "That guy is always on drugs. Don't."

"Who are you?" Eusebia asked Hudson.

He turned away from her, ignoring her question. He walked over to the store, phone in hand. They heard him describe what happened. Tony and the men who had been playing dominoes all moved toward the store, shaking their heads as they surveyed the damage along with Hudson. The Tongues made their way over to where Cuca and Luz stood, expressionless faces regarded Eusebia. She nodded at them, letting them know it'd been planned. They were hurt she hadn't included them in the planning, she could tell.

Raúl stepped out of the building moments later and went over to the Tongues with a look of bafflement. Pretty convincing, in fact. It was his store, he said into the phone, send the police fast. He headed to the store.

Soon as people got over the novelty of the broken glass, most began to leave. Nothing like the threat of a couple of cop cars to remind people it was a work night, the summer stretching ahead of them in languid weeks; no one needed a ticket or summons.

Vladimir came out of the building. Eusebia greeted him with a chin that pointed at Luz and this new friend. But Vladimir didn't react to that. No. He went over to Raúl, and by the speed with which he took his phone out of his pocket and the commanding voice he used speaking into it, Eusebia could tell he was on with buddies at the local precinct. When Vladimir finally joined them, he was visibly upset.

"What the hell just happened?"

Eusebia threw her hands up in the air. "This neighborhood is going straight to hell."

"I sure hope not," Luz's friend said, extending a hand toward Vladimir. Vladimir extended his hand instinctively, puzzling between Eusebia and Luz. Hudson stepped closer to Luz, waiting for an introduction.

"I don't understand why you're here," Luz said instead.

"I work here," he said. "I was at the construction site."

"This is Hudson," Luz said finally, trying to cut him off before he said anything else.

"Vladimir," Vladimir said, shaking his hand. "I'm Luz's father."

"This is Eusebia," Vladimir continued. "Luz's mother."

"We just said hi," Hudson said, in perfect Castilian Spanish. "I'm sorry we're meeting under these circumstances."

The two men were the exact same height.

Cuca bit her lower lip at Eusebia in a knowing

way. Maybe this is why Luz had said those terrible things? Eusebia let go of her anger momentarily, felt herself grow with pride, admiration at Luz's beau. It may have been his height, or the suit, or how handsome he was. Eusebia softened toward Luz. Good job, Luz. Vladimir, suddenly relaxing at the sight of this man, also softened his tone. He spoke with resignation.

"I called the precinct," he said to Hudson, polishing his Spanish to sound more formal in front of this stranger, "and they say a break-in isn't priority. It'll be hours, if anyone even shows up. Better to just report directly to the precinct, they said. Like that's going to dissuade estos hijos de putas from striking again."

Hudson nodded knowingly.

"What did you say about the building across the street, Hudson?" Cuca asked.

"I work there," he said. "I mean, my firm owns the new building. Today was the first day of excavation, so we'll be building up in just a couple of weeks. It's very exciting."

Eusebia attempted some words in English, to show this gringo she could speak English just as well as he could speak Spanish, but choked on the attempt. When would this building be completed? she wanted to know. How much time did they have? But then, as Luz brought her hand to her forehead, Eusebia grew speechless. Sunday night, her daughter had spent the night away from home. Now here was this man, placing a hand on the small of her back. "Are you okay?" he mouthed.

Her daughter, dating the developer? Luz shifted her weight from one foot to the other. Vladimir beamed at the gentrifier. Of course he would.

Angélica and the Tongues quietly observed the scene from a distance.

Eusebia made her expression that of something dry, cold, hard.

"You want to go?" Hudson asked.

Luz nodded. "I'll grab an overnight bag."

"I'll swing the car around," he said to Luz, then turning to Eusebia and Vladimir said, "I'm so pleased to meet you." He sauntered away and after a moment so did Vladimir, heading over to speak to Raúl.

Luz stood in front of Eusebia.

"Ma," she began.

"No," Eusebia said. "We don't have anything to talk about. You're independent. Do what you want."

Hudson turned around, stopped mid-stride, an eyebrow raised at her tone.

"Don't overreact," Cuca said to Eusebia. "Let her have fun."

"Ma," Luz started again. But Eusebia raised a hand.

Luz gaped at her, annoyed. Then, as if she'd made a real effort to apologize, she shrugged, giving Hudson a nod so he would go get the car. She disappeared into the building.

When Hudson pulled his Tesla up to the entrance,

Cuca was the one who strolled over to him, made light conversation. Tony was standing by the sidewalk, sharing conspiring looks with Angélica. "Tesla," he mouthed, giving her two thumbs-ups. Eusebia overheard the tail end of what Cuca said to Hudson. "Dominican moms are mad extra," she said. Everyone clamored around the white man, like he was something special.

Luz came out with a small gym bag and her purse. She'd changed into a pretty yellow sundress. That wild hair all around her, like rays of sunshine in the night, and Eusebia was sure this ridiculous white man had never seen a prettier girl. Just look at the way his entire face lit up with lust disguised as wonder. She was so foolish, so young. Had the nerve to lean down, give Eusebia a kiss. Eusebia didn't return the kiss. Luz rolled her eyes at Cuca before rushing into Hudson's car.

Tony placed an arm around Angélica's shoulders as the other two drove away. It was Angélica's voice that pierced Eusebia, such a high-pitched sound.

"See?" Angélica said. "This is what I've been telling you. Some people have all the fucking luck."

As Vladimir predicted, hours passed and still no cop cars. Raúl paced the block, worried. There was no other source of income in the house, Eusebia knew. She nodded at him. It would be okay. The first question she'd asked him was about insurance. They found out he could add an endorsement for business interruption, so he would get a check if reconstruction took long. Plus, she had savings to see him through. She didn't care about Luz and her developer. Let her daughter live in the clouds, with the enemy. Whatever they did next, it had to make a real impact. It would have to be unmistakable, big. Who said they had to go down the list in order, one at a time? It was time to pick up the pace.

"We should go get dinner, somewhere nice," Eusebia said to Vladimir, reminding herself of that huge house, of how he'd being lying to her.

"That's a great idea," Vladimir said, putting an arm around her. "See how things work out? Luz has someone new, the landlord is ready to write us our retirement check, and you don't have to worry about Cuca anymore. Life has a way of working itself out."

Life? As if she would leave her future up to that unseen, giant hand of God.

CHAPTER THIRTEEN

Luz Guerrero

A HUMAN FITS INSIDE
A HUMAN-SIZED EMPTINESS

It took a few moments for her heart to slow down.

"Are you okay?" Hudson asked.

"Why would you think it a good idea to show up like that?" Luz asked.

"I didn't hear from you for hours," he said. "I wanted to see you. I wasn't expecting your parents would be there. That's not the way I wanted to meet them."

The way? He couldn't possibly mean he'd thought about meeting them. They'd met and gone on a first date just two days ago.

"People are having a hard time with the construction. People are scared. Mami is one of those people. Shit, shit, shit," she said. Her hand was on her forehead and her eyes were closed. She kept thinking about the way her father looked at her. What was that? Yes. Certainly, he'd beamed. And Mami, so pissed off.

Hudson's hand rested on the back of her neck, the spot she'd tapped on their first date. "I'm really sorry," he said, massaging the part that hurt.

She nodded. So, they had gotten off to a rough start.

"I missed you," he said. "You left so abruptly yesterday."

Luz didn't respond, even as his eyes searched hers for an explanation.

"I thought about you all day," he went on, focusing on the road.

"I couldn't stop thinking about you," she said, feeling the heat rising on her body. She took his hand from her neck, held it in hers. She wondered what it was about it that made her feel so comfortable, as if she'd known him for so much longer than she had.

"I'm sorry I didn't reach out earlier. It was such a busy day. Crisis after crisis. My dream project in London was approved. Likely I'm going to split my time between this project and that one, eventually be spending all my time there. And we're having a huge naming problem. Another project, a huge mall in Midtown already registered Hudson Yards, so we'll have to come up with a new name."

Luz was disappointed he'd glossed over the news of his impending time away from New York. She put a little extra oomph into her voice. "Sounds like you're about to be very busy."

"No," he said. "That's not what I meant."

"I got the job," she said.

"Oh," he said. "They already made the offer?"

She nodded. Outside, the streets were crowded; two young men kissed as people rushed by. It was a movie kind of kiss, a swoon-inducing kind of kiss. Her own love affair? Over before it started, she thought.

"How do you feel about it?" he said, a tightness in his voice.

"Sure it's not what I want," she said.

"And?" he said.

"I'm going to take time," she said. "Figure out what I want to do."

"Good," he said. "That's really good. What about London with me?"

She laughed. "Right. Like we didn't just meet and go on one date together. Let's go on vacation together."

"It's not a vacation for me," he said. "We can spend time together at night, dinners, enjoy a fun city. My friends will be there, you'd get along with them. A little distance and you'll see things so clearly. You can take a week or two to yourself away from all of this pressure. Excavation is the worst part of construction. It'll be hell around the park for the next couple of weeks."

Luz unlocked her phone, stared at her social

feed. Her friends were globetrotters, foodies, overachievers—sunsets in Fiji, a rare steak at a restaurant in Buenos Aires, a first marathon in Beijing, a successfully summited Kilimanjaro. Angélica popped up. A picture of the twins—all that broken glass on the sidewalk behind them. La familia primero. Hold on to what you love, she wrote. Today had been such a hard, long-ass day. She was glad they'd had that time, in the kitchen. Maybe not all her friends were globetrotters or foodies or overachievers, but a lot were. All had obviously figured something out that eluded her.

What if she went with him? Just for a week? Not like she didn't have a passport, and credit cards to come back fast if things went south.

"There's no pressure between us," he said, as if reading her thoughts. "Come if you want, don't come if you don't. Your choice."

"I'm not going with you," she said. "That would be running away. I have things I have to sort out."

Yet. How heavenly if she could go. If she did. Her deep inhale in that moving car was all of him, that sweet spicy scent, a reminder of his mouth on her hip. He'd lightly bitten her hipbone, sent a chill that hardened her nipples. To shut the world down, to run away with him. Why would she say no?

"I missed you today," Hudson repeated, a palm on her thigh. "Today was rough. It's like everything is going wrong."

"This has been the longest day of my life," she said.

"I wish I could hide away from the world with you."

"We can," she said, turning off her phone. "At least for one night."

He pushed the button in the car that opened the gates to the stone driveway of his house. And she told herself, yes. Maybe all they'd get was this night.

WITH HER TONGUE, SHE FELT HIS PULSE

Later, brokenhearted Luz would remember the ease of that start. How his home had flooded with darkness when they'd gone inside. How that abundance was a gift. Could he have been more awkward when she went up to him, wearing that yellow summer dress? He held out his hand, which she thought was a first attempt at pulling her to him, but instead just stood there, studying her.

"I love your hair down."

Still he kept her at a distance, his eyes a brush, the air a canvas between them. Had she ever felt more precious? Worthy of a frame? She tried to pull him to her, but he resisted. He tasted his lips like maybe it was her body, lingering there.

"Why are you so weird?" she asked, getting closer, kissing him. "You don't want to?"

They'd come so close, a day ago.

"I don't want to mess things up," he said. "If we go too fast, that can happen, you know. A mess."

"And all I want is to get messy with you," she said, raising her eyebrows up and down comically. She took his hand, brought it under her dress, between her legs. His mouth fell open. No underwear was her surprise for him.

"You're crazy," he said, laughing.

And then her fingers made his fingers curve, and the laughing stopped. She could feel him giving in to her. Pulling her against him, his hands no longer gentle, no longer soft, all of him against her, hard. That little yellow dress up over her head in one movement, just as she'd imagined, and there she was, naked. His house sensed the heat, and a current of cold blew from a vent above them. Sharp.

He inhaled and she thought she might disintegrate, turn to powder, dust, all of her in him. Her mouth on his neck, feeling his pulse with her tongue. His mouth on her mouth, tender, tentatively locking her in. She'd been so hollow. Now, his hip against her hip, a throb. Now all of her—hungry, feral, blind. She flipped him over, fingers traced and unbuttoned his shirt, felt skin now slick with sweat. He followed suit, pants down with one motion and one hand always on Luz. "Maybe so?" Hudson said, grabbing the condom from the nightstand. "Definitely so, let me," Luz responded, a command. Back atop, hip against hip, bodies thick with longing, she guided him into her. Her body anchored him. Then. Her body inflamed, light, floating. She couldn't think past it. Beyond it. All of it—a burst.

CHAPTER FOURTEEN

Eusebia de Guerrero

CANDELA

Vladimir didn't mention the house on the mountain as they drove from Nothar Park to the restaurant where they were to have dinner. A secret house he'd been building behind her back, in cahoots with their daughter. Why?

Maybe because he genuinely wanted to surprise her, since this had been a dream they'd shared for so long. Maybe because he knew, deep down, she didn't want to go—and didn't want to deal with the resistance.

No matter the intention, deception. He's a liar, Eusebia told herself. During the drive to the restaurant, Eusebia watched him intently as he chatted on instead about what happened to Raúl's store, how unacceptable it was that no one from the police department had bothered to show up, even after he called the local precinct. Vladimir looked good, sounded confident. He was invigorated by the latest win, capturing that truck driver. This was his moment, he must have thought. To end his career on a high note. She could see it, the way he tapped the steering wheel: **pa, pa—papapa.**

They went to Harlem because Vladimir wanted her to eat Dinosaur BBQ, which he'd had for the first time up in Syracuse when he was chasing that bad guy, and because, as usual, they did whatever Vladimir wanted them to do. Always ate whatever he wanted them to eat. They parked a few blocks away from the restaurant, on 12th Avenue at 132nd Street, beneath the West Side Highway overpass. It was a dark part of the city, a place she'd never been to before. To her right, the river was dark, and slithered metallic, a little sensual, like a dangerous serpent about to strike. Across the river, the New Jersey skyline blinked prettily, which made her think for a moment of Verónica García and her family, and how they likely were now settled in Teaneck, along with a growing group of Dominicans who were all cowards, ready to allow the city to push them out.

"You okay?" Vladimir asked as he reached for her hand. "You've been so quiet. Why do you look angry?"

She turned her best smile on him, softened her features, firmly held his hand. "Just a bit of a headache," she said.

Vladimir wasn't upset at all about Luz dating the developer. She'd seen his relief.

"They made this pathway that goes by the river, all the way to Battery Park," Vladimir said, pointing through the darkness. "Maybe we should go by the water after dinner?"

She nodded. "We used to love going for walks," she said, deciding to turn on that different part of herself, the part he would recognize. How long had it been since she'd seen water? Allowed relief in it?

She noticed a few women jogging on the path, followed by a few men running faster to catch them. Who would run this late at night? Didn't these women understand the danger that lurked behind them? That those men would do them harm at the first chance? They'd been fooled, these women, into thinking their bodies were safe to move about the world, that they were free. Just the way Luz had been fooled by that developer, with his killer good looks and all his wealth. Just the way Cuca had been fooled into doing unnameable things to her body.

Steady, she said to herself, under Vladimir's gaze, can't show him this anger that bubbled, that threatened to make her scream. They entered the restaurant. The brightness inside hurt her eyes. They played her favorite Buena Vista Social Club song, loudly. Candela as in flame, candela as in candle. She wasn't expecting that.

Sweeping the room for someone to share a knowing smile with, at the strangeness of a rib joint playing this beautiful song, she was struck numb. Everyone white. Every single table filled with them, not one Black or Brown face among the patrons. Over the sound of Vladimir's voice, she told herself she shouldn't be surprised, she shouldn't grow more upset. She allowed the shock to morph into outrage. The only Brown people were the servers, the kitchen staff visible through the open kitchen, the hostess. Our people always cleaning and serving, she thought.

The pretty hostess had a big afro and a necklace so thin it was like the delicate string from a spider to the wall, pendant a Dominican flag hanging from gold. The kind of gift a mother gives a daughter, so she doesn't forget where she's from. She gave them a beeper that would buzz when it was their turn.

"Señora," she called after Eusebia, when she neglected to take the beeper as they turned away.

They grabbed a couple of empty stools at the bar. Vladimir caught her up on the conversation he'd had with Luz that afternoon. Not about the mansion on the side of the mountain but how he, already, had decided they should move out of their home, away from the people Eusebia needed to protect at Nothar Park, because he had made them into the gentrifiers in their own country. Did he think she was an idiot?

"If we can get a big enough payout for our lease," he said, "we can finally do what we've been talking about for twenty years. Go back. Go home."

Eusebia felt a sting in her eyes. Those words had been carved in the flesh of that young boy, José

García. And his small body was only the newest manifestation of the older José García, the one shot dead like a dog in the lobby of a building back in 1992, who was also someone this city thought of as disposable.

The bartender came over and took their order. Vladimir got a Johnnie Walker Black with Coke. She got a Presidente Light. The beer was really cold, just the way she liked it, and foamed when she put the bottle down. Vladimir finally shut up, staring at his drink. Overhead, Marc Anthony crooned about a woman who betrayed him, who he was sure would be back.

Siento pena, pena porque
Te quise de veras

She sang along, smiling because she was supposed to be having a great time. Because she knew his silence meant he awaited a response from her, about how close they were now, after waiting over twenty years for the moment they could live their own life, and not live in order to provide a life for their daughter.

"Muñeca," he said, "why do you look so worried? It's going to be all right."

Gulp, gulp, bitter beer. Who was she most angry at? Maybe Cuca. She looked so strange in that tacky catsuit. No. It wasn't her sister. Luz. Yes. Spiraling away from a life they'd built. But why was she lying to herself? Why did she have such a hard time admitting she was mad at Vladimir? Her husband, plotting behind her back. She imagined him drawing the plans, coming up with the configuration of that house. She realized now, thinking back on it, how often he'd asked her details about their retirement home, how she'd answered distractedly, quickly, to get the conversation done with, not realizing he'd been taking notes all along. She had difficulty recalling the guidance he'd followed to build their forever home. And just like that, anger gave way. Eusebia—seized by an overwhelming urge to cry. In that moment of stillness, she noted how earlier that rage had made her want to fight, where now the sadness made her want to surrender.

"I'm more worried about Isabel and the Tongues," she said, biting down on her lip. "What are they all going to do?"

"Tony has a good job," he said. "I'm sure Angélica could do more than be a server at a restaurant. Christian is off to college in a few months, so that's one less mouth to feed. Some people live off much less than what they have coming in the door. They're going to be all right."

No, Vladimir, she wished she could say. Everyone would not be all right. The beeper on the bar remained still. Eusebia motioned the bartender over, ordered another round.

"Remember the last time we went?" Vladimir

asked her. "The weather so perfect, peaceful. How beautiful each night? How gorgeous the beaches? The fish, everywhere, so fresh. Do you remember?"

She drank her second beer much faster than the first, trying to figure out how, since each of the moments he described happened while she was by his side, they could have such different memories. When they'd first landed, the heat had been so oppressive it'd been hard for her to have a clear thought. On the way to their town from the airport, they'd stopped to buy sugarcane from a young boy who'd been so devastatingly thin she had given him a twenty-dollar bill for something that cost fifty American cents and not asked for the change back. Luz had paid for their stay at a resort in Cap Cana, and after a few days there, they'd headed to the mountain. Stayed at her mom's old house, which admittedly had been falling apart the last time they were there. And the garbage. How bad everything smelled. They said it was a mystery to do with climate change. The ocean, regurgitating refuse on the beach. There had been miles and miles of garbage on the waterfront. And even as the government launched a massive cleanup effort, there was no relief from that stench. Vladimir had been so unaffected. Back in DR, he seemed able to rest, relax. It was only on vacation that Vladimir ever picked up a brush, painted. On those days when the smell hung heavy in the air, threatening to suffocate them, he painted still lifes. The soursop's skin, spiky and soft at once, made her want to reach into his painting, devour the fruit. What to do?

"We couldn't possibly leave Luz," Eusebia said. "She just lost her job."

"This is definitely not the perfect time," he said, reasonably. "But, if you think about it, when will it ever be? We can't possibly afford to buy that apartment. For that amount, we can live in DR worry-free for years. And if they're willing to buy us out for the lease? How can we turn free money down?

"Look at me," he continued, and she turned her head slightly so they faced each other. He grabbed her hands and gently held them in his, which were chilly from the drink he'd been holding. "Luz is going to find a job. She's going to get married and have kids. Soon, she won't have time for us, like it's supposed to happen. This is the time for us. Our chance. You still want to retire out there, right? You still want to go home?"

At that moment, there was such an earnest, eager look to his face, it was as close as he would ever get to begging. But. How to explain she already was home, that Nothar Park filled her with a sense of peace she'd never had back in DR? That these people were now her family, that their worries, their fight, was her fight? Could he possibly understand?

There was no way through she could see.

"Of course," she said, "it's time for us to go back."

"So, we're agreed? I'll tell Luz to begin negotiations?"

She nodded.

"I'm going to need verbal consent," he laughed, his face boyish with joy.

"Yes, yes, yes," she said. "But let me deal with Luz."

She allowed herself to kiss him back. Yet the voice in her head grew ever so loud. Yes, it was time for Vladimir to go home. Luz was right about how hard he'd worked, how much he'd given up over time. But what about what she needed? What she wanted? What she'd lost?

The plan needed to escalate. She needed to move through the remainder of the list. Fast.

#4. DESTRUCTION OF PUBLIC PROPERTY

Three days after their BBQ dinner, on the television, a newscaster stood in front of Nothar Park. Watching the live segment, Eusebia had an odd sensation as she heard the noise of the jackhammers outside in real time, echoed, delayed on the television by a heartbeat, as if the television were watching her and not the other way around. The pretty woman with her straight blond hair strained her voice to be heard, pressed a delicate finger against her tragus, closing the ear canal. She explained the incredible scene behind her, the trash cans that had been set on fire, a mural defaced. Then she turned, let her hand sweep the cars, the park, ending at the construction—disbelief accentuating her features.

Eusebia turned away from the television as the

anchors in the studio bantered lightly about the shame of such a terrible act in such a vibrant neighborhood. Someone said the weather was perfect—a comfortable 69 degrees. She grabbed a light jacket, went down the hall. She paused in front of Luz's empty bedroom. She hadn't seen or heard from Luz this entire week, ever since the night Raúl's store was vandalized. She went inside the bedroom. She'd made the bed so it would be clear as day if Luz came home while she was out coordinating the next item on the list. But there was no sign her daughter had been back, not even to pick up clean underwear. She'd texted Vladimir, Cuca—to say she was staying with a friend for a few days. A friend!

Right before Luz left the car with the developer, after she'd tried to apologize, Eusebia caught her expression and still didn't know what to do with it. Luz had rolled her eyes at Cuca, ready to be whisked away. Would that man give her the right guidance? Push her to get herself back on track? Of course not. He'd love an unattached plaything. She pulled the comforter off the bed, threw it on the floor.

She went downstairs, knocked on the Tongues' door. They weren't home. When she went outside to look for them, the heat was an open mouth that swallowed her. Slowed by the thick saliva, she moved against its constraint. Knowing this too was a lie, that her mind lied. She took off her jacket, went on. Half the windows around the park had a

Dominican flag in them. Some were made of fabric, others of paper, a few spray-painted directly on the windows. Pride, yes. Nationalism, yes.

Raúl was on the sidewalk. He offered her a worried, furrowed brow. The check from the insurance company had not come. The claims representative casually explained there was an exclusion for vandalism. Eusebia mentioned she'd help, they'd fight back. She'd have to go to the bank later, get him some money before rent was due, to tide him over. But then what? he pressed. Couldn't work long-term.

Bah! She'd come up with something soon. "I got it under control," she said. She waited for him to say something else. At his silence, she moved on.

Eusebia surveyed the remaining signs of the newest damage. The windshield of every car had been broken; rearview mirrors had been struck with baseball bats, some coming clean off, while others hung by wires. The shards of glass that remained on the ground shimmered rainbows in the blinding sunlight. The tires had been slashed, making cars look like they were taking a knee. The fire that was supposed to have been contained inside the garbage cans had spread to some cars, ignited gas tanks. But mistakes always happened. You couldn't anticipate every possible outcome, and maybe it had turned out better, not worse, than expected. The explosions a bonus.

Several stores along the park had been broken into, looted, merchandise damaged or missing. Silly teenagers, she was sure. Just crimes of opportunity.

This! Finally, national coverage. Nothar Park on every news channel.

René had done such a great job with the mural. Over a black background, white letters exclaimed what'd been written on the young boy's back. **Go Home.** On the other side of the wall, a Dominican flag had been painted by people in the community without her prompting. A response that said, This is home. Maybe they were beginning to feel the rage she felt.

As she turned away from the mural, she was rewarded for her visionary work by the silence she'd hoped for. The machines were turned off right at that moment, after all those days of nonstop drilling. The drilling, the banging, the sawing, taunted them each day that week. When she'd planned this latest crime with the Tongues, they'd warned her about relying so heavily on René. A drug addict, unreliable by nature, would be hard to control. She asked them to tell her again about the first wave of women who had left to go to DR and get the procedures Cuca had so enthusiastically endorsed. As she hoped, the Tongues spiraled away from discussing the details of the crime, disgusted at the insecurity of the women. They talked on and on and on.

When the fire department showed up to put out the fires, they'd inadvertently ended up spraying too much water in the direction of some apartments. A few windows had broken, and a handful of people had been displaced. The Tongues told her they had to be more careful. There had to be a way to prevent these kinds of mistakes. Of course, she said, she'd plan with more care. But it wasn't true. Collateral damage was to be expected.

She did it. Construction had stopped.

Ahead, beneath the monkey bars, René sat as if waiting for her. Even a hundred feet from him, and with his back to her, he was undeniable. That stench growing worse by the minute. Eusebia thought it must be a survival trait, how the body got so close to smelling like death. She noticed a few people hurrying away from him, how they avoided looking his way. The truth was that people would rather not look at René or think about him; in some ways, he reminded them of all those things they'd hoped for and lost, of the absolute worst that could happen to each of them if they gave in to despair.

"I have to show you something," he said when she reached him.

With a quick step, he took her across the park and up the stairs of the building adjacent to the construction site. The same building she'd climbed with the Tongues. That was nearly two weeks ago.

When they made it all the way up, Eusebia didn't hesitate to go over to the railing and lean over to see what lay beneath them.

Six floors below, the excavation was complete. A

cavity so large it could house half the neighborhood. It was deep, too, a lot deeper than seemed necessary. Eusebia stared, unbelieving, at the darkness of the hole. Hadn't Hudson said a couple of weeks? He'd said that Tuesday night. There was so much wind up here, it thrashed around them, sending her hair into wild spirals. The hole pulled at them.

"What're we gonna do?" René asked now.

It must be because Hudson felt threatened. He'd accelerated his pace. Which meant she had to go even faster. More and more landlords around the park had mailed their manila envelopes. People had gone around to the Bronx and the farthest reaches of Brooklyn and Queens, only to find out what Eusebia had told them all along. The only places they could afford were horrible. There was a growing sense of panic in the neighborhood. She could tell more were poised to be asked, to be brought in.

"Don't worry," she told René now, knowing she'd have to leave the Tongues out of all plotting going forward. "I already have a plan."

Before he left for work that morning, Vladimir had said he had something special to show her. When she asked what it was, he said he'd rather wait until he was back from work, not rushed or distracted. She suspected he'd finally tell her about the house, ask if she thought it was time to put in his paperwork for retirement. Luz, gone this week, had texted him directly not to worry. That she was spending a few days at a friend's house.

Like they were born yesterday. And Vladimir had been so happy. Hudson seemed like a fine young man, Vladimir said offhand, as he left for the day. Not worried about how their only child was ready to throw her entire life away, talking about needing time. All he wanted to do was go away. Leave all these people they loved behind. She? Surer than ever. She wasn't going anywhere.

CHAPTER FIFTEEN

Luz Guerrero

THE SEED THAT HALF OPENS

The glass-paneled doors parted silently as Hudson entered the room. Other than the muffled creak of his bare feet on the wooden floors, the entire space was completely devoid of sound. Luz awoke as Hudson sat on the bed. In the darkness of the room, the only familiar object to orient her was his body. They'd been hiding from the world for days. It had been so good.

He handed her a cup of coffee, and almost immediately the pressure building in the back of her head from the wine they'd drunk the night before went away. She sipped, admiring his body. He was wearing a loose-fitting T-shirt and the shorts he'd worn to the hot yoga class. His black hair so striking against his pale skin, those blue eyes. His raw pink lips, chafed from all their kissing, made her touch her own mouth. She liked the soreness she found there. His shoulders so wide, his torso so long, made her conscious of her body, swelling, wanting more.

"You're looking at me like I'm food," he said.

She nodded greedily.

From his alertness, she could tell he'd been up for a while. Her body was still in a pleasure trance. Didn't want to move much. But she felt the stirring. Felt the jolt of caffeine as it spread.

"You want to go to hot yoga today?" he asked, as he reviewed his work calendar and showed it to her. He'd blocked out most of his Friday afternoon.

Her phone vibrated on the bedside table. She glanced at the screen. **Come home, Dulce,** Papi wrote.

"I have to go home," she groaned. **I'll be back in a few hours, promise,** she wrote back.

She was sorry to break the spell. They'd been in and around this bed since Tuesday night, curtains drawn; she'd lost track of her cares before the end of her first night with him. In and out of sleep, eating a little bit, drinking a little bit, mostly sated with his body. Her time with him: a revelation.

SINVERGÜENZA

After that first electrifying night, Hudson had turned to Luz. There was a question that lingered on his tongue, and she could sense him working up the nerve to ask it. Knew what it was, even before he asked. Do you do this often? she'd been asked, time and time again, by men she found herself naked with. It was a dance she was supposed to allow herself to be led through, where she was expected to claim a bold, voracious sexual appetite or, maybe more often, shame. It was the question that would guarantee no second meetup, no text exchanges in the future. She preferred to remain a sinvergüenza in theory if not fact to the men who asked her—she never graced her lovers with a response.

"Let's stay in bed all day tomorrow," he'd said instead.

"Don't you have to go to work?" she asked him, surprised.

He shook his head. "I haven't taken a day off in a decade."

She'd felt unsettled but intrigued. While they had sex, he'd met her fervor with his own but had also touched her with so much tenderness. There was a loneliness she recognized in the care his body took with hers, but also a need for space. They'd been able to understand each other, in a deep, important way. Luz drifted back to sleep.

When she next woke up, Hudson had settled close to her in bed, reading a book.

"What's it about?" she asked, reaching for it. The title of the book was imprinted on the cover, and she fingered the depth of each letter. It was an old book, and the pages had a musty smell. She liked its weight.

"Two people meet and then they make love very shortly thereafter, and they never spend a single night apart. My favorite love story."

She didn't respond, yawning as she considered the point of the story, of any fairy tale. To be convinced anything was possible, anything could happen. That two people could fall instantly in love and be happy against all odds? A story to reassure her that the human-sized emptiness in her life could be filled with any human being, even this one next to her.

"Should we read it together?" she asked, suddenly feeling a surge of energy.

Taking turns, they read to each other, pausing now and then to weave themselves into the lovers' story. In the book, the two strangers hadn't felt an immediate attraction for each other, but during this fateful night, after witnessing a horrible accident, they allowed what each expected to be a single moment of intimacy. The love story only began when first one, then the other, admitted their deep solitude. Hudson opened up to her about his childhood, about his isolation. He said to her, while her hand folded a page as a bookmark, that he'd always felt the emptiness inside him was human-sized, and her breath caught in her throat. She was scared to tell him those were her exact words for the emptiness that lived inside her. Because his sadness, his loneliness, permeated the entire house. Because from the bit she'd seen, she already knew everything was so perfectly ordered, lacking the warmth of someone else's touch. There was something about this house that felt like it had been made for a purpose that hadn't been fulfilled, and she wondered about the girl who broke up the engagement, wondering if the sense of sadness lingering in the space was her presence gone or her presence wanted. Maybe this house had been made with her in mind? Maybe his human-sized emptiness actually had a human it belonged to? This, then, evoked such emotion.

She felt self-conscious, wished she had done more living, more loving.

She spoke casually of the times of her truest loneliness—never tied to another person. Harvard, Columbia, the firm—achievement had become her companion. Striving had fueled her. Even now, as she recalled Frances, and the picture of those gorgeous women, she felt a pull to fall into lockstep next to them. As if there was promise in their company that remained to be fulfilled. Because wealth had always seemed the thing that would cure her, but the more money she made, the hollower she became. She pictured Raenna in that beautiful brownstone, but drunk and alone. She'd pushed it away, she told him.

"Pushed what?" he asked.

"The emptiness," she said. She remembered standing in the bathroom of the restaurant the day she thought she was about to get promoted and feeling, in the midst of her excitement, a sense of emptiness and despair. Every time that feeling neared, she'd pushed it away. Convincing herself perhaps she just hadn't done enough yet, hadn't made enough money to get to the feeling she'd been sure was waiting for her. She told Hudson how often she forced herself to mimic everyone around her. Their clothes, the way they spoke, even their sense of humor. She thought if she became more like everyone else, this emptiness she felt might go away.

"And instead?" he asked.

"Just keeps getting bigger," she said. "I'm such a coward. Never had the guts to ask myself why."

She didn't wipe her tears, as they filled and spilled, just turned back to the book. Hudson took the book away, placed it on the floor.

"I think you're the bravest person I've ever met," he said. "To succeed in those places, to even make it there, you know how many people I know who couldn't cut it? You're amazing."

He was so earnest it made her snort loudly.

"I'm trying to have a moment with you, why are you laughing?"

"Tía Cuca would say you're just pussy-whipped," Luz said.

"So what if I am? Sprung, whipped, wrapped around that sexy little finger." Then, as he hovered above her and nibbled on her pinky, she let the smile fall away, gave in to the feeling of having finally found some shelter. They didn't turn their attention back to the book for several hours after that.

YOU CAN'T TOUCH THAT

"Do you really have to go?" Hudson asked, as Luz brushed her teeth in the bathroom.

"Not like I want to," Luz said, spitting out toothpaste.

"Norma," Hudson said. "Open the blinds."

The bedroom flooded with sunlight when the curtains parted; the brightness stung her eyes in the bathroom where they stood.

The entire house was voice activated, with sensors that heard, watched, reacted. They'd had so much fun playing with the lights, using a computer program Hudson had created himself that mimicked daylight or nighttime with astounding accuracy. Luz had discovered Hudson was a legit genius. He had created sensors that reacted intelligently to anyone in the room—if you were hot, the AC went up, and if your skin dimpled from too much AC, the temperature adjusted automatically—to keep you comfortable at all times. The program listened to them speak, and if either said they were hungry, and Norma had been activated to speak, she offered options from nearby restaurants and could soundlessly place an order for delivery. So, you're a developer by day and a nerd by night? she'd asked, so amused. Something like that, he'd said.

He followed her movements closely. She tried to figure out where the yellow dress had ended up, what she'd done with her overnight bag. His silence drew her to him. His eyes changed colors. They went from blue to this color, almost gray. This happened throughout the day, depending on his mood. This among the many things she learned about him.

"Stay a bit longer," he said. "At least let me get you some breakfast."

He extended his hand to her. It was palm-up, fingers lightly curved upward, the pinky parted slightly away from the rest of his fingers. She let her hand fall into his hand and welcomed the corresponding warmth. He pulled her back onto the bed.

"What kind of breakfast did you have in mind?" she said, into his mouth.

"I make really good omelets," he said.

I've never liked anyone the way I like you, she almost said. But didn't.

They smiled, teeth against teeth. He told Norma to close the blinds. Darkness again. Next to Luz, her phone buzzed, vibrated, rang.

Hours later, a text from Mami. Did you see your dad's text? Stop ignoring us, Luz. Where are you? We need to talk about the lease buyout. At least let us know you're ok.

She texted Cuca first, to find out how pissed everyone was at home.

Haters gonna hate, Cuca texted, then told her to delay, delay, abort, abort, that she was sitting next to Eusebia, who had fire coming out of her eyes. Her mother, in a much too serious tone Luz could hear through the text said, I'm worried about you.

She wrote Mami back, shocked Eusebia was truly concerned.

Ma, I'm better than ok. [Tongue-out emoji, gymnast-doing-a-cartwheel emoji, hearts-for-eyes emoji.] Sorry, was sleeping. See you in a little while.

She waited for Mami to respond, even with a cursing emoji, but nothing came her way. While she and Cuca preferred acting the fools, Eusebia was in no playful mood.

Time to face the music. Luz showered, put her yellow dress back on. But when she came out of the bedroom, he'd made breakfast, and she stayed, just a little while, to eat. It would have been rude not to after he went to all that trouble. And after they ate, he offered her the tour. How could she resist? They'd been wrapped up in each other for days, up on the fourth floor. A labor of love, he'd said the first night. Surely, she would learn something new about him.

He showed her his house.

It was remarkable. Upstairs, in his living room, he kept his precious collection of rare first-edition books. When she noticed a book of poems by Pablo Neruda, she shrieked loudly, grabbed it off the shelf. Started to tell him how Neruda featured in her parents' love story.

"You can't touch that," he'd said quickly, grabbing it from her, placing it back where it belonged.

"Why?" she asked.

"It's such a rare book," he said. "Just to be looked at, not touched."

"That's the most ridiculous thing I've ever heard," she said. "You and Raenna, both buying beautiful things just to look at. Ridic!"

"It's a collector's item," he said, a little hurt.

"Sure," she said, "you look like you're really hard up for the increased value over time."

There were several bedroom suites, used mostly by his friends who lived abroad and visited often. But she could tell his proudest accomplishment was down on the ground floor, where his meditation room could also be used as a hot yoga studio. Behind a case of glass, a gorgeous fabric in a luminous gold, overlaid with intricate red stitching. Trees, with roots intertwined, a vast sky. She went up to it, awed at its beauty.

"Why would you put this behind glass?" she asked.

Same with the collection of sculptures, paintings, rare records. She quickly noticed that the more meaningful and valuable the item was to him, the less likely it was he ever touched it, or would ever let her touch it. It made her laugh, to think of him as so peculiar about the acquisition and care of things he loved.

"Conservation," he said, "assures longevity."

He was nuts about the environment, sat on the

boards of international organizations dedicated to the preservation of the environment, of animals, of the planet. When, two days ago, she'd called him on his bullshit, for driving an SUV and living in a house that sucked so much energy, he'd been genuinely struck silent.

"It isn't duplicity," he'd said.

"It's fine with me," she'd said. "But wild you have this duality in you."

He'd been quiet. "The car is electric."

"Still, a car in a city with 24/7 transport? I'm not hating the player, just the game."

"You can't win if you use clichés."

"Don't really care about winning."

It was their second night and he'd leaned quietly back, as if he was weighing something heavy in his head. She didn't press. When they reached the ending of the love story, he'd volunteered what happened to the elephant, to him as a boy. At seven years old, his father took him hunting with his uncles for the first time. It was his shot that killed the elephant. And he had been so upset the entire trip, and even more so when a few weeks later his father gifted him that trophy. He'd never eaten meat again. Never gone hunting again. It made her want to hug that little boy.

Last night, he'd asked her exactly what happened at the firm. Her time to share a story she herself had been holding. And she'd told him the truth, how angry and upset she'd been, because she was the only one affected.

"And you're the associate who happens to be a woman of color," he said. "The only immigrant?"

She nodded, but explained no way, it wasn't that.

"Then why did they let you go? Talk to an attorney. I bet you could get a higher severance package, at the very least."

But no, she wasn't going to do that. She stopped short of telling him how many people had made errors that cost them cases, had only received a light reprimand because of their connections, which everyone else murmured about during happy hours. Even if she knew her firing was most likely related to her race, she wasn't going to burn any bridges. What connections did she have?

"You're letting those people get away—"

"Stop it," Luz snapped. "It's my life. I'm not going to accuse people of something I don't think they did. I'm not sure I get it, but I know it's not that."

"Whatever you say," he said. "But think of what you're letting them get away with. What they'll likely do again now they see that they can with such ease."

She knew he was right. That if a great injustice had been done to her, it would likely be repeated. But so what? Bad things happened to good people all the time. Papi saw it in his line of work, had said so since she was a kid. And she knew it would be a stain on her, if she called out discrimination, hostile work environment.

"At least think about talking to a lawyer," he'd said. "One of my best friends is an employment lawyer. Get a consultation."

Luz hadn't responded and he'd let it go. But she'd been upset enough that she'd reached out to Laura, the HR director, via email. Told her she had some concerns about the language in the release and that was the holdup. Laura wrote her back within minutes, telling her she'd welcome a chance to chat about any concerns, offered her personal cellphone number in case Luz needed to call after work. Luz had promised to call within the next day or so.

Still, what they hadn't talked about again was his trip to London and whether or not she would go. When he said he wouldn't pressure her, he meant it, but his silence around it pressed harder than if he'd just brought it up again. The sex marathon was, in her mind, the way he was trying to persuade her, in this super-physical way, that the connection was real, that she was a priority. She loved his house and she loved spending time with him.

At the end of the tour, as if to prove to her what she meant to him, he took that precious Neruda book off the shelf and gave it to her as he recited his favorite poem, from memory. It didn't get old, how good it felt, hearing him speak Spanish. The words from the poem he chose floated from his mouth into hers, and she swallowed hard, making room for them somewhere in her chest. So moved she thought she might faint.

"That's it," Luz said, excited.

"What's it?"

"The name for your building—it should be named 'Neruda on the Park,'" she said.

And he nodded, like, of course, and he emailed someone. "Just like that"—he snapped his fingers—"you named your first building."

That's the thing about falling hard, fast. Even the parts of him she didn't yet understand were rooted in something she found precious and charming. Like inside the courtyard, with the cobblestones, he had all these different-sized pots with orchids, their faces turned toward the sun, spots on the petals making them look like animal skin. He watered the plants, lips forming words she couldn't hear, while his finger touched the gnarled roots.

Staring at all the beauty around her made her aware how little there was to hinge her in place. She brought it up as she prepared to leave, wondered aloud what would happen after he left.

"Whatever you want to happen," he said.

"How long will you be gone?"

"I never know for sure. A week, a month. Have you been to London?"

She'd been there, if one counted a cab ride from the airport to the hotel, and then nonstop trips

between the hotel room and the conference room
with a dinner interruption now and then. The silence between them stretched.

"The invitation is there," he said.

Luz thought about how everything could change
so drastically in the space of a morning, of five
days. And if fate had conspired to lay this at her
feet, well . . .

"I shouldn't," she said, but it was the smallest
opening he needed.

"If it's the money you're worried about—"

"Who said anything about money?"

"Let me finish," he said, holding her by the waist
again, giving her small kisses on her neck from behind. "If you choose to come, you wouldn't have to
worry about any expense."

"I'd only consider coming if I was paying my own
way." She unwrapped herself from him. "Just to be
clear, I have my own money."

Could he tell she was lying? Building her parents' dream home, paying her parents' bills, keeping up with the women in the office who made
four, five times as much money as her, had left her
broke. Beautiful jewelry, designer shoes, purses that
changed with each season, for no adequate reason—
she'd been living in the red as soon as she stepped
onto a college campus.

"I can take care of myself," she said.

"I know that," he said. Hands up, don't shoot. It

was her uncle JJ's favorite gesture. "I never meant to imply you didn't. Just that I own a flat there, and we have a private plane. And the flat's in a hotel, so whatever we eat, it's on my tab. So, you wouldn't have to worry about not having extra money for travel, if you didn't, which obviously you do, so this conversation is moot."

"I gotta go," she said.

"Wait," he said. "You can't leave mad."

Angry arms folded over her chest.

"I'd really like you to come with me," he said, seriously. "It'll be fun. An adventure."

He pulled her into him—face-to-face. She didn't hug him back.

"You don't have to come for the whole time I'm there. Whatever you want. Two weeks, one week, a few days, a few hours. Seconds even. I'd take anything you give me. What would Cuca say? Whipped, sprung, wrapped around—"

She chuckled. Fingers met behind him, a fetterbush's slick vine, seducing as it glued itself to this manly trunk. Behind her closed eyelids, the world was red.

"We okay?" he asked.

She squeezed his butt.

"Come away with me."

"Def not," she said. "I gotta work my own stuff out."

He kissed the crown of her head.

"Crazy how much life can change in a matter of days," she allowed herself to say.

"Say you'll come back tonight," he said. "Say no nights apart."

"No nights apart," she said, putting away her worries. "At least through tonight."

His hands tightened around her, and that hug felt so good. Maybe it was the best hug ever.

"I can probably delay the trip, anyway. Go next month."

"Stop it," she said. "You have to go, you just said that."

They were both aware of the wild beating of her heart.

"I mean it," he said.

"I know," she said.

"What we have . . ." He trailed off, then spoke again, with confidence: "What we have, is it not a once-in-a-lifetime kind of thing?"

She thought so, too. Understood this to be a rare kind of connection. Yet. She had worries. Couldn't really allow herself to get completely lost in this feeling. She had to go back to work. Eventually, someone would call. She was certain of it. She, a rarest find. A woman, Latinx, Black, Ivy League–educated twice over with glowing recommendations from her old firm. Surely there were jobs out there for her. So, what of this find? This man she already cared so deeply about. The strong current between them was real. No nights apart? she thought. This, then, another path she could choose. She wasn't one for fairy tales. Would make an unlikely heroine. Could hardly salvage tensions in her own yard. And what about what waited for her at home? This was her true test of courage. She couldn't keep hiding from Mami. Who knew exactly what she'd find? She didn't have to decide. Nope. But knowing he'd be waiting for her at the end of this day made her feel like she could face anything.

A WARRIOR, FOR SURE

Raenna wanted to know what was going on. **Why aren't you writing me back, Luz?**

Luz had no response. Been holed up under a man for days and days, she wanted to text back, but that wouldn't do.

Mami had written her several times. The lease buyout had to be dealt with. When was she coming back home? But no words in her phone screen about the other thing they weren't talking about. That last terrible fight? If Mami was willing to act like no big deal, she could, too.

As Luz made her way across Nothar Park that Friday afternoon, the construction site was quiet. Hudson said it was unprecedented, how quickly they were able to get through the excavation.

Everywhere it smelled like burnt rubber. She was stopped in her tracks by the mural. Go home? This is home, she thought. Who would do that? She lingered in the park, called Vladimir. No answer. Exasperated, she crossed the street and stood in front of the building, and like a coward, she leaned against the wall, the same one that had that sticky moisture, and waited to see if Papi would call her back. She touched the wall and found it dry.

A bunch of putas were in the park, messing around with Diablo Cojuelo masks. They were painting different patterns on the horned devils; one in particular caught her attention. Henna-style drawings completely covered the black background. She couldn't help but think of the mural, of whoever was urging, threatening them all with this demand. Go home! Yet, here were these young girls, oblivious to the harshness of that message. Taking the masks worn on Dominican Independence Day and making them into something completely new— the flowery femininity of the henna design elegant, giving the devil masks a completely new meaning. What new creature was this? A warrior, for sure.

"But this is exactly what I got that policy for," she heard Raúl shout in frustration.

Over to her left, Raúl was in the front of his boarded-up store. There was a suited-up woman clicking through an iPad. Luz made her way over and was in earshot when the suit said that due to the exclusions in the policy, this damage would not be covered. Against her better judgment, Luz got closer.

Raúl was agitated, his slight overbite exaggerated in his frustration.

The woman said she was very sorry. And then abruptly stopped speaking. She put the iPad away in her purse, extended her hand to him. Like they were done.

Without thinking, Luz went over, extended her hand to the suit.

"I'm so sorry I'm late," she told Raúl, who was clearly confused by her presence. The woman shook her hand, and Luz introduced herself as Raúl's attorney. "I had a personal emergency, so didn't get a chance to change. Can you explain what's going on now?"

The claims person was clearly unprepared for the words that came out of Luz's mouth then, dressed as she was in the yellow sundress. "Are you declining coverage, or are you reserving the right to decline? Which endorsement is this declination based on? Do, please, email me the coverage letter directly and I'll review it with my client." She took Raúl to the side, asked him a few questions about the claim, and when he told her he'd just added business interruption, which the company refused to pay until there was a full investigation, she felt her face grow oh-so-hot. She turned her outraged—Ivy Leaguer tone on full blast as she pivoted back to the woman.

"Don't you think this is unacceptable," Luz said, tilting her head just so, "to delay payment of the business interruption when my client obviously has this coverage?"

The woman agreed, apologized. It had been an error to delay payment. "Look," she said, fatigued, "he still doesn't have a police report, is the bottom line. It has to be documented as theft because right now we have it noted as vandalism. I have a checkbook, let me review your earnings, it'll be just a minute and I'll calculate what we owe you."

They went inside the store, where the calculations happened and an initial check was signed. When the woman left, Luz wrote a list of what Raúl needed to do. He read it. Got it.

Raúl couldn't stop gushing. The entire time, he had quietly marveled at Luz, he told her, so impressed at how effortlessly she'd switched to her lawyer self. Luz smiled. This isn't a big deal, really. And no, certainly no need for any Brugal, as he pushed the bottle with its yellow mesh and insisted she take it.

"Yo, you loved rum and Coke when we used to hang," he said. Luz shrugged, remembering those teenage years in the burnt-out building.

"You used to love art," Luz said, matching his tone. "Always thought you'd end up doing something more artistic."

Raúl explained he had to take over the business; they needed money and his spending four years learning about art didn't seem like the best idea.

"This may be a chance for you to slow down," Luz said, looking around at the boarded-up store. "Do what you want, not what you have to do."

He shook his head, dismissing her words. "Who gets to do what they want to do?"

Luz didn't respond to that.

"Would it be too much to ask you," he went on, once outside, "to read the letter for real when the insurance company sends it to me?"

Luz glanced around the neighborhood, made sure no one else was around to see, then, reassured, nodded. She would make sure they paid him what they owed him.

"But please," Luz said, "don't tell anyone I helped you."

Abogada del Pueblo Redux, she could almost hear Angélica laughing at her, pointing behind her at a line that would mysteriously appear out of the blue, swinging around the block—every person's hand outstretched for help. No way. No how.

SHE REACHED FOR HER SHARPEST KNIFE

Upstairs, Luz found Mami taking groceries out of plastic bags. It was obvious she was about to make pasteles. She had all the ingredients spread out on the kitchen table. Over the years, Luz had asked Eusebia to teach her how to make them, had even bought her a food processor so she wouldn't have to do all the hard work by hand. Her mother refused to use it, just as she'd refused to teach her how to make it, how to cook at all. **Not put on earth . . .**

Eusebia insisted it didn't taste the same when you used a machine to do something meant to be done with hands, anyway. Now Luz cleared her throat to announce herself, and Eusebia, though surprised, didn't utter any sound.

"I'm glad you're finally here," she said.

"Where's Papi?" Luz asked, wishing for a referee.

"He's out," she said.

Luz went to give a hand, taking a glass bottle of ketchup out of the bag that remained on the floor.

"Don't touch that," Eusebia snapped.

Startled, Luz dropped the ketchup. Both women studied the thick red liquid on the floor. When Luz made no immediate effort to clean it up, Eusebia mumbled under her breath, how this was exactly what Luz always did, dirty what was clean, make more work for her.

"I'm sorry." Luz kneeled next to Eusebia. She touched her mother's hand, then said: "I'm really sorry I said those terrible things to you."

Eusebia shook her off. "Please stop," she said, voice terse. "Let me clean this up."

As her mother cleaned up, Luz went over to the sink to wash the ketchup off. She spoke to her mother about how things had gotten out of control. Couldn't the two of them talk this through, find their way back to their old place?

"We've had fights before," Eusebia said. "I already forgave you for saying those things, you couldn't possibly have meant it."

Luz let out a sigh of relief. Damn it, she really did need to stop being cowardly. She might have solved this with a phone call to Mami days ago.

From outside, the sound of new machines reached the women in the kitchen. Concrete being poured? Eusebia straightened up, tilting her head just so, expression one of disbelief. With hands red from all the ketchup, she hardened her jaw.

"I thought they'd call off the construction," she said.

Luz searched the refrigerator for a bottle of the sparkling water she liked. Finding it, she twisted the cap. "The opposite," she said, between sips. "Hudson said there was even more demand for the building. They're not even ready to accept applications yet and they've gotten so many inquiries. Guess because of the news exposure?"

Something strange happened then. While still cleaning the floor, without once looking up at her, Eusebia said they'd decided to pass on the lease buyout. Her voice sounded gravelly, like she had an itchy throat, as she went on about how Papi would retire now, and they would split their time between the two countries, wintering in DR, then spending the warmer months in Nothar Park. When she finally stood, she still avoided looking directly at Luz. At the sink, Eusebia washed all the red off her hands.

"Oh," Luz said. "Papi sounded pretty sure he wanted the buyout. You're going to give up free money?"

"Are you calling me a liar?" Eusebia said, standing up to her full height, staring her up and down.

"No, no," she said quickly. "Not at all. On Tuesday we were sitting on the fire escape, and he was ready to call just then, to ask about settling the buyout."

"The two of you were ready to call the landlord without speaking to me, this week?"

Luz took a sip of her water. Shit. "No, just to find out the details."

Eusebia unrolled a paper napkin and dried her hands slowly.

"You know what I haven't been able to work out?"

Luz opened her mouth but Eusebia continued before she could speak.

"I get why your dad wouldn't tell me about the construction for so long. He didn't know I'd changed my mind. But I confided in you. You knew I didn't want to go."

Luz placed the bottle back in the refrigerator. She took her phone out of her pocket. Checked her email. Maybe if someone from a job had inquired about an interview, she could change the conversation? Get the hell out of this jam?

"Why don't you put the phone away, Luz."

Luz put the phone away.

"Why did you go along with your dad, instead of telling him I didn't want to go? That I'd confided in you that I never want to move back? You know how much I love it here. You know, these women, around Nothar Park, they're my family, too. I told you about that last time, how I couldn't catch my breath. I told you that mountain doesn't feel like home to me. Not anymore."

There was nowhere to hide. And Luz decided this was the moment to be truly honest with Mami.

"I know what you said, Mami, but I didn't believe you. I still think you were just having an off day, that it wasn't a great trip. But this is what you've wanted your entire life. How can you change your mind? You have to go; you owe yourself to at least try it. You both deserve it."

"Both? You mean Vladimir deserves it. What about what I want?" Eusebia's voice faltered.

"Come on, Ma. Be serious."

Eusebia didn't respond. Her expression an amalgam of emotions: anger and annoyance, sure. But even more than that, she seemed genuinely puzzled, as if she was truly trying to understand.

"I thought making us happy made you happy," Luz said. "You can't blame me for this. You have a responsibility to tell your husband the truth."

"Lately, I keep asking myself who you are. You seem like someone else entirely. Selfish, self-centered. Of course, I'm sure that's my fault, too. Shit away your life"—here Eusebia made a gesture with her hand—"waste your time as that white boy's plaything. But what you will not do is ruin my life."

"You're being so melodramatic, Ma. I'm ruining your life? By giving Papi all my savings so we can build your dream house? That is selfishness to you?"

"You didn't have to send me away to get me to stay out of your life, you know?"

Halfway through that sentence, Eusebia's voice broke. Her expression tore at Luz. Had she ever seen her this hurt, this upset? Luz was quiet. "That's not—"

Mami handed Luz the house phone. She instructed Luz to call the landlord right then and there. "I want to hear you tell them we're not ready to sell the apartment. The only thing you owe me right now is some time to sort this out with your father."

Luz left the kitchen to call her father but then stopped. In the hallway, Eusebia had hung all the diplomas and pictures she'd removed from the china cabinet after their last fight. Luz had been so distracted when she'd first walked in, she hadn't even seen herself, at each stage of her life. Each diploma, each accomplishment, she'd told her mother, this is yours, too, Ma. It was a reminder of all they'd gone through. Now Luz steadied herself, reminded herself this relationship was the single most important one of her life. She returned to the kitchen. Under Eusebia's watchful eyes, she called the landlord and said they weren't ready to sell the apartment. The building manager said they would need to vacate the apartment within sixty days ("six-oh," the woman said on the phone, like Luz was an idiot). The letter would come in the mail, as a reminder of this conversation, and their agreement to vacate.

"We don't agree to vacate," Luz said, growing firm in her own voice, no longer just a mouthpiece for her mother. "Please document this for your records clearly. We intend to take you to court if need be, to fight. You can avoid litigation if you leave us alone."

Eusebia nodded at Luz, and momentarily, Luz felt the warmth of her approval. She knew they both needed time to settle into the new dynamic of their relationship. Surely, things would change.

"They likely will come back," Luz said, "offer even more money. So this is a good tactic."

"Not everything is for sale," Eusebia said.

Tired, Luz leaned against the doorframe.

"Ma," Luz said, "I don't know what's going on with us lately."

Her mother wasn't herself, hadn't been herself for a while. What was it? Outside, the noise grew louder, more insistent. She was sure her mother could say the same thing about her.

"Don't be ridiculous," Eusebia said, glacial in tone. "We just need to give each other a bit of space."

Eusebia went to her with a raised hand. Luz steeled herself. But it was softness she offered. Eusebia smoothed her kinky curls with a warm hand.

"Maybe we should stay out of each other's way," Eusebia said, then gave Luz her back. Eusebia turned her attention to setting up her various vegetables, neatly arranging them before she reached for her sharpest knife.

Luz nodded. She tried hard not to cry. Cuca had joked from time to time that one day their codependency would come bite them in the ass. Well, here they were. She pivoted and made her way to her room, where she changed clothes and promised herself to spend as little time as possible with Mami.

She searched her phone for Laura's cell and called the HR director as she packed a bag to take a few things over to Hudson's.

Laura picked up after the first ring. She got right down to business. What were Luz's concerns with the paperwork?

"I'm concerned about the way I was released," she said. "I'd rather not get lawyers involved. I'd like you to take a closer look at my severance agreement and find out what's the best you can do."

"Well, what is it that you want?" Laura asked, her voice still surprisingly friendly. Her tone reminded Luz of how each year at the holiday potluck, Laura proudly told the story of her Italian immigrant grandmother, who taught her to make lasagna from scratch.

"I want two years' worth of salary plus my full bonus for this year," she said.

Laura was typing furiously on the other line. When she spoke again, she was curt.

"Thanks for not getting lawyers involved. I should be able to get back to you within a few days."

Luz hung up the phone and felt the knots in her stomach give way. She was proud of herself for standing up but doing it her way. But she had to admit she wouldn't have done it if Hudson hadn't pushed her to hold them accountable. No nights apart, Hudson had promised.

She went back to the kitchen and found her mother hunched over the root vegetables.

"I'm going to head out," Luz said, placing a hand on her mom's shoulder.

Eusebia put the knife down and turned to face her. "I'll be here, waiting, when it all falls apart."

Luz took a step back, studied her mother for a moment, then turned to exit the apartment, more certain than ever she'd find her way.

In a few hours, she'd work her network, step up her game, and find a job. Give in to Hudson, to the passion that was at her fingertips. She was waiting for a car when Laura called to say the best they could offer her was eighteen months' worth of salary, but they agreed to give her a full bonus.

"Is this good for you?" Laura asked.

Luz thought of Hudson, how he'd made the decision to rename the building without a second thought. It was as if he was showing her that once you had the right answer, you made the decision and moved on.

"Yes, it works for me. Thanks for the quick turn-around, Laura."

Laura cleared her throat, spoke quietly into the phone. "I'm happy you called, Luz. You had to take a stand."

She thanked Laura for the reassurance, the kindness. She'd prove her mother was wrong. She could manage on her own. This was her life. Hers.

CHAPTER SIXTEEN

Eusebia de Guerrero

LA OTRA

On this day: excavation was completed over at the construction, demolition began in the downstairs apartment, and Eusebia became two people. Pastel making started out as it always did—hours peeling skin, grinding the flesh of plátanos, yautías, and yucas until the grainy yellow paste was smooth enough to be mistaken for cooked cornmeal. To her side, on the stove, three pots filled with beef, pork, and chicken she'd cleaned, seasoned, and cooked to be put inside the paste. In front of her, on the kitchen table, the first six of twenty-four plantain leaves waited to receive the paste and the meat. Her right arm throbbed, complained at the joint. She'd been ignoring it for hours. Then—a shudder on that arm traveled to a spasm in her back, forcing her to stop and grasp the edge of the table to brace herself against the familiar pain. But how? Her entire body a fist, her stomach cramped sharply.

A quick glance at her body told her all remained as it had been—strong, the belly firm. She forced herself to return to the task at hand. Once done spreading the yellow paste onto the plantain leaf, she smoothed the edges with her fingers, scooped the cooked meat onto the center of the rectangle, and folded the plantain leaf so it created a cocoon around the meat. When she went to tie the twine around it, she had to stop. What followed was more than a contraction: it was a hollowing of bone that curved her spine to a perfect C, returned her stomach to the concave shape of her teenage years. Next came the expulsion of a fume so vile it stung her eyes, filled the kitchen with a distinctive odor that was hers and wasn't, of something putrid, dead, leaving her. Another vision? No, this was different. A presence unfolded from her body as Eusebia held her breath against the stench.

It left her feeling dimensionless, and though she stayed quiet, there was a ringing in her ears, a white noise that circled her eardrums. She'd been waiting for this moment, though she hadn't known it until now. From the burst of that gorgeous red in the park, to Juan Juan's slimy hands, to the silence the day the twins had almost been struck dead in the street, she'd been waiting.

She told herself immediately to offer no resistance to whatever was going on in, through, her body. It was like the first day over twenty years ago, in this apartment, when she'd been scared of what would come at her in this new land. When she had convinced herself that all she needed to do was tuck away her old self. Become whatever this new place required. Maybe it was cowardice, but she had survived, hadn't she?

Frightened, she considered leaving. She held her breath for a cry, or some other movement that might let her know how big or small this presence was. But other than the sense that there was someone behind her, nothing. Eusebia wanted to run. She wished she could yell out for help. Surely, the workers downstairs, in the apartment under renovation, would run up to see what was happening. Instead, Eusebia stilled herself.

A moment passed and the pain was gone; she straightened her body and got back to work, still not brave enough to turn around. Nimble with adrenaline, she got through assembling the rest of the pasteles quickly.

This presence, behind her, took a gulp of air and Eusebia was slightly relieved—it sounded big, female, and as if it'd survived drowning. There was another sound that followed—strangled and feral, and Eusebia knew then this was, impossibly, another one of her. She imagined this other self, called her La Otra in her mind. Eusebia paused to consider whether La Otra was from the future or the past. But all she had to do was smell that pungent fume, an embroidery of death and sadness, to know. Her old self had come loose.

Behind her, La Otra's breath calmed down as hers sped up. Eusebia grew aware of her hesitation. What next? Eusebia didn't turn around to look at the other, though she knew they both wanted it to happen.

There was a rustling behind her. If Eusebia moved her chin above her shoulder, she'd see her. But she didn't.

"Why do you think I'm here?" La Otra said.

Her own voice, for sure, but also not. A coarseness in it that bothered the ear.

It was a good question. Why today of all days? Not the day she fell in the park. Not the day she decided to come up with a plan to stop the construction of a luxury condo across the street. Not the day the other boy died, or when she talked Raúl into vandalizing his own business. Not three days ago, when she'd talked half the neighborhood into letting their cars be destroyed, or afterward, when they went around setting fire to a bunch of trash cans. Any of those days would have made sense. But maybe it made **some** sense. Today was, after all, the day her daughter had decided to leave, make her own life.

Done with the pasteles, she stacked them in the freezer. Each bunch so neat. Twenty-four meals ready to go—you only had to drop them in a pan of boiling water and cook them for an hour. So, no matter what, Luz and Vladimir would always have a meal ready. Eusebia wouldn't have to agonize. Though neither of them deserved it, she still worried they might fade if she wasn't around to nurture them. She could do this small thing for them. Make sure they didn't yearn for too long. That even when she wasn't around, they might feel the way she always loved them.

Next, she focused on the dust particles that lined the frames of the photographs in the hallway. Duster in hand, she gently cleaned them. The photographs tracked Luz, from nine years old through this year, at her twenty-ninth birthday. Graduations, award ceremonies, each achievement memorialized not only as Luz's but her own. Her own. From downstairs, the Garcías' old apartment, a cacophony of familiar sounds—today was demo day. Destroy the old in favor of the new.

La Otra sighed loudly, sounding bored.

"If you're not going to look at me or talk to me," she said, "at least look out the window. You have some decisions to make."

Eusebia's face came closer to the photograph on the wall. Luz at nine years old, missing her front right tooth. This picture had been taken on her first day of school in this country. Eusebia had been the one most scared that day, thinking of her young child, not one word of English inside her small frame. How would she make friends? This same hallway she'd paced, hour after hour, reminding herself it had to be done. Luz's entire life was at stake.

Familiar hands rested on her shoulders and froze her to the spot. This touch comforting yet disturbing. It was a bony-fingered grip. She'd been much thinner long ago.

"Eusebia," La Otra said, "Luz came home after school that day, and what happened?"

Luz came home happy, excited a girl in her class lived right downstairs. Angélica, she said. An angel is my friend.

"And you worried," La Otra taunted. "You made yourself sick that day, didn't eat all day. And she came home, and she was fine."

It was true. She'd felt so foolish.

"There's a chance you're putting in all this work," La Otra said, "all this effort to save the neighborhood, and none of it will matter. Just like that day. Worried all day. For what?"

"It matters," she said.

"It hasn't made a difference yet."

"We made the news," Eusebia said. "The place looked like a war zone."

"Look out the window. Do you see any camera crews now?"

Eusebia wasn't going to be bullied by this younger self. She commanded herself to stay away from the window. Her feet didn't accept her command. There went her body to the window, there her hands, releasing the gate from its lock, there her neck, sticking her head out. The air smelled like something wild was dead—another echo, now from inside to the outside. The sidewalks had dark stains like a splintered body, and each shape shifted down the concrete, writhing. There was absence, too. No cameras, no police, no shocked developers throwing hands into the air, no white cloth flag waving defeat. Just a bunch of teenagers, painting masks, wasting time. Teenagers she'd once held as babies, fully grown, reminding her of her biggest loss.

"More cameras will come," she said.

"Coño," La Otra said. "Everything with you has to be the hard way."

Time collapses and is unmovable even when there isn't another self. But now the past was her, and La Otra took her back to that day, her first day in the apartment, and then further back, to the worst days.

BENT ALIVE

Eusebia couldn't pretend the seven years she and Vladimir had spent apart were made up entirely of bad days. But on the day she arrived with nine-year-old Luz in Nothar Park to be reunited as a family, she'd calmly tallied the cost of his absence. What was the balance?

Vladimir waited for her in their bedroom, whistling along to the song he was playing on the stereo, his favorite song. She walked toward the bathroom, the pitch-perfect melody a wave that followed her. The artist's voice, and that of the second voice in the song, a coating on her body, so that even when Vladimir stopped whistling and she was too far away to hear the words out of the stereo, the voice permeated, echoed in her.

They'd danced to that salsa song on their wedding day. Back then, she'd wondered if anyone would ever come up with a song as beautiful. The duet's perfect harmony made an entirely new voice. Willie Colón's song must be the greatest love song of all time, she'd said to Vladimir. She didn't know back then the song was about a short-lived love affair, the kind that leaves both lovers worse off for all the future longing. She only heard the words she loved, the ones in the chorus, the part of the song that repeated, that talked about two bodies becoming one. And in Vladimir's arms, on their wedding night, she said to herself: This is what it means to live. To give yourself up, surrender dimension, bodiless—love.

Se fundan en una sola tu alma y la mía

Listening to the words on that first night, in their new home in Nothar Park, together after so many years apart, she wondered if anyone had written a sadder song. The words floated in her mind fragmented, incomprehensible. The choice of song by Vladimir proved what she'd suspected all along. A song about bodies that merge to make a new body, forced to depart from each other before they're meant to, didn't invoke in him any visceral reaction. Even after all they'd been through. He didn't remember. Or had chosen to forget.

Moments before, when he'd patted the space next to him in bed, she'd pretended she had a new bedtime routine just to buy herself a little bit of time. Then, standing in the tub, she let the water fall, messing up her salon-straight hair. It coiled back to its natural state: bent alive. She bit her cuticles until she couldn't anymore, until she drew blood. The easiest thing to do is give in, she'd said to herself in that tub.

Yes, she'd given in. But it wasn't her first time.

In the Dominican Republic, when Luz was only a few months old, Eusebia realized she'd gotten pregnant with their second child. When Vladimir got home and she told him, his eyes darted away from hers but not fast enough. She saw the panic. True. It was a bad time. Both of them so young. Vladimir had lost his job at the ginger factory, and on some days, she had to ask Soledad, her neighbor, for a cup of rice so they could eat.

He never told her he was going to apply for a visa to the USA. He never told her he got called back for an interview, or that against all odds, he'd gotten the visa for permanent residence. It was his friend Juan Juan who sponsored him, who vouched financial responsibility, who would house him and promised him a job in the bodega when he arrived. When he finally told her the plan, he laid it out so logically it was difficult for her to disagree. There was no life for their children in the Dominican Republic. He held her shoulders and shook her, with a roughness that surprised her. Look, he said, there is nothing here. She knew he was right. This little room was their life. It held their bed, a three-drawer dresser, and the small table with two chairs in a corner. Luz's little crib. The door led to a back-yard they shared with the other tenants, a small dirt patch that served as a communal space for a dirt-floor kitchen that wasn't much more than three walls open to the elements, no roof to speak of. Even the latrine was communal.

He would work in the bodega and learn English, Vladimir explained, then who knew? He could be an architect, a writer. They would have a great life. We make the decision together, he said.

It wasn't until she lay down in bed that night that she recognized that, short of leaving him, nothing would change the trajectory of her life. Her pregnant belly moved around, the baby pressing against her skin. She felt the pressure of a tiny elbow and imagined a tiny flat hand pushing against her flesh, just to the right of her jutted-out belly button. Another human being inside her body, motioning a stop. Luz was in her crib, blowing bubbles with her spit. Together we'd decide, he said. A lie. Vladimir made the decision without her when he set the thing in motion.

Months later, the day Vladimir was set to leave, Luz had a fever so severe Eusebia couldn't go to see him off at the airport. Luz's thin lips blistered and she had a yellowish liquid dripping out of her eyes. He'd looked at Luz with detached worry and gone on packing his suitcase, his mind hardened in a way she hadn't ever known it could. He would be okay without them.

"It's the exact same thing Soledad's baby had, right?" he asked her.

It was.

"She broke the fever and was all better within a few days?"

Right.

"We can't afford to postpone," he said, finally sitting with her on the bed, taking Luz into his arms. Eusebia stood and walked away from him toward the backyard.

"Wait," he said. He told her he'd had a dream that was exactly like this moment, only Luz was much older, maybe three or four years old, and the baby in her belly, a boy, had already been born and both kids were almost the same size, and each took turns on his lap, asking him to swing them up into the air. And she'd stood in the doorway, just like she'd done when he took Luz right now, and leaned her back against the opened door.

And even though it was supposed to be daytime in that dream, he went on, the sky had turned gray and the outline of her face and the swelling of her pregnant belly with their third kid made the perfect profile outlined in gold. "This dream is a sign. I'm the one who's going to take the first risk and we'll all be better for it."

She couldn't remember if she nodded or if she shrugged, but she remembered how hard she'd been crying, because the memory had been with her after all these years and the sobs were coming again now, from a deep place in her chest, a place where time didn't matter and the only thing that was recognizable was pain.

There might have been different things they could have done to make a life. They'd already survived for so long on so little.

The day after Vladimir left, her water broke, and even though they induced her, labor didn't progress, and even though they did a C-section at the hospital to get the baby out, it died. The dream had been right: it was a boy. A fully formed boy with ten fingers and ten toes and a strong nose just like Vladimir's. His eyelashes were so incredibly long, almost impossibly so.

DOES IT ACHE?

Eusebia shook herself free of the memory, found herself back in the apartment staring out through the fire escape at Nothar Park. The teenagers were gone. The sky had darkened; it appeared as if rain was on the way. Dizzy, she went to the refrigerator, filled a glass of water from the tap. It was cloudy. As it settled and became clear, she remembered holding the baby, who was so light and so small and so perfectly made. She remembered the feeling that overwhelmed her that day, a certainty she would drown at any moment. La Otra clicked her tongue.

"Can't let you look away now," she said.

Weakly, Eusebia sat down at the kitchen table, finally drank the water. She went back to the memory.

That terrible day was the worst day. Eusebia's mother came to look after them while she recovered, and brought Luz to the public hospital a few times that day so Eusebia could feed her. In between feedings, her mother took Luz home. The maternity ward wasn't the kind of place for babies or mothers to be at for long. The sounds were of the living but the smells were of the dead. There weren't enough beds for everyone who was waiting to give birth. Some women waited out in the hallway. There were moans and screams and pleadings. There was cursing and yelling and tears. In the ward, ten single beds on either side of the wall faced each other without sheets—patients were expected to bring their own—or privacy curtains between them. The mattresses were stained from so much use, and two exhausted nurses paced back and forth between the patients. The row of windows in the room was high up on the wall, by the ceiling, and useless against the heat of the day. Whatever breeze came through stayed above the beds. Eusebia couldn't even see clouds or sky or sunlight, as the branches of a nearby tree blocked the windows closest to her. It seemed unusually cruel they would put those windows so high in the wall when you considered the difference sunlight might have made. All around her, women held their newborns. She was the only one who lost a baby that day. The nurse said some days it was half and half.

That afternoon, Eusebia knew it must be about time for her mother to arrive by how tight and full her breasts were, by the painful and constant drip of milk coming out of both nipples. To the right of her, a woman in her late twenties, just a few years older than Eusebia, proudly held a baby that was ten pounds. Directly across from her, a girl who didn't look old enough to have her period sat up with a baby who wouldn't stop crying, who no matter how hard she tried to get him to latch onto her flat chest refused to do so.

Eusebia lay on her bed, stunned. They'd run out

of painkillers and she liked that just fine. She tried to get up to go to the bathroom, but the pain was a bolt that pinned her to the bed. The smell of her own body nothing she'd ever smelled before. It was pungent with blood and urine and she had the suspicion she'd shit herself and whoever wiped her hadn't done the best job. The hospital didn't serve food, but her neighbor, with her giant baby, kept trying to get her to eat. They had brought mashed plantains with codfish and eggplants, and the salty smell of the fish lingered inside Eusebia's nostrils, forcing her to flare them, filling her mouth with saliva that pooled underneath her tongue. She shook her head over and over.

She lay on that bed, still and stunned. Yesterday, she thought she knew loss. She'd been suffocating with her sobs over Vladimir, tears and snot hot in her mouth. Today, it seemed absurd that she'd thought that was pain.

Her mother arrived with Luz. When she got close enough to smell Eusebia, she winced. Luz's fever had broken overnight and she was alert, reaching for Eusebia as soon as she saw her. Eusebia sat up with her mother's help and held Luz, whose weight settled right on the stitches in her lower abdomen. Luz was over a year old and liked to clamp down on her breast when she fed. Her mother showed her how to squeeze Luz's nostrils shut, to force her to unclamp. Luz's eyes widened with surprise and she unclamped immediately, struggling to breathe. The next time, Eusebia let her clamp until she was done. Eventually, the clamp turned into greedy swallowing. Eventually, she would let go.

The nurse spoke to her mother in a whisper and left. To this day, the only thing Eusebia remembered about the nurse was that she was there every moment of every day and that she was missing part of her index finger on both hands. The line so perfect it looked like someone had set up her hands side by side, then cut. Her mother told Eusebia they had the option to take the baby with them the next day when she got released.

A dead baby, Eusebia thought.

"No," Eusebia said.

"We'll bury him in our backyard," her mother said. "Maybe we find a spot down by the beach."

"Bury him for what?" Eusebia said aloud to her mother. Silently, to herself, she said, This boy is already buried inside my body. She touched the stitches, raw flesh still moist, like wet earth. Holding him in place. Whatever had exited her body was the casing of what had been alive. What had lived in her boy never made it out of her body.

When the nurse returned with a small basin filled with cold water and a small, abrasive towel, her mother went about the business of giving her a bath. Her neighbor's mother took Luz away, hands smelling like codfish. There were a lot of people around: women and men, babies and visitors, nurses and doctors and people cleaning up someone's vomit. Eusebia was naked on a bed—sobbing hard enough she could taste snot in her mouth—getting a towel bath from her mother and not caring who looked. Once clean and dressed, she felt more like herself. She cried quietly, unable to stop, feeling an uncontrollable spinning, an endless descent.

As her mother held Luz, readying her to leave for the night, she leaned over to Eusebia, whispering so the neighbors wouldn't hear.

"When I went through this," she said, "my mother told me what I'm about to tell you. You don't have to cry. This pain, it will find a place, and you'll be able to move on. Just let your body do what it already knows how to do."

Eusebia nodded. There was comfort in knowing her mother understood, and her mother's mother had known this pain, too.

A third of the way through that night, with Eusebia's breasts full and aching, the girl across the way started sobbing almost as loud as Eusebia had been crying over Vladimir just a day ago. Her baby was crying, still refusing to eat, and the women around the girl kept yelling at her to shut the fucking baby up.

Eusebia got out of the bed, grinding teeth through the bolt of pain, and leaned over the girl.

"How old are you?" she asked.

"Twelve," the girl said.

"Where is your mother?" Eusebia asked.

"I don't have a mother," the girl said. "I don't have anyone."

"Give him here," Eusebia said.

Eusebia reached for the boy, and the girl gave him right up. She fell asleep even before Eusebia waddled back to her own bed. She felt his cold, wet nose against her cheek, how his head swung back and forth toward her, lips puckered to suck. These were the kisses of a newborn. She put this other boy, who was also small and light, and perfectly made, on her breast and let him take the milk. He slurped, and choked on it so that Eusebia had to take her nipple out of his mouth, a spray of milk arcing to the floor. Shhhh, she said, there's more. It's okay. Her body was making enough milk for two children.

She fell asleep with him at her chest. No memory of anyone taking him away.

When she woke up, the nurse was bending over her with a gentle hand on her face. She stood up with a rosary in her hands, and in the complete darkness Eusebia could somehow see that she held the cross and stroked the miniature Jesús at its center with the maimed finger, as if the missing part were still there.

"You were screaming," the nurse said.

"What happened to your fingers?" Eusebia asked.

"I was bad when I was little," she said. Eusebia could tell she'd used that line many times, it came out so automatically. As if it were normal to mutilate a girl who ran too fast inside the house. Or was it for saying no?

"I have to ask you a few questions about the pain," she said. "Then I'll see if anyone can spare some medicine to help you."

Eusebia nodded. Across from her, there was complete stillness. The young girl and the boy were gone. It was silent, too; not one baby cried.

The nurse dragged a chair and sat next to Eusebia. She pressed on her belly, around the incision area.

This pain: Does it ache? Does it throb? Does it pulse? Is it inflamed? Is it sharp or is it dull? Is it moving like a current or is it quiet and still? Is it tender to the touch or is it hollow and cold? Does it make you light-headed like you're floating above yourself or is it heavy, anchoring? Is it locking you in? Are you under it? Can you see it? Is it blinding you? Is it lingering or does it come in short bursts? Can you think past the pain? Can you get beyond it? Does it make you feel desperate, or feral, or crazed?

Eusebia wasn't sure how the nurse could tell when she nodded or shook her head. The tears that filled her eyes and made her vision blurry remained unspilled for the first time ever, and no matter how hard she blinked they just stayed right there, until later on she felt them gone, maybe absorbed back into her body. She wasn't quite sure about anything other than she fell asleep moments after the nurse shot something into her arm. The next day, she couldn't work up the nerve to ask her if their conversation about her pain had happened or if she'd hallucinated it. Instead, she asked about the girl and the nurse shrugged. Another already in place.

Eusebia made her way out of the ward with her mother's help. So many women in the hallway, screaming and waiting for their turn for a bed. Was it a coincidence that the darker the woman, the farther away from any available bed she was? The Haitian women weren't even inside the hospital but waited in the heat on the street. Eusebia turned her gaze away from them.

Back at home, Luz's infection was back, her eyes shut dry with the yellow discharge. The doctors said it was a common infection. Best source of treatment? Breast milk. The fever went so high she had to run her to the hospital, and things were so bad Eusebia forgot about the pain from her scar, the pain from her breasts, the pain in her heart. And just when she thought she'd have a chance to lie down for a while, to close her eyes and let herself feel something, because there was something urgent lingering nearby, a different heartbeat that wasn't hers, that she heard sometimes, that beat inside her body, Luz was sick again, this time dysentery, and the doctors again said the best source of treatment was breast milk, and Eusebia gave up on the thought there would be time to rest, to listen. For Luz, she thought. Forget everything, grow numb, and focus on her.

It was better that way anyway because it forced

Eusebia to learn how to pretend. That if you controlled your breathing, you could cry tearlessly on
the phone and the person on the other side wouldn't
know the difference. She learned that if you took all
the pain and disappointment life had thrown your
way, and put it in a place inside of yourself where it
further muffled the other sound, that urgent sound,
no one would ever wonder or ask if you're okay.
Vladimir's dream had been prophetic: the family
in the dream only existed in this land. She remembered tucking the rage she felt at life, at Vladimir, in
the same place where she had hidden that pain and
disappointment. When he promised time and time
again that in just a few months they'd be together,
she told him she couldn't wait. It would have been
ridiculous to be mad at Luz. She was just a baby.

"You should have buried him," La Otra said, caressing Eusebia's arms. Up and down, her skinny
hands went. Down and up. "Might have saved
yourself some pain."

Eusebia focused on the sensation of those
dry hands. Her own hands had always been
comforting—warm from cooking even if the skin
on her palms was tough from life. Her mother used
to say that. La Otra was taking something from
her, she felt the current, it was a relief. For so long,
she'd been the one laying hands, making life better
for others—Cuca, Vladimir, Luz. Now La Otra's
dry hands were on her. Like tiny suction cups, or,
maybe, a tiny mouth relieving pressure.

She only felt rid of that pressure when she floated in water. Her mother had been right. The beach would have been the perfect place to bury the baby's body. There was a caoba tree whose gnarled roots snaked aboveground toward the water. But she didn't think La Otra was right. There was no saving herself from this pain.

That first night in Nothar Park, her wet hair dampening the pillowcase, Eusebia had given Vladimir her back to preempt any move he might try. In the darkness, he put his hand on her hip, so tenderly, and waited. When she didn't react, didn't turn around, he told her he knew it would take time for things to go back to how they used to be. There is no pressure here, he said. We go when you say. He removed his hand from her hip, but she felt as though he hadn't. Its absence heavy. The tears were warm in her eyes as they pooled. She blinked hard with the hope they would fall but they didn't, because they never fell. Her body knew what to do. She turned to face him, gave him her mouth.

THIS IS A DANGEROUS PLACE

Downstairs, one man screamed for a hammer and the other man ignored him, by the sound of it, because the first guy yelled again, his voice clear.

"Get your head out of your ass and pass me the hammer, pendejo," he said.

That guy sounded angry. He was ready to break things. Eusebia imagined the other guy was lost in thought because of the song that played on their radio. That old salsa song about two bodies becoming one wasn't the most beautiful love song of all time, after all. It wasn't the saddest song ever written, either. It was a reckoning, a promise that would shortly be fulfilled.

She'd avoided this pain for so long. Thinking it would drown her. But she wasn't dead. Eusebia's calm was a calm she hadn't known in years. There was no body dryness or body heat distracting her from rational thought. Behind her, La Otra slammed a hand against a wall. Eusebia wasn't startled by the sound. She thought it a cheap tactic, really, to try to frighten her in that way.

"The thing about loss," the other said, "is that it creates a memory in your body, a shadow that remains with you, and it's that shadow that recognizes whenever the loss, or another one like it, is about to be repeated."

Eusebia nodded but she wasn't listening. She sat at the table in the kitchen of an apartment where she'd lived for two decades, with a mysterious spirit who was forcing her to remember things she'd rather forget.

"Your body brought me here," La Otra said. "I'm the shadow who understands loss isn't just the choice you make but also the choices you don't get to make. Each possibility leaves a trail ahead of you, and behind you, illuminated with the gold tint of pain. Loss will compound. You should avoid it at all costs."

This spirit was talking nonsense. Everybody knew pain was red, not gold. And how could the possibility of something you never had also be considered loss? No, what mattered was what you actually had, what could never be recovered.

"What are you going to do if all your efforts fail?"

"Sadness is rage locked inside," Eusebia said. "Turned loose on oneself."

"Are you listening?" La Otra said.

"We always do this. Hurt ourselves instead of the people who deserve to be in pain," Eusebia said.

"Who deserves to be hurt?"

"We've been going at this the wrong way. We haven't made people scared they'd lose their lives if they lived here. That this is a dangerous place."

Silence behind her. She thought the younger self was shocked. Shocked silence loaded with doubt.

"Meaning what?"

Eusebia didn't know if she would go through with it. She didn't know what she would do if this new plan didn't work. Did La Otra know? She turned to her.

Thirty years from now, this would be her face. Not the face of her younger self. She'd assumed wrong. This was a future self in front of her.

La Otra's nude body seemed so frail Eusebia wanted to embrace her, shelter her. Those eyes darted from side to side, avoided hers. They were sunken deep. A constellation of freckles dark as charcoal, big as dimes, covered the bridge of her nose, then curved to cheekbone, scattered down to jawbone. The wrinkles in her face were deep. Her hair was startlingly white, bright as the heart of ice, and so thin she saw scalp through it.

"You're saying the right words," La Otra said. "But you're not sure if you're ready to do what needs to be done. Are you going to let others take everything that matters from you?"

"No," Eusebia said.

La Otra came close enough that Eusebia was forced to look directly into her eyes, then so close she lost focus. The woman in front of her had the same soul inside her body. That was clear. In a mirror, she'd never been so certain as she was in that moment the image was her. Had she ever seen anyone so sad? So lonely? Was that the way she looked to anyone who paid attention?

"What will you do if everyone you love is about to lose everything they love? Will you let someone just take it take it take it all away? Vladimir is talking about retirement. But really this is just him doing what he does best. What he wants. Are you going to let Vladimir drag you back? Backwards? For what? Do you remember how quiet it is on the mountain?"

La Otra stopped. When she spoke again, it was slowly, enunciating each word like a hand reaching out in the dark for a wall.

"Do you remember how you can grow to hate a person who takes you from the place you love most?"

The tightness in Eusebia's chest was pressure made weight. The weight of her entire life.

"What will you do if everyone you love is about to lose everything they love? Will you let someone just take it all away?"

"No," Eusebia said.

"What will you do?"

"I'll destroy it before I let someone else have it," Eusebia said.

She repeated it silently to herself.

"Say it again," La Otra said.

Eusebia didn't say it again. This was the moment. She knew what she had to do next.

"You say it," she told La Otra.

"You will destroy it all before someone else takes it."

"Why are you here?"

La Otra swallowed hard, stepped back. Eusebia moved forward, narrowing the space between them.

"Why?" she repeated, searching La Otra's face.

"There is a version of this where you won't go far enough," she said.

On a crumpled piece of paper, inside her kitchen's messy drawer, two added crimes she'd listed, then erased. Eusebia thought of the impression on the paper, how the words remained in place. Don't tempt the devil, the Tongues had warned her.

"How far am I supposed to go?" Eusebia asked. Then shook her head before La Otra could speak.

"All the way," Eusebia said, certain. Invisible words from a crumpled paper appeared before her.

With the other staring at her, she reached for her cellphone, called Vladimir.

"My love," she said, in her sweetest voice, "I spoke to Luz. She called the landlord and put in the request for the contract to sell the apartment."

"Oh, great," he said. She could hear his smile through the phone.

"How long is it before you're released, once you put your retirement papers in?"

"Sixty days," he said. Of course it would be sixty—six-oh, she thought.

"Put the papers in today," she said.

"Are you sure?" he said. "At the restaurant, you didn't seem like you were all the way sure."

"I'm sure now," she said. "Matter of fact, you should also book a trip to DR. Go oversee the last part of the construction, get the house ready for us. You have so much vacation left."

"I was thinking we should do that together," he said.

"Of course," she said. "You're right. Just thought it would take twice as long if we're both there and then we have to deal with the sale and everything else when we come back."

Vladimir was quiet. "I'm sure we can figure it out. With technology, we can make most decisions together, even if you were to stay . . ."

"Whatever you think," Eusebia said, smiling into the phone.

"Yeah, right! Like we don't know who's the real boss. We'll need a lawyer who knows about this. Maybe Luz knows someone. I can call her, ask?"

"I got Luz," Eusebia said, knowing this was him trying to force them to make peace.

They hung up. Eusebia made a fist, flexed her arm—relieved the soreness was completely gone. She would come back to this moment, to this feeling again. Powerful. Purposeful.

La Otra was shorter than her, what with the spine curved and all, thin enough her body would easily break with a hard shove. Eusebia reached out and touched her skin. Hands jerked back on instinct at the touch. She marveled at how her eyes could no longer be trusted. She saw the soft wrinkled skin of an old woman. But as she forced herself to place her palms on either side of La Otra's arms again, run them up and down, down and up, Eusebia's hands felt what was actually there. The bark she'd found growing inside the wound weeks ago. Here was the genesis.

"You need to fold back in," Eusebia said.

La Otra nodded, her turn to offer no resistance.

Eusebia gave the other her back. She braced herself for the pain. Then reconsidered. Would coming together be nearly as painful as breaking apart?

PART III
GROUNDING

CHAPTER SEVENTEEN

Luz Guerrero

The June air was thick with heat, delicate with the fragrance of sugar. Luz opened her mouth in wonder—only to shut it immediately. Delighted to taste cotton candy on her tongue, like she'd walked into a cloud of powdered sugar. In through her nostrils it went, melting, meeting at the curve of her throat. The taste, blending with the scent, became so overpowering it slowed Luz's quick movement up the steps to Hudson's home. Disoriented, she grabbed the handrail for support. How could the air taste so sweet? This—every good memory of childhood, of summertime parties in Nothar Park, when her parents were too busy with cold Presidentes and each other to pay attention to just how many times she went back to JJ's bodega for a handful of this, a nibble of that. Only later, at bedtime, aching with the sweetness, as she'd curled into a ball, they'd stop to ask her: How much candy did you eat? Luz pushed away thoughts of her parents, of Nothar Park. She embraced the dizzying feeling, allowed herself to float in it.

Lightness. Buoyancy. Sweetness as intoxication. Despite the handrail, she stumbled as she went up the steps. Hudson caught her before she fell.

"What is that smell?" she said.

"What smell?" he said.

"All that sweetness," she said.

He shook his head, unaware of the extraordinary smell.

"Have you been smoking pot behind my back?" he joked.

If there was no sweetness in the air he breathed, what was there instead? She felt silly at the thought of asking him again, demanding he take a deeper breath.

He steadied her, then let her go.

They both carried cloth tote bags filled with all the groceries Hudson needed to make dinner. As they made it up to the top floor, Luz stole furtive glances at Hudson. Him? Cool as a cucumber! Her? Hallucinating the sweet smell of cotton candy.

"You're about to tug that earlobe off." Hudson gently pulled her fingers away. She helped him empty the various bags onto the counter, lining up the many-colored veggies next to each other. For a moment, she stared listlessly at them. "Are you okay?"

Calm down, she told herself.

"I stay better than okay," she said.

She, in fact, wasn't better than okay. His best friends were coming over, and they were bringing their wives. Luz was going to meet everyone for the first time. Hudson kept acting like it wasn't a big deal; even as they shopped for impossible-to-find vegan ingredients, even as he grabbed bottle after bottle of expensive red wine ("You don't understand how much my friends drink," he said), he went about the errands as if they were for another meal for the two of them, just as they had been doing night after night for the past month.

It was a big deal to Luz. She knew how these things went, that if his friends didn't like her—if she didn't fit in—whatever they had would fizzle out, even if it happened gradually.

"Give me your best smile," she said, and took a selfie of the two of them, background filled with the strange-looking veggies.

On social, she posted, tagged it #FirstDinnerParty!!! Three hearts, all green for all the veggies they would consume.

"Stop posting our business," he said.

But she could tell he was pleased. She opened a bottle of wine, served them each a glass. They said cheers and took the first sip without breaking eye contact. She'd taught him the Dominican superstition, that breaking eye contact during the first sip would bring years of bad luck. The liquid went down all butter, all smoothness, spreading warmth all over her body.

"I'm going to jump in for a quick shower," Hudson said. "You?" He leaned down to kiss her, sending bits of electricity that immediately hardened her nipples. She tasted a bit of salt—he was sweaty. She was tempted but held back.

"You know what," she said, "I'm going to run to say bye to Papi now. Thought of going tomorrow before his flight, but maybe just get it over with? So we can sleep in?"

He nodded. "Do you want me to go with?"

She snorted loudly, thinking that's exactly what she needed to make things even more tense with Eusebia. Hudson left the room and moments later she heard the rain shower on full.

Luz lingered, savoring the wine, the silence of his home. She glanced at her phone, checked for likes. Already, dozens of people—mostly her old colleagues—had pressed a heart at their photo. She imagined the associates at the firm, looking at her post, sending each other green-face-about-to-vomit emojis, secretly dying of jealousy that Luz was dating the hunk millionaire. She texted those who reached out that she was being selective with her job search, would take all the time in the world to find the right opportunity. She'd been careful not to let on how devastated she'd been by the lack of callbacks. Raenna had been furious she'd requested a more generous exit package.

Nice job pissing away your entire career, Raenna had texted.

Luz hadn't responded and that had been their last exchange—now several weeks old. She didn't know where to go next with Raenna. She'd started to think it was somehow Raenna's doing, that she hadn't gotten any calls. The silence stretched until it became the only solid thing there was between them. She downed the last bit of wine, grabbed her purse, and headed back home. She wondered, when the heat of the day slammed into her face, if today was the day she'd break the silence that had thickened into a wall between her and Eusebia the last two weeks.

DOMINICAN SPARKLE

The severance check had been direct-deposited into her account, so she stopped by the bank, withdrew the amount the contractor told her was needed to upgrade the pool. By the time she arrived at Nothar Park, she embraced the oh-so-good feeling that wrapped itself around her any time she was generous to her parents. She called Vladimir while she sat on a bench, legs crossed at the ankle, told him she had a big surprise for him.

"Come down quick, Papi."

Papi stepped up to her smelling fresh, looking fit and strong. She rose from the bench and lingered in his hug before leaning back, whistling at him. He had gotten a haircut in anticipation of his trip, and with his newly shaved face, he sported the Dominican sparkle of those about to head home for pleasure. She told him he better be careful with all those putas back home, as she handed him the fat bank envelope.

"There are no grillos on the mountain," he said, "except the insect kind. Look at you! So pretty and relaxed."

When he unglued the flap of the envelope, he whistled at so many one-hundred-dollar bills. He pressed it back into her hand. She explained about the upgrade to the pool. Papi thought heating a pool was a total waste of money. He told her so.

"It's the Caribbean," he finished. She could almost feel his hand patting her head, even though her hands were sandwiched between his, pressing the envelope between her palms.

As they sat down, he withdrew his hands. Luz strategized the best way to get him to take the money.

Around them, the neighborhood bustled with city noise—buses and cars and people rushing to and fro. The school year had ended, so there were children playing around, teenagers hanging on corners just to be away from their parents. The warmth of the midafternoon annoyed the hard hats around the park, so many Black and Brown men, who lingered on park benches and moved with the leisure of someone in no real rush to get back to work—mandatory fifteen-minute breaks could be made to last an hour, the way they strutted.

"You'll appreciate it when you're wintering there, Papi," Luz told him, reminding him the temperatures dipped at the end of the year. She held the envelope out to him again.

She'd hoped mentioning the seasonal move would prompt him to have a more detailed conversation about timing, about the lease buyout, that somehow, she could broach the subject without betraying Eusebia's trust. They really did need this money. She expected Vladimir would have noticed, by then, the tension between the two most important women in his life. They hadn't been in the same room alone in so long. But when Papi spoke again, it wasn't to talk about the house. His eyes pierced her.

"Be careful with this money, cielito. I don't want you to be pressed to take the first job that comes along. Do you understand?"

At his seriousness, Luz groaned, and started to make the running joke with her father about the need to settle down, that this wasn't the 1950s—and she wasn't **pressed** to focus on her budding relationship with Hudson—but his hard, tired tone stilled her.

"That's not what this is about," he said. "Look at

me. I don't want you stuck doing a job you hate. Don't make the same mistake . . ." And then he trailed off, snapped his mouth shut.

The dust from the construction lifted particles into her eyes, nipping, forcing her to close them. She could feel the remainder of that sentence as if her father had said it aloud: Don't make the same mistake I made, he would have said if he'd allowed himself to say it. The snap of his mouth was that of someone unwilling to feel sorry for himself.

"Papi, the winter months get cold on the mountain. When I go I want to be able to swim at night. Is it too much to ask, for you to let me have this one thing in the house? I told you how much money I have. I won't rush into a job I don't want. I promise you that."

He cleared his throat, giving in to the extravagance of a heated pool. He folded the fat envelope, tucked it into the back pocket of his jeans. Luz felt twice as torn—there was no simple way to think of sacrifice in their family. He changed the topic then, pointing to the grounding of the metal structure that had gone up, the machines screwing the bones together miraculously.

"I'm amazed how fast this has happened," Vladimir said. He was right. Neruda on the Park was moving at furious speed, all in response to what'd happened around Nothar Park. First, a series of thefts. Then the horrible day when all those cars had been vandalized, garbage cans set on fire.

Hudson had explained that because of the crime spree, the investors were worried. So the development firm had tripled the workers, upgraded equipment, simplified the construction plans—which he shared with her. They'd even risked fines, extending the workday.

All that effort had paid off. The structure in front of her, same six stories as the tenement it replaced, somehow seemed more menacing, regal—strangely, the exact orange rusted color of the dirt of the mountain where the house was going up. There were cork-like wooden walls that covered the first few floors. Those wooden boards would soon be covered by concrete, which would be laced with bricks, in honor of the heritage of what stood before.

"Are you coming up?" Vladimir asked, standing. Luz shook her head, made the excuse about needing to meet Hudson, they were having friends for dinner in a few hours.

Vladimir paused, as if he was about to call her out for her excuse, then nodded with resignation. And just like that, she saw it. He, with the wisdom of a long line of men before him, knew just when to walk away, leave an issue untouched.

She gave her father a big hug.

Luz had spent most of her free time with Hudson the past few weeks, avoiding the tension at home. She would put off confronting this standoff with Mami, for just another day. Her father made his way back to the building, pausing now and then to regard her, as if it pained him to leave so many things unsaid.

RICH KID SHIT

When she arrived back at Hudson's, jazz filled the room. Luz sighed loud enough he'd hear it. She still hadn't gotten used to his taste in music. He laughed in response because he considered her playlists—made up of whatever was popular and danceable—to hardly be music at all. Each time one of them had put music on over the past few weeks, they'd laughed and debated, eventually allowing their bodies to make melodies of their own. Now, as she stood by the kitchen island, Hudson maneuvered between the refrigerator, the oven, the sink. He'd changed into a loose T-shirt that accentuated his broad shoulders and jeans that fit his body just right. She reminded herself she could withstand the cacophony of sounds for all of that.

"One hour to showtime," he said.

"How can I help?" Luz said. She moved around the island, stood really close behind him, made sure he could feel her braless chest against his back.

He turned around, held her by the shoulders, and walked her back to the other side of the island. "Maybe a little bit of space so we don't get . . . sidetracked?" He poured her more wine and topped off his own glass, which he'd hardly touched before he went to shower.

"I mean, I wasn't about to start anything!" she said, face flushing a deep red. "We're a big hit," she said, showing Hudson the screen of her phone. By now, hundreds of people had liked their picture. He held her phone in his hand, furrowed his brow in an odd way, then clicked the screen off. "We look really good together, don't we?" he said. She could tell that wasn't what he was thinking, but she didn't push. Maybe she should cool it on the posts?

"Give me the dirt on your friends," she said, taking small sips of the wine.

Hudson took a big gulp, then set the glass down. "My friends," he said, and trailed off, cleaned the bit of wine that had accumulated on the rim of his glass with the side of his thumb. He stared at her glass, which he often did. On this day, Luz followed suit, and wiped the bit of wine, too.

But before he could start, her phone rang. "Hold that thought," she told Hudson while she answered, walking away for privacy.

"I got my insurance check," Raúl screamed into the phone, and Luz could picture the overbite, his eyes slightly bulging out the way they did when he was happy. Overhead, Coltrane's **A Love Supreme** came on, and she let it wash over her, the only one of his albums that had the power to move her, transport her. In front of the bookshelf and out of Hudson's eyeshot, she fingered the spine of that Neruda poetry collection. She opened the book as she listened to the music in the foreground and

Raúl in the background; he went on about how he'd never seen this many zeros in a check, how her act of generosity had changed his life. Luz inhaled the musty scent of the old pages, thinking of the first few days she and Hudson had spent in bed, reading to each other from that love story; those pages smelled just like these did. And she thought of a time long before that, when her father used to recite poetry to her mother, his devotion such an important part of how she came to know their apartment in Nothar Park as home. A story inside another story, and in this moment, she felt certain she was on the right path—she hadn't felt this free, ever.

"If it wasn't for you," Raúl said, "I wouldn't have gotten a dime."

"It wasn't that big of a deal," she said, putting the book back, sitting down in a nearby chair. She marveled at the feeling she'd had earlier, of floating, and lightness, and now this, a weight—it was grounding her. An injustice had almost happened to Raúl, when the insurance company tried to deny him a claim they should have paid. And she had helped him, not wanting anything in return, and in a way, being able to do something without needing to get anything back from it, well, that felt like part of the reason she'd endured so many years of school and all the hardship of her corporate job. To do just this small thing. In all the years she'd helped forge multimillion-dollar settlements back at work, she'd never felt this way. What did that say about her?

"You're amazing," he continued, telling her how he'd already told the landlord he was taking the buyout for his apartment. "You were so right, when you told me to really think about what's next. This windfall, shit, Lulu. I'm going back to school, to take art. Some rich kid shit."

"Wow," Luz said. This was unexpected news. It made her a little sad, Raúl leaving the neighborhood. But it was right, that he should do what worked for him. From the other end, the sounds of Nothar Park came through clearly. An ice cream truck, and kids laughing in the background. A loud Fefita la Grande song, interrupted by Cardi B, overcome by the incomparable and always great Celia Cruz. ¡Azúcar! Then the loud sirens of a fire truck. She could almost smell the pastelitos in the corner, the multicolored yun-yuns' artificial flavor beckoning. It made her miss home. She should have gone upstairs.

"You haven't seen my mom around, have you?"

"Yeah," he said. "Just rushed by me. Solid, Luz. I owe you big. I'ma let you go. Unless you need me to find your moms? Tell her something for you?"

"No. I'll try her phone."

She hung up, listened to the music overhead. There was something so tidy and neat about this life with Hudson. The nearness of her purpose, it was rushing toward her, she could tell. Luz made her way back to the kitchen island slowly, knowing she wasn't going to try Eusebia's phone. She missed

Mami terribly, it was true—but it was also true they both were probably a little better off for giving each other space. She sipped her wine quietly, feeling slightly removed from the conversation as Hudson chopped and peeled and went on as if he'd never been interrupted.

Hudson became more animated as he told Luz old Harvard stories about his friends. There was Liam, who worked in Hudson's firm, and his wife, Adele. There was Luca, who was an investment capitalist, and his wife, Ruby.

"You're going to like them," he said. "They're good people."

He took for granted that they would like her, she noted. A given in his mind.

"What if they don't like me?" she asked, in spite of herself.

"Impossible," he said.

"But if they don't?" she insisted.

"Throw you to the curb," he said. "How does that Beyoncé song go? 'To the left, to the left'?"

"Stop it, please don't ever do that again. Ever!"

He dropped what he was doing and came to her. He held her hand and they were quiet together for a while. This felt good. So easy.

"I'm glad you're here," he said.

"Me too," she said.

They'd fallen into a routine over the course of the last month. He worked all day, and because they spent no nights apart, she'd leave in the mornings with him, go to the library and apply for jobs, researching different companies in anticipation of interviews she hoped would come through, but hadn't yet. At night, they often met downtown, where they ate out or just walked around. They'd walked all over New York City. All the way down to the World Trade Center memorial, where they'd made their way without a plan, where she'd traced the indented letters of the names of all the people who'd died, struck most by those names of women followed by the words "and her unborn child." Hudson had been transfixed by the structures, the vacant bases of the buildings, with water flowing endlessly into the emptiness. The sound of waterfalls reminded Luz of that beach back in DR, at the foot of the mountain where her parents had grown up. She told Hudson about it, how she hoped one day to take him there. Maybe, if I'm not too busy, he'd said. He'd stood a little taller, that half smile on his face, the way he smiled whenever she posted a picture of them together, whenever she imagined them into the future.

On the subway home that day, they'd gotten caught in the rush, and among the slightly unpleasant smell of summertime sweaty bodies, and the uptight suits coming from downtown, and the busy moms who were rushing home to take care of their kids, Luz pressed her body firmly against Hudson, who kissed her hard, among so many strangers, including a few who screamed **Get a fucking room,** and when Luz felt his hand on her ass, she surely agreed with the hecklers. She couldn't wait to get him in bed, told him so as soon as they went through the doors, high from a day of so much emotion. I can't believe you grabbed my ass in public, she said. What? he said, surprised. I never grabbed your ass.

Oh, New York City.

Luz puzzled daily at how easy it was being with him, only because she'd never experienced it in a relationship before Hudson. What came before? Flings, half attempts at finding people interesting, feeling that human-sized emptiness growing bigger and deeper inside herself. She'd certainly never had this level of chemistry, this level of immediate connection. She claimed him, claimed a future with him, in a confident way that said of course they'd be together forever. Of course one day he'd visit her family's hometown, stand on the precipice of those rocks, waves crashing loudly, splashing them both in the face. It was easy because they both agreed, and all you needed to do when it came to love was decide and move on. This was exactly where she wanted to be. Even her old fantasy, of living on Seventy-ninth Street, had dissolved over the last month—what a superficial desire, to cement her idea of success on place and not people. The doorbell rang and Hudson went to welcome his friends. Luz held back, drinking her wine, until he turned around and extended a hand.

"Come on."

And so she did, feeling at ease, knowing with him by her side, she needed to be no one but herself.

A STORM

The first sign of Adele and Liam was the puppy who preceded them into the house. A ball of bright cinnamon fur with a face like a small-toothed lion, he attempted to climb Luz's legs, then rushed over to Hudson, then back to Luz. She kneeled to receive him and the puppy energetically licked her hand with a shockingly blue tongue.

"What in the world!" Luz screamed in delight.

"What the hell, Adele," Hudson said.

Adele stepped in. She was striking. Her long blond hair, which stopped at the small of her back, had a wide streak down the middle the exact color of the puppy's tongue. She had a piercing in her lip, the ring a silver hoop with three tiny balls that rotated. She was lean and long, her body appeared prepared to eject toward the ceiling.

"Hudson," she said, leaning over to grab the puppy from Luz's arms, "I told Liam not to tell you. I knew you'd be a total pooper."

Right behind her, Liam came along, carrying Adele's handbag in one hand and a tote with several bottles of wine that clinked in the other. He was just as tall as Hudson, similar athletic build. His dark brown eyes rested on her, then he turned to Hudson.

"Damn," he said.

Hudson shook his head, ignoring Liam.

"Adele," he said, "you can't bring a dog to dinner."

"Why not?" she said. "I just got Moby two weeks ago in Buenos Aires. We can't leave him by himself, he'll eat through all my Louboutins. Can't leave him with strangers. He hates strangers. Don't know how he took to you so fast."

Adele leaned over to Luz, gave her a kiss on each cheek.

"Hudson has no manners. But I'm sure you know that already. It's so lovely to meet you. You are stunning. Look at that skin! Look at that bone structure, Liam. Moby is a chow chow, Hudson. I love saying that. Chow chow. Doesn't even bark. I swear. He's going to be good."

Moby wiggled out of Adele's arms. Tried to climb Luz's legs.

"We can't speak to his level of loyalty yet, obviously. Traitor."

Adele took his furry paw into her hands.

"Adorable traitor," she said in a baby voice. "It's okay, Moby. We know you can't help yourself. Men! Am I right, Luz? Where's the lie?"

Luz nodded helplessly. Hudson stood up. Exasperated but trying not to smile. He introduced Adele, his good friend. And Liam, who instead of shaking Luz's hand gave her a hug. All three graduated from Harvard the same year, Hudson said. They already knew she went there, too. She could tell by how quickly Liam started reminiscing about campus, old professors, favorite bars. Luz went along, smiled, pretended the Harvard years had been mostly good.

"What's for dinner?" Adele asked, going right inside the house and climbing the stairs like she was home. She put her purse above the book-shelf (Luz imagined to keep it away from the puppy), and as she did, she exposed her flat, pale stomach and a belly chain that went around her waist and connected on both ends to a belly button ring. On her stomach, there was a splattering of cir-cular dark spots, old scars. When Adele noticed Luz's gaze, she pulled her shirt down self-consciously.

Luz stole a glance at Liam. There was something so familiar about him, she wondered if he was a model or had appeared in a movie at some point. Was it possible she knew him? He caught her look-ing at him and gave her a big smile.

"Luz," Adele said, "don't look so surprised that Liam is Black."

Luz laughed aloud.

"You're crazy," she said to Adele. Then, looking at Hudson, she mouthed the words "I like her."

"Everyone likes Adele," he said.

"The guys are going to try to bore us to tears," Adele said, sitting across from Luz. "Building cri-sis, dream underground lair, blah blah blah. Let's just drink until we can't understand what they say, yeah?"

"Sounds like a plan," she said.

Luca arrived by himself. Handsome, like Hudson and Liam—three Ken dolls. Didn't they let any short, fat people into this group? As soon as he sat down, Moby walked over, growled at his feet.

"No," he said to Adele. "Don't let that dog touch me."

Adele got Moby.

"Easy, prima donna," Liam said.

Adele handed Moby to Liam. She poured until all the glasses were full, the first bottle empty.

"Where's Ruby?" she asked.

"She went to get her hair done," Luca said. "Can't waste a sitter on just one event. She'll be here soon."

Hudson was tending the pots. Everyone stared at Luz. Waiting.

"Is anybody else hot?" Adele said, and then yelled into the air, "Norma, only monitor Adele's body temperature."

Hudson came back to the group, repeated the command. The room began to cool instantly.

"Did he tell you Norma was his Black nanny?" Adele said. "That he was in love with her from the time he was a baby up through college?"

Hudson groaned. Luz raised an eyebrow. "Am I the new Norma?" she said. All three of his friends guffawed.

"Def not," he said. He wrinkled his nose and between them rested the knowledge of how she didn't clean, didn't cook, hardly ever picked up after herself. His holding that between the two of them made her want to kiss him.

Hudson's finger made a vine up Luz's arm. All three of his friends gaped—transfixed by this movement. Luz had it on the tip of her tongue to ask if the reason they stared was because she was the first woman he'd brought around. Or if maybe he was never very affectionate with his lovers. But she held back.

"Buenos Aires was amazing," Adele said, turning to Luz. "Have you been?"

"Not yet," Luz said.

"The people are so warm," she said, "so kind. Last time we all went, Hudson took us to rally against single-use plastic."

"Nothing changed," Hudson said.

"My point," Adele said, "is that it's much more fun to visit Argentina without Hudson. He didn't even let us go to Mendoza."

Hudson went off. Speaking about the impact of eating red meat, of how the entire world was in denial about the progression of the earth's warming.

"Not tonight," Adele mock-screamed. " 'It's already too late, the world is ending!' Hashtag climate doomers so boring. ¡Hoy se bebe!"

Luz was surprised that Adele spoke Spanish, and with a Dominican accent, no less. But there was no way to ask how she'd learned. Adele talked nonstop. By the end of the first glass of wine, they'd broken into two distinct groups, the men over in the kitchen, preparing the food, and Luz and Adele over by the bookshelf, drinking the wine.

"He's at ease," Adele said. "It's good to see him do something other than work himself to death."

Luz smiled, didn't respond.

"So, Hudson mentioned you're currently looking for work?"

Without letting her respond, Adele then spoke of the organization she and Ruby led, whose mission was tied to helping children escape war-torn areas. "We could really use some help," she said.

"I need a paying job," Luz said, knowing "help" meant free labor.

"Not if you play your cards right," Adele said, pointedly looking from Luz to Hudson.

Luz ignored that.

"He's head over heels," Adele pressed on. "You know this, right?"

"We're both having fun," Luz said.

"It's not just fun for him," Adele said. "We've all been hoping he'd meet a nice, down-to-earth person. Someone like us."

"Ain't nobody like you, slut," someone screamed from the doorway.

Adele shrieked, and ran over to embrace the newest arrival, who Luz assumed was Ruby.

"You slut," Adele said. "Where you been? Getting hair did, nail did, everything did?"

Ruby's big smile was warm, showcasing the prettiest dimples. She turned her head just so, and the cascade of her waist-length dreadlocks spilled over her shoulder.

"Is she harassing you?" Ruby said, turning to Luz. "It's so nice to meet you. Why are we segregated? I'm starving."

Back in the kitchen, the meal was done. The space got loud quickly, with everyone speaking over each other. Ruby and Luca linked arms around the waist. Liam had a metal straw he apparently carried with him everywhere and was using it to take sips out of Adele's glass any time she looked the other way. Hudson kept stealing worried glances her way. So, while she'd thought he'd been cool as a cucumber, he'd been worried she might not like his friends. It made her want to kiss him more.

Adele pointed at Luca, said, "Half Japanese, half Chinese."

Then pointed at Ruby. "Half Black, half Korean."

Pointed at Hudson. "Plain white."

Then pointed at Liam. "All Black, all mine."

Then pointed at Luz—"We've been missing a Latina. And Afro-Dominicana, YASSSS!"

"You need to tone it down like ten notches," Hudson said. He turned to Liam. "What is she on today?"

"Listen," Adele said, taking Luz by the arm. "We've all been really worried about Hudson. He has been so lonely and sad since—"

"That's enough, Adele," Hudson said. There was an awkward moment. "Let's eat."

Everyone grabbed a plate, served themselves. Moby started jumping up and down, smelling the food. Adele somehow got him to calm down on her lap. After murmuring compliments to Hudson, Ruby turned her attention to Luz.

"So, what kind of work are you looking for?" Ruby asked her.

"Ummm," Luz said, "I'm not really sure. Just know I don't really want to go back to practicing law."

Ruby nodded. "I worked as a doctor for years before having kids. It was so stressful. When we finally decided it just wasn't worth it, that it was better for me to pursue my passions and take care of my family, that was such a moment of liberation for me."

"Doesn't sound so liberating, having to take care of four kids," Hudson said.

Luz was surprised at his tone. "You don't want kids?" she asked.

Everyone grew quiet.

"Probably not."

Ruby cut in. "Adele and I run this organization."

"Yeah, Adele began to—"

Ruby went on, interrupting Luz. "We were both so burnt-out. 'Cause it's all bullshit. And you have these women, you know, who act like you aren't doing shit unless you're shattering ceilings and working yourself to the ground. Well, fuck that. There's this other way, you know. To be able to work toward social change without doing it the way men have done it. We help people directly. And we have enough time to spend with our loves."

Adele raised her glass in cheers.

"No pressure," Adele said, tone a little softer, smoother, after her second glass of wine. "But it'd be great if you can give us a few hours and learn what we do. Eventually, there could be a paying job in it."

"She doesn't need a paying job," Hudson said.

Adele nodded, and smiled at Luz, an I-told-you-so kind of smile.

Luz stilled her tongue. She ate, waited patiently for the dinner to end and his friends to go home.

"You were the girl," Luca said. "The girl on the fire escape. The day of the mural painting!"

"You were all there," Luz said, remembering Adele's blue hair. "Why were you all there?"

"We do a volunteer day for all of Hudson's projects," Luca said. "To beautify the community. But Hudson couldn't stop staring at you that day."

Hudson blushed crimson red. Luz remembered him waving at her. She thought about what her mother had said the first day of demolition. If they'd been talking to each other, she would have called her, said you won't believe this, Mami, you were right.

"It's always the same," Liam butted in. "We always have to clean up. It's like, how come these people don't give a fuck about their own neighborhood?"

"What are you talking about, 'these people'?" Luz said. "Most people care."

Luz thought of Angélica, even the Tongues, who spent more than what they had in order to make their apartments nice. Who were terrified of being displaced.

"No offense, Luz," Liam said, "but these people literally set the neighborhood on fire. You can't defend that. We might lose millions of dollars because a bunch of thugs are angry they can't afford to buy a nice apartment."

Luz stared at Liam, then turned to Hudson. He was obviously not going to speak. Why? Because Liam was Black? And she was, too? And he wasn't?

"I'm not defending the behavior of people who vandalized my neighborhood. But I'm also not accepting you sitting here talking shit."

"What did you have to do, Hudson, to convince our investors not to pull out of this shit show?" Liam said. "We need to get back on track, Luz, maybe some of these great people can tell the bad guys to chill the fuck out."

The tension made the atmosphere taut, but suddenly, as if they were on the set of a movie, a storm of air cooled the room.

"Norma wants us all to cool off," Ruby said. The friends laughed but Luz didn't laugh along. She sipped her wine, glanced with disappointment at Hudson, then turned her attention to her phone. Cuca had sent her a text while she was busy chatting with everyone. They as stuck up as I thought? she'd asked. Luz started to write, then stopped. What could she say? Moby came over and she busied herself playing with him.

By the time the group made to leave, Luz had grown somber. Hudson came over, asked gently if she was okay.

"Fine," she said. She got up and gave each person a hug, even Liam, who drunkenly said it was his bad, that he didn't mean to sound like a dick, but that she knew, like he knew, some people were T-R-A-S-H.

Luz got out of her clothes and into bed in the time it took Hudson to see his friends off. When he came upstairs, he slipped inside the bed without changing, and put his hand on her waist. "I know you're not asleep," he said.

She turned over and looked at him.

"What was that about?"

"I just didn't think it was my place to get in the middle of that conversation."

"Not your place."

"You've purposefully avoided anything to do with race in our relationship. From our first date, you made it obvious you didn't want to have these conversations with me. You can't blame me for not stepping in, defending you."

"I don't need you to defend me. But you need to check your friends when they're talking crazy. But whatever—that's not even why I'm upset.

What the hell was that about? Saying I didn't need a paying job?"

"Because you don't," he said.

"Not for you to say." She thought of those two women, of how smart Hudson had been, how calculated in all his plans. He wanted her to get sucked into the clique with Ruby and Adele. He wanted her to see this path as an option. She told him that.

"I wanted you to meet my friends," he said. "There was no ulterior motive. I'm not trying to brainwash you."

He removed his hand from her waist. Turned his body to face the ceiling.

"It wouldn't be the worst thing for you, Luz. To understand there are different ways to live a full life."

"You hardly know me," Luz said. "We've been dating for a month and a half. For you to—"

Hudson's sharp intake of breath made her stop talking.

"I don't know you?"

"You don't," Luz said. "If you think that I'm going to just fall in line with these women? Travel the world with you and volunteer on the side?"

"Is this because I said I didn't want kids?" Hudson asked, sitting up. "Because if that's what it is, we can talk about it. I just didn't think we were ready to have that conversation."

Luz knew they were both drunk. She knew she shouldn't have said anything else at that point. The room was spinning, and she thought she might get sick, right in this bed, in the beautifully soft white sheets. A month ago, he'd decided to cancel his trip to London when she told him she needed a place to stay for a few days. Had made an excuse about his oversight being urgently needed at Nothar Park. But they'd both known it was because of her.

"You'd change your mind about kids? For me?"

But Luz already knew the answer.

"Why can't you consider me an option for your future? Would it be so terrible, Luz, to make a life together? We just have to decide. There are people who decide to build a life together with a lot less than what we have. The passion is there, Luz. Most people never have a connection like ours."

Luz felt her anger dissipate in service to nausea. How to explain she wasn't ready to pick him, that she had to first pick herself?

"Hudson," Luz said, "I can't have this conversation with you right now. I'm not ready to make this decision. And I don't think you are, either."

Hudson stood up, went back to the living room. She felt the overhead speakers play Coltrane again, softly. In the swirl of motion in her body, she felt the weight of the day land on her. What Hudson had done to her, no matter how well intentioned— wasn't it exactly what she and Vladimir had done to Eusebia? Nauseous, she rushed to the bathroom, the entire meal up, hurling out of her.

CHAPTER EIGHTEEN

Eusebia de Guerrero

THE BOYS HAD LOST BOTH PARENTS
SEPTEMBER 11

Eusebia served René oxtail soup leftovers. Sitting at her dining room table, beneath the watchful eye of the campesino, he ate slowly, slurping soup like someone with a toothache. From time to time, he rested the spoon on the rim of the bowl and inserted his index finger beneath the collar of his shirt. Scratch, scratch, scratch.

René looked better than he had in years. Was it the responsibility? He'd taken a shower, cut off his hair, shaved his scraggly beard. He'd borrowed some clothes from his brother Raúl. If he didn't open his mouth to expose those rotted black teeth, one would think he was a normal person. Not a drug addict. Not a criminal. Not a vagabond.

"Mami used to make the most delicious oxtail soup back in the day," he said. He smiled self-consciously and she saw his effort, how he tried to fold his lips over those teeth, so darkened at the root.

"I gave your mom that recipe when you were ten years old," she said. He beamed at her, touched by the disclosure, before his gaze softened into the past—there, in his eyes, still the boy he'd been once, full of wonder at the magic of a good meal, and the man he was today, cognizant of and gutted by the absence of such comfort. It was his mother who had said she was going to lie down in bed for a bit after her husband's funeral, where Eusebia had contributed this exact meal. It was his mother who had never gotten out of bed again, except to use the bathroom from time to time. The boys had lost both parents September 11. Eusebia rose from the table—to get away from his breath, from his past.

"I have another job for you," she said. Looked out the open window, feeling that mid-June breeze on her face, hearing it rustle the branches of the trees. The London planetrees that would light up in brilliant yellows, oranges, burnt gold come fall were now majestically clothed in an emerald green. Her honey locust tree was dwarfed, surrounded by them. In the park, on the streets across the way, moving through the wide floors of the new construction, so many hard hats—the workers, a complete infestation. The construction went on. The drilling from weeks ago had been replaced by hammering. The frame was up—now they were erecting walls. Building actual apartments.

Her phone rang, back on the table, and René held it up in his hands, showed Luz's photo: illuminated, radiant. She shook her head and René sent the call to voicemail. Last night, while Cuca splayed on this floor in hot-pink short shorts, bicycling her legs and arms, she'd mentioned lightly that Hudson and Luz were hosting his friends for a fancy dinner. She'd paused from the exercise momentarily to show Eusebia her daughter's post. Luz's skin had settled into the darker tones of the summer—cafecito rich and warm, hardly any milk there—making her teeth startlingly whiter. Her eyes sparkled, mischievous, a dare in the parted mouth—her cheekbones even more pronounced in bliss. How long had Eusebia worried about Luz? Fearful if she wasn't around to take care of her, she'd somehow fall apart? Look at her now.

Feliz como una lombriz, Cuca had said, as if reading her thoughts, chuckling, speaking between labored breaths about how inconsolable Luz had been, at having lost her job, at not getting any calls back. Sometimes pain is the only way to carve your path to a happy life, Cuca said. Eusebia was about to ask Cuca if all her pain had sculpted a happier life, but Cuca had gone on, after stopping her exercise at last, tapping the phone with force—now, **that,** that's the look of a woman getting her back blown out regularly. Won't you miss Vladimir? she'd asked.

Eusebia wouldn't miss Vladimir, who was overloading his suitcase in their bedroom as Cuca went on and on. Vladimir, eager to leave, eager to deal with the final details of the construction. She wouldn't miss their past either, whatever younger self she used to be, always with her head in the clouds—allowing herself to be so easily led down a road she'd rather not travel. She would be fortified by Vladimir's and Luz's absence. Already, it was as if her bones encased stronger bones, her skin covered steel. Cuca picked up speed on the ground, the array of scars wrinkling and releasing with the strain. Eusebia wondered briefly if her sister could tell that her body was now different, too.

A bit of wind made its way to Eusebia's neck as she rose to offer Vladimir a hand with his packing. She found him finished, suitcase zippered and upright. She felt a delicious row of goosebumps down her spine. Beyond him, through the window, the wind rustled the leaves outside. She had a strange premonition then, that unless she acted fast, she would never see the trees outside change colors, bare their limbs as they reached outward, upward. It would be her clothes inside a suitcase, locked up. And there would be many different sets of eyes enjoying the view. Was it La Otra, sending her a reminder from deep inside her own body?

La Otra had made no further visits in the last month. At first, she'd been disappointed. But over time, Eusebia saw that, too, as a sign that she was good on her own, armored with the will to triumph over dire circumstances. The headaches, that sense of malaise, were a thing of the past, too. Had been replaced by a tightness in her skull as if her head inflated a bit more each day. But even that feeling—of an ever-tightening expansion—beat the old debilitating headaches. Her moods didn't swing as high or low. She'd become steady, cold in a way that alarmed her from time to time. Now, across the distance, she saw Christian messing around with a bulldog, throwing a raggedy rope that the dog brought back. It was hot enough that beads popped on her forehead, and she allowed her face to relax into the heat of the day—the crickets were out and about in the park, shorts even shorter than what Cuca wore last night, cropped tops showing their bellies; even from up here, she could see how their body piercings shimmered in the sun. Children laughed, music blared out of open cars, people talked in Spanish and English, paying no mind to the beast of the building as it rose up against them. Eusebia turned away, suddenly impatient with them all, exasperated at their sheer cluelessness.

René finished eating the soup. She picked up the bowl, gratified there was nothing left—he had licked the bowl clean. She rewarded him with a cup of coffee. He inhaled the nutmeg when she placed the cup and saucer in front of him.

"You're so fancy," he said, raising a pinky up in jest, eyes taking her in—the hair, the red lipstick, the silk blouse colored the soft pink of a tongue.

She hardened toward him immediately so that

there would be no mistake. This was business. She spoke as if she'd had this conversation before, used a frequency that didn't bounce sound outward, but injected itself right into his bloodstream. René perked up. He did not ask why she wanted him to beat up Francesca. He did not blink shock or curl a lip in trepidation. She got a feeling maybe he had done much worse.

"That's going to cost you fifty dollars," he said. "I need twenty-five now."

She was disappointed he didn't ask for more. Gave him payment in full so he would know it. She was sure this was the incident to make a second set of headlines. That would get Nothar Park back in the news cycle. A beautiful young woman battered and abused. She would give pause to anyone considering a move.

"Make sure you do it at night," she said. "As fast as possible. No broken bones."

"What if she changes her mind?" he asked.

Eusebia paused to consider.

"Stop," she said.

"No money back," he said, wagging a finger at her. There was grime under his fingernail. "If she changes her mind, I'm not giving you the money back."

There was a slight tremor in his face that traveled from his eyelid to his cheek, and he blinked harder than seemed necessary. Before this day, she'd thought it was a lie, that addicts scratched so much. But look at that. René couldn't seem to get at that itch at the soft indentation of his neck, right by his protruding collarbone. He accelerated his fervor, fingernails digging out bits of flesh. Eusebia held a napkin against his neck, stilling his hand, and noticed, as she brought the napkin to her lap, bits of him that came away like grape skin, curling.

#5. PHYSICAL VIOLENCE

Eusebia faltered when she walked into the hospital room and saw Francesca's face. One hand went to her own forehead in horror, the other to her mouth. Francesca's left eye was swollen shut. The right side of her face was bruised, scratched. On her chin, a cut had required stitches. The scar there would remain, even when the rest of her face healed.

"I did good?" Francesca lisped, words barely above a slur, mouth barely moving.

"You did real good," Eusebia said. Her C-section scar, after so many years numb, began to throb.

Francesca had volunteered without question, had offered her body and face, once Eusebia mentioned the U visas meant to protect undocumented immigrants who witnessed or suffered crimes. Francesca had lived in the neighborhood most of her life, since she'd arrived at eight years old. But her parents, who even became US citizens when she was in high school, didn't sort out their child's expired visa, out of carelessness or laziness—who knew? Back then it didn't seem to matter that much, Francesca had said.

Francesca explained she'd been calm with the cops, following precisely the script Eusebia had come up with, the one that ended with her saying there are many other women like her, who get abused in other countries and then here by extension, who seem to be under the protection of no one. How it was that abuse that prompted her fleeing—saying her husband had pursued her from the Dominican Republic to the USA. The cops were very confused as to why she spoke English so well.

"What did you say?" Eusebia asked.

"I told them the entire world wants to live in America," she said. "That pleased them. But they said they didn't know anything about the asylum process. They said they would send someone from ICE."

Eusebia had left the Tongues in charge of contacting the news outlets. The women had stopped her midway through her instructions—have you lost your fucking mind? they asked. You can't have Francesca beat up. But there was no stopping now, she told them, explaining she'd volunteered. The women stared at the floor while she continued speaking to them, only nodding tersely when she asked if they were up to the task.

She told them firmly what she expected: by the time Francesca was released the next day, the cameras must be waiting. She asked them again if they were up to it. The women finally consented verbally, though they fidgeted with their eyeglass chains instead of getting to work at once.

"Am I safe?" Francesca said.

Eusebia nodded without hesitation.

"I'll make sure nothing bad ever happens to you."

Eusebia stayed with Francesca most of the day, despite the odors that reminded her of death. She worried La Otra would suddenly appear or start speaking to her in such a way she'd be forced to respond. But she remained inside, silent. When Francesca fell asleep, Eusebia adjusted the blanket so it would keep her warm. She touched the side of her face that remained unharmed, whispered, "Pobrecita."

She headed back to Nothar Park.

After the initial quiet, the noise of construction was back on. She'd asked Vladimir to point out each machine in the days before he left to go to DR, requesting that he teach her their names in English, so she could identify each distinctive noise without having to look out of her window. Bulldozers, hydraulic hammers, excavators, cranes, cement mixers, road rollers, dump trucks, backhoe loaders, asphalt pavers, water trucks, forklifts, manipulator trucks, trenchers, concrete pumps. Each machine a part of their arsenal. She had her own weapons.

Today, as she made her way through the park, she could hear distinctively the trencher cut through metal, didn't even have to turn her head. Before that? There'd been concrete poured out of those concrete pumps, fast enough, loud enough, one could almost mistake it for the sound of waves crashing. Almost. Even more men than before showed up each day, loitered on the sidewalks, invading their stores, their park benches. The metal frame had gone up so fast, so high. There it stood, dark orange and indestructible like some kind of skeleton of an alien ship.

She stopped in front of the growing structure. Sat on the spot where she'd fallen, right on the grass. Sitting beneath the tree, it seemed neither small nor frail, as it had looked from her window. She raked the root of the tree with her fingernails, right where it had been bruised by her laundry cart. That root hadn't recovered, the ridges were still there, like it had been just yesterday she fell. She dug into the fleshy root and the bark pushed back into her flesh. Splinters. It hurt. Another wind tunnel swept up her hair. The gust swerved around the trunk, a coil up through those branches, pushing the bright leaves down, then lifting them up. Water, snow, sunlight all get absorbed, but when wind hits a tree, the tree splits it in half like a pair of opened legs. Eusebia thought herself the tree. She was stronger than she looked, could be dangerous when it was needed. She rose, split the wind.

The Tongues watched her from their spot in front of the building. They were waiting for her, and by the set of their jaws, she could tell it wasn't good news.

She had her own bad news to contend with. Should she tell them? There would be no asylum for Francesca. At the library, she'd asked a woman at the front desk to show her how she would find information on U visas, after they mentioned it on **Primer Impacto** as a true path to citizenship. It had taken a lot of time to understand the process, to get an operator to pick up her phone call, answer her queries. There was a backlog of tens of thousands of people who had applied. She found articles online of people who'd gotten deported after they'd come forward, before their application had been reviewed. She'd have to get back early, make sure she got Francesca out of the hospital before the police sent ICE. What in the world had she done to this girl?

There's a version of this where you don't go far enough, La Otra had said.

Eusebia knew it must have been this moment she'd been talking about. Seeing Francesca so hurt had left her feeling revulsion—at herself. But revulsion at Francesca, too, for being so trusting. Why hadn't that silly girl looked up the information? Figured out Eusebia didn't know what she was talking about? Francesca as a stand-in for Eusebia herself, who'd always trusted that hard work, faith, and focus would be rewarded. That life had an internal logic that should bend toward justice. But did it? If anything, the last month showed her how small she was, how small they all were. She'd orchestrated several additional rounds of theft, the looting of private property—she'd paid for people's insurance herself, to ensure they'd be able to replace what was stolen. And what did she get for that? There was now an open investigation, the insurer claiming fraud because there were too many similarities in the way the crimes had been conducted—too short a time line between getting a policy and filing a claim. But most devastating: the building itself. Nothing she did slowed it down. Look at the indestructible metal crawling up toward the sky. Helpless people get squashed daily by less powerful structures than this, she reminded herself. There was no room to waver now. She invoked the gravelly tone of that old woman. Eusebia shied away from focusing on the hurt she'd caused Francesca physically; if she dug too deeply there, that raw expression on Francesca's face, that helplessness, would remind her of herself. She welcomed the numbness that encased her.

June weather now felt like July—it had grown humid, oppressive. Across the way, she noticed Juan Juan and Cuca, sharing a mango, back and forth, juice dripping down their chins. Sometimes pain is the only way to carve your path to a happy life, Cuca had said.

Every person she loved would lose everything they loved if she didn't stick to the plan. So, never mind the trepidation in her heart. Never mind the bile burning in her throat. Never mind the news that waited for her when she reached the building. No news channel would touch a story of domestic abuse; newspapers didn't consider it news. The Tongues looked at her with fresh appraisal, as if it only just occurred to them she might not know what she was doing.

"We tried our best," they said, meaning their list was complete, each fear checked. One through five. Even number five, which she'd sworn they'd never get to. They were standing right in it.

"It's time we stop," they said. They were exhausted, defeated. Their voice the white flag.

She agreed with them. They had done their best, which wasn't Eusebia's good enough. She still had more to do but no need to get into it with them. Would they even understand? Her body felt sharp enough, strong enough to splinter. Metal, concrete, flesh.

WHAT HAPPENED TO SANCHO PANZA?

At the kitchen table, she served herself a cup of coffee. Vladimir had set up the tablet so they could speak each night and see each other. And each night, at this same time, she made her coffee and sat down, called her husband, sipped until she finished her cup. Most days she didn't have to speak much. Most days, Vladimir didn't notice that she was so quiet.

"Look at this," he said, showing her the cabinets in the kitchen, their fixtures simple nickel knobs she knew would corrode in the salt air without regular maintenance. The video kept cutting in and out, and at that moment, the view she had was of the floor, shiny ceramic tiles that would be cold no matter how hot the day, how much sun came through those gorgeous bay windows.

"Like it?" he asked when the sound came back on.

"Pretty," she said, not sure what he was talking about.

His excitement was palpable. Yesterday, he'd filled up the pool, and showed her why it was called infinity, water lapping down a wall, eyes no choice but to lift, then drop at the heart-stopping view— all never-ending ocean and sky. The bathrooms would be finished next. Some days he shared the options for the finishes, and she chose based on the inflection of his voice, always a tell in the question itself. Sometimes she picked the options he didn't want, to give him something to chew over until the next day, when he'd show up on her screen and talk about how the sun struck a certain paint color just so, how going a bit darker would make a statement.

Vladimir referred to his conversations with Luz and she acted like no big thing, even though her heart hammered each time. Did he know? Had he figured it out? But somehow the lie still held. He thought they were about to get a big fat check, that they'd live off it for years into their retirement.

What happened to Sancho Panza? She still hadn't worked up the nerve to ask. She kept hoping Vladimir would offer the information, reassure her he'd just moved a bit farther down the mountain. What was that about? Here she was, the strongest, most powerful she'd ever been, and still, when it came to Vladimir, she couldn't say the things that needed to be said, couldn't ask the questions that needed answers.

"We've accomplished so much in just the week since I touched down. The new appliances should arrive tomorrow."

She smiled brightly, so glad this had worked out as she intended. "I can't wait to see it. Hope they don't mess them up."

"Can't wait to show you," he said.

She blew him a kiss, hung up. Look at that, last sip of coffee, not warm. Hot.

Her phone rang, and she picked it up immediately without noticing who was calling, thinking Vladimir had forgotten to show her some other ridiculous thing in that damn house. But no. Francesca, crying on the phone. They were releasing her early, something to do with her medical insurance not covering overnight stays.

"Calm down," Eusebia said. "I'll come get you right now."

One of the nurses had said this might be a godsend, then confided to Francesca the police had recently changed procedure and were arresting undocumented patients right out of the hospital. "They have my home address," Francesca said, voice rising.

"I have it all under control," Eusebia said. She grabbed her purse and rushed out of the apartment. What would she do if ICE came to get Francesca right out of their building? Well, she wasn't going to worry about that. Raúl had been overreacting just like this, and in the end it all worked out the way she intended. To make Francesca's sacrifice worthwhile, she had to put the remainder of the listed items in play. The ones she'd erased so carefully, confident they'd never have to resort to that. But what could she do next? She knew she had no option, otherwise everything else would have been for nothing. Wouldn't that be a bigger violence? Letting those people win?

CHAPTER NINETEEN

Luz Guerrero

ADMISSION

Raenna eyed her manicured fingernails for a long moment. When she raised her eyes, Luz couldn't help but admire her makeup, those false lashes that extended forever, how even when she was annoyed as all hell, she was still the most elegant person in the room.

"So, even if I can talk Frances into increasing the salary," she said slowly, "you wouldn't go work for her?"

"I wouldn't," Luz said.

"And what is your plan?" Raenna said, savoring her red wine. Luz swallowed the last of the tres leches flan. Luz took her time, slowly considering her words, worried less about offending Raenna and more about being able to explain how she felt. The Pinotage in Raenna's glass was the richest hue of burgundy—so deep it was almost black. Raenna closed her eyes in pleasure.

"You sure you don't want a glass of wine?" she asked. "This vintage is superb."

This was Raenna, offering peace, a way back in. Around them, the scene was familiar, soothing in its regularity. They were back at the Secret Place, where Luz had first found out she would be losing her job. The waiters hurried about, just as they'd always done, only this time, there were new faces. Henry gone, struck with the lightning good luck of a smashing art debut. Won't have to work another day in this shitty job in his life, Raenna had said. The branches of the trees had been replaced with full floral arrangements, striking, extravagant, a mixture of Caribbean-inspired flowers and fruit. Birds-of-paradise, a branch holding lemons. It reminded her of Cuca's dress, when she came back from DR.

Luz had finally agreed to meet Raenna to talk about her choices because she felt they both deserved some closure. And after that fight with Hudson, she realized it was important to speak for herself, to confront the people she feared disappointing. Now she questioned that decision.

"Rae, I don't really have a plan," Luz said. "I'm going to take some time to figure out what to do next. Thanks to the new severance package, I can take time."

"What do you call the time you've been off work?" Raenna said. "What has it been? Two months?"

"A bit less than that," Luz said. "I'm going to figure it out. Please don't worry about me."

"I'm not worried," Raenna said sharply, "I'm sharing the privilege of hindsight. I've put so much energy into helping you grow, thinking you were a different person. But this? Makes no sense. You're pissing away your life. Your education. Your talents."

"You keep saying that," Luz said.

Luz scraped the plate with her spoon, licking the last bit of her dessert.

"You're going to regret this decision," Raenna said. "I know that."

"Maybe," Luz said. She left it like that, feeling Raenna's judgment closing in around her like a full-body cast. She needed to get away from this conversation.

"I thought for sure, when you lost your job, you'd get angry. A chip on a shoulder can be a great motivator to do more, achieve greatness. You know the fight we have ahead? As women? We all need to have a fire in our belly, let it ignite every decision. Only way we can multiply."

Luz was quiet, and then, like a lightbulb: "So, you had me fired so that I would get angry, and become great? Become your duplicate?"

"I didn't get you fired, Luz," Raenna said, in a tone meant for a petulant child. "But I didn't argue against it, which I could have done. I thought it would be good for you, to wake up, to get more aggressive, develop edge. Never in a million years could I have thought this would be the outcome."

"I'm making my own way," Luz said, surprised that she wasn't hurt by the news, that somewhere deep inside, she'd known a version of this was likely what had happened. "It's my life. I just don't understand why I was chosen. I still don't get it."

"There was a favor owed by one of the partners, a young lawyer we had to bring in. We just had to make room. No one thought you'd sue or raise a stink. Or say anything, really. You'd always been so reserved, falling in line without question. Unfortunately, you made an easy target. I thought it would help you grow. Don't you want to be great? Very few people get a chance to truly be great at something in their lives. Don't you want that for yourself?"

Soft music came out of hidden speakers. Luz allowed herself to appreciate it. There were drums, a güira, the music decidedly Caribbean. At the tables round them, everyone was so focused, so serious—even the ones who shimmied their shoulders to the beat—with a stance that said they were ready for battle, everyone poised for triumph. Today, she didn't mistake that poise for power. She noted how strained people were, at each table. How dull their skin, how quickly they drained each glass.

Luz had taken the terrible shoes off under the table when they'd first sat down, and now, as she put them back on, she wondered at all those years she'd punished her feet. For what? She'd even worn a suit, because she knew she was going to be in this place, among these people, and didn't want to be mistaken for the help. Now she found the silhouette so restrictive. She knew it was lame, not having the best, most perfect plan in place, but it occurred to her, as Raenna yawned—not a fake yawn, a real, bored yawn—to accept her own insight as wisdom. Rejecting the path she wouldn't follow was perhaps more important than knowing the one she did want to follow. She was proud of herself for that. She raised a hand at the waiter, asked for the check.

"You don't have to pay for lunch," Raenna said.

"I know," Luz said. She decided this would be the last time she saw or spoke to Raenna, for the rest of her life. "But I insist."

A POLICE VEST, WITH WHITE LETTERING

As she left the restaurant, a cryptic text from Mami:

I need you for a few hours today, come straight to Francesca's apartment.

Luz, grateful to finally hear back from Eusebia, grabbed the subway uptown. She'd left her mother a voicemail just that morning because she'd decided enough was enough—her mother had been ignoring the texts she sent asking if it was okay for her to drop by. Whatever distance, space, her mother thought she needed had turned into an impasse. Some people she willingly let go of, but Mami? Now was the time to dig in, resolve their issues, move on. She could acknowledge she'd made a big mistake, had been taking her mother for granted, and she would do whatever she could to get things back to normal.

Before she rang the bell to Francesca's apartment, Eusebia opened the door as if she'd been peeking through the peephole. Eusebia kissed her cheek, pausing to frame her face in her hands. "¡Qué linda!" she said, taking in the suit, the shoes.

Luz knew she was full of shit for not explaining in that moment that the suit didn't signal a return to her old life. But she wanted to savor this moment of intimacy between the two of them as long as she could.

"You look too skinny, Ma," she retorted. "Already missing Papi so much you're skipping meals? And why are you in here in the dark?"

Luz kicked off her shoes, hung her expensive purse on the back of a nearby chair. Francesca's taste hadn't changed much since they were kids growing up in Nothar Park. Everywhere in her apartment, bright girly décor—pink chairs, and fluffy pillows that sparkled even in the dimming sunlight. When she asked where Francesca was, Eusebia pointed to the bedroom's closed door. Francesca had been asleep for hours, she said, under the influence of heavy painkillers.

"Painkillers for what?" Luz asked, flipping on a light switch.

Eusebia squinted. She mentioned offhandedly there'd been an incident—Francesca had been assaulted.

"What? By whom? When?"

But Eusebia ignored Luz, told her she had an important errand to run and would be right back.

"Don't let anyone in here," she said, "under no circumstances, no matter who."

Eusebia froze, and Luz heard her say something under her breath about invisible number six. Then she turned around, scratched her forehead, said, "I really hope we don't have to get to invisible number seven."

"Are you all right?" Luz was puzzled at Eusebia's odd behavior. She thought her mom was talking about the Dominican lottery, or maybe a dream. Did she hear right? "What do you mean, invisible numbers?"

Eusebia inhaled deeply. "Never mind," she said. "Just don't let anyone in. Not anyone. Not for anything."

Eusebia's eyes were set deep in their sockets, dark circle bruises on her skin. Maybe she hadn't been sleeping well since Vladimir left? Or was something else going on?

"You don't look so good, Ma," Luz said.

"I'm better than I've been in years," Eusebia snapped,

staring hard at Luz until she was forced to look away. "I'll be back."

As soon as Eusebia left, Luz called Vladimir.

"Something is not right with Mami," she said, and on the other end, Vladimir was silent. "Have you noticed anything strange lately?"

"Nothing strange," Vladimir finally said. "She's been excited about all the work in the house. I would have noticed if something was off. She'll be much better when she's breathing clean air, relaxing in this pool. Wait until you see it, Luz."

Luz was about to tell him what just happened, about Francesca being assaulted and Eusebia's strange reaction, but Vladimir flipped the camera, went full steam into construction mode, discussing all the minor details that had to be taken care of that day. She decided to keep it to herself. What would he be able to do from DR, except worry?

"Hearing someone talk about paint drying is way worse than watching paint dry," Luz said.

"Fine," Vladimir said, flipping back to his face, "I will speak to you tomorrow."

How did it go with Raenna, Hudson texted, soon as she hung up.

She's still an asshole.

You ok? Want to talk?

In the quiet of Francesca's apartment, Luz placed the phone face-down on the coffee table. Surely this was what happened when you stopped working with someone, eventually you drifted apart? But she felt uneasy, unsettled by Raenna's admission—even if at the moment she'd heard it, she'd been anything but surprised. In retrospect, she felt she should have reacted with outrage, but knew that would have been posturing—hoping to elicit respect from Raenna. She was done trying to prove herself.

The morning after their fight, she'd woken up to find Hudson scooped behind her, his arm a little heaven of warmth around her. She, the little spoon. He'd woken up moments after she had, maybe sensing her restlessness. Still fired up from the night before, she'd turned to him, ready to get back into it. But his expression had stunned her—he seemed afraid of what she was about to say, bracing himself—for what? Did he think she'd walk away that easily?

I don't want to be anywhere else, she'd whispered. He breathed a sigh of relief. But she continued, I can't move as fast as you're moving. Can we go one day at a time? He'd nodded, a shadow of a new expression passing his features so quickly she hadn't been able to catch its meaning. She didn't push for an explanation, knowing it was his turn to figure out what he was willing to accept and not accept when it came to her. With their feelings deepening each day, she had no doubt they'd work it out.

The past week had felt like a new beginning. She allowed a proud smile at herself. "Check me out," she said aloud. She'd released herself from whatever expectations Raenna held over her—which were really expectations she'd shackled onto herself. She had established her boundaries with Hudson—**she** would be the one setting the cadence. And now here she was, ready to tackle the most important relationship of them all—as soon as Mami came back.

Her phone buzzed again. Ruby this time. Any chance you want to meet up for coffee this week? Everyone feels like shit about dinner.

Luz wondered if Hudson was aware that Ruby had reached out. She hadn't shared her phone number at dinner, so he must have given it to her. Had he asked them to make peace?

Just as she made to call him, the front door opened.

"Did you forget something?" Luz asked.

Eusebia summarily dismissed her. "I got it from here," she said. "I'll stay with Francesca." As if that's all it would take to get rid of Luz. She'd hardly been gone for half an hour.

"Ma," Luz said, "don't you think this has gone on long enough? Can we try at least to have a grown-up conversation?"

Eusebia took a step back and leaned against a doorframe. By the raised eyebrow, Luz knew what she was about to say—only one grown-up in this room. And she was thankful Mami held that tidbit back.

"Being with that man is a mistake," Eusebia said.

"How can you say that?" Luz asked. "You don't know him."

"I know men like him," Eusebia said.

"You don't know anything about him. There's so much more to him than you think."

"All men like him do is take, take, take."

"I'm in love with him, Ma," Luz said, surprising herself. She swallowed hard, went on. "I want you to get to know him, maybe see why?"

"You don't love him. You love the freedom you have right now. He's just a part of it. You will regret it if you stay with him, believe me. Can't you see how big of a mistake he is? This is?"

"Any way you look at it, it's my mistake to make. Anyway. I don't want to talk about Hudson, Ma. I want to talk about us. We've had enough space, don't you think?"

Eusebia sat next to Luz on the girly pink love seat. She took Luz's hand, sandwiched it in her hands. Luz's body relaxed, and for a moment, it was as if they could find their way back to the way things used to be between them. Luz remembered that afternoon on the couch, her mom's soft hands oiling her dry scalp. The way her mom had always been the scaffolding, giving her strength to be upright.

"Time," Eusebia said. "You said you needed some time to figure out what you're going to do with your life. Have you figured it out? Are you closer today than you were a month ago?"

Luz felt as if she'd been struck. Her bare toes dug into the shag rug.

"I don't want you to be embarrassed. I want you to ask yourself these questions. How is running around with some rich man helping you figure out what you should do with your life? From where I'm standing, it just looks like you're being someone's toy, not much better than a whore."

"Wow," Luz said. She removed her hand from in between her mother's. They were quiet for some time.

"That came out wrong," Eusebia said, eyes skirting from side to side, unfocused, a bit frantic. "I don't think you're a whore, but you're acting like a whore."

"That's not much better," Luz said. She wished she could keep all the emotion from thickening her voice. It was as if Raenna and Eusebia had coordinated their attacks, aimed right at her gut. Luz stood, picked up her purse, put her terrible shoes back on. "How does dating a man I like make me a whore, anyway? I'm really sorry you're having such a hard time with my decisions."

"Look, it's not like I don't want things to go back to normal between us," Eusebia said, as if she hadn't heard a word Luz had said. "I could use your help here, in the neighborhood. There's so much that has to get done if we want to keep everyone safe. The Tongues, they're useless, you know? You're kind of the only person I can trust."

"Of course you can trust me. I'd love to help," Luz said. "But what are you talking about?"

"I can't talk to you about it unless you break up with him. Can you agree to that? For me? Can you let that terrible man go?"

"He doesn't have anything to do with us, Ma. I will help in any way I can."

Eusebia smiled, stood up, did a little dance. "I knew it! I knew you'd agree."

"No," Luz said, "I'm not going to break up with Hudson. What do you need help with? I'll do that."

"You're being selfish," Eusebia said, pacing back and forth. "You're wasting your life. Wasting it!"

Eusebia turned her back on Luz. Then turned to face her again. Screamed, at the top of her lungs, "You're a total waste!"

Just then, a hard knock on the door. Luz, who stood closest to it, opened it and several men rushed into the apartment. They wore helmets, and black vests with the words POLICE and ICE in white lettering.

"Which of you is Francesca Ruiz?"

Eusebia froze in silence, then pointed toward the closed bedroom door.

One of the men aimed his gun at the door as he opened it. He disappeared into the room and emerged moments later with a sleepy Francesca stumbling next to him, still half asleep. He was trying to handcuff her but was having a hard time.

Luz's hands went up to her mouth, shocked at Francesca's injuries. Her face was bruised asphalt black; she was almost unrecognizable. Then, suddenly sobering to what she was witnessing, Luz stood to her full height.

"Where's the warrant?" she said.

"Excuse me?" one of the men said.

"I need to see your warrant," Luz said. "You can't just grab someone out of their home without a warrant."

"I'm going to need you to back out of the way unless you want to be arrested, too," he said.

Luz turned her cellphone on, started livestreaming on her social.

"I'm a member of the New York State Bar," Luz began. "You're on a livestream," she said, shocked that her voice sounded so calm. She hoped they couldn't see her legs shaking. "I need to see your warrant. It's a reasonable request."

The two men shared a look, let Francesca go. "Turn the phone off," one of them said.

"Unless you show me a warrant, I demand you leave this apartment right now. You can't return until you have a warrant for her arrest."

One of them nodded, asked her again, slowly, to turn off the phone.

Luz complied, hearing something in his voice that she could trust, but that also scared her.

"We're going to wait outside until another officer brings the warrant, but no one can leave."

The women nodded. One of the men gestured for Luz to come help him put Francesca back in the room, while the other got on his walkie-talkie, spoke loudly about the status of the warrant. Francesca was so out of it she rolled over on her bed, went back to sleep as if nothing had happened.

The men left, and Luz immediately texted Angélica, asking if she could step outside the building, tell her what was going on. Within moments, Angélica wrote back, said there were a ton of other officers standing by the entrance. WTF is going on? she asked.

"Ma," Luz said, shaking. "Did you know ICE was coming here? Is that why you said not to let anyone in?"

Eusebia was distracted, looking at her phone. "I bought her a ticket so she can go back to DR. I filled out a U-visa form for her, it's been received." She turned her phone over so Luz could see a confirmation email.

"Francesca isn't undocumented, Ma," Luz said.

"What?" Eusebia said. "Yes, she is. She said it herself."

"No, she's not. Her parents became citizens when she was a teenager, we were all in tenth grade. She was underage. Their status immediately transferred to her. She doesn't need a U visa. It's a different process. She just needs to put in some paperwork that shows the dates, that she was in the USA as a resident at that time, she had an active visa back then. She didn't break any law. It's the fastest process to citizenship."

Eusebia was quiet. "I knew there was a way to resolve it."

"You were about to put her on a plane? She never would have made it back here."

"All right already." Eusebia twisted her mouth.

"I'm going down to explain to them that she's not who they want. But, Ma, look at me."

Eusebia turned lucid eyes to Luz. Had she misunderstood her mother's manic episode before? "Ma, I think something is wrong with you. The rage, the secrets? I mean, you never got checked out, something is wrong."

Eusebia shook her head. "Nothing is wrong with me. I've had a hard time sleeping the last few weeks, is all. Because I'm trying to do something about the crisis happening here, in our neighborhood. There is something you can do, to help me, Luz. Are you willing to do it?"

Luz felt sick. Between Francesca's situation and now her mom, she felt torn. Who needed help first?

"Ma," Luz said, "I want to hear what you have to say, but first I need to straighten this out."

Eusebia's eyes bored into hers, insistent. It was as if she'd completely forgotten what just happened to Francesca. No, Luz had to trust her gut. Something wasn't right here.

Outside, the block had grown desolate with the presence of so many police, armored trucks. She identified and spoke to the officer in charge, explained the situation. The officer didn't buy her story for a minute, and told her so. She looked at his name tag. O'Sullivan.

"She's not an undocumented person, Officer. This is an administrative error, not a crime."

Maybe it was her unwavering voice or how tall she stood as she spoke to him. It couldn't have hurt that she was wearing her thousand-dollar suit, with her thousand-dollar shoes on. That her hair was slick tight on her head, and she had the right inflection to her voice. He stared her down a long moment before he turned to the other officers, told them they weren't going to get the warrant today, that they would be back tomorrow.

"Your best bet is this judge," he said, taking her phone, typing a name. "There's a temporary stay that can be granted for situations like this, to make sure we don't make mistakes. Your best bet is to keep her from being arrested. If she is, it won't matter whether it's an error or not."

Luz took her phone back, tried not to let on how touched she was. Quietly, she thanked him. She'd find what she needed in Francesca's apartment, no doubt. The girl had been the most organized person they'd known as kids. She would still have every report card from third grade on. Luz would get her parents to locate the originals of their naturalization papers. With precision, she'd sort this out. Without a second thought, Luz grabbed a taxi, determined to find and talk to this judge.

CHAPTER TWENTY

Eusebia de Guerrero

#6. [. . . .]

As soon as Luz left, Eusebia rushed to the Tongues'
apartment. When she mentioned that word the
first time, all three women collectively gasped, gave
her a horrified look. But Eusebia would not be dis-
suaded by their reaction. She was certain, short of
someone's death, this single act would put a stop to
all the nonsense around the park. Eusebia asked the
Tongues: What was a body worth, in the end, when
they were never safe?

She reminded them of José García, how those
words had been carved in his small back. She tried
to get them to understand, how the ICE agents
had barged in, guns loaded, triggers ready to be
pulled. They'd looked at Francesca as if she wasn't
even a person—just a worthless bug. They'd looked
at Luz and Eusebia the same way.

"No one is safe," Eusebia said. "Don't you

understand? None of us. At least this would be a sacrifice worth something."

Eusebia forced stability against the feeling of expansion and contraction in her head.

She told them that in the USA, people had always used their bodies in protest, in order to gain rights—it was the only effective way to make real change.

Not one of the Tongues made eye contact with her. One of them fiddled with her cellphone. Another turned the television off. The third drummed her fingers against her thighs. Until, she thought, finally! Her words had worked as intended, woven a spell around them, a coil tightening around and around, bringing them closer to the mission. She was sure that in the end, they'd be horrified but accepting, willing to volunteer. There was logic in what she said! Like in any real community, the old women always know when it's their time to acquiesce, to make room for the younger generation to take over; it is because of their sacrifices the rest of us get to live a better life, Eusebia reminded herself. They had a clear responsibility.

"What if we use the weapon that has been used to terrorize us, to win?" she said.

When they finally peeled their eyes off their distractions and confronted her face, sadness carried weight. So much disappointment that Eusebia thought it might crush her.

"For you to ask that of us, it's unforgivable, Eusebia."

Which one of them said that? Eusebia was dumb-founded. She couldn't respond. She tried to gather thoughts to further move them, to make them see.

"It all ends now," they told her silence. "We've done enough."

Done? Eusebia ignored their outrage, dismissed their questions, was unmoved by their hurt. She pointed a finger at them. "A bunch of fucking cowards," she said, in a gravelly voice that wasn't her own. "You and you and you. Cobardecobardecobarde."

CONSENT

On the last Friday of June, Eusebia cooked the best meal she'd made in her life. She roasted a pig shoulder and boiled root vegetables. The rice had coconut as a base, and black beans so tender they'd dissolve on touch, on any tongue. She cooked egg-plants right on the stove, letting the smoke alarm ring on and on and on as she charred the flesh. She fried green plantains, smashed them, then refried them. She sliced through a head of cabbage and made the thinnest bed for a salad, and on top of it there were carrots and tomatoes and cucumbers. Only at the end, when she'd finish boiling the beets, and held them in hand, slicing them into perfect bite-sized cubes, and laid them with the rest of the veggies on that salad, only then when she was done, and she saw the red on her hands, such a vibrant red, did she remember that day in the park. The day she fell. The day something in her broke open.

The mistake had been in the performance of the crimes. That had been her misstep.

On her tablet's screen, Vladimir's face appeared. She'd been avoiding him for a few days, but couldn't do so any longer without raising suspicion.

"Guess you're feeling better," he said. "Luz mentioned you were under the weather."

She nodded solemnly. "I invited some of the ladies over," she said, never taking her eyes off her stained hands.

"Oh," he said. "I can smell the delicious food from here."

Much too quickly, he reversed the screen, moving through this new house so fast the screen froze in and out, put her on edge. When he finished his ascent, he flipped it again, and in his eyes she saw the energy that had been missing for so many years. He plodded through the doorway and her heart did a flip—he'd treaded out onto the balcony. Lingered at the edge, so she could get a 360-degree view. The slab of rough concrete he stood on was wide open, beneath it a precipice that made her immediately fearful for his safety. He showed her options for their balcony that were up against a wall—there was clear glass, there was black wrought iron in twirling designs, and there was even bamboo, stalks tightly bound to each other that didn't let her see anything behind it.

"Which one do you like best?" he asked her, and stopped the screen on the glass, made a joke about him not giving her any hints which one he preferred. He zoomed in and out of the glass sample as he said that. His cheerful voice held the excitement of the young boy he'd once been. Right in that moment, it was as if time went backwards, revealing him as he was almost thirty years ago, pacing excitedly as he prepared for the future. He'd taken such care with his packing, making sure he was traveling light as possible as he reached for the unknown. Confused, she felt time slipping away.

She tried to say she liked the glass best, because then they'd be able to see the sea from bed. But her voice grew thick in her throat, choked her on the way out.

"Are you sure you're okay?" he asked, reversing the camera again.

She took his face in carefully. The rosy skin, now a deeper, richer brown after just a short time back home. His broad forehead wrinkled in concern, and she wanted to ask him how it was possible he'd already moved on, that he'd so easily removed Nothar Park from his life, as if their lives were a suitcase so easily transferred from place to place. Did he forget? This, the place where they'd gotten another chance at love, at finding a home in each other. Didn't he realize what they owed to the walls of this apartment? Didn't he know that without this place they would never have found a way to this day?

"Don't you miss home?" she asked him finally, over the humming of her heart.

"I miss you. Wish you were here right now."

He flipped the camera. The view was breathtaking—the ocean glistened prettily in the distance, the sky was full of fast-moving clouds. "Paradise is waiting for you, muñeca," he said. "Believe me, you won't miss Nothar Park once you get here."

She nodded agreement, told him she'd rather the tight bamboo—the view would be impenetrable. When he asked if she was sure, she told him she wanted no distractions when they were in bed— she'd have eyes for nothing but him. He seemed hurt, disappointed, and she was glad about it. Let him feel an ounce of the pain and disappointment she felt.

She threw him a kiss, made it extra loud, told him they'd have to finish this conversation when the women left their apartment, promised to call him back. When he asked her again if she was sure everything was all right, she spoke with confidence. Nothing was wrong. Not one thing. It was easy to lie to someone who preferred not to know the truth. Eusebia hung up the phone. She banged her hand against the kitchen table, each time thinking how it was just like him to let go, to pivot away from their home, their life, again, just like he'd done before. She, a rag doll, going wherever he wanted? Not this time.

RECRUITER

The women arrived. Cuca out front and Angélica bringing up the rear. There were dozens of them. No one asked how come no Tongues. By then, everyone had received notice that their buildings were converting to co-ops, or condos, or been hassled by landlords who put pressure on them to move on, move out. Eusebia bought the women beer, and played music, and let the entire thing go on until they were so full of good food and cheer, they would have consented to anything.

"So much ugliness in the world," she started. They all agreed. Who could argue with how unfair the world turned out to be? How no matter how hard they worked, they were locked in place? The little they managed to have could be taken away so quickly. Were they supposed to willingly hand it over, without a fight? Everyone shook their heads no.

She explained what they'd been doing. How a handful of them had volunteered to form a crime ring, just to scare the rich white people away. That was the root of the problem. She asked Francesca to stand up, congratulated her on how brave she'd been. All one had to do was look at her face, black-and-blue all over, to know this wasn't a joke. Eusebia told them how close they were to stopping the entire thing. But now, it had to be bigger. Only Angélica looked alarmed as she went on.

"I need your help," she said. A deep silence

enveloped the room and she knew she had them. No one moved, no one blinked. Had Luz consented to breaking her relationship with the developer, Eusebia would have invited her. They could have worked together. But Luz had made her choice. Now it was time for Eusebia to make hers.

"What would keep you from moving into a neighborhood? Whatever that thing is for you, do it or expose it. We all know enough people who privately do things they're not supposed to do, that are harmful or wrong. Make sure to call the police. We get enough reports and I bet you that building across the way won't be finished. I bet you these apartments won't sell. Our objective is to scare people. We want them to look at us and think we're monsters. Whoever is ready to sacrifice themselves, just let me know. We'll take it from there. It's all voluntary. If you don't want to be involved, it's okay. But don't get in our way."

That last part was directed at Angélica, who seemed more agitated the more Eusebia spoke. She held Angélica's gaze until she nodded agreement. Around her, each woman nodded. She saw the wheels turning, scheming under way.

Oh, what she planned to unleash into the world.

. . . ___ . . . ___ . . . ___

That night, the park lit up with cop cars like it was the Fourth of July. The news trickled to Eusebia courtesy of all her recruits, who were keeping a close tally on each incident reported, each incident exposed.

Marta from across the street called the police on her stepfather, who had been beating her mother for years while everyone looked the other way. Samantha, who found a home attendant stealing from her father's rare collection of baseball cards, had the woman arrested. And what about that pervert uncle, who everyone knew touched little girls? He went down, too. Building by building, apartment by apartment, the secrets of the neighborhood hung out to dry, torched by the light of day. Some who didn't even know what had started the series of events turned an honest eye on each other in retaliation, and in so doing made telling the truth a contagion in Nothar Park. Family members or not, if you were doing something wrong, someone was going to tell on you. The next day, Eusebia saw the telltale sign of a news camera crew in front of the dentist's office. He'd been exposed for performing illegal abortions. The dentist got taken away in handcuffs.

The Tongues confronted her. Right in front of the building, in broad daylight.

"This thing is spinning out of control," they said.

Eusebia had seen the men, the ones people had been talking about. Men no one knew, who weren't there for the construction, who didn't live there. They just showed up one day, started frequenting the park.

Taking it over, making people uncomfortable. But it didn't matter. She had everything under control.

The women went on and on. About the danger, about how she had to stop immediately. Eusebia could see what they weren't saying, fearful of losing so close to winning.

"We've almost won," she said to them, reasonably.

The women stopped speaking. Their shocked silence went out, past the neighbors who looked on curiously, across the park, until it settled on the wilting branches of her tree.

"What will you sacrifice?" she screamed at them, loudly, so they'd hear through their cotton ears. "I need a bath, get out of here."

The Tongues seemed helpless, searching beyond her, into Nothar Park for help. She made a motion with her hand, dismissing them. She crossed the street, went over to the construction site, and stared at the signs that had been posted. Telling them to stay out, of course. That it was all private property. The men continued to walk into the construction site each day. She'd seen them from her window. Would continue to come every day unless this thing ended. Now.

She walked past the Tongues on her way home, hoped they'd leave her alone, or else. And she threw them daggers with her eyes as she went past, so they'd get the message.

In the tub, she asked herself why people were such

a disappointment. All her life, she'd given those women so much, and look at them now.

As she toweled herself dry, her movements slowed down. She was tired. Tired. But this last step would put an end to all of it. A peaceful protest, a hunger strike, would bring needed attention from the media. What says sacrifice more than that? Bunch of women linking arms for their community, refusing to eat? And then, camera in position, she'd blast them off their feet with invisible number seven. They'd be on every news channel, on the cover of every newspaper.

Eusebia put on a simple dress. She went up to the safe, typed in the date she'd arrived in this country. 1-1-2-5. The gun was cold, and heavier than she expected. It was comforting, that weight. She locked it back inside the safe where Luz's birth certificate, the death certificate of her second child, and her passport all kept it company. Eusebia went out on the fire escape, enjoyed the heat of the sun. La Otra spoke softly, right from her itchy C-section scar. All the way, La Otra said. You must. On Eusebia's hand, the cold of the gun and its heaviness remained.

She had a thought. Like a premonition reaching to her from the past. A warning? Or a congratulations? She couldn't tell. And then something happened in her body; she was stuck between thought and action.

When she emerged from this strange place, she knew the truest part of her was getting farther away. She created a new list then, to hold herself accountable, to remind herself why she shouldn't ask for help or alert the others. She was deteriorating, sure. But also, look at her body, so strong, growing bigger inside of herself. People couldn't tell. She went through the list again, to remind herself why she shouldn't ask for help or alert the others. Wait. Had she had this thought? Yes. The list. What was that cold, spreading? Head? Scar? An ache, a pulse. Where was it coming from?

Eusebia, calm down, La Otra said. The list. Remember the new list, she said.

For the women and the children dead in that truck.

For the boy who had those words carved on his back.

For that nurse who had her fingers cut off.

A man's body down, for each of their bodies.

Hardly sufficient, but a place to start.

For them. For them. For them.

THE TONGUES' INTERLUDE

Of course, we had to call Vladimir, and ask him to get back as quickly as possible.

We told him Eusebia was keeping something from him, that we couldn't tell him over the phone, to buy a ticket and get back fast. Eusebia's life depended on it.

CHAPTER TWENTY-ONE

Luz Guerrero

RAIN IN THE AIR

While the entire country readied to celebrate Independence Day with fireworks, Hudson celebrated her success, which preceded July 4 by one day, with a bottle of champagne. The bottle? Same as in the restaurant. She savored the champagne along with her satisfaction. Francesca, granted full citizenship, with unprecedented speed. Over the last few days, Luz had chosen not to respond to the cryptic text messages and missed calls from Angélica, because after the last bout with Mami, she needed a break. Now it felt odd to relish this victory away from Nothar Park. Today, Luz felt rooted. To make a real difference like that, in someone's life. It was a crazy, humbling feeling. She wanted it again and again.

Since the night of the dinner with his friends, things had intensified between them. So Luz wasn't surprised when Hudson told her he wanted to show her something special. He wanted to respect her wishes, to go slow, he said. It was a feeling he shared, wanting to relish each moment. They walked across the courtyard, past the nymph, through the double doors he had said housed storage. He unlocked the set of doors and led her into a windowless room with a high ceiling; it looked almost like a film studio space under construction—the ground beneath their feet was covered with soft grass.

"What is this place?" Luz asked.

"It's my life's work," he said.

He took a flat device that was slightly bigger than a television remote control. The room became illuminated with what seemed like soft sunlight, revealing a small park, with trees and a few benches on the side. There was a cobblestone path that led to a small fountain like the one that was in his driveway.

"I know things between us have been kind of weird since, well, whatever," he said. "But I've always trusted my instincts. I want to show you something." He clicked a few buttons on the control and then started speaking to the empty space.

"Wind," he said.

Luz felt a soft breeze on her skin.

"Rain," he said.

A light drizzle fell on them both. Luz smiled, relaxing, giving in. She took off her sandals, felt the soft wet grass on her feet.

The rain began to dampen her Frida Kahlo tank top.

"At the rate the world is warming," he said, "humans won't be able to live on the surface of the planet for long. I think in another twenty years, we'll have to spend most of our time indoors. We've been working on creating what that life will be like."

"We who?" she asked. "And what life will be like? For whom?"

Luz touched a nearby tree. The color of the bark was perfect. But there was something about the feel of it. Her fingertips could tell it was plastic.

"I don't want to scare you. I know it's early. But you should know how I feel."

As he spoke, with the soft rain drizzling around them, Luz felt the moment couldn't be more magical. Standing in this otherworldly space in her favorite shirt, mist all around, while the man she loved kissed her. It gave the moment a shimmering evanescence. And when he told her that he thought of her as his home, she said she felt the same, that just like him, she wanted to be together all the time.

She was fascinated by what he'd built. But she couldn't deny it made her uneasy.

"I want you to understand my calling," he said, "so you'll understand me. I'm not in the business of making tall buildings. I'm working to transform the way humans live. To mirror the experiences we have today, like smelling fresh air, or feeling rain, but indoors, underground, for when the time calls for it. There is going to be a day, in our lifetime and not that far away, when we won't be able to experience weather outside."

Luz felt the force of his ambition.

"As soon as I'm done with Neruda on the Park, I'm going to move out of New York. The London project is a large-scale replica of this. That's what I'll be doing."

"This is insane," Luz said, clearing her throat. "What does that mean, large-scale?"

"We're going to start with a self-contained residential neighborhood."

"I don't understand."

"We already have the funding, it's massive. We're going to create the first underground community, and we'll select the people who come as part of this first project. I want you to come with me."

"To live in an underground community?" Luz took a step away from him.

"You don't belong in Nothar Park, Luz. With those people. This neighborhood brimming with criminals. They destroy what they're supposed to love. You belong with me."

"Whoa. Slow down."

"You don't have to say anything. Neruda on the Park is still at least four months of work for us. I want you to know how serious I am about you."

"Why? Why are you saying this now?"

"I don't want you to get sucked into all the drama

of the people from your past," he said. "I'll support you, in whatever you want to do, but I want to be sure you understand my plan for us."

She was quiet. Of all the ways she thought things might have turned out . . .

"You don't belong in Nothar Park," he repeated; then, after a moment: "Why do you look so sad?"

"Because you've given up. This entire place, this amazing gift you have, you could still use it to save what we have. You want to hide away, instead of working to fix the problem."

"There's no hope, Luz. It's too late for that."

"If you used your talents to work on dealing with our current climate, a breakthrough could happen. One that turns things around."

"No. What I'm showing you here, this is the future."

Could she do it? Could she leave everyone, everything behind? Go with him? They sat on a bench as she looked around in both awe and fear at what he'd created. The roof above them was a series of screens that masterfully created the illusion of sunlight. But she could see the seams. They sat there for a long time. Finally, she shook her head.

"What does that mean?"

"I'm not ready to give up or run away. I know that."

"I'm going to leave New York City, for good, and I really hope you come with me."

"But who gets to live in this trial community?

I mean, it must be astronomical, the amount of money it costs to make this work."

Hudson was silent.

"It's for rich people, and whomever the rich bring with them?"

"The homes will go up for sale. Whoever can afford them can come."

"But you said there was a selection process. Who makes the selection?"

Now that they'd been down there for a while, she could smell the artificial scent of everything. It smelled like a new toy.

"It's not a conspiracy. We want to make sure we are cultivating the right group of people, that's all. You could help with that part, with the criteria, if that makes you happy."

"I'm still wrapping my head around it all. But I know that I'm not ready to give up and hide," Luz said.

They made their way up the stairs. The harshness of a heat wave underlined the relevance of his work. One day, the entire world would likely be looking to him to build underground shelters. He was offering her a place in that future, beside him. When he reached over to kiss her, she kissed him back. She would have so much time to decide what to do, ask all the questions. And she didn't underestimate her ability to persuade him in a different direction, either. Who had the power to control her own fate? She did, of course.

HUNGER STRIKE

The mural in Nothar Park was eerie. **Go Home,** in blinding white letters. That black background made it pulsate. Ahead of her, Luz watched the construction. The building was tall, towering over the neighborhood. The concrete walls were messy, rough, all the way up five flights. Above that, it was still metal frames, jutting up.

She turned and bumped into Angélica, recalled the missed texts and unattended-to voicemails. She'd been standing too close to her for what probably had been several moments, by the way Kenya and Paris were laughing. She imagined Angélica making funny faces behind her as Luz gawked with derision at the building.

"Hilarious," she said, leaning over to give her a kiss on the cheek. Kept on walking ahead.

"Wait," Angélica said. "We have to talk."

The girls ran ahead of them as they slowly made their way west. They passed the construction site, and Luz counted the women who stood with linked arms, chanting a song she couldn't make out. The sight gave her pause. These women, many of whom had been at Cuca's party, had gotten so much work done in the past two months. Luz noticed their surgically tiny waists, the glute implants, all slightly square, that made them all identically oddly shaped. She remembered saying to Mami, to Papi, that the women had a right to do whatever it took to feel good about themselves. That it couldn't go both ways, the women being criticized for not being perfect, then criticized for doing something to match the standard. But seeing these women—what they'd done to their bodies to fit in—it made her sad. What about a world where they could just be the way they were?

"What the hell is going on here?" Luz asked.

"The women started a hunger strike three days ago, because of the construction, the lease buyouts."

The heat moved up from the concrete, made Luz feel dizzy. "I have to head home," she said.

"I'm really worried about your mom," Angélica said.

Luz turned to her. "That makes two of us. But why are you worried?"

"You know all the weird stuff that's been going on in this neighborhood? It's all been her. She's the mastermind behind it."

"What do you mean, all the weird stuff?"

They headed to the front of their building. When they arrived, Luz leaned her hand on a wall, feeling faint. The wall was wet, and the moisture had the same white, powdery consistency she'd felt on that day long ago. She raised her fingers to her nose. Same powdery scent.

"It's going to sound crazy, I know," Angélica started.

"Just say what you're going to say."

"It's a long story," Angélica said. "The whole thing started from a good place, you know. She thought if she did a few minor crimes around the neighborhood, they would stop trying to sell the apartments, maybe stop building the luxury condos."

"That's insane," Luz said. "It would never work. Is that why you've been calling me?"

Angélica nodded.

"I'm so sorry I didn't call you back."

Angélica shrugged. Went on: "I'm worried about what she's planning to do next. I'm worried something is wrong with her. She was talking to all of us and it was like she was someone else. The whole thing is out of a fucking movie, or a front page." She made quotation marks with her fingers and said, "Rolos-Wearing Doña Coordinates Major Crime Spree."

Luz couldn't laugh. She thought of the day she'd been in Francesca's house, the way her mother had sounded so unhinged. With a chill, she thought about what happened to Raúl's store. And then, more alarmingly, what happened to Francesca. "You don't mean Francesca's injury?"

Angélica nodded. "All of it."

A sinking feeling engulfed her. What to do with it? Mami came down the street, and walked right past them into the building, looking calmly at Luz as she went on, smiling in a small way without recognition, as if they were strangers.

"Holy shit," she said at Mami's retreating back.

"El diablo," Angélica whispered. "You want me to come with you? In case you need help?"

"You got your hands full," Luz said, hurrying after her mother. "Just don't go far."

IDIOT ROBOTS

"Ma," Luz called from the hallway. No response. From the bathroom, the sound of water running. When Eusebia emerged, she was smiling.

"Who are you?" she said. "Why are you in my apartment? How did you get in here?" There was something in her voice that made it thick, raspy.

"What's going on with you?" Luz asked. "I'm Luz, your daughter."

Eusebia's eyes warmed in recognition. "Oh, Luz? For a minute you didn't look like yourself."

She went to the kitchen. "I have to get back to the women on the line."

"Ma," Luz said. "Stop. We need to get you to a hospital."

Mami stopped.

"No. I'm not going to a hospital. I'm not sick. Do you know what I've lost in a hospital?"

"Is it true?"

"I don't have time for you, Luz. It's all going to end today."

"What's going to end today?"

Luz felt sick. There were growing needles in the nape of her neck. Mami's voice was calm, steady.

"I gave Christian Vladimir's gun," she said. "René is okay with the plan. Once real blood spills, they have to stop building that thing. Right? And the women can get back home, to work. I did it for them. For the little girl in the hospital, and the nurse. You remember them? You were so little. The nurse, who do you think cut her fingers? I bet you it was her father. Imagine what else he must have done to her. Of course you don't remember them. You were so little. Still on my breast, so greedy, you were. Do you remember how you used to clamp down on my nipple? Even back then you were so selfish. Why are you crying? It finally will end today. Is that why you're crying? That happens to me sometimes, I get so tired the only thing that helps is a good cry. But you know my eyes, they won't let the tears out. Holding it all in! It took so much work to pull it off. But today, it'll end."

Luz was shaking; the sick feeling had transformed to a chill. It made her shiver.

"Ma," she said, speaking slowly. "Where is Christian going to do it?"

"Okay," she said, with a childish shriek. "You got me! That lawyer brain is so smart. René didn't agree. I just told Christian he did."

Luz sat down. She put her face in her hands. From downstairs, the sounds of reggaetón blasting out of a car radio grew loud, then receded, like a wave hitting a seashore.

"Eventually," Eusebia went on, with that deadly calm, "we had to take the choice away. We had to say, What's worth more? The life of a drug addict or of everyone else? To avenge history? You know the answer. You know how much I adore everyone in this neighborhood. René, you know, he had so much potential, and you know what happened to him? Tragedy happened. That's how he became an addict, you know? He has no conscience, not anymore. He's willing to do anything, to anyone, to get high. What kind of life is that? I thought long and hard about this. It wasn't a decision I made lightly. Because there are others who deserve to die. You know who I mean. If we thought of death as an end. But death, you know, Luz, death sometimes is a gift. And I asked myself, Who deserves this gift? Who deserves to be set free?"

"Where, Ma? Where is Christian?"

"Christian just wants to get the hell out of this neighborhood. You remember how you were at seventeen. Looking around here like you deserved so much better than this. I remember that. It wasn't even hard to convince him. I said, Listen, this mess isn't going to clean itself. How can they afford an apartment? Tony about to get fired. Angélica can't keep a damn job. Isabel, God bless her, but not the best super. I told him it was his last chance to help his family, make sure they're safe, at home. He's supposed to be heading upstate at the end of August."

"That was smart, Ma. It's Christian's best chance. It will allow them to do something good with their life."

Outside, there was the sound of metal screeching against metal.

"Stop it," Eusebia screamed, in the direction of the construction.

Settling down, she twirled to the stove, turned it off, and without flinching, dipped her fingers into the boiling water, lifted the pastel by its string. With a quick twist of the wrist, she undid the knot, unwrapped the pastel, and placed it on a plate. Dropped a glob of ketchup on the top, then ate it slowly.

"We will keep our homes. I mean, they said go home on José's back, they threw him on the street like garbage. Do you remember that? It was the day you got fired. You lied to me, Luz. Pretended like you still had a job. Embarrassed me in front of the Tongues." Eusebia turned toward the stove, said to the emptiness there, "She got dressed to go to work like I was a damn fool."

Eusebia looked back at Luz. "Why do you keep crying?" she asked, this time her voice tight. "With everything I've done for you, do you think you have a right to cry?"

"Ma," Luz said, "I'm crying because I'm scared. Who were you talking to just now?"

"That old lady," she said. "The one who lives inside my body. Don't tell anybody. But she's me, in the future. Why did you lie to me? Why did you pretend you still had a job? The old tree lady came from the future to tell me I'd be a coward my whole life if I didn't go all the way. You know what your future self would say to you? Don't lie to your mother, that's what."

"I was afraid you'd be disappointed. I never should have lied. How can I help? To stop the construction, to make sure your plan works?"

Eusebia was quiet, observing Luz. She got a glass of water. Gulp, gulp, gulp.

"You're going to try to stop my plan, aren't you?"

"No," Luz said. "It's a good one."

"I know you. Always trying to do what's right. That's what I raised you for. You think their lives are worth more than our home? No, Luz. There's no stopping this. I'm not going to let you."

She stepped up to Luz, slapped her mouth, hard. Luz winced.

"You were so greedy. Are you really here to help me?"

"I swear it," Luz said.

"I believe you," Eusebia whispered. "You took my side on the lease. I know you're still loyal to me, even if you're a constant disappointment. Christian is at Juan Juan's bodega, right now. René is supposed to go in there, to rob it, but it's not a robbery, you know what I mean. Christian thinks René is in on it, because I lied. It's number seven. Invisible number seven."

She laughed.

"These people are idiots. I mean, every single one

of them. The women haven't eaten in days." She took a spoonful of her pastel. "Did you see them? Every single one of them had surgery done, after Cuca. All of them look like a bunch of idiot robots."

Luz bolted out of the kitchen, out of the apartment, the elevator working for once, down the block, inside the bodega. There was René rifling through the cash register, taking money and putting it into his pockets. Christian stood on the opposite side, with a gun pointed, their eyes closed. Luz pushed René to the side. She tried to find the words, to tell Christian to stop, that it was all a great mistake. She couldn't speak at all.

A loud sound went off and Luz was thrown against the window behind the register. She stood back up. Christian held the gun, their eyes drawn to her neck in horror. The force of the gun had pushed them back, too, and Luz could tell by the way they grimaced, dropped the gun on the floor, and cradled their limp wrist that they'd been hurt, too. Instinctively, Luz touched her collarbone and felt it then, both cold and warm, but mostly wet. There was no pain.

"I'm fine," Luz said. "Stop looking at me like that."

René recovered from the push. His expression forced her to look down, too, and see the blood, spreading on her Frida Kahlo shirt. Christian ran out of the store, leaving the gun on the floor. How could the blood spread so fast and yet her skin feel completely dry?

"Jesus fucking Christ, Luz," René said. "Why did you do that? Why would you step in front of me? It was all pretend. He was going to miss."

He wove around Luz, grabbed the gun, and ran outside. Luz followed him, trying to figure out what just happened. Down the block, Mami rushed toward her, face disfigured with screams Luz couldn't hear.

Then there was a gushing, and the blood became wet. Down her body it slid, dripping off her, puddling by her feet, covering the dark gum stains on the sidewalk. She saw it form the rivulet she'd felt on her body earlier with sweat, just this time on the sidewalk, red filling in, then filtering through each of the cracks. Had she ever seen a red that vibrant, that gorgeous? Yes. But only from her own body. This part of the street had sparkling concrete. How had she never noticed that? She touched her collarbone again and realized there was a gap of softness where once there used to be the hardness of bone. That's where the bullet had struck. When she looked toward Mami, she was amazed it was taking her so long to make her way. Then all she saw was sky, no ground beneath her feet. And how strange, when the sky turned red, too.

CHAPTER TWENTY-TWO

Eusebia de Guerrero

Eusebia stood on the fire escape overlooking Nothar Park, poised to jump. The Tongues stared intently at her from the street level, not moving, not speaking. She imagined the Tongues' reaction if they witnessed her body splattered on the asphalt. How startled they would be by the sound. Eight floors: a long way to fall. Would there be peace? The silence held peace in it, she anticipated that. She grew certain it was past that silence she'd meet her real self. The thought settled her into calm. Suddenly there was only stillness around her.

"What are you doing out there?" Vladimir asked. He extended an arm toward her.

She looked at the arm, then at the ground below.

"Muñeca," he said. "Come on."

It was as if his voice had never aged. Like maybe they were still standing in the doorway of that one-bedroom dirt-floor house back in DR. She would have said no if that had been so, I don't want you to go, I don't want to go. She would, she would speak up, if she had the chance to go back in time.

She took his hand.

Inside, they sat on the couch. He leaned back, neck hanging over the back of the maroon couch, and closed his eyes. "The pot with the pasteles was boiling over when I came in. Why are you making pasteles? The Tongues sent so much food just a few hours ago. I knew something . . ."

His voice trailed off. He breathed in and out, evenly. Maybe he'd fallen asleep? Neither had slept in the one week since Luz had been hospitalized. Eusebia listened for that hissing sound and found it missing. He must have turned the stove off.

According to the doctors, the surgery had been a success. But, inexplicably, over the last week, Luz's skin had grown gray, her eyes had sunk deep into her skull. It was her size that most alarmed Eusebia, the most chilling of all the visions to date. She'd shrunk overnight, as small as she'd been as a sickly infant. When the medicine didn't work, they turned to prayer. When the prayers didn't work, Eusebia knew what she had to do—my life for hers, she'd told God, right before she left the hospital. This was a promesa she meant to keep.

"Don't tell me I have to worry about you, too?" Vladimir asked, opening his eyes.

On her palm, right underneath her thumb, there

was a dry spot of skin filled with a bit of air. She wasn't sure how it'd happened. Other than drop those pasteles in the pot, she hadn't cooked for a while or ironed any of Vladimir's shirts or pants. But it resembled a burn of some kind. She went into their bedroom and got a needle. She punctured it and was surprised when a clear liquid emerged. It was thick like goo. It made its way down the side of her hand, and when she raised her wrist a bit, it changed direction. When she put her nose closer to it, the smell was of something dead. Smelled just like La Otra, who'd disappeared, who'd also abandoned her.

Vladimir seemed to gather himself.

"What were you doing outside?" he asked.

The phone rang. Eusebia picked it up.

"Are you okay?" Isabel asked. "I just heard you were out on the fire escape."

"I'm fine," she said, and hung up without another word.

"What were you doing out there, Eusebia?" he asked. She tried to remember the last time he called her by her real name and couldn't.

She told him. Everything.

When she left Luz hours ago, her daughter looked like she was already dead. Vladimir had embraced Eusebia before she left, each holding the other without making a sound. On the way here, she'd been asking herself whether he would ever come to learn what she'd done. What would he think? What would Vladimir do? She had no plans to be around to find out.

She considered it. Maybe he'd raise his hand to her, a thing he'd never done for as long as they'd both known each other. No, he wouldn't do that. Would he take the gun out of the holster and shoot her? No, he'd never do that.

When she was done explaining what had happened over the summer, how the events unfolded in such a way that their daughter ended up shot in Juan Juan's bodega with Vladimir's own gun, he appeared unaffected. For a moment, she feared someone else had beaten her to it. The same ones who'd commandeered him back from DR, timing nearly perfect as he'd arrived right as Luz came out of the operating room. Had he known this whole time? Over the last week, as they sat side by side, worried their child was about to die?

"All of this," he said, "because you didn't want to go back to DR."

His tone, what was in it? Heartbreak? Resignation? He was hearing this for the first time, she was sure. And now what? How to explain there was so much more to it than that? She wanted to explain the rage that had filled her, that blinded her, at having choices stolen from her, over an entire lifetime, but also that new house, the way he and Luz had planned a life she didn't want. She wanted to explain to him, about the list of the crimes that became another list of different wrongs. She couldn't find the words in her body. Maybe because the rage was gone. But no, not quite gone. She wished that headache would come back now. That throbbing fullness had made her feel powerful, in control, remorseless. The things she'd gotten people to do! And where was La Otra now? So quiet, vanished from the world, from her body. In her place a familiar hollowness.

"Yes," she said, knowing there was no space for cowardice. "That's the way it started."

"How will you live with yourself?" he asked. "Knowing if Luz dies it was your fault?"

It was a familiar effort, to take that image of her daughter on that bed, so tiny, and sew it inside herself. Luz's translucent skin allowed Eusebia to see things she'd never seen in her daughter's face, like where the veins rested. Her Luz so wilted. Eusebia pulled at the dead skin on her palm. She didn't stop at the edge, where she should have, and pulled too much skin until the edges bled.

He looked at her hand. He did not stand to get her a napkin to wipe at her blood, or some peroxide to clean it with, or a Band-Aid to cover it. Was it because he was tired?

"How am I supposed to live with the fact that you made this my fault, too?" he asked her bleeding hand. "Because I was too selfish to realize it wasn't what you wanted? And Luz, so many times she told me she thought something was wrong with you. And I said no, she's fine, nothing to worry about."

The pressure on her head came back slowly, then plunged. Was he really blaming himself? Was he fucking kidding? Was he a fucking saint?

He got up from the couch and for a moment she was hopeful he was going to leave her, so she could finish what she'd come to do. But he went to their bedroom instead and returned with her purse, his keys. He put the bag next to her on the couch, careful not to touch her.

"Were you about to jump?" he asked.

She nodded. She owed him that. The doctors said there was no explanation. Luz should have woken up. They removed her from the ICU and put her in a regular room right before Eusebia left. Maybe her body needed a bit more time, they said. But Eusebia understood she was in control. Not the devil. She knew what needed to be done, what her ultimate sacrifice needed to be.

When Vladimir first started as a cop, years before Eusebia and Luz joined him, they'd given him the George Washington Bridge as one of his routes. The entire time he was there, he would tell her years later, he was talking people out of jumping. You could always tell who the jumpers were, he would say. Those people would end up sharing why their lives were so miserable, what had driven them to that moment, standing so far above the water. Ninety percent of the time, it was loneliness, confronting a broken heart, that drew people to that edge. He used to boast that in the time he patrolled the bridge, not one of his jumpers jumped. If this police thing doesn't work out, he could get into shrinking head, his cop buddies used to joke with him. Was he thinking now how none of those people had done the things she had done? If they'd had this conversation first, would he have reached for her? Would he have pulled her back into their home?

There were lines around his eyes that extended toward his hairline. He was grayer than just a week ago, than maybe just ten minutes ago. Then with a flash she saw the truth. Contempt clouded his vision as he looked at her, unflinching. She had done that. But maybe what was worse than the contempt was the way he'd responded. He hadn't been surprised, because he knew things about people. Everyone was capable of shocking cruelty.

She contemplated the past twenty years, each of Luz's accomplishments along the way. Had it been worth it?

The house phone rang. They both stayed as they were, neither prepared to move, relieved when at last the person gave up.

Eusebia left Vladimir on the couch, spiritlessly staring into space. In the kitchen, she untied the twine, and placed each of the pasteles in Tupperware. She glanced at the pot, still steaming though Vladimir had turned it off. She heard La Otra's voice not inside her body but outside it, far away. **Don't be a coward, Eusebia.**

In one movement, she took the pot with her bare hands, felt it burn burn burn her palms. She put it high over her head, ready. Vladimir walked in right at that moment. He took the pot from her hands, and as they struggled, the hot water fell on the side of her body, burning half her stomach, all the way down to her hip. She was stronger than him for once, and so it was her force that pressed the bottom of the pot, the hottest part, against his forearm, his hand.

"Goddamn it," he said. He took the entire pot off her hands. He slammed it far from them, toward the hallway. Hot water vapor rose from the floor.

They were both breathing heavily. She felt the heat on the side of her body, fabric stuck to her side. Burn burn burn.

You gotta finish the job, La Otra said. Eusebia looked around, trying to place her voice. She sounded like she was far away, but where?

When Vladimir's cellphone rang, he picked it up. Cuca's high-pitched voice: excited, happy. Eusebia could hear it clearly: Hurry up! Get your ass over here! Luz woke up!

"Luz is the only one who matters," he said, after he hung up. "Not you. Not me. She'll need everything we have to get better."

And with that he went on ahead. Luz was the only one who mattered.

A loss is a loss. Then why? Why did Vladimir walking away from her feel so devastating? The worst loss of all. When she learned about the house on the mountain, she'd been prepared to let him go, to let him move on without her. She wiped the blood on her palm against her pant leg. Not caring that the blood would stain her pants, that the stain would never come out. She didn't bother changing. She didn't care at all about the sting of all the burning skin. She welcomed it.

CHAPTER TWENTY-THREE

Luz Guerrero

Luz awoke to the distinctive scent of burnt sugar she'd once confused with cotton candy. The source? A lidless Tupperware filled with pollo guisado right next to her bed. The caramel on the meat was the sweetness she'd been smelling for months. Not cotton candy. Caramel. And then she remembered. The scent of the first meal the Tongues had made for her family when they arrived in this country. The women had shown up at their door, a little out of breath from walking all those flights since the elevator had been out of order, bearing gifts. Mami had opened the Tupperware, and the scent had filled their apartment. Maybe we'll be okay in this place, Mami had said to Luz, pinching a piece of the sweet meat and placing it in Luz's mouth. When she tasted that sweetness, it had immediately reminded her of the sweet earth from her abuelita's mountain, the earth she used to eat by the handful, and Luz had agreed with Mami. They would be all right.

"Smells good in here," she said to Hudson, who sat at her bedside. Cuca was beside her moments later, a half-chewed chicken bone hanging out of her mouth. Luz's voice was hoarse. It hurt to speak.

"What's good is seeing you awake," Hudson said, as he reached for a cup of water with a straw and raised the bed so she could take a sip. The pain from the movement was searing, forcing her eyes closed. He pressed the call button to summon a nurse, promised her the pain medication would make it better in no time. "You're on the home stretch," he said, kissing her forehead.

When she next woke up, Mami and Papi were in the room. Luz knew everything was wrong. Papi and Hudson were on either side of her, each holding a hand, each asking how she was feeling. Alarmed at the burn on Papi's hand, Luz asked what happened, but he dismissed her worry. Mami hung back, sitting by a window seat that had no cushion, with a pained look. Her hair had been pulled tightly, hair follicles strained at her temples. She wouldn't make eye contact with Luz.

"What day is it?" Luz asked, feeling disoriented. The sweet smell grounded her.

"The accident happened a week ago," Vladimir said.

"What accident?" Luz asked.

Everyone in the room was quiet. Where could anyone start?

"You were shot," Hudson said finally, in a strained voice. "No one has been arrested."

Every time Luz tried to move her body, no matter how small the movement, she was newly shocked at the levels of pain it brought about. The heart rate monitor signaled her rising distress. She tried hard to remember the last thing that happened before she passed out, but there was no memory of a gun. She remembered Eusebia running toward her, both of them underneath a red sky.

Now, there was Hudson's jaw set hard, determined in a way that scared her. Had she ever seen him look so angry? Qué va. Vladimir rushed out of the room to go get a nurse, while Mami leaned over the bed and pressed the nurse call button on the side of the bed. One, two, three times.

The nurse arrived, asked everyone to leave the room. Everyone acquiesced except Hudson. A shot of morphine into Luz's open IV line, and within seconds, the pain was gone. Her body floated away from all that unpleasantness. From a distance, she heard the nurse say the next few days would be difficult. Hudson asked how quickly he could get her out of this damn place, and she wondered if he meant the hospital or New York City.

JOSÉ GARCÍA'S MURDER: SOLVED

The next day, Luz woke up feeling much stronger, a bit more like herself. It had taken so much effort to get Hudson to leave the hospital room, to go take a shower and get a proper night of sleep. Before he left, his last words to her had been thick with emotion. I'm going to do all I can to keep you safe, he'd said.

She was well enough to speak to the detectives investigating the case. They crowded the room, greeting her father by name. The older one, a Dominican woman with short wavy hair and a Brooklyn accent, introduced herself to Luz as Detective Ramos. The younger guy, somewhere closer to Luz's age, said she could just call him Lorenzo. Out of the room, through the glass window, Tía Cuca motioned at Detective Lorenzo with a kissy mouth. She made an X with her arms, mouthed the words "Lock me up" to Luz. Luz shook her head at her aunt, tried hard to remain serious.

They asked what she remembered.

"I don't remember anything," she said. "It's so strange."

The detectives raised their eyebrows as if they weren't buying what she said. They left their cards, promising to check in on her in a few days.

"I will call you if I remember anything," she said. "I know how important it is to put criminals away." The last part she said for Papi's benefit.

"Maritza gave me the news," Lorenzo said to Papi as he got up to walk the detectives out. "Congrats on the retirement."

Papi glanced back at Luz as they left the room,

stoic. Luz gave him a blank stare back, but she could see what was coming. So many things she could see now that she'd missed before. Her parents weren't speaking, could hardly be in the same room together. They'd taken turns in the last day, doing a silent dance where one left the room after speaking to her about when they'd be back, while the other came in and sat down, enjoyed the views of the Hudson River and the skyline of New Jersey, some-times the lit-up George Washington Bridge. Mami never entered the room without Cuca, and while Luz was getting used to the new reality that was her body, understanding it would be months before she felt good, or strong, or able, she wondered how she'd have an opportunity to confront her mother about her mental break. She could tell her father intuited what had happened; saw the rupture that had started so long ago. Luz had chosen to shift her gaze the other way, instead of facing it head-on.

Papi was heartbroken but he still didn't fully understand the seriousness of Mami's situation. Mami seemed oddly distant; upset but bored. Her only sign of emotion the open hostility toward Hudson when they happened to be in the room at the same time. Luz felt if she allowed herself time, she could work out a way to fix everything.

Vladimir returned to the room after saying good-bye to the detectives and sat next to her. Papi's hand over her hand was light. He didn't ask any questions.

"The pool," Luz asked, "is it as good as we thought?"

"Better," he said, pained, "so beautiful. Such a waste."

Luz didn't know what to say. A waste of what? Money? Time? Love?

When Mami came to the hospital later that night, without Cuca for once, Papi spoke some words to her outside the room before he left for the night. Luz saw her nod.

Sitting next to Luz, Mami leaned forward, whispering though there was no one else in the room.

"This pain," she said, "it won't last forever. And you don't have to cry. Your body already knows what to do, if you let it. My mother told me, and her mother told her."

Luz imagined her great-grandmother, and all the women before, suffering great losses, great pain, and each telling her body not to cry, not to feel, to instead be hard like steel and stone. And then teaching her daughter that lesson.

"I knew he was bad news," Mami continued. "It's his fault, su culpa. All of it. The entire neighborhood fell apart. So many people hurt."

Her mother's jaw set hard—just as hard as Hudson's had been when Luz first woke up. A vein pulsed on Eusebia's neck. Her eyes filled with tears of rage that failed to fall, that disappeared moments later. Luz thought of all the times, over so many years, when her mother had turned her face away as soon as she was about to cry. Luz had never questioned it. Just like she'd never questioned her

mother not ever eating with them, always waiting in case they wanted to eat her portion, too. In
her calm madness, in the kitchen, devouring that
pastel—that was the first time Luz had seen her eat
something that wasn't a leftover. Now she saw her
mother's tears being absorbed back, just like her
anger and her disappointment, and, maybe, just as
her dreams had been.

"You in this hospital," she continued, touching
her shoulder tentatively, "he put you here."

The rage that filled Luz was electrifying; her em-
pathy fled fast. She snapped up off the bed and
pushed her mother's hand away.

"He didn't put me in here," Luz said. "You put
me here."

From the television, a picture of a young boy silenced them both. José García's murder had finally
been solved.

Eusebia and Luz simultaneously had the same reaction to the news of his assailant, as if the shock
calcified the pain they each suffered. José García,
a beautiful boy who had so much life ahead, had
been murdered by his own mother.

Eusebia was the first to break the silence. She let
out a scream.

Luz stared at her mother's open mouth, the sound
so tremendously loud, and felt helplessly, childishly
paralyzed. When a nurse rushed into the room
to see what had happened, Eusebia slammed the
nurse against a wall.

My boy, Eusebia screamed, my boy. The nurse hit a red button, and an alarm rang out, and Luz understood there would be trouble, that the police would be in the room momentarily. She found her voice, then.

"Mami, please, stop. Cálmate."

Eusebia didn't calm down. She proceeded to the same wall and began to slam her head against it, over and over and over, until there was blood, until the blood poured over her eyes. Then she collapsed.

No security came. No police. Several other nursing staff arrived, went to her mother's side. Her will to reach her mother was strong enough to propel her out of the bed. But it wasn't strong enough to keep her standing. She fell. The last thing she heard was the metal on her collarbone snap. The last thing she felt were stitches tearing and the now-familiar cold-warm feeling of blood as it spread all around her. The last thing she saw was her mother, a few feet away, also on the floor, eyes open, blankly staring at her.

With relief, Luz gave in to all the silence that surrounded her. Inside of the silence, she understood how easy it would be to blame herself for not having realized what had been happening with Mami this entire time, to turn that mistake, that disappointment, into an acceptance of pain as the only way through her life. To run away with Hudson, to say goodbye to all the work that lay ahead, would be one way to say no to the pain. But there ought to be another option. Another way to make room in her body for her mother, for herself. But what her mother offered wasn't the way for her, either. In tranquility, she trusted her body was evolving, would lead her to a new course. And when tears filled her eyes, she let them fall, into the present and the past. And she promised herself she'd never hold the pain inside her body. That wasn't for her. Or the women after her.

THE TONGUES' LAST INTERLUDE:

HER DOING? OR OUR TELLING?

Luz was the one who called us to the hospital. She said, Mami está enfermera. She meant sick, not nurse. She meant Eusebia might not make it. In her broken Spanish, she sounded younger, like a kid. As if she'd been reborn.

We sat in front of her in the hospital bed where she was still recovering, watching as her boyfriend held her hand, seemingly as unprepared for these circumstances as the rest of us. We listened to her try to explain what had been going on with our dear Eusebia all summer long.

"We speak English," one of us said, to put her, and ourselves, out of that misery.

A nonmalignant tumor had taken root in Eusebia's brain. Luz called it a fancy name. We rolled the words with our tongues—**brain growth,**

meningioma. It had been growing slowly, maybe over many years dormant, but likely triggered by the fall three months ago. It then became invasive due to stress. She'd suffered hallucinations, uncontrolled rage, a lack of impulse control. These kinds of tumors are most common in women, Luz said. Eusebia's reaction was rare, extreme, and the doctors thought it might have been an inherited nervous system disorder, likely passed down by the women in their family.

"But why did she act normal some of the time?" we asked.

"Think back," Luz urged. "Did she?"

We thought back through May, June, and what had gone of July and realized the only time she was normal was when she remained silent.

Then the crux. If they operated, there were risks: She might lose her ability to function, might have more severe personality changes. The hallucinations might remain, might even grow worse. Radiation as the main vehicle brought about so many complications, up to and including death. But to let her remain as she was?

Luz started crying then, and we were just as awkward as her boyfriend was. That white boy was in way over his head. That's to say, none of us knew what to do. How to offer some comfort. Hudson folded her in, letting her cry it out until she settled. At least he was making himself useful.

Where is Vladimir? we wondered.

"Where is Vladimir?" we asked.

Luz said he was with Eusebia, by her side.

We tried to get Luz to focus on the alternatives. Medicine? Yes. Drugs were an option. It would require a combination of medications to combat swelling and psychosis. It would likely cause some personality problems, but it was an option.

Vladimir came into Luz's room. Back curved, aged years and beyond in the last few days.

He kept saying their goal should be to get her to her old self. Her normal self. It was Luz who said no.

"We have to give her the medicine so she can decide, Papi," she said. "This has to be her choice."

We went to visit Eusebia in the hospital. There was a wound on her forehead, a mess of loose skin shaped like petals of a big flower, decomposing, curling on itself: oddly labial.

Eusebia took her medications over the next three weeks, and as the swelling went down, we noticed she was neither her old self nor that new self. Once, in a moment of lucidity weeks into her stay, she looked at the three of us, and at Luz, who was there in a wheelchair with us.

"If they cut my brain, I won't make it," she said. And then, after a few moments, "As soon as I can travel, I want to go back home. I need to go home with Vladimir."

WHAT FALLS AND WHAT FLOURISHES

The day Luz and Eusebia got released was August 3. We know because it's our birthday, but we never told anyone. It was enough gift to have them out of there. We made them a good meal. It wasn't Eusebia's cooking, but it was still pretty good.

In the hospital, and in the weeks to follow, we got to see a different side of the girl. Was it that terrible wound that helped her become someone else? Who knows? We heard the conversation with the boyfriend, who was telling her Neruda on the Park had been placed on hold until things died down. We heard him tell her now was the perfect time to go. And we could tell he meant far. Would she?

Tell me your stories, she said, about what happened before, in Nothar Park. And we spoke; we cut open the stitching that held the past in place, told her of the times when the activists used to come here, when Nothar Park was the epicenter of activism in New York City.

She wrote down what we said. She scrutinized us, said, You got any proof? We brought photos, and the old newspaper articles, and letters we'd kept. It took some time for us to work up the nerve to ask what she was up to.

"I'm going to make our neighborhood into a heritage site," she said. "So no one can touch it."

And she filled out forms, and she submitted those forms, and days later, when the forms were returned because there was something incorrect, she resubmitted them. We were there when Hudson told her it was too big of a fight, and she said, "Not for me." Neruda on the Park is the only thing keeping me here, he said, and she nodded, understanding. Was this her goodbye present, to all of us?

It was at that point the old boss came to visit, brought her a check from her old firm, saying they'd all decided she was def the biggest loser. Luz refused to take the check, said, "I thought I'd never see you again." Eusebia was the one who spoke up: "You've earned that," she said.

The old boss told Luz if she ever snapped out of it and decided to get her head out of the clouds, there was a job waiting for her—she'd decided to start her own firm. "It will be different," she added softly.

Luz shook her head.

"I'd rather get shot again," she said. And the two women laughed, in a way that meant this time it was for real, this goodbye.

She called us over and told us Hudson was right, this was a big fight. We needed additional arms. That we had to get the others. To bring her the stories of why they loved this park, this neighborhood. And everyone had stories, some we never heard— the women and the men, everyone came—and she listened to each of them, and asked them all these questions, and laughed at the funny parts and cried at the heartbreaking parts, and without faltering said bring me proof. There were videos and photographs and recordings that weren't about fighting for justice, or standing up for rights, but about creating something new—new dances, music that blended cultures, in this big city where nothing stays the same for long. And we could see, then, how the things some of us brought from our mountains and our beaches and our tin-roofed homes were in those Diablo Cojuelo masks, the scandalous dances, the strange-tasting food. Shit! Of all people, esa mocosa was the one who showed us how a community can thrive, transform, while still honoring the past.

Just look at Christian. When they showed up ("they" 'cause esa mocosa was quick to correct when we said "he"), wrist still bandaged, dressed in another strange outfit that looked like a wolf had bitten through it, we perked up. Those two hadn't seen each other since the day Christian shot Luz. Christian carried marbled notebook upon marbled notebook and they offered them to her, sheepishly, and quickly turned to go. She said, "Slow your roll," and padded the spot next to her so they'd sit down. She leafed through those pages, turning them just so we could see. The notebooks meticulously documented the comings and goings of the neighborhood, with some words and some strange hand drawings that showed all of us as we'd once been, as we'd become.

"Holy shit, Chris," Luz said. "This is amazing."

Some of their entries took our breath away. **Wilfredo finally figured out nobody's gonna buy his dirty-ass-water hot dogs and changed it to a**

pastelito cart. The oil drips on the sidewalk and makes outlines like ghosts about to take off.

"I'm sorry I hurt you," Christian said, finally, moving the way young people move, like a flag, falling, then floating back up.

Luz tenderly held the part of their arm closest to her, the one that'd been hurt. "Now we're a set," she said, touching the scar on her clavicle.

Then the two of them turned to each other in hushed tones, going through the notebooks together, and as she asked them about this or that day, pausing at the striking drawing of Christian's father as a young man, or Eusebia's body facing the park, or Angélica laughing, holding the twins, or Luz on the fire escape looking over a shoulder at them, we realized it was time for us to leave them alone. So we did.

When the news came that the park had been designated a heritage site, we looked at that mocosa with her big smile acting so proud, like it was her doing and not our telling. We said, Fine. We supposed we were a **little bit** proud of her. All that intelligence, finally, used for a worthwhile cause.

Eusebia? Like a robot, she just sat through all of that, sometimes her hands made a motion like she was floating in water, hands gently caressing waves. We could tell she was just waiting, waiting to be cleared by the doctors. Waiting to get the hell away from Nothar Park.

It was Luz who told her, Teach me how to cook.

And it animated her, a little bit. And recipe by recipe, she showed the girl how to cook, until the food tasted almost as good. And we knew it had to have hurt, the girl moving her arms as the collarbone healed. We had underestimated her strength. The entire building filled up with the aroma, until we really couldn't tell whose hand had made the food.

José García haunted us. We didn't believe it was true, that the mother had done such a terrible thing to her own son.

But since Luz had been shot, the neighborhood had undergone a drastic transformation. People around the park hardly looked at each other as they crossed the street, hurried home. There had been an attempted rape: men who knocked on a random door rushed in to attack, only to find a group of men playing dominoes behind the woman who'd walked in moments before, carrying groceries. There had been a brawl, and the would-be rapists had been beaten within an inch of death. Once word got out on what happened, it put a stop to people popping in, as no one bothered to answer their doors anymore. It was quieter earlier, no one out and about doing sidewalk BBQs or playing music real loud. Who wanted to walk through the park late at night?

The stores around the park had also become a target. Juan Juan's bodega had been broken into at least three times over a few weeks. Each time, he'd handed over the money, put his hands up, against actual thieves this time.

The mural. We stared and stared.

Go Home.

In the building, word had made it around that a few folks had signed the contract, had agreed to be bought out. Raúl said he'd be back. But we knew what happened when young people left. With Vladimir and Eusebia leaving, Luz would finally be free to go with her man. What could possibly keep her here? We felt the familiar truth of the city—for some, a gateway to inconceivable wealth; for others, a path to unspeakable struggle; but for most of us, company among concrete, metal, trees, wind. Neighborhoods turn over and over again. We were relieved that we hadn't been ousted, at least not yet. But we'd lived through enough, had been through worse, knew what came next. It was the natural course of things and so the natural rules applied. The only ones who earned a stay would be the most obstinate.

CHAPTER TWENTY-FOUR

Eusebia de Guerrero

It was hard to keep track of time. The pills came in different colors. Some were as thick as her ring finger. Those choked her. But she forced them down. Her body wasn't her own. It moved slowly. Vladimir was relieved; each night, he told her so.

"Things are going to be so great when we're back," he said.

While they were hospitalized, July had turned to the hottest August on record. The heat this year unlike anything anyone had seen. Any time Luz convinced her to wander out for fresh air, Eusebia felt as if a pillow were pressed down hard against her face.

So many people in those days, in and out of their house. Luz listened to the neighbors who came by, to the stories they told, while Eusebia thought it was the saddest thing she'd ever heard—how everyone had transformed their music and their food and their bodies to make a home in this new place. Shameful, really.

Eusebia tallied her losses, expected the drugs, this new numbness, would elicit remorse, but each time pivoted toward what she hadn't lost: she hadn't lost Luz, and though the bodies of some had been torn, bodies mend. Everybody was alive. She'd won. The building had been stopped. Why would she feel regret?

When Luz asked her to teach her how to cook, she thought this would be her gift to her daughter. Something to outlast them both.

At the end of their first full week back home, she was cleared for travel, but Vladimir and Luz worried. They watched over her as she placed each pill in her mouth, but it wasn't hard, as she tucked them under her tongue, withstanding the dissolving bitterness, to accept that this was the price for the two of them to feel confident she was on her way to better. She felt it a small victory when Vladimir finally booked their trip. In two weeks, they'd leave Nothar Park. Fourteen days and she'd go back home.

When Luz brought out that old book of poems and started reading them in her bad Spanish, Eusebia understood what she was up to, as the words spread in the air and adhered to her skin, like Eusebia's skin was paper and Luz's mouth was quill. Could words heal? Maybe. But Eusebia wasn't having it. She put something solid around her heart so the words wouldn't reach. But those words, like wind, spread wildly. She couldn't help it, with her daughter's voice, how those words were absorbed into her heart.

One day, in the bathroom, she fell. A thunderous boom in her own ears. The shower was on, full blast, and the water made her hair coil, like it was alive. It reminded her of the first day she spent in this apartment.

Luz came into the bathroom, asking if she was okay, and even though Eusebia insisted she was fine, Luz helped her out of the shower, reached for a towel, and stopped dead when she saw the skin of her stomach so badly disfigured from the burn, not quite healed.

"When did this happen?" Luz said.

"It was a kitchen accident. They treated it in the hospital. It's slow to heal but doesn't even hurt anymore."

"Ma, that looks terrible. Maybe I can find a specialist," Luz insisted, "a hospital that specializes—"

"I'm done with hospitals," Eusebia said, cutting her off.

Luz dried her skin, gently massaged coconut oil on her legs, applied it gently to her burn. When she helped her put on her undergarments, Luz stared and stared and stared at her C-section scar.

"I thought I was a natural birth," she said cautiously. "What's the scar from, Ma?"

What do we owe each other? Eusebia asked herself, allowing the words to come out. She told her daughter about her boy, and how he was the reason she never had a brother or a sister. She told her daughter about the pain, how she'd buried it inside.

"You called out to him, in the hospital, when you hurt yourself," Luz said.

"I think a scar is the reminder a body can survive great pain," Eusebia said. "How even if a part of you dies, you can go on."

Luz hugged her, told her she was sorry about the boy, and about how lonely she must have been, all these years, carrying such sadness inside. Eusebia felt gutted by her confession to Luz, reliving the trauma as she told her daughter about her son. She called to the other self but never got a response.

There could be a different beginning, she supposed. Could she repent? Should she let them cut the brain tumor out? Could she stand to go back to the person she'd been? She contemplated those questions, and those two weeks passed the way hours passed when she was a child. Some days interminable, some gone in a blink. She reached certainty the day before they were set to go back to DR. No way. She could not return to the woman who did not control her own destiny. Eusebia stopped taking the pills. Every single one.

* * *

Luz helped her downstairs, where Vladimir waited in the car to take them to the airport.

When she got in the front seat, next to Vladimir, he slid the car into drive and hit the accelerator. Behind her, Luz reached out through the headrest in the seat and gently caressed the sides of her head.

"Going home will be good for you," Luz said. "I'm going to come visit you soon, and we can go for a long swim."

Eusebia patted her hand. Wondered if that would ever truly come to be.

"When you were very little," Eusebia said instead, "I used to wonder how to keep you safe. You were so wild at two years old, como un ciclón. You used to climb furniture and hurl yourself into the air. I couldn't understand where that recklessness came from; even after you hurt yourself, maybe scraped a knee, you would cry for a little while and then be back at it, climbing higher than the last time. There was such force in your spirit. And I thought, The world will break you. I thought, Better I do my job to contain you. I thought I was doing the right thing, trying to make you more cautious, to be wary of the world."

Such dryness in her throat, her entire body a drought. Would that ever go away?

"Whatever you hold inside," Luz said, "you gotta let it out. I'm fine. I turned out great."

It was true. Her Luz had turned out great.

Vladimir reached for Eusebia's hand. His hair was completely white. She tried to remember when that happened. His hand on her hand. Eusebia saw no scars, but understood perhaps Vladimir had scars she couldn't see. On her stomach, the burnt skin had created a new layer, thick like bark, spreading like scales up her body, even to the parts that hadn't been burned. She'd been happy Luz hadn't checked the burn again. At that moment, she felt it spread. Her body, hardened.

"Things will be better at home," he said.

They arrived at the airport and Eusebia leaned her head on Luz, so tenderly, making sure there wasn't any force or weight to her touch.

"None of the things that happened here were your fault," Luz said, reminding Eusebia that people who love you sometimes lie to spare, to protect. "You should let yourself off the hook. Think about what you got away with, Ma. You terrorized an entire neighborhood and now you get to go on vacation. You're the most incredible human being to ever live."

She laughed hard and Vladimir laughed hard but Eusebia couldn't laugh. It had been decades since she'd felt the warmth of tears on her own face, how they paused on her chin, staying there for a while before falling onto her chest. How, as the moisture dried on her face, her skin felt tighter. How exquisite the soreness around her eyes, the lightness in her chest, to let the past exit, to let the pain go. It made sense the tears would fall right now, for Luz. And it was right, that her daughter got to see that. Eusebia wasn't prepared when Luz leaned over and kissed those tears, kissed Eusebia's eyes.

She'd miss her daughter. But look at her now, standing on her own, making her own way. So much stronger than Eusebia had ever been.

CHAPTER TWENTY-FIVE

Luz Guerrero

NOW, GO

At the airport, right before her parents went through security, Luz handed Eusebia Vladimir's book of poems. At first, she took it from Luz, but then quickly shook her head no, handed it back. Eusebia told Luz to take it back to Nothar Park and give it to the Tongues instead.

"They'll understand," she said.

Papi looked momentarily hurt, but when Eusebia took his hand in her hand, he nodded, content. And Luz understood that at this point her parents were beyond words.

She stood on the side, watching them slowly make their way. Vladimir came back once, then a second time. He gave Luz a hug each time, reminding her they'd be together soon, that they would talk each day. Luz noticed her mother calmly looking ahead, as if the important goodbye between them was already in the past, as if what needed to be said had already been said. The unease Luz had felt for days dissipated as Eusebia stepped up to the security guard who checked her passport. There, before Eusebia went through, she glanced behind at Luz and held her gaze. Eusebia smiled, waved at her in a silly way that begged a response. Luz followed suit, waving back, throwing her a kiss. Eusebia placed her hand gently against her heart, nodded as if to say, Now, go. Luz received the blessing, the permission to make her own way. She was convinced, finally, that Eusebia was getting on that plane for herself and for no one else.

EACH WORD, A BRICK

Hudson was waiting for her in her apartment. How weird to think it—now hers, hers alone.

Luz had been practicing the words she would say, to explain what she needed to say. Even as she stepped off the elevator and unlocked the door, she hesitated. There was total certainty that her decision was the right one. But it was her turn to feel protective of him, to worry about what her words would do to Hudson when she was gone.

Those days when she'd been trying to soothe her parents, she had asked Papi for his copy of Neruda's love poems and started absentmindedly reading from it aloud, and pretended her Spanish was worse than it was. She could hear both Mami and Papi correcting her pronunciation, their mouths open long enough that the words of those poems could sneak in, carve a way into their hearts, mend them. How was it possible she'd never noticed how sad these poems were? How beautiful they were? When she'd gotten to the one poem that would forever be lodged in her heart, the remembered words—out of her mouth in real time but also leaving Hudson's mouth when he recited that poem by heart on that fateful day—made her understand that love, like loss, was as much a choice made as the shadow of the choice not made. Already, her choice left an indentation inside her, like the title on the cover of Hudson's favorite love story.

When she reached the living room and found Hudson looking out of the window toward the construction site, she felt the warmth of his body still nestled in her chest with those words, pulling, pulling.

"There you are," he said, smiling.

Later, she would agree with him, that it was cruel, to take his large hand in her hand, to guide him to her bed. She found herself unwilling to explain it. Because understanding she needed to let him go didn't make it less painful. How to admit her body let her know, with a certainty that scared her, that she would never feel about any other man the way she felt about him? Yet still, she had to say no. Her place was here, in Nothar Park.

He tried to be gentle but she didn't let him, she

wanted it fast, rough, all-consuming, so that by the time he took her ass in his hands and lifted her hips off the bed, it was her teeth that bit into his shoulder before they both screamed. They momentarily left their bodies in motion on that bed, levitated toward a blocked sky.

Sated, he began to speak of what it would be like, when they moved to London.

Luz had hoped there would be more time for them but knew this was the moment. She spoke the words she'd been dreading speaking aloud: "I am not leaving with you. My place is here."

He kissed her shoulder right where her scar ended. He smiled, like he was humoring her joke. At her expression, a coldness settled between them.

"This fucking place," he said, "you don't belong here."

But also, he could tell that there was no convincing her, because even as she cried, her resolve was rooted. He got out of the bed and put his clothes on. His distance from her lengthened, nailing her in place like an undertow. In her lips, she could still taste his skin, the ginger, the salt. He hung his head and quietly closed the door to her bedroom. Moments later, she heard the closing of the front door. And she imagined his footsteps, too impatient for the elevator, running down the stairs, across the park, into another life.

Of course, Luz picked up that book of poems. Of course, she went to that page, though by now she'd memorized those words, never mind that she stumbled over the pronunciation here and there.

She imagined those words following Hudson, following Eusebia and Vladimir into the air, how each sound slid through the accordion-like gate, out the open window, touching nearby buildings— each word, a brick—through the park, hanging on the branches of the trees that held the vibrancy of summer tight. Some of those words would trickle through the cracks in the boardwalk, eventually meeting earth. She thought those words would heal the burns on Papi's hands, on Mami's stomach, in the park, in the neighborhood. Mami had said scars were the way we carried the dead parts of ourselves with us, a reminder we could go on. And Luz thought that was true, but also, perhaps all scarred tissue was porous, letting in what the body needed, sealing out what didn't serve it. She rested the book of poems on her night table. She searched for and found the application materials she herself had written on the way to getting Nothar Park certified as a heritage site. She wondered if maybe these words, examples of imagination and ingenuity, would restore the people she loved. Maybe they'd help Hudson find hope. Help Papi find rest. Help Mami let go.

Luz walked outside. The park was slowly coming back to life. There was Uncle JJ, with the sidewalk BBQ, smoke of hot dogs and burgers floating up, then remaining there, suspended in the air. Tía

Cuca and JJ always made extra food. Most people in the neighborhood did.

"¿A buen tiempo?" René said, just then.

"¡Buen provecho!" Tía Cuca responded, handing him an extra burger.

That's what the extras were for. The music was loud, so loud. Christian waved at her from across the street, yelled at her to come over and help. In a few days, she'd be going with them up to Cornell, to drop them off for freshman orientation. She'd volunteered to drive.

It had been her idea to paint over the mural. To ask the putas to bring their masks and brushes, and see what they all came up with together. Already, she could hear the ones who'd gathered laughing as they painted over the words that were there—they painted over the black and white. Soon there would be so many colors.

Soon, the days would grow shorter. But today, darkness was still hours away. She thought again of the way Mami had smiled at her at the airport, of her nod. You will be okay, her mother meant, just like I'll be okay.

Across the street, in the park, Paris and Kenya were in the swings, and Angélica waved at her to come over to where she was standing with Tony and Isabel. Despite the light rain, they drank beer in a leisurely way. Luz motioned to wait; she'd be there in a minute.

The Tongues sat in front of the building, in their

beach chairs, wearing their matching eyeglasses with those beaded chains. Luz went over to them. Their eyes on her were gentler but still had bite.

"Mami left."

The women nodded. As in, We saw.

"But I'm here," Luz said. "I'm staying."

They didn't offer thanks or show any appreciation whatsoever. It was the opposite. They looked at her like she'd finally started behaving. Like she finally was paying them back what she owed them.

"Mami said to give you this," Luz said, handing over the book.

"Wait," the Tongues said.

One of the women went inside the building and came back moments later. She handed Luz a few tattered books. **In the Name of Salomé,** by Julia Alvarez, Toni Morrison's **The Bluest Eye,** a third book whose cover was so worn she had to open it to read the title of the book, the name of the author.

Luz thanked them, and as she made her way into the park, she saw the silver sign for Neruda on the Park and thought, What about Salomé on the Park, or Alvarez on the Park, or Morrison on the Park, or this other, mysterious writer, the one she'd never heard of?

"Mil gracias," she said, but knew it came out more like "mir" and had to laugh at the women, shaking their heads at each other, at her awful Spanish.

Up above, the overcast sky was gray and it reminded her of Mami. This is the best color for inspiration, for new beginnings, she always said. She wondered if others saw the unfinished building the way she saw it. It was a raised fist, threatening. The construction loomed over Nothar Park, messy concrete in spots like scar tissue, with bricks, with glass, with metal spines, shooting up toward a cluster of clouds. She touched her own scar, and there was no difference between it and Mami's stomach. A reminder she carried her mother in her body. In a quiet voice, she heard Mami's voice again, not the demented voice of the last few months but her voice from Luz's entire life, so heavy with sadness and joy and wisdom. Even after she left, she remained. Lived on to fight. She felt the Tongues in the distance behind her, turned her neck to catch their silhouettes as they slowly rose from those beach chairs, took all but one of them away. Suddenly not so raggedy, not so absurd. Once the mural was finished, she'd sit down in that single chair the Tongues had left behind, just for a little while. Take the shortest of rests.

EPILOGUE

They arrived on that mountain in the Dominican Republic and the house was bigger than Eusebia could have imagined, grand in a way that stole her breath. She wasn't quite sure what to do. Vladimir so proud, so excited, hung back—expectant. When they were kids, he used to draw houses with a stick. She'd had a sense, back then, that his capacity to create couldn't be contained within his body. When he'd drawn the painting of the campesino, so full of feeling and melancholy, she'd had the same thought, though back then she'd seen it sadly as a capacity that was diminishing in intensity, in power. But as she made her way through that house, with its vaulted ceilings and wide stairways, those endless views of nature—she knew he'd somehow ended up doing exactly what he was meant to do. It was as if all the years he'd spent on stakeouts, bored to tears waiting for the moment to strike, hadn't been wasted. He'd been daydreaming greatness. She couldn't possibly tell him the house made her claustrophobic, gave her an awareness of how much time she had wasted, how much time he would gain.

At her request, they spent what was left of the day walking around the grounds, admiring the beautiful views of the mountain. When she kneeled, late in the evening, and touched the pool with the lightest touch, Vladimir told her to pose for a picture, for Luz, and so she forced a smile.

"What happened to Sancho Panza?" she finally allowed herself to ask.

"He died," Vladimir said. "The day he moved off the mountain. I didn't want to upset you. Didn't want you to think it had anything to do with us."

It had everything to do with them. Eusebia wished she hadn't asked.

When they woke up the next morning, with the sun bright and shining, Vladimir held her hand, showed her to the balcony off their master bedroom. They were on the highest peak of the mountain. She leaned over the bamboo railing she'd selected, took in the immensity of the sea. It was a writhing, shimmering, dark blue mass with slashes of turquoise. The water's transparency and clarity beckoned.

"It's beautiful," she said, and meant it. She was awed and surprised to find her vertigo gone.

She reminded herself she owed him a perfect day. And all he wanted to do was drink coffee, and hold hands, and float on a pair of ridiculous inflatable swans Luz bought them. When he offered her a beer, she said no. She was done drinking. Vladimir fell asleep early that evening, right after dinner. Eusebia remained awake.

In the darkness of dusk, out the floor-to-ceiling windows, she stared at the dark hole that was the ocean and let it pull her. On the bed, Vladimir slept softly on his side, all chrysalis. She turned away. Outside, the feeling of the dirt under her feet cooled her. Through the dirt tunnel, her bare feet left footprints as small as when she was a girl. At the mouth, the beach waited—narrower than she remembered. The imported white sand so gentle on her feet. All around her, darkness. Silencio.

Luz, Vladimir, Nothar Park, the atrocities that befell women, children, here and far away, now and long ago. She'd done what she could.

She went in. The water was colder than she expected. Her clothes dragged, so she took them off. Naked, she moved through the seaweed, beyond the shore. She touched the side of her ribs, where her skin had become tree bark. In the water, her skin grew soft. She pulled a bit and the skin gave way, like the first layer of a tightly wound cigar. If she kept going . . . would she be able to use the skin to form yet another self?

When the vision arrived, transforming the world around her, she was aware of the change. Waste formed a layer in the water, and the stench filled her nostrils. She breathed deeply, telling herself she could control the vision this time, and for the first time, she could. She pushed a path through the waste, swam farther, leaving it all behind. When she stopped swimming, and stood, she felt the waves slowly lap at her C-section scar, which pulsed. There, a small life stirred.

There, a boy, perfectly made, with impossibly beautiful eyelashes, with Vladimir's strong forehead. She reached for him, lifted him from the water, felt in her heart the falling stillness she remembered so clearly from that day, so long ago. She gently placed him against her shoulders, though he squirmed against her, pushing as if to say, Let me go.

She thought of all the things she'd held inside, of the sadness she'd carried in her body for so long. Of the kisses she hadn't given him, of the tears she hadn't been able to shed or wipe. Could she ever let go?

By the time her limbs grew tired, a familiar mourning came from the joints of her arms, her hips. She let him slide down, dissolve into the water around her.

She swam for a long time, made her way out to where the water was the clearest, where it smelled of her childhood. How it energized her, a release. She picked up speed—this, the moment she'd been waiting for. Arms straight and tight by her hips, she let all the force come from her legs—where she'd pulled what was dead off her body, only softness remained. For me, she thought. This, just for me. In silence, Eusebia swam, thinking herself the sea.

ACKNOWLEDGMENTS

I wrote this novel over the course of fifteen years. There were countless moments when I feared the book would not reach her readers. I am grateful for the people who helped, guided, inspired, and believed. If I left your name off the list that follows, lo siento.

This book would not exist if it were not for:

My literary agent, PJ Mark, who didn't let me get away with a damn thing, no matter how hard I tried. I love you for it (now). My Janklow & Nesbit Associates family, who've done so much to support me, especially Ian Bonaparte and Kerry-Ann Bentley.

My brilliant editor, Chelcee Johns, whose wise questions led to the discovery of more layers, more depth, more humor, and more life in Eusebia's and Luz's stories. My Ballantine Books family: Sydney Collins, Cassie Gonzalez, Diane Hobbing, Luke

Epplin, Quinne Rogers, Allison Schuster, Michelle Jasmine, Jennifer Garza, Grant Neumann, Pam Alders, Kim Hovey, Jennifer Hershey, and Kara Welsh, who lovingly and respectfully ushered **Neruda on the Park** to readers.

The unrivaled public-school teachers in the Bronx, Harlem, and Lower Manhattan who helped me learn English and love language, and the librarians on 125th Street who helped me fall in love with reading. My creative writing teachers, who transformed me into a lifelong learner and a teacher proud to hand down their gifts as legacy: Steven Millhauser, Robert Eversz, Mat Johnson, Noy Holland, Jenny Offill, Taiye Selasi, Cristina García, M. Evelina Galang, De'Shawn Charles Winslow, Vanessa Martir, Breyten Breytenbach, Nicholas Christopher, Brian Morton, Chuck Wachtel, and, most of all, the late E. L. Doctorow and Paule Marshall.

Marita Golden and Sandra Gúzman, who have been fierce mentors of great tenderness and skill.

The organizations who supported me: PEN America's Writing for Justice Fellowship under the leadership of Dru Menaker and Caits Meissner changed how I think as an artist and an agent of change. The Virginia Center for the Creative Arts provided stunning space in the United States and France. Bread Loaf Writers' Conference under the leadership of Lauren Francis-Sharma and Jennifer

Grotz helped me understand that the real magic is in revision. Disquiet International Writing Program under the leadership of Jeff Parker and Scott Laughlin helped widen my lens. Juniper Summer Writing Institute under the leadership of Noy Holland set my imagination (wildly) on fire. Voices of Our Nations Art Foundation under the leadership of Elmaz Abinader and Diem Jones made me feel at home as soon as I walked in. The NYU Creative Writing Program is the first place where I ever considered myself a real writer thanks in large part to Melissa Hammerle and Russell Carmony. **Kweli,** under the leadership of Laura Pegram, gave my first short story a home. The Kenyon Review Writers Workshop under the leadership of Elizabeth Dark and Nicole Terez Dutton provided a wonderful virtual space to generate seeds of what I hope will be a future book. The Dominican Writers Association under the leadership of Ángela Abréu— whose tireless passion and advocacy lifts the voices of all Dominican storytellers across the diaspora— provided connections that have fed me, en mi alma. The entire crew at the Brooklyn Caribbean Literary Festival: Marsha Massiah-Aaron, Mellany Paynter, Melissa Harper, and Christopher Aaron have linked Caribbean writers to one another and to a broader network of readers who love Caribbean literature across the globe. Love As A Kind Of Cure, under the leadership of my co-founding partners

Magogodi oa Mphela and Courtney Montague, was instrumental in teaching me to dream the impossible when women decide to change the world.

The Dominican writers whose work and imagination filled me with pride and made me believe I could: Julia Alvarez, Josefina Báez, Junot Díaz, Angie Cruz, Nelly Rosario, and Naima Coster.

¡Dime con quién andas y te diré quién eres! The women who've held my hand, without whom I would not be as brave as I've become: Xochitl Gonzalez, Peggy Bourjaily, Elizabeth Francisco Calenda, Judy Francisco King, Kristen Lepore, Shamsa Khan Visone, Margaret Green, Alison Mariella Désir, Kianny N. Antigua, and Sofija Stefanovic.

To my closest friends, who constantly stun me with their faith, loyalty, and love: Harry Marte, Ángel B. Pérez, Jonathon White, Judy Gúzman, Evelyn Vásquez, Kalyani Sánchez, J Reuben Shango, and Phillip J. Ammonds.

I worked at CNA Financial Corp. for two decades and ascended from an administrate clerk to an executive. I'm grateful to the family I made while I worked there and the ways they each supported my work as a writer, mother, and an almost-professional athlete: Karen Stuttman, David Perry, David Dwares, Stephanie Solomon, TJ Alexis Kittles, Susan Scharf, Charnett Brown, Sherry Anaya, Victoria Chen, Tara Acosta Porter, Tony Vranas, Joy Sable, Diane Silverman, Kerry Maguire, Ann Birdsell, and Rebecca Toffolon.

To the friends and writers who read this novel in parts or in its entirety: Katie Sciurba, Elizabeth Nuñez, Jacqueline Lucas, Nicole Callihan, Olivia Birdsall, Katie Berg, Maaza Mengiste, Nicole Treska, Caleb Gayle, Diana Marie Delgado, Joseph Riipi, Robb Todd, TJ Wells, and Marco Navarro. My deepest gratitude goes to Carrie Cooperider, whose keen eye, humor, and big heart transformed this novel. My book club read this entire novel at the beginning of the Covid-19 global pandemic and offered light when all around us the world dimmed: Natasha Friedrichs-Fapohunda, Amanda Pérez Leder, Jean M. Reich, and Rachelle Lahens Harris. The PEN America Writing for Justice cohort offered a family that extends beyond words: Justine van der Leun, Vivian D. Nixon, C. T. Mexica, J. D. Mathes, Jonah Mixon-Webster, Sterling Cunio, and Arthur Longworth.

Thank you to the writers who have shown this novel early support: Dawnie Walton, Elizabeth Acevedo, Kimberly King Parsons, Zayika Dalila Harris, Gabriela Garcia, and my brother, Robert Jones, Jr. The biggest heartfelt thank you to Mitchell S. Jackson, who has been there from the very beginning.

My family and I have survived immeasurable pain, loss, joy, and love as immigrants in the United States. A mi madre, Nicolasa Lucas, que sobrevivió tanto trabajo para ofrecernos una oportunidad de vivir mejor. A mis hermanas, Evelyn Natera y Nuris

Natera, y a mi hermano, Cristian Natera: thank you for your unwavering belief. Un fuerte abrazo to my tías: Milagros; Daisy; Mary, aka Cutuca, aka Batatica; Suneica, whom I spent my entire life calling Suleica (why?); Míriam, aka La Gringa; Judy; Dominga; y a mi madrina, Sylvia, aka La Chica; and tíos Pin, aka Felipe, and Julio, aka Delo, and cousins and neighbors who always made me feel loved and destined for greatness even when there was little evidence to support that belief. I'm deeply thankful to my husband's family for lovingly stepping in when I needed you: Josephine Tucker, Sheryl Tucker, Kyle Tucker, and all our cousins, aunts, and uncles. I love you deeply.

My children, Penelope and Julian: thank you for injecting me with purpose and strength and the kind of love that continually threatens to explode my heart. To my husband, my best friend, my entire life, Kevin Tucker: thank you for everything.

This book would not exist without the people I've lost. I first learned to tell stories as a ten-year-old, when we called Papi from calling centers in New York City back in the late 1980s. When he died, I felt his presence toughen my resolve and strengthen my heart. My grandfather spent most of his life tending farmland and taught me perseverance and humility in harvesting all I can grow but offering the world only the very best I have to offer as sustenance. My grandmother, Regina "Masona" Lucas, was a force of nature. Ella fue la que me inculcó que yo soy el tronco, no una rama.

This book would not exist without you, the readers. I hope every one of you who has ever been transplanted, made to feel unwelcomed, who faces hostility at home or beyond, embraces my abuelita's words: Let us grow rooted in love of all our homes, let us rejoice in our strength and never shy away from it, let our stories change the world with the power and beauty of our imagination.

ABOUT THE AUTHOR

CLEYVIS NATERA was born in the Dominican Republic, migrated to the United States at ten years old, and grew up in New York City. She holds a BA from Skidmore College and an MFA from New York University. Her writing has won awards and fellowships from PEN America, the Bread Loaf Writers' Conference, the Kenyon Review's Writers Workshops, and the Virginia Center for the Creative Arts. She lives with her husband and two young children in Montclair, New Jersey. **Neruda on the Park** is her first novel.

cleyvisnatera.com
Twitter: @CleyvisNatera
Instagram: @cleyvisnatera